HIGH PRAISE FOR
ROBERT J. RANDISI AND
EAST OF THE ARCH!

"Another exceptionally entertaining and riveting mystery from genre stalwart Randisi."

—*Booklist*

"[Randisi] doesn't waste a phrase or a plot turn. . . . His prose is supple and never flashy."

—*Publishers Weekly*

"A skilled, uncompromising writer, Randisi knows which buttons to press—and how to press them."

—John Lutz, author of *Single White Female*

"Randisi knows his stuff and brings it to life."

—*Preview Magazine*

"Randisi has a definite ability to construct a believable plot around his characters."

—*Booklist*

"This is the hard-boiled detective story as it ought to be: tough, fast, savvy, with a touch of sentiment, but without pretension and fake moralizing. Enjoy!"

—Dean Koontz on *No Exit From Brooklyn*

A KILLER'S DEADLY GAME

Andrew Judson watched the report of the press conference on KPLR's nine o'clock news with interest. None of the men who spoke impressed him, except for Detective Keough. This man stepped up and took charge confidently. He would be a daunting opponent—and an opponent was what he would be. After tomorrow, Keough would be doing everything in his power to keep Judson from making new friends.

That wasn't something that Andrew Judson was going to allow to happen, though. Not now that he'd just gotten started.

EAST
OF THE
ARCH

ROBERT J. RANDISI

LEISURE BOOKS NEW YORK CITY

For Marthayn,
my North, my South, my West, and my East

A LEISURE BOOK®

August 2003

Published by

Dorchester Publishing Co., Inc.
276 Fifth Avenue
New York, NY 10001

Copyright © 2002 by Robert J. Randisi

ISBN 0-8439-5244-X

Printed in the United States of America.

Visit us on the web at www.dorchesterpub.com.

EAST

OF THE

ARCH

AUTHOR'S NOTE

While the Southern Illinois cities of East St. Louis, Collinsville, Belleville, Fairview Heights, Lebanon and others mentioned in this book actually do exist, the author does not claim to have been 100 percent accurate in their description. The same applies in the descriptions of the procedures of their municipal governments.

As usual, Joe Keough's procedures are all his own.

The Mississippi River will always have its own way;
no engineering skill can persuade it to do otherwise. . . .

—Mark Twain

Prologue

THE MISSISSIPPI RIVER annually deposits four hundred and six million tons of mud into the Gulf of Mexico, causing one famous riverboat captain to dub it "The Great Sewer." It is then reasonable to assume that, should one dump a body into the river—a body that one did not want found—it would end up mixed in with all that mud, never to be seen again.

Unless, of course, the body got snagged on one of the many pieces of flotsam that also float down the Mississippi each year.

That's what happened to Mary Ellen McKay's body. Her dress got itself tangled in a tree branch, and instead of floating straight and true down the Mississippi to the Gulf, the branch spiraled, twirled, and eventually deposited her on shore, where she was found by a homeless person sleeping on the dry half of a rusted out Volvo.

Detective Marc Jeter, of the East St. Louis Police, stared down at the body, aware that wet mud was seeping down into his shoes. He knew this was the end of the line for the woman—and probably for his career, which had seemed to be going nowhere fast, and now had probably gotten there.

Depending, of course, on who she turned out to be.

He stood up and looked at the uniformed cop standing next to him.

"Go up and down along here and find me her purse," he said, "preferably with a piece of laminated ID in it."

"Fat chance," the cop said. "That would be sheer luck."

" 'It is strange the way the ignorant and inexperienced so often and so undeservedly succeed when the informed and the experienced fail.' "

"Huh?"

"Mark Twain," Jeter said.

"ME's here!" another cop shouted out.

"Go and look," Jeter said to the cop.

"Yes, sir."

Jeter turned and saw the medical examiner slogging through mud towards him, backlit by blinking red and yellow lights. It had been raining steadily for days, the river rising steadily with it. Maybe that had something to do, he thought, with her ending up on shore.

"Goddamned rain," the ME complained. "You in charge?"

"Yes, sir," Jeter said, and introduced himself.

"How'd you get stuck with this one?"

"Low man," Jeter said.

"Figures."

The detective noticed that the ME had been smart enough to cover his shoes with plastic bags, tied around his calves, and that the man was also wearing rubber gloves. Very neat, he thought, for a man who always looked so sloppy. Jeter didn't know if it was because the ME bought cheap Kmart apparel, or because his body was so lumpy, or maybe a combination of both, but the man never looked comfortable in his clothes.

"Okay," the older man said, "let's have a look."

He trudged over to the body, the bags keeping his shoes and pants dry and clean. Jeter looked down at his own. They were ruined, and he had no room in his budget for new ones.

Uniformed men were either standing around watching or searching the ground for something that would help. Footprints were out of the question, because the mud was too wet and loose. But maybe they'd find something partially submerged. Every uniformed cop hopes to find an important piece of evidence at the scene of a homicide, one that they might be able to parlay into some kind of promotion.

Jeter looked around, knowing that some of the men thought they'd find something that would get them into the detective division. Like that was a big promotion.

"Jesus," the ME said. His tone of voice betrayed the fact that he had found something unusual, maybe something even he had never seen before.

"What?" Jeter asked. "What'd you find?"

"It's what I'm not finding," the doctor said, as he leaned over the body.

"And what's that?"

The ME turned his face up to the detective, and even though most of the illumination available was red and yellow Jeter knew that most of the color had drained out of the man's face.

"Her belly," the ME said. "It's . . . missing."

One

KEOUGH ROLLED OVER in bed and bumped into the woman lying next to him. Surprised, he sat up and looked at her, then at the clock on the nightstand beyond her. Three o'clock in the afternoon. Now he remembered. Marie Tobin. He'd met her two years earlier, when he was working on his first case in St. Louis, the Mall Rat thing. She was a very attractive brunette with a seriously sexy body who had come on to him during the case. Back then he'd avoided her because he made it a habit not to fool around with married woman. Also, he was just beginning a relationship with Valerie Speck at the time.

Earlier that day he had run into Marie in—of all places—a mall, and the next thing he knew they were back at his house desperately going at it in his bed. Both of the obstacles that had kept them from this when they first met were gone. Oh, she was still married, but he didn't care now. And his relationship with Valerie had ended a few months back, right around the time he'd discovered he had diabetes, and his partner had been killed.

There were a lot of things he didn't care much about, these days.

"Marie," he said, gently. He touched her shoulder and she turned over onto her back. Her big, brown-tipped breasts were as

sexy as ever, but right now he just wanted her to get up and leave.
"Marie!"

"Hmm?"

"It's after three."

"Hmm? What?" she asked, sleepily. She lifted her hands to her face and her breasts were no longer leaning to the sides.

"Three o'clock," he said. "It's after three. You said you had to pick up your daughter at school."

She opened her eyes, looked at him calmly for a moment, then her eyes widened and she said, "Oh shit."

She was a flurry of activity then as she sprang off the bed and started searching for her underwear and clothes. She found her panties first and slipped into them, then grabbed her bra from atop a dresser where it had landed when he tossed it, and fitted herself into the cups. After that it was her sweater and jeans, until finally she started looking for her shoes.

"Downstairs, I think," Keough said.

"Shit, shit, shit," she swore, charging from the room. She was a big girl and made noise pounding down the stairs. He got up, put a robe on to cover his nudity, and went down after her.

When he found her she was hopping on one foot, pulling on her second shoe. She looked around, spotted her purse and grabbed it.

"Keys, damn it!" she snapped.

"In the purse, I think."

She stuck her hand in her purse, rattled around a bit and then came out with the keys.

"I'm sorry I have to rush, Joe," she said, giving him a fleeing kiss on the lips as she passed on her way to the door.

"It's okay," he assured her. "We shouldn't have fallen asleep."

That stopped her. With the door half open she looked at him and smiled.

"We didn't have much choice," she said, "did we? I mean, we went at it . . . like . . . wild, right?"

"Right," he said, "wild." Although the word "desperate" still said it for him.

She took a moment to look at him and asked, "We're not gonna do it again, are we?"

"I don't think that would be smart, do you?" he asked.

"Maybe not," she said, "but doing it this time wasn't smart either, was it?"

"I guess not."

"Well . . . maybe we'll see each other again in a mall sometime and . . . who knows?"

He smiled back and echoed her words.

"Damn," she said, looking at her watch. "Bye, Joe."

He said, "Bye," but by the time he got to "Marie," she was gone, and the door slammed shut.

He stood at the front window and watched her drive away, then remained there, staring. Something had changed in Joe Keough. He was making decisions lately he would never have made before, like a spontaneous romp in the hay with a beautiful young married mother. For Marie Tobin it had just been another stolen moment—or afternoon—from an otherwise predictable existence as a wife and mother. For Joe Keough it represented a major change in the way he led his life.

Keough thought he was unhappy about where his life had taken him over the past year. His move into the mayor's office had not worked out as planned. He thought that as the mayor's top cop he'd be able to pick and choose his cases. Instead most of his work had involved security for the mayor at fund raisers and political functions, not what he had signed on for at all. He was a detective, not a bodyguard or security specialist. The mayor had a security specialist, and the man didn't like Keough at all. Most of the cops in the city didn't like him much either, because he had become the mayor's "Top Cop." In fact, a recent issue of *St. Louis* magazine had featured him on the cover with that very sobriquet beneath his picture. He had done the accompanying interview at the mayor's behest, but naturally the mayor was thinking of his own political future when he made the request.

Since arriving in St. Louis just over two years ago, Keough had been involved in two very high profile cases and had closed them both out. He was a media darling, and a valuable asset to the mayor's office. His own life, however, seemed to have been put on hold.

And then there was the diabetes. Diagnosed about six months ago, during the case that landed him in his present job—a political murder where the body had been found at the base of the Arch—he had not yet come to terms with it. Oh, he thought he had. He took his pills, and drank diet soda, and thought he was unhappy about it, but in reality he wasn't dealing with it at all. He had stopped checking his sugar levels each day, and he constantly broke his "diet" with donuts and beer and other forbidden items. He thought he was dealing with it, but what he was feeling was unmitigated anger, and an immeasurable resentment that this had happened to him before he was even forty.

And that was another thing. In a week he would be forty, and where was he? In a job he didn't like, a city far from home—Brooklyn, New York—with no relationships to speak of, not even a partner. His last partner had died of a heart attack during their last case together and shortly afterwards he'd made the move into the mayor's office. He hadn't had a partner in six months, and the romp in the hay with Marie Tobin was the first time he'd had sex in—well, since he broke up with Valerie. The diabetes, the death of his partner, Al Steinbach, and the breakup with Valerie had all occurred during the same tumultuous week in his life. But as bad as all of that was, at least something had happened. That had been the last week in his life that he'd actually felt useful, and alive.

He turned away from the window and looked around the living room. Boxes. He'd been there two years and was still surrounded by boxes he had not bothered to unpack since moving from New York. Was that because he knew St. Louis would not be his last stop? That he'd be moving on, again?

And if so, what was his next stop?

Two

A MONTH EARLIER Joe Keough had been complaining to the mayor about not having done any real police work—that is, detective work—for some time. Neither one of them could have known how quickly that situation would change.

"I need someone experienced with serial homicides, Your Honor," Will Emery, the mayor of East St. Louis, said into the phone. He stared down at the Japanese garden his twin teenaged daughters had given him on his last birthday—the Big Five-Oh—to help manage his stress. It wasn't helping, especially now.

"Well, I have just the man for you, Will," his counterpart across the river said.

"Your man Keough?" The hopeful tone was plain in the other official's voice.

"Exactly."

"That's what I was hoping you'd say."

"Of course," the mayor said, shrewdly, "we'll have to discuss the terms of the, uh, loan."

"Well, of course," Will Emery said. "What kind of terms did you have in mind?"

* * *

When Keough got to City Hall the next morning he got the word that His Honor wanted to see him right away. Maybe, Keough thought, today should be the day he quit. He'd been tossing around a lot of possible scenarios for a change in his life, but it had come down to two. He could quit the mayor's office and go back to working with the St. Louis PD. Or he could quit altogether and start again in a new city. Every time he thought about that last possibility, though, he thought about the unpacked boxes in his living room. How could he move to another place when he'd never really unpacked for this one? Maybe he just hadn't given St. Louis a fair shot. But had he really had time? His life had seemed to literally explode from the moment he first arrived, right from three-year-old Brady Sanders wandering into the Richmond Heights Police Station leaving a trail of bloody footprints behind him, to the death of his partner, Al Steinbach, and his move into the mayor's office.

Bottom line was, as he walked to the mayor's office, he hadn't made up his mind yet.

He was ushered directly into the mayor's office. That meant the Man really had something important on his mind. Normally any-one waiting to see him had to do just that. Keough had the feel-ing it was more a superstition with the mayor than anything else.

As he entered the office the mayor was seated behind his desk, talking on the phone. He looked up at Keough and waved him to a chair. Keough sat and watched as the handsome black man talked to some political crony, charming the pants off of him. Working for the mayor was not a bad job. It paid well, and the man was okay, for a politician. It had just gotten so . . . stagnant. He wondered again, for the umpteenth time, if going back into the regular department on any level was a viable option. Would they take him back?

"Well," the mayor said, hanging up, "I'm glad you came in early today, Joe."

"Your Honor," Keough said, "I've got something I want to talk to you about—"

"It can wait," the mayor said, cutting him off with a wave of his hand. "I've got something for you."

"Sir?"

"Something you can sink your teeth into."

"And that would be?"

"I got a call yesterday from Will Emery, the mayor of East St. Louis," the mayor said, sitting back in his chair. "He wants to borrow you."

"Borrow me? You're sending me to Illinois?"

"That's right. He's got a problem and he needs a good detective to solve it."

"Doesn't East St. Louis have their own police department?"

"They do, but he needs a homicide specialist," the mayor said. "That would be you, right, Joe?"

Keough's heart began to race. Was he actually going to get to do some real police work? "Maybe you better tell me what this is all about, sir," he suggested, trying not to seem too anxious.

"It's about murder, Joe," the man said. "Actually, more than one."

"A serial killer?"

"I think," the mayor said, "that will be for a man of your expertise to decide."

Keough listened while the mayor told him what he knew, which didn't seem to be much.

"There was a story in the papers a few weeks ago about a woman's body found on the Illinois side of the river," the man said. "Do you recall that?"

"Vaguely," Keough said. "I don't remember any particulars."

"Well, to tell you the truth neither do I," the mayor said, "but it will be for them to fill you in when you get there."

"Get where?"

"I promised Will Emery you would be in his office this morning," the mayor said. "I assume he'll have all the particulars—and all the people involved—at your disposal."

"Let me get this straight," Keough said. "Am I off the clock for this?"

"You are," the official said. "For the foreseeable future you'll be working for the mayor of East St. Louis. That is, if you think you can handle the job after you hear about it."

"You said murders," Keough said. "Was there a second one in the papers?"

"Not that I know of," the mayor said, "but he did say there were two. They might be keeping the second one quiet. You can find that all out when you get there. I don't think there's anything else I can tell you."

"There's one thing."

"What's that?"

"I know what the relationship between you and Mayor Emery is like."

"I don't know what you mean," his boss said. "We're friends."

"Friendly adversaries, is more like it," Keough said. "You like reminding him that there's an 'East' in front of *his* St. Louis."

"That's ridiculous."

"Is it?" Keough stood up. "I know you're not just loaning me to him out of the goodness of your heart. What's the deal, Your Honor? What are you getting out of it?"

"I thought you'd be happy, Joe," the mayor said. "You'll be getting to do the work you love again."

"I am happy, but—"

"Then why don't you stop looking a gift horse in the mouth," the man said, "and get over there."

"Yes, sir!" Keough said.

"And keep me informed on your progress," the mayor said. "I don't mind helping my esteemed counterpart out, but I don't want you to be over there forever."

"Yes, sir, Your Honor. Anything else, sir?"

"No," the mayor said. "You can go. I don't like when you get . . . sarcastic. It makes me think I'm losing your respect."

"I may get sarcastic sometimes, sir," Keough said, seriously, "but it never means that. I'll keep in touch."

"Thank you, Joe."

"No," Keough said, "thank you, sir."

Because, in the end, the man actually was giving him something he wanted, wasn't he?

Three

KEOUGH KNEW THAT like most of the smaller cities and townships in the St. Louis area, East St. Louis housed most of its municipal services in the same complex. He parked his car among the other police vehicles in the parking lot—leaving his mayor's office ID in the window—and crossed the street to the municipal building. A secretary immediately saw him into the mayor's office as soon as he announced himself. When he entered, he found three men waiting for him in a small office.

"Detective Keough?" the man behind the desk asked.

"That's right. Mayor Emery?"

The mayor stood up and extended his hand. "Just call me Will. Everyone does."

"Nice to meet you, Will," Keough said, stepping forward and shaking the man's hand. He seemed fit, and had a firm handshake. He thought the man was smart to allow him the use of his first name. It cut the tension a bit.

"This is Sergeant Ben Benson, our investigative supervisor," the mayor said, pointing to an older man with white hair who was wearing gray slacks, a white shirt and a blue tie. His jacket was not in the room.

The sergeant stood and shook hands, but it was with obvious reluctance.

"Sergeant," Keough said.

The man grunted and sat down.

"Our chief of police, Adam Clark, wanted to be here, but he was called away," the mayor said. "This is Detective Marc Jeter." The mayor indicated the youngest man in the room.

"Detective Keough," Jeter said. "It's a pleasure." The sharply dressed young man pumped Keough's hand with barely contained eagerness. He had a powerful grip and the smoothest ebony skin Keough had ever seen. "I've read a lot about you, sir, and I know I can learn a lot from you."

Keough reclaimed his hand and looked at the mayor.

"Am I giving a course or something?"

Mayor Emery laughed uncomfortably and said, "Detective Jeter has been working on this case, uh, up to now."

Keough looked at Jeter, who, to him, appeared not to have turned thirty yet, or seen the sharp side of a razor.

"No offense to Detective Jeter," Keough said, "but you didn't have a more senior man to put on this . . . case?"

"No one with your expertise in homicides," the mayor said.

"I'm sorry," Keough said, "but East St. Louis . . . when I moved here a couple of years ago didn't I hear how dangerous this city was? How there was more crime here per capita than anywhere in the country?"

Now it was the young mayor's turn to frown.

"We've been trying to change that."

"I understand," Keough said, "but you must have had men working in your department who had experience with violent crimes."

"With violence, yes," the mayor said. "Carjackings, robberies, assaults . . . even murder, but certainly not *serial* murder."

Keough looked at Sergeant Benson, who seemed to be either extremely unhappy or afflicted with a bad case of gas.

"Did your boss tell you why we need you?" Will Emery asked,

reseating himself behind his desk. He picked up the little mini-rake of his Japanese garden, then dropped it as though it was hot. To Keough, this was the only outward sign that the man was anything but calm and in control. Suddenly, Mayor Emery seemed almost jittery to him.

"No," Keough said. "He said you'd fill me in."

"Before we start can I get you something? A coffee, or—" Emery asked.

"I had breakfast, Your Honor," Keough said. "I'd really just like to hear what it is you want me to do."

"All right, then," Emery said. "I'll have the sergeant and Detective Jeter fill you in. Sergeant?" He leaned back in his chair, as if relieved he no longer had the floor.

Sergeant Benson shifted in his chair and hesitated. "Borrowing" Keough from the St. Louis police obviously was not sitting well with him.

"About two weeks ago we had a dead woman turn up—a girl, actually."

"Where?"

"She washed up on our side of the Mississippi," the sergeant said. "Needless to say she was dead, but it was how she died that was . . . disturbing."

"And how was that?"

"Well, according to our medical examiner—" The sergeant took a moment to look at the mayor and then said, "We didn't have to borrow one of those from St. Louis," before he continued, "—the woman was pregnant when she died. Apparently, the uh . . ."

"Baby," Jeter said, at the same time the mayor offered, "Fetus."

"Yes," the sergeant said, "the, uh, fetus was taken from her, which may have been the cause of death."

"You mean her baby was delivered, and then she bled to death?" Keough asked.

The sergeant frowned, then looked at Jeter and said, "Detective? You were on the scene, and in the ME's office."

"Yes, sir," Jeter said, and took up what could hardly, at this point, be called a narrative. "Detective Keough, the woman's baby was taken forcefully from her, not delivered naturally. The ME said it looked as if—these are his words—her belly had exploded."

"I see," Keough said, "so the baby was forcibly removed from her."

"Exactly," Jeter said. "And then, obviously, she bled to death."

"Was she dead when she went into the river?" Keough asked.

"Yes," Jeter said. "The ME found no water in her lungs."

"All right," Keough said, "so we have a dead woman and a missing fetus."

"Similar to the case you had when you first arrived here," Mayor Emery said.

"No, sir," Keough said. "In that case we had live babies and missing mothers. Quite different."

"Um, yes, I see," the mayor said. "I was hoping that, well, it might be the same man."

"Eric Pautz is still in prison, sir," Keough said. "I check up on him periodically."

Keough looked at Jeter. He decided to talk as much with the detective as he could, and leave the two politicians out of the loop.

"And there's been a second girl?"

"Yes."

"Found where?"

"In a garbage dump," Jeter said. "Tossed there like just so much garbage."

"And her condition was the same?"

"Yes, sir," Jeter said. "Exactly the same."

"Was she the same age?" Keough asked. "Or age group?"

"No, that was something we noticed right away," Jeter said. "The first woman appeared to be in her early twenties, and the second in her early thirties."

"Have you identified either woman yet?"

"No," Jeter said. "We ran their prints and came up blank."

"What about missing persons reports?"

"We went through our files on the first girl, and we're going through them on the second."

"When was the second woman found?"

"Two days ago," Jeter said. "It was exactly two weeks after the first body was discovered. We've kept it out of the papers."

"That's good," Keough said. "You don't want to encourage a serial killer."

"So we do have one?" Mayor Emery asked, his voice cracking at the high end.

"It's too soon for me to say, sir," Keough said. "I'd have to see all the reports, visit the scenes—it would take some time. I'd need a place to work—"

"We can supply you with everything you need," the mayor said. "Detective Keough, we would really appreciate your help on this. We know your reputation with serial killers both here and in New York."

"I read Mike O'Donnell's book on the Kopykat case in New York," Jeter said.

Great, Keough thought, *that book again*. Of course, he couldn't be too upset about the book because Mike O'Donnell, the reporter who wrote it, still sent a percentage of his royalty checks to Keough.

"We'll give you a place to work, all the equipment you need," Emery went on, "and Detective Jeter can assist you."

A two man task force, Keough thought. He could use Jeter, if just to drive him around East St. Louis.

"I might need more men."

"We'll try to give them to you," Emery said. "Just make all your requests to Sergeant Benson. If there are any problems, you'll have a direct line to me."

Keough looked at the sergeant again. If there was one thing he didn't need it was problems with the top cop in town. If the sergeant thought Keough was going to go over his head every time they had a problem this wouldn't work, at all.

Keough walked over to the sergeant and looked down at him.

"This is your department, sergeant," he said. "If you don't want me on this, I'm gone. Just say the word."

The sergeant looked up at Keough, then stood so they were eye to eye.

"To be honest, Detective Keough, I don't want you . . . but the mayor and the chief both feel we need you. I wish we didn't, but maybe we do. So whatever you need, you let me know."

The man still looked unhappy—or gassy—but his words rang true.

"I don't think I'll be needing that direct line to you, Your Honor," he said to the mayor. "The Sergeant and I can come to an understanding."

"Then you'll work on this?"

Keough nodded. "I'll see what I can do."

Four

KEOUGH LEFT THE mayor's office in the company of Detective Marc Jeter.

"They don't have an office set up for you yet, sir," Jeter said, "'cause they didn't know if you'd say yes or no."

"How old are you?"

"What?"

"Your age?"

"I'm thirty. Why?"

"I'm not forty yet," Keough said, "so stop calling me sir."

"Yes—uh, okay."

"If I don't have an office, where are you taking me?" Keough asked as they walked through the halls.

"To my desk," Jeter said. "That's where the files are."

"Okay," Keough said. "The files are a good start."

Walking through the East St. Louis Municipal Building reminded Keough of when he first walked into the Richmond Heights Police Station two years ago. Then it was all new to him, and surprising. Since then he had come to accept each municipality's ability to house all its services in the same structure or complex.

"I'm in here," Jeter said, and guided Keough through a doorway that was marked simply, POLICE.

Inside it was more like a police station Keough was used to. Uniformed men went about their business, the sounds of the radio dispatchers doing their jobs—voices, static and such—in the background.

He followed Jeter to another room. The sign over the door said INVESTIGATION ROOM. There were three desks and the young black man pointed to the one in the corner. "That's mine. Yours, too, for a while, I guess."

"And you don't mind?" Keough asked.

"Mind?" Jeter asked. "Why should I mind?"

"Well, it's your case, and your territory."

"Detective Keough," Jeter said, "I meant what I said. I can—and will—learn a lot from you. I want to be a good detective."

"Well," Keough said, "your attitude is admirable and . . . rare. Why don't you show me the files?"

"Yes, sir."

"How about if I call you Marc," Keough suggested, "and you just call me Joe?"

"Okay, Joe," Jeter said. "That works for me."

The young man picked up two files from his desk. He'd obviously placed them there before going to the meeting at the mayor's office. Maybe he'd even thought about taking them with him.

"You can sit here and look through these, if you like. I can get you some coffee."

"Just let me take a quick look," Keough said, seating himself behind Jeter's desk. From this vantage point he could see two other men in the room, looking at him. He ignored them and opened the first folder, leafed through it, and stopped when he came to photos of the body. Then he opened the second folder and did the same, stopping again when he came to the photos. When he looked up, he was alone in the room with Jeter.

"Sometimes, I can't believe the violence that we're capable of," he said, looking up at Detective Jeter. "I mean, the human race . . . and the violence we're capable of visiting upon each other . . ."

" 'The joy of killing. The joy of seeing killing done—these are traits of the human race at large.' "

Keough looked up at Jeter, puzzled.

"What, a black man can't quote Mark Twain?" Jeter asked.

"I didn't know it was Twain," Keough said. He replaced the photos in the folders, stood and picked them both up. "I'm going to take these home with me and go over them more thoroughly. I'll come back tomorrow morning at nine. At that time I'd like to visit the locations where both women were found."

"Okay," Jeter said. "Uh, what do I do until then?"

Keough shrugged and said, "Do your job."

"I've been taken off the chart to work only on this case," the young black man said.

"Then, my friend," Keough said, "take the rest of the day off."

Keough started for the door, then turned and looked at Jeter. "Mark Twain?"

"Greatest writer who ever lived," Jeter said.

"Okay," Keough said, and left.

After he was gone the other two men reentered the room.

"Is that the great expert?" one of them asked Jeter.

"That's him," Jeter said.

"Don't see why we need him," the other man said.

Jeter looked at them. "I need him to learn. God knows I'm not learning anything from you jokers."

"Bite me, Jeter."

"If anybody's looking for me," Jeter said, heading for the door, "tell them I was given the rest of the day off."

Five

KEOUGH RETURNED HOME and dropped the files on the dining room table. He called the mayor's office, but wasn't able to get the man on the phone, so he left a message with his secretary saying that he was now "working" with the East St. Louis Police, and that he'd keep the mayor updated on his progress.

After he hung up he noticed the message light blinking on his machine. When he played it back there two messages, and they both floored him.

"Joe, it's Valerie," Valerie Speck said, her tone very tentative. "You're probably surprised to hear from me, but I'm not calling for myself. It's about Brady. You remember Brady?" Of course he remembered the little boy he'd met his first day on the job, bloody footprints and all. He was living with a foster family out in Florissant—or was it Sunset Hills?—the last time Keough had seen him, but that was more than a year ago. He wondered if the boy had been adopted.

"I got a call from the family Brady is living with now. They're thinking about adopting him, but they said that Brady wanted to talk with Detective Keyhole." That was what Brady had ended up calling Keough. "You can call me back, or I'll just give you the family's number." She said their name was Rodman and gave him the number. "They know that they might be hearing from you or me about this. You can call them . . . or me . . . it's up to you, Joe. I, uh, well, that's it, I guess. I . . . g–good-bye."

He hadn't seen Valerie since that day in the park, after Steinbach had been killed, when he was flying a kite and she walked away from him. He had reacted badly to both Steinbach's death and to the fact that he had diabetes. She said she couldn't be with him if he didn't want to share his feelings.

The second message cut into his thoughts of Valerie, a momentary reprieve for which he was grateful.

"Detective Keough? A voice from the past, here. This is Special Agent Harriet Connors."

Connors had been the FBI agent he'd worked with on the Mall Rat case. Her partner, Hannibal, had been an asshole, but he had gotten along okay with Connors.

"I'm in town and thought we might get together for a drink, or dinner. I'm staying at the Drury Inn downtown—FBI expense account hasn't gotten any better. Anyway, give me a call, I'm in room two fourteen. Oh, and this isn't all pleasure. I've got some business to discuss with you. Call me."

Another shocker. Two women from his past in one day. He made notes from both messages and then erased them. Did he want to talk to either woman? That was something he'd have to decide over dinner, and maybe even after he had gone through the two files he had brought home. He picked up the folders and carried them into the kitchen with him, dropped them on the table and started rooting through the refrigerator and freezer. He had recently taken to keeping the freezer stocked with frozen dinners for evenings he didn't feel like eating out—like tonight.

He put one chicken and one beef rice bowl in the microwave—they were small—and set it for fourteen minutes, then sat down at the table with a diet Coke and started going through the files. When the rice bowls were done cooking, he was still reading the first report. He dumped the contents of the plastic bowls onto a plate, mixed it all together, got another diet Coke and continued to go through the files while he ate.

The women were very different from each other physically. One was older, one was taller, and heavier, one had been very pretty in life, one plain. The only similarity between the two was that they had been pregnant, their fetuses seemed to have been taken from them violently and their bodies had been discarded in places where—the killer hoped—they would not be found.

Keough grabbed one of the blank notebooks he kept in a nearby closet and started making notes. On one page he made a THINGS TO DO list and at the top he wrote: "Talk to the ME." Next he wrote: "Visit the scenes."

He looked at the photos again, but they only refueled the anger he'd felt earlier in the day, the first time he'd seen them. What had been done to these women was monstrous, and who knew what had been done with their babies?

But to work on any case effectively, anger had to be put in one of those compartments in his mind, locked away until he needed to take it out again, when the case got so frustrating he wanted to give up. That was when that anger, that deeply indignant fury, was necessary.

He put the photos away, shuffled the papers until they all fit neatly into the folders, and then got up to make a pot of coffee. That was when he started thinking about Valerie, Brady and Harriet Connors again.

He tipped the mug, sipping his coffee, and over the top of it checked the clock on the kitchen wall. It was the coward's way out, he knew, but subconsciously he'd felt that if he waited until after he had read the files, and eaten his dinner, and made coffee, it would probably be too late to return the calls. Alas, that was not the case. It was barely eight P.M., and most people—the ones who lived those normal nine-to-five lives—were still awake.

However, neither of the women who had called him led those kinds of lives. Valerie took her work home with her, he knew, and he suspected Harriet Connors did the same. Still, eight o'clock was eight o'clock, and he had to do something about those calls.

The only one he knew he shouldn't call was Brady himself. How old was the boy now, anyway, five? And what could a five-year-old boy have to say to him that was of any importance—especially in the face of a case involving two dead women?

He decided calling Harriet Connors would result in the least trauma, picked up the phone and dialed her hotel. He gave her room number to the operator and waited. She answered with the customary, "Hello," and he recognized her voice right away. Their relationship on the Mall Rat case had begun in an adversarial manner, but in the end they got along and were able to work together. Hell, he even ended up liking her.

"Agent Connors," he said, "Joe Keough."

"Detective Keough," she said, "thanks for calling me back."

"What brings you back to St. Louis?" he asked. "A case?" Could it be the case he was working on, that he had only just begun to work on? No, that would have been too much of a coincidence.

"Not exactly," she said. "Look, I know it's late . . ."

"It is for some people."

"Can you meet me for a drink?" she asked. "I'd like to talk to you about something, and I don't know if I'll still be around tomorrow."

"Sure," he said, "why not?" Going out to meet with her would be the perfect excuse not to call Valerie back, wouldn't it?

"Where?" the big coward asked.

Six

SINCE IT WAS his town, Keough picked their meeting place. He knew the bar at the Drury Inn and vetoed it. Instead he chose the Morgan Street Brewery on Laclede's Landing. It would be easy for her to find.

Keough got there first, scored a table near the front window and ordered a pale ale. It was a weeknight, so it wasn't hard. He saw her walking down the street and recognized her right away. Forties, kinda solid, kinda plain, but not unattractive. A good cop, too, from what he saw last time. She was wearing dark pants and a lavender blouse with pearl buttons and cap sleeves.

When she came in the door the hostess approached her and Connors pointed to Keough, who waved. She smiled and walked over to join him.

"Hope you don't mind these tall bar tables," Keough said, standing to greet. "We could get a booth, if you like."

"No, this is fine," she said. She stuck her hand out and he shook it. "Good to see you."

"And you."

A waitress came over and smiled expectantly.

"What've you got?" Connors asked.

"The pale ale."

"I'll have the same," she said to the waitress.

"Would you like anything to eat?"

Connors looked at Keough.

"I could snack," he said.

"Order some appetizers."

He ordered them a sampler—chicken fingers, cheese sticks, that kind of thing—and two orders of the Unique Corniques.

"What are those?" Connors asked, sitting.

"These potato thingies," he said. "You'll love 'em."

"They won't love me, though."

"You look good."

"I look solid," she said. "I blame my mother. She was big-boned."

The waitress arrived with the drinks and promised to have the food over pronto.

"This is good," Connors said, after a sip.

"While we wait for the food, Agent Connors," he said, "why don't you tell me what's on your mind?"

"Harriet," she said. "I thought we left each other on a first name basis last time . . . Joe."

"All right, Harriet," Keough said. "Do we want to catch up on each other's lives and careers, or get right to it?"

"They're both a little bit the same," she said. "For instance, I know you're working for the mayor now."

"Are you investigating me?"

"No," she said. "I was just being nosy . . . but somebody's investigating you."

"You're talking about Internal Affairs," he said. "I haven't heard from them in a while. They still interested?"

"Apparently."

"Detective Mason?"

"Angela Mason, and her partner, Jack Gail."

Keough nodded.

"What did you do to piss them off?" she asked.

"They couldn't nail me last year. I guess they took it kind of personally."

At that point the waitress came with their appetizers. She set them down, took an order for another round, smiled and walked away. She was cute, but Keough wasn't interested in girl watching tonight.

Connors tried one of the "potato thingies," and nodded. "They *are* good."

Keough snagged one and said, "Told you. You want to tell me why you were nosing around about me?"

She picked up a cheese stick, stuck it in the little plastic cup of sauce and took a bite. It left a little smear at one corner of her mouth. He didn't tell her about it; it made her seem softer. She pointed at him with the other half.

"I have a new job."

"In or out of the FBI?"

"Oh, still in," she said. "I still have my Bureau credentials, but I'm part of a larger unit now. It's a multi-agency national task force. We have members from ATF, NSA, other federal agencies and some local departments."

"Sounds impressive."

"It will be," she said, picking up a chicken tender, "but I'm getting ahead of myself. I should be saying that we *will* have members from other agencies and departments. We're still in the process of interviewing people."

Keough grabbed a chicken tender for himself and dipped it in some plain ketchup.

"Are you in command?"

She popped the chicken into her mouth.

"Don't I wish," she said, with feeling. "No, I'm just in on the ground floor."

He washed down his chicken with a swig of beer and asked, "The ground floor of what?"

She leaned forward and said, "A new era in law enforcement . . . maybe."

Seven

KEOUGH LISTENED WHILE Connors explained that this new unit was the brainchild of a senior agent in the FBI, who had asked her to join as one of the first members. The rest of the unit would be made up of the elite—the finest detectives from all over the country. He then asked her to suggest anyone she knew who might be an asset to the unit, it didn't matter what other law enforcement agency he or she was with.

"I immediately thought of you," she finished.

"Well . . . I'm flattered, Harriet, but—"

"Don't be flattered," she said, cutting him off, "and don't say 'but.' After what you did in New York with the Kopykat case, and then here with the Mall Rat, you're somebody this new unit needs."

"You haven't told me what this unit is supposed to do."

"It's principally a serial killer unit," she said. "We'll answer calls from all over the country to assist locals in apprehending serial killers."

"I'm not a profiler—"

"We'll have profilers, Joe," Connors said, "and agents, but what we need are good detectives, and that's where you come in."

She told him more. While ostensibly they were being assembled to try to put away the hundreds of serial killers who were active in the country at any given time, they would also work on other violent crime cases, specifically ones where the local law enforcement personnel were stymied.

"When they're facing a stone wall and are at their wits' end," she finished, "that's where we'll come in."

"Let me ask a couple of questions," Keough said.

Connors popped the last Cornique into her mouth and said, "Go ahead."

"If I agree to join this unit, will I be in the FBI?"

"No," she said, "with the permission of your boss you can maintain your St. Louis credentials. My boss has asked a deputy sheriff from New Mexico to join the unit and he's just gonna hang on to his sheriff's badge and ID. You will, however, be carrying a special unit ID—we all will. And we'll have jurisdiction wherever we're working."

"So this won't be an FBI unit?"

"No," she said. "It's inter-agency, or multi-agency—it's still kind of complicated, but it will give you a chance to work on some amazing cases around the country. I, uh, understand you're working out of the mayor's office, right now?"

"That's right."

"Are you getting the opportunity to work the kind of cases you want to work?"

"As a matter of fact," Keough said, "I just got a case today. Seems my boss is loaning me to the mayor of East St. Louis to help clear it up."

"Really?" she asked. "Isn't that in Illinois? How does that work with you employed in Missouri?"

He explained about being "on loan" to East St. Louis for this case.

"Is it an interesting case?"

"I'm not sure yet," Keough said. "I'm just getting started on it."

"Want to tell me about it?"

"Not right now," he said. "I mean, I'm not ready to call in a special unit yet."

"Oh, don't worry about that," she said. "It's going to take some time to get this under way. You'll have plenty of time to settle your affairs here."

"So if I agree to join this unit I'll be living . . . where?"

"Somewhere in the D.C. area. Take your pick. Virginia? Maryland? Maybe Alexandria? That's real pretty."

"I see."

"Is that a problem?"

"I've only lived here a couple of years."

"Not long enough to put down roots, right? You, uh, still got that same woman friend?"

"Not really."

"This job at the mayor's office . . . would that keep you here?"

Keough studied her and had the feeling she knew more than she was saying.

"I'm going to have to think this over, Harriet," he answered, "and I'll definitely have to finish what I started today."

"I understand that," Connors said. "We're prepared to give you a month, Joe, to get yourself to D.C. It should take us that long to fill the unit."

"Well," he said, "I'll give you an answer as soon as I can."

They finished their appetizers and beer. Keough insisted on paying the check. "My town," he said, and she relented.

They walked out. It had started to rain. The cobblestoned street gleamed with it.

"Did you walk?" he asked.

"No," she said, "took my car. Didn't trust myself not to get lost. I'm in that big parking lot."

There was a public lot right in the center of the Landing, where Keough had also parked his car, so they walked into it together. They went to her car first.

"This is me," she said, as they stood next to a rented Toyota Camry. "Thanks for coming out to talk to me."

"Look, Harriet," he said, "I don't want you to think I'm not . . . well, that I don't appreciate the offer. I've just got a lot of things on my mind lately."

"I understand," she said. "A lot has happened to you in the past year or so. I heard about your partner. I was so sorry to hear it. He seemed like a good cop."

"He was," Keough said. "Damned good. And speaking of partners, is yours going to be part of this unit?"

"Hannibal?" she asked. "Jeez, no. Even I didn't recommend him for the job."

She unlocked the car door and opened it.

"Take care of yourself, Joe," she said. "Diabetes is nothing to play around with. My old man had it. He didn't take care of himself, and it killed him."

She got in the car, closed the door and rolled down the window.

"I'll be waiting to hear from you."

"Soon," he said.

"I look forward to working together again," she said. "We worked well on that Mall Rat case."

"Yeah, we did," he said.

She released the handbrake, rolled the window back up, waved and backed up. He watched her drive to the booth, pay the parking attendant and then drive off.

He walked to his car and got in. He stated the motor, but sat there for a few moments reviewing every aspect of their conversation in his head.

No, he thought, he didn't once mention anything about the diabetes. She definitely knew a lot more than she was letting on.

Eight

KEOUGH SHOWED UP at the East St. Louis Municipal Building
the next morning around eight fifty-five and found Detective
Jeter sitting at his desk in an otherwise empty room. He'd
returned home the night before too late call Valerie Speck, but
he vowed to try her as soon as he got home this time, and get it
over with. The coward's way out was good for one day, but that
was it.

He walked in with a bag containing two coffees and a couple of
bagels with butter.

"Didn't know what your routine was," he said, setting the bag
down on the desk.

"That's okay," Jeter said. "I drink tea, and I don't eat donuts or
bagels."

"Don't like them?" Keough asked.

"They don't like me," Jeter said. "I work out, can't hack the
extra calories. Takes too much time and effort to work them off."

"Well . . . that's admirable," Keough said. "Guess that means
twice as much for me."

He'd drink the two coffees, but only eat one of the bagels.
That was his concession to the diabetes—that and taking the
pills.

"You want to sit?" Jeter asked, preparing to rise.

"Stay there," Keough said. He looked around and hooked an empty chair from another desk. "This is fine."

He sat down next to the desk and dumped the two files in front of Jeter.

"I went through those last night," he said, taking the plastic top off the first coffee and unwrapping the bagel. "The one from two weeks ago still hasn't been identified?"

"Not yet," Jeter said. "I can check again, though."

"With missing persons?"

"I can use the computer."

"Are you well versed with that thing?"

"Very much so," Jeter said. "I have my own system at home that I built from parts."

"So you're an expert, then."

"Well . . ."

"And a modest one," Keough said. "Okay, you check on that and then I want to see the medical examiner."

"His reports are pretty complete," Jeter pointed out.

"I have some questions for him that aren't covered in the reports."

"Really? Like what?"

"I'll let you hear them when he does," Keough said.

Jeter turned to his computer, switched it on and said, "Okay. This shouldn't take long."

It took one bagel and one coffee to determine that an ID had not yet been made. Before they left Keough had an idea.

"Can you tap into the St. Louis PD system and run a check there, too?"

Jeter turned and looked at him with his eyebrows raised. "Can I—or am I allowed to?"

"Can you?"

"With a computer," Jeter said, "I can do anything."

"Do it, then."

"If it's traced back here—"

"I could make some calls and get the information, but I'd

rather use that time to talk to the ME and look at the scenes where the bodies were found." He popped the top off the second coffee. "And I'd like to finish this second coffee. Run the check, and if it gets traced back to you I'll handle it."

"You got it."

He watched the young detective's fingers dance over the keys while he finished the second coffee quicker than the first, since it had cooled off. As he tossed the empty container into a nearby trash can, Jeter said, "We should have an answer by the time we get back."

"All right, then," Keough said. "Let's go."

"I want to make one stop," Jeter said, and picked up the left-over bagel.

Keough followed him out of the room and down the hall to another doorway. Jeter ducked in and reappeared without the bagel. From inside the room a woman's voice said, "You're a sweetie, Marc."

Jeter's smile was shy. Keough didn't know if black men blushed, but Jeter sure looked like he was.

"Making points?" Keough asked.

"One can only hope," Jeter said. "Come on. We'll go out the back and take my car. It's got a radio."

"Lead on."

Nine

IT DOESN'T MATTER whether a morgue is in St. Louis, East St. Louis or New York, it smells and feels the same. This was Keough's thought as he followed Marc Jeter into the morgue beneath St. Mary's Hospital.

"The Doc responded to both scenes," Jeter had told Keough in the car on the way over, "and he gave us some pretty complete reports on the bodies."

"I know, I read them," Keough said. "I still have some new questions for him."

"These I've got to hear," Jeter said.

"Why's that?"

"Because then I can figure out why I didn't think of them."

They entered the ME's office after Jeter knocked on the door.

"Eh? What? Oh, it's you. I sent you my report."

The man's back had been turned when they entered and as he wheeled around Keough got a quick image of—a mess. He was wearing a white lab coat, unbuttoned so that Keough could see the white shirt beneath it was half tucked in and half out of the man's trousers, which were ill-fitting for a man of his girth. They were stretched so tightly across the front that Keough wondered why the zipper had not given up, and they were worn so low on the man's hips that his belly hung over the waistband. Keough was glad he had not paid any attention to how they stretched across the man's buttocks.

"I know that, sir," Jeter said. "I'd like to introduce Detective Joe Keough, from the St. Louis PD. He's on loan to help us with these two murders."

"Eh? Keough?" He slammed the file drawer closed and peered myopically at them first through and then over his bifocals. "I've read about you. So you're the serial killer expert, eh?"

"I have some experience," Keough said.

"Well, you'll need it, if I'm any judge," the man said, "which I'm not, because I haven't seen a serial murderer in East St. Louis in all my years here." Abruptly, the man stuck his hand out and Keough took it. "Doctor Edward Meeks."

"A pleasure, Doctor."

"I told Detective Keough that your reports were pretty thorough, and he's read them, but he says he has some questions to ask you, anyway," Jeter said.

"I'm sure he does." The doctor moved his gaze from Jeter to Keough. "And I suppose you want to see the bodies?"

"Yes, sir, if I can see both."

"Questions first, or viewing?"

"Questions—" Jeter began, but he was cut off by Keough.

"Any reason we can't do both at the same time?"

"I don't see why not."

Jeter made a face. He thought he might get away with hearing the questions without having to view the bodies—again.

Victim two was in a steel drawer, but victim number one had to be put in a freezer to keep her from "fermenting," as the good doctor put it. Keough viewed them in order.

"I'll stay out here, if you don't mind," Jeter said, as the doctor opened the door to the cooler.

"Squeamish, Detective?" Meeks asked.

"I was there the night we found her, remember, Doctor?" Jeter asked. "As it happens I'm sensitive to the cold."

"That's okay," Keough said. He took some plastic gloves from his pocket and pulled them on. "Stay out here. We won't be long."

"I'll keep the door open," Jeter said, hurriedly. "I want to hear everything."

The doctor removed the sheet from the first victim. Keough's stomach clenched when he saw the gaping wound in the woman's belly. He'd never seen anything like it before. The body had obviously taken a beating from being in the river, but despite this the face seemed recognizable enough. He quickly examined the body. Her arms resisted as he lifted them to examine her hands and wrists.

"It's the cold," the doctor said, explaining her resistance.

"All of a sudden," Keough said to the doctor, "I'm kind of sensitive to the cold, too."

"I don't blame you," Meeks said. "Let's step outside."

He covered the body and they exited the cooler. The doctor closed the door behind them.

"Her wrists, Doc," Keough said. "There are some marks . . ."

"I noticed those," Doctor Meeks said.

"What?" Jeter asked.

"Looks like strap marks to me," Keough said.

"That wasn't in the report," Jeter stated.

"My error," Meeks said. "I was looking for ligature marks, bruising . . . these are just some indentations."

"So she could have been strapped down, but did not strain enough against her bonds to cause bruising."

"Yes," Meeks said. "Come and look at the other one."

He took both detectives to a steel drawer to view the fresher corpse.

If anything, the wound in the belly of victim two was even worse for being fresher. It didn't help that the sutures in her torso were also new.

"What are the similarities, Doctor?" Keough asked while he examined the body.

"As I said in the report, both were pregnant, both had their babies torn from their bodies violently, with no regard for the safety and health of the mother. And, as you can see, she also has those indentations on her wrists."

"And ankles," Keough said.

"What?" Meeks said.

Keough held up one leg and said, "Look."

Meeks came closer, looked over and through his glasses and then mumbled, "Yes. I didn't notice that on the other woman."

"Neither did I," Keough said. He set her leg down gently. "Can you tell from the condition of the bodies how far along their pregnancies were?"

Meeks looked at Keough with respect. "No one's asked me that before. As near as I can tell they were each almost to term, perhaps eight or nine months."

"And what else is missing?"

"What do you mean?" Meeks asked, frowning.

"What other body parts are missing?"

"None," Meeks said. "They have their arms, legs, fingers, toes . . . the girl in the river was battered, but intact . . . other than the babies being taken—"

"What about the umbilical cords? The afterbirth? That sort of thing?" Keough asked.

Meeks stopped a moment and thought, then looked directly at Jeter. "Another question no one else has asked me. No, you're quite right, Detective. Both cords and placentae were removed."

"How is the umbilical cord removed, doctor? I mean, when the baby is born I know the cord is snipped on the baby's end, but I have to admit I don't know what happens on the mother's end."

"It comes out with the placenta," Doctor Meeks said. "In these cases when the babies were torn from their mother's bodies, the cords and placentae would have come with them."

"So we're not dealing with the removal of a fetus, in either case, but a child—a child who could still be alive."

"That would be correct."

"So in addition to murder," Keough said, looking at Jeter, "we can charge this mutt with kidnapping when we catch him?"

"*When* you catch him?" Meeks asked.

"That's right, Doctor," Keough said, "when we catch him. I plan on bagging this sonofabitch."

"Well," Meeks said, "I hope you get him before he does it again. Two cases like this are quite enough for me."

"Hopefully," Keough said, "these are the only two, so far."

"Hmm," the doctor said, "I see what you mean. There could have been some killings before these that we don't know about."

"If there were others," Jeter said, "we would have heard by now. I mean, East St. Louis is a small—"

"Two things, Marc," Keough said, cutting him off. "There might be others from other parts of Illinois, or Missouri, or other parts of the country. . . ."

"I hadn't thought of that. What else?"

Keough tossed the sheet back over the young woman. "There could be others that simply have not been found, yet." Keough looked at the doctor. "You were at both scenes, Doctor." It was a statement, not a question.

"Yes, I was."

"I need you both to think, then. How were the bodies situated when they were found?"

The doctor and the young detective looked at each other.

"Were they on their backs, on their sides, could they have been posed in some way, were they hidden, raped, or ejaculated on—"

"You're looking for a signature," Jeter said, suddenly.

"Very good, Marc," Keough said. "Yes. Not all serial killers are also signature killers. If this one left a signature it would come in handy identifying him if and when other bodies are found."

"Well," Meeks said, "I can tell you they weren't raped, or ejaculated on."

"There's no sexual element to the crime, then. The UNSUB is not getting off on this, unless he's doing it when he gets home. Now, what about the positions of the bodies?"

"They weren't hidden," Jeter said. "The first one, found on the banks of the river, was lying on her back. The second one was on her stomach, arms and legs spread, as if she had simply been tossed on top of all the other garbage."

"Are we certain she was in the river?" Keough asked.

"Why would we—" Jeter started.

"She could have simply been dumped there," Keough said. He looked at Meeks. "No water in her lungs?"

"No, none. My God, she had to have been dead by the time he threw her in the river, just from the blood loss—"

"You're assuming she—they—bled to death."

"They did bleed to death," the doctor said. "That's a fact."

"Then the babies were ripped from their bodies while they were still alive?"

"Undoubtedly."

"Sick," Jeter muttered.

"Then I'll ask again," Keough said, turning to Jeter, "how do we know she was in the river?"

"She was snagged on a large branch," Jeter said.

"And, as I said," Meeks offered, "the body was battered and torn, more consistent with damage that would have been sustained through contact with river debris, than from a beating. That had to have happened in the water."

"Bruising?"

"No," Meeks said, "any bruising was inflicted while she was still alive. This is actual damage to the flesh."

"And what about number two?" Keough asked. "Bruising?"

"Some."

"Consistent with the first?"

"Well . . . they could both have received blows from a blunt instrument at some point . . ."

Keough fell silent, and deeply into thought. Both of the other men were so impressed by the depth of his questions that they remained silent for fear of interrupting his thoughts.

"Doctor, can you go over both bodies again for me?"

"Looking for what?"

"I don't know," Keough said. "Something you . . . or I . . . might have missed." He was tactful enough not to mention the slight strap marks on the second victim's ankles.

"Well . . . I can do that, I suppose. Putting in a little overtime won't kill me."

"I'd appreciate that, Doctor. Please let me know as soon as you've done so."

"Where can I reach you?"

"You can leave a message at Detective Jeter's office. I'll be working out of there, for now."

"All right," Meeks said. "I must say, Detective, even in the midst of this . . . carnage, it is a distinct pleasure to watch you work." His compliment came grudgingly. He was still miffed at having been caught out on the second victim's ankles.

"Thank you, Doctor." He turned to Jeter. "Time to go."

Ten

MARC JETER STARTED the car, and as they pulled away from the morgue he said, "Uh, is it okay if I ask questions?"

"How else are you going to learn, grasshopper?"

Jeter stole a glance at Keough and said, "Huh?"

Obviously, he didn't watch much TV—not old reruns of *Kung Fu* on TNT, anyway.

"Go ahead and ask," Keough said.

"What's the difference between an MO and a signature?" the young detective asked. "I mean, I know what a *modus operandi* is, but I haven't run into any signature killers."

"They're pretty close to being the same thing," Keough said. "I'm not an expert—"

"You could have fooled me."

"Hey," Keough said, "I couldn't write a book on the subject, like John Douglas has—"

"*Mindhunter*, right? The guy they based Jodie Foster's boss on in *Silence of the Lambs*?'"

"Right," Keough said. "You want to hear from an expert, read his books. Me, I operate on instinct and logic. As far as I'm concerned an MO and a signature are almost the same. It's just that a killer's signature is more . . . personal."

"I can understand that."

"Good, because I don't know if I can explain it any better."

"Can you really tell if there's a signature, or a pattern, from two murders?"

"Sometimes," Keough said. "It's easier to track when there are three or four cases, but you also want to catch this madman before he gets that far."

"Do you already think he's mad?"

"Don't you? You saw those women's bodies. Only a madman would do that."

"'Of course, no man is entirely in his right mind at any time,'" Jeter said. The tone of his voice betrayed the fact that it was a quote, and not his own words.

"Mark Twain?"

Jeter nodded and said, "From *The Mysterious Stranger*."

"How much Mark Twain have you read?"

"Everything he's written," Jeter said. "I discovered him in college and devoured all I could find."

"And does he have a quote for everything?"

"Just about," Jeter said. "There's even a website dedicated to his quotes."

"Interesting," Keough said. "What else does he have to say about madness?"

"Well . . . there's 'When we remember we are all mad, the mysteries of life disappear and life stands explained.'"

"Don't know that I agree with that," Keough said. "We may all be mad, but some are worse than others."

"Serial killers."

"Too bad," Keough said, "there aren't any Twain quotes about them."

"'If the desire to kill and the opportunity to kill came always together, who would escape hanging?'" Jeter quoted. "From Pudd'nhead Wilson's New Calendar."

"Well," Keough said, "I don't think Pudd'nhead knew anything about serial killers."

"Well then, there's—"

"I've got some questions, if you don't mind," Keough said, having gotten his fill of outdated Mark Twain quotes.

"Uh, all right."

"I'm not noticing a lot of burnt out buildings," Keough said. "When I moved here I was told that East St. Louis had the highest per capita crime rate in the country. I was warned not to ever drive over here if I didn't have to."

Jeter shook his head and said, "That's old news. In nineteen sixty-nine we had a population of ninety thousand. By nineteen ninety-six it had gone down to thirty-five thousand—and then things started to change."

"How so?"

"Well, first we got a mayor who wasn't a crook," Jeter said. "In fact, it went even further than that. He's a deeply religious man."

"And that made a difference?"

"Big time, but not just that. In nineteen eighty-seven Wyvette Young, a black legislator from this area, challenged the University of Illinois at Champaign-Urbana to prove their commitment to urban service. As a result the university president committed money and time for a group to come into East St. Louis and assess the problems."

"And that changed things?"

"Not at first," Jeter said. "See, the people of East St. Louis were suspicious. They thought the university was just using us to justify grants that they received."

"So what changed?"

"Kenneth Reardon."

"Who's he?"

"An assistant professor from the university who came up with an idea," Jeter explained. "He decided that the university should go into small communities, one at a time. They interviewed residents and asked for their ideas for making things better. They allowed the people of these neighborhoods to control their own destinies—and it worked. The university formed the East St. Louis Action Research Project. Students and professors joined in with the citizens to start clearing out crack houses and burnt out buildings, put new faces on old buildings, add what they called 'vest pocket parks' here and there. That's what worked. We went into neighborhood after neighborhood and made small changes, until they added up to big ones. Absentee owners were forced to make changes, or sell."

"We?"

Jeter looked at him. "Yes. I was a student back then. I lived here, went to the university, and then came back as part of the ARP project. After graduation I joined the police department and came home to stay."

"I see."

"Now we have an extension of the St. Louis Metrolink so that there are stops on this side of the river, and we expect communities to expand around those stops. So you see, this is no longer the East St. Louis you heard about when you got here—but you can't tell that to people from the St. Louis side of the river. They don't buy it. They're clinging to a stereotype. We're a predominantly black community, so we must be riddled with crime." He shook his head. "When this hits the papers it sure isn't going to help."

"Hey, St. Louis has had its share of murders, just in the two years I've been there."

"But St. Louis isn't saddled with a reputation for crime." Jeter blew air out in disgust. "This is going to set us back but good."

"Unless we catch him before he hits again."

"Do you seriously think we have a chance to do that?"

Keough considered his words carefully, then said, "Not with what we know now, no."

Eleven

THEY STOPPED AT the site where the first victim was found, and had to park some distance away before walking down to the edge of the water. Keough didn't think he'd been this close to the Mississippi since moving here—he'd certainly never had the muddy water lapping at the toes of his shoes.

"If you want to see exactly where the body was found," Jeter said, "I've got some plastic bags in my pocket."

"Plastic bags?"

"For your shoes." Jeter had seen the ME use them, and the young detective usually only had to see something once to retain its value.

Keough looked around. Finding any kinds of tracks here was obviously hopeless, and it did seem logical that the body had come down the river and ended up here on the water's edge by accident.

"That's okay," he said, "let's go back to the car."

They walked back and leaned side-by-side against Jeter's Plymouth Reliant.

"What about up here, where we're parked?" Keough asked. "Any sign of tracks?"

"If there were," Jeter said, "all the emergency vehicles pretty much wiped them out. I didn't have enough uniforms here to rope it off until it was too late."

"That's okay," Keough said, "You're probably right about the body coming down the river, which brings up another point."

"What's that?"

"She was found in East St. Louis," he said, "but not necessarily killed here."

"Wait a minute," Jeter said. "You're right—and the same goes for the other one. She was left in an East St. Louis dump, but not necessarily killed here."

"So the question is," Keough said, "why dump them here, in a smaller city, where they'd get noticed faster? Why not take them someplace larger?"

"He wanted them found here?"

"Either he wanted them found," Keough said, "or he's not as smart as the profilers say serial killers are supposed to be."

Jeter looked at him. "You don't sound very confident in profilers."

"Let's just say I'm skeptical of anyone who treats serial killers as something other than criminals. That means doctors, who claim that they have an 'illness,' and profilers, who see them as 'subjects.'"

"Wow."

"Why 'wow'?"

"You have a reputation for being able to catch these . . . monsters," Jeter said, "but you don't adhere to any of the popular opinions."

"I suppose I don't." Before Jeter could go any deeper into the subject, though, Keough pushed off the car. "All right, let's go and see the second site before we try to figure this out."

"But this is great," Jeter said, as they got in. "If they weren't killed here, then the crimes may not have as drastic an effect on East St. Louis's reputation as we feared."

"Don't count on that, Marc," Keough said, as the younger man started the car. "They were found here, and that's what sticks in people's minds."

"But if we can prove—"

"Let's just head for the second site and see what we can see there," Keough said, cutting him off.

It was a garbage dump, plain and simple. It looked like a dump and smelled like one, only on a smaller scale than others he had seen.

At least he could walk around this site and study the ground, since the body hadn't been found practically in the damned river, which offered no evidence whatsoever. After only a few moments, though, it was clear that this river of garbage was not going to offer up any helpful hints, either.

"Let's go," Keough said. "We're not learning anything here."

They got in the car and Jeter started it up and pulled away.

"But we did learn something, didn't we?"

"You tell me."

"Well . . . that the women may not have been murdered here in East St. Louis."

"That's not something we learned," Keough said. "It's something we agreed was a possibility. It's just a theory."

"So what do we do next?"

"We're going to use that computer of yours to find out if there have been any other bodies found in this condition anywhere in the country."

"And what about the world?" Jeter asked. "I can find out about other countries, too."

"That's a long shot, but let's do it," Keough said. "And then there's a call I want to make."

"To whom?"

"To someone who offered me their help on this last night," he answered, "and I should have accepted it then. I only hope she's still in town, and still willing."

"She?"

"A lady FBI agent," Keough said. Then he looked at Jeter and asked, "Any Mark Twain quotes about lady cops?"

Jeter thought a moment, then shrugged and said, "Not a one."

"Well, that's refreshing."

Twelve

WHILE JETER SAT at his desk and worked furiously at his computer keyboard, Keough called the Drury Inn, hoping Harriet Connors was still registered. He'd been foolish the night before not to bounce this off of her. If these kinds of murders were happening anywhere else in the country, she'd probably know.

When she answered the phone he said, inanely, "I guess you're still here."

"I decided to stay another night," she replied. "I figured I could use some R-and-R."

"Then I'm sorry to break in on your down time, Harriet," he said, "but it turns out I could use your help on my case, after all."

"The one in East St. Louis?" she asked.

"Yes."

"Is that where you are now?"

"Yes, at their police station, but I can come to you—"

"Just give me directions," she said, cutting him off. "I was never very good at R-and-R, anyway."

She followed his directions to the letter and made it from downtown in fifteen minutes. He was waiting for her outside, in front of the building, and waved as she parked her car in the lot and got out.

"Come inside," he said. "I want you meet my young partner on this. I think you'll like him."

"How many victims are we talking about?" she asked, as they walked along.

"Two," he said, and hurriedly gave her the salient details. She was about up to speed when they reached the investigation room. Jeter and one other man were in the small room when they entered and he stood.

"Detective Marc Jeter," Keough said, "Special Agent Harriet Connors, FBI."

"It's a pleasure, Ma'am—I mean, Agent Connors."

Harriet put out her hand and after only a moment's hesitation Jeter shook it. The other man slipped out of the room wordlessly.

"Nice to meet you, Detective," Connors said.

"Has Detective Keough filled you in?" the young man asked.

"For the most part, I guess," Connors said. "He just hasn't told me exactly what he wants me to do."

"Here," Keough said, pulling a chair over for her. "Have a look at these files, just as an unofficial observer, and tell me if you've ever run into this before."

"We're running a computer check on the, uh, MO right now," Jeter said.

"But I trust you more than I trust the computer, Harriet," Keough said.

"I'm flattered," she said, sitting down. She was wearing the kind of pants suit she had worn all during the Mall Rat case: dark, with a white blouse. It occurred to him that last night had been the only time he'd seen her dressed in something without a jacket.

She set her purse down on the floor next to her chair, pulled the files over and started to examine them. Each time she came to the photos she stopped short and shook her head. Finally, she closed both folders and pushed them back across the desk.

"I'm sorry," she said, shaking her head.

"What do you mean?" Jeter asked, but Keough already knew.

"Nothing?" he asked.

She looked up at him. "I've never seen anything like this," she said, waving a hand at the files. "It's . . . barbaric."

"Yes, it is," Keough said. "Well, it was worth a try. Thanks for driving over."

"That's it?"

"What else is there?"

"Well, maybe I can . . . make some suggestions. Maybe there are some questions you haven't asked."

Keough realized that Connors not only wanted to help, she needed to. There was something inside of her that drove her, which was what made her a good agent—but it probably also kept her from having a private life.

"Excuse me!"

They all looked up and saw Sergeant Ben Benson standing in the doorway, looking more unhappy than he had when Keough first met him.

"Sir?" Jeter said.

"Can I see you in my office, Detective Jeter?"

"Yes, sir."

Benson turned and left. Jeter looked at Keough, shrugged and followed his superior.

"Who was that?"

"Sergeant Benson, the investigative supervisor."

"Is the kid in trouble?"

"I don't know," Keough said. "I thought I had things smoothed out yesterday."

"Maybe it's me," she offered.

"Why would it be—wait. There was another man in here when we arrived."

"Yes," Connors said. "He slipped out as soon as you . . . right after you introduced me to Jeter."

"That sonofa—he must have gone running to the sergeant to tell him the FBI was here."

"So the kid is in trouble," Connors said.

Keough nodded. "And I'm going to have to get him out of it."

"Maybe I can help."

He looked at her and said, "I guess it remains to be seen whether you can help, or if we've done irreparable damage."

Thirteen

UNDER NORMAL CIRCUMSTANCES there was local resistance whenever the FBI came into a case. Even Keough hadn't liked it when they had become involved in the Mall Rat case, but later he realized how vital their involvement had been—specifically Harriet Connors's involvement. However, she was only here now at his request as an unofficial observer. He knew he was going to have to explain that to Sergeant Benson.

While he waited for his turn to speak, he thought back to the phone call he had made that morning before leaving the house. He'd left it til the last minute, when he was showered and fed and dressed and ready to go, to actually pick up the phone and make the call. . . .

"Hello?" Valerie's voice said.

"Val—Valerie," he said, changing at the last moment. He didn't feel he had the right to call her "Val," not anymore.

"Joe?"

"Hi," he said. "I'm sorry I didn't get back to you right away last night. I, uh, I got busy."

"Oh, sure," she said, "that's all right. I understand."

"It's . . . nice to hear your voice." He didn't know what else to say.

"Yes, yours, too."

There was an awkward silence then before he cleared his throat and asked, "You said the call was about Brady?"

"Oh, yes . . . his foster family called. He says he wants to talk to Detective Keyhole."

"Is he all right?"

"He seems fine," she said. "I saw him last week, though, and he didn't say a word about you. Then I got a call yesterday from the family."

"Is this family going to adopt him?"

"It looks like it," she said.

"Finally. How many families has this kid bounced around to?"

"Too many," she said. "He's such a sweet boy, Joe."

"I know," he said. "All right, uh, let me see when I can . . . how about later today, after school?"

"I can arrange that. Say around four?"

"Yeah, four would be good. Should I go to his house?"

"Why don't I meet you there?" she asked. "I mean, you haven't met this family, and . . ." She let her voice trail off.

"Well, all right," he said, when he realized she wasn't going to say anything more. "Just give me the address." She rattled it off and he wrote it down on a pad by the phone, then tore off the page and put it in his wallet. "I'll see you there, then."

"Yes," she said, "I'll see you there."

There was another awkward silence and then she said, "Joe?"

"Yes?"

She hesitated a few beats. "Um, I'll see you at four."

"All right," he said, and they hung up. . . .

"Detective Keough?"

He looked up at Jeter, who had reentered the room. "The sergeant would like to see you now."

"Is it about me?" Connors asked. "Maybe I should go with you, since it's about me."

"Let me talk to him alone first," Keough said. "I'll call you in if I need backup."

"Well . . . all right."

"Come on," Jeter said, "I'll take you down."

In the hall Jeter hissed urgently, "He's really pissed that we called in the FBI without checking with him first! He says he's going to get your ass shipped back across the bridge."

"Well, first of all I don't think your mayor would go for that, and second we didn't call in the FBI, I just made a call to a friend. Did you tell him that?"

"I tried," Jeter said. "Mainly he just reamed me and then sent me out to get you. I could hardly get a word in."

"Okay," Keough said. "I'll handle it, Marc."

"It's right there, on the left."

"Why don't you go back and keep Agent Connors company? Talk to her a while. Maybe you'll learn something."

"I'm learning a lot," the younger man said, "I'm just not sure it's all good."

Fourteen

As KEOUGH ENTERED Sergeant Benson's office, the man looked up at him with the same sour expression on his face. It seemed a safe bet at this point that he always looked that way. The Sergeant wore a wedding ring, which made Keough wonder what all the little Bensons looked like.

"I think I know why I'm here, Sarge—" Keough began.

"I thought we had an understanding, Keough," Benson said, cutting him off.

"We do—"

"Then why would you bring the FBI in on this without consulting me first?"

"Look, Sarge," Keough said, "Agent Connors was just in town on another matter. She and I had a drink last night, and today it occurred to me that we could use her opinion on this thing. Her being here is completely unofficial. In fact, she happens to be on leave, right now." That last part was almost the truth.

Benson touched his stomach, which made Keough wonder if there wasn't another reason for his sour puss.

He waited while the Sergeant scratched his cheek and mulled over want he'd just been told.

"I don't want the FBI rushing in here and taking over," the

man said, finally. "It took me a while to accept the fact that *you* were coming over here from the other side of the river."

"I appreciate that, Sarge, I really do."

"Well . . . did she?"

"Did she what?"

"Give you her opinion?" It seemed as if the resistance part of the conversation was over—for now.

"She did," Keough said. "She's never run into anything like this before."

"Oh, that's great," Benson said. "We're gonna be on the map for coming up with a whole new class of gruesome killer."

"That's not necessarily true."

"Why not?"

"Because the victims were just *found* in East St. Louis," Keough said. "They didn't necessarily live here, and maybe they weren't even killed here."

"Then why would they be dumped in my city?"

"Only one was dumped here, Sarge," Keough said. "The second one. The first one was apparently dumped in the river and she just happened to make her way to shore here."

"That's a good point," Benson said. "Have you been to the scenes?"

"I have, and I didn't learn anything from them."

"So what's the next step?"

"Well," Keough said, "other than waiting for the killer to hit again, the next step has to be to identify the victims."

"And how do we do that?" Benson asked. "We haven't had much luck with fingerprints, or with missing persons reports."

"The newspapers."

"What about them?"

"We've got to put their pictures in the newspapers, and maybe on TV, and ask people if they know either of the women."

"That's gonna be pretty rough on their families," Benson said, "to find out that way."

Police departments almost invariably withheld the identity of a crime victim from the press until family was located. However, this did seem like a time when it would have to be done the other way around.

"I don't think we have a choice, Sarge," Keough said. "I'll need your okay before I talk to the press. Unless you want to make a statement."

"Our chief might want to do that," Benson said, "but let me check. Since you have the lead on this it might be better for you to do it."

"Well, talk to him and let me know," Keough said. "The sooner we get it done, the better. If we can ID these women and establish some kind of motive, maybe we can catch him before he hits again." He didn't really believe that, but it sounded good.

"I'll get ahold of him right away," Benson said. "I'll let you know when I know."

"Okay. Is that it?"

"Yes, that's all."

Keough was at the door when Benson said, "Look, uh, I tore into Jeter pretty good. Tell him for me, uh, I'm, uh . . ."

"He's young, Sarge," Keough said. "He'll get over it—but I'll tell him."

"Thanks," the man mumbled, apparently embarrassed at having to apologize to a subordinate—but a big man in Keough's eyes for doing it, anyway.

Keough left the supervisor's office and walked back down to the investigation room, where Jeter and Connors were deep in conversation. They stopped and looked at him as he entered.

"It's okay," Keough said to Jeter. "He's sorry he tore into you."

"He said that?" the young detective asked, looking surprised.

"Almost."

"He understands I'm here unofficially?" Connors asked.

"Yes."

"Good," she said. "I'm glad I didn't cause too much trouble."

"It would have been my fault anyway, for calling you over here," Keough said.

"Joe," Jeter said, "Agent Connors has come up with a logical next step."

Connors looked at Keough's face, then said to Jeter, "I think I've been scooped, kid."

"Huh?"

"IDing the victims?" Keough asked.

"That's right," Jeter said. "You thought of it?"

"I've already talked to the sergeant about it," Keough said. "He's talking to the chief right now about going to the press with photos."

"I told you he was pretty smart," Connors said to Jeter.

"I'm flattered," Keough said. "Harriet, the least we could do is buy you lunch while you're here."

She looked at her watch. "You got a deal."

"Where to?" Keough asked Jeter.

"The Casino Queen's got a lunch buffet," Jeter said. "Not great, but not bad, and we won't have to wait to be served."

"How's that sound?" Keough asked Connors.

"I like the part about not waiting."

"Okay, then," Keough said, "why don't we leave our cars here and let the kid drive us over."

"Are you guys going to keep referring to me as 'the kid'?" Jeter asked.

Keough and Connors exchanged a glance and he said, "Probably."

"At least until you catch up to us in age," she added.

Jeter thought it over a moment, then said, "Okay, I can live with that."

Out in the parking lot, as they were getting into Jeter's car, Connors said, "You aren't going to expect me to gamble, are you?"

"Why not?" Keough asked.

"Because I have the worst luck of anyone I've ever known."

They got in the car and closed the doors. As he started the engine, Jeter quoted, "'It is strange the way the ignorant and inexperienced so often and so undeservedly succeed when the informed and the experienced fail.'"

Connors, sitting in the front with Jeter, turned in her seat and looked quizzically at Keough.

"Mark Twain," Keough explained.

Fifteen

ANDREW JUDSON KEPT his eyes on the woman. Of all the mourners in chapel number nine, she was the one who had the look of a "casket jumper." It was odd, he thought, but from what he could tell she was not one of the family. She was seated in the back row while the immediate family of the deceased man—his parents, his wife, and his children—were in the front. They all looked calm and resigned to the fact that the man was dead. This woman, however, had the *look*. She must have been close to the man in another way. A friend . . . or a lover.

Probably a lover, he thought, which meant there was a scene in the making unless he did something about it.

The woman was young—younger than the dead man's wife, and much prettier, which convinced him even more that she was the deceased's mistress. It had probably taken a lot of nerve to come here and not go up to the casket, but moment by moment her nerve was waning and he was sure that, soon, she was going to charge the casket and try to jump in it to "go with" her lover.

Not if he could help it. He'd worked too long and hard to get this account. For a mortuary as small as his was, jobs were not easy to come by, anymore.

He had only this one showing going on until tomorrow, when

a second would begin. Luckily, this was the last day of this particular wake. Working alone, he had to make sure he scheduled carefully because he liked to devote as much time as he could to one "client" and one family. Sadly, this was becoming less and less problematical.

Judson moved into the room and positioned himself behind the woman's chair. He could feel the energy radiating from her, knew that it would soon drive her to her feet. When it happened he moved immediately. A big man, he grabbed her by the elbow and surreptitiously hustled her from the room.

"Let me go—" she started to say, but he shook her and said, "Behave!"

She quieted down and he spirited her away into a nearby lounge with a dripping coffee maker and a cheap table and chair set he'd been meaning to replace.

"Sit down," he said, and she did, contritely.

"How did you know?" she suddenly asked.

"I can tell. I've been in this business a while."

"I—I just wanted to go with him, you know?" she said. "I—I loved him so much."

"He's gone, Miss . . ."

"Julia," she said, "Julia Cameron."

"He's gone, Miss Cameron."

"Just call me Julia."

He stared at her a moment. The dead man had been sixty-three when a heart attack took him from his family and friends—and, apparently, from a thirty-year-old lover. She was pretty, rather small and slender, pale-skinned with a gentle voice.

"Julia, you don't want to make a scene in there. You want him to go with dignity, don't you?"

"Yes," she said, sniffing. "Of course."

"Then I suggest that you leave before we remove the casket."

She stared at him wide-eyed and said, "But . . . I want to go to the cemetery with him."

"Wouldn't that be difficult to explain to his family, Julia? To his wife?"

"B–but, he has to know that I was here—"

"Believe me," Judson said, "he knows."

"You think so?"

He crouched down in front of her and took both of her clasped hands in his. "I'm sure he knows that you were here, and he knows that you loved him. I think it's time you went home, don't you?"

She stared at him, her lips quivering, and when she squeezed his hand he knew he had her.

"You're very kind," she said.

"You're easy to be kind to." He released her hands and stood up. "Are you parked in the lot? I'll walk you out."

"A–all right."

He helped her to her feet, walked her outside and watched while she got in her car and drove away. She was pregnant, he knew that. It was something he could tell, even though she was barely showing yet. He wondered if her lover had known before he died? Had he provided for her, at all?

He went back inside thinking maybe he'd look her up and see how she was doing—in about six or seven months.

Sixteen

AFTER LUNCH, THEY dropped Agent Connors back at her car so she could return to her hotel. She'd be checking out tomorrow, she said, and heading back to Washington.

"No other candidates to interview?" Keough asked.

"Not this trip," she replied. "I came all this way just to see you. Don't keep me waiting too long for your answer, Joe."

"I'll try not to," Keough said. "I'm going to be busy with this a while, though."

"I'll ask around when I get back," she offered, "and see if anyone else has any ideas."

"Thanks."

As she drove off they stood in the parking lot watching her car. "Decision about what?" Jeter asked.

"Just an offer she made."

"Neat lady," the young detective said. "Smart. Whatever she's offering, I'd say yes if I were you."

Keough looked at him, waiting for his next Mark Twain quote. When it didn't come they went back into the municipal building.

* * *

There were no MO matches on the computer when Jeter checked for replies. Keough only had a couple of hours left before he had to go meet Valerie and see Brady. He used the time to coordinate with Sergeant Benson and Chief Clark. They successfully set up a press conference for the next morning, in the lobby of the building. Even though he had not yet met Clark, he made the arrangements through the chief's secretary.

"I've got to go," he told Jeter as 3:30 rolled around.

"I'll stay here," Jeter said, "and play with the computer a little more. Do you have a cell phone in case I want to reach you?"

Keough made a face. He did have a cell, but he kept it in the glove compartment of his car. He didn't even have the number memorized. He only used it to keep in touch with the mayor when the need arose.

"Just call my home and leave a message," he told Jeter. "I'll check in from time to time."

"A cell phone would be a real help—"

"I hate the things, all right?" Keough said, cutting him off. "They ring at the wrong times and people talk loudly into them to impress everyone around them. Then if they see you listening they give you a dirty look. If they're going to yell into the things, then I have a right to listen—and comment—right?"

"Okay, okay," Jeter said, backing off. "No cell phone."

"I'll be in here at nine A.M. tomorrow morning," Keough said. "The press conference is set for ten."

"Do I have to be there?"

"I'd like you there, yes," Keough said, "and make sure we have photos of the victims ready."

"Um, I won't have to say anything, will I?" Jeter asked. "I mean, I'm not so good at public speaking."

"You won't have to say a word," Keough assured him. "In fact, I probably won't, either. The chief will do most of the talking. Just like any politician, he'll relish the opportunity."

"You don't know our chief," Jeter said. "You'd better be ready to do most of the talking."

"Whatever," Keough said, stealing another glance at his

watch. He knew it wouldn't take long to get to Sunset Hills, but he wanted to make sure he wasn't late. "I've got to go."

"Hot date?"

"Important appointment," Keough said. "See you in the morning." He started for the door, then turned back. "You always dress like that?" Keough asked Jeter.

"Like what?"

"Like *GQ*."

Jeter looked down at himself. "Hey, I'm a single guy with nothing to spend money on but myself. I like to look nice."

"Do me a favor," Keough said. "Dress like that for the press conference tomorrow, but after that try and dress down a little. You make me feel too Kmart."

"Where do you shop?" the younger man asked.

"Never mind."

He pulled up in front of the home of Brady's foster family with ten minutes to spare and found Valerie already there, sitting in her car. He took a deep breath and assumed she was doing the same.

They'd met because of Brady, had gotten along well and had fallen into a fairly comfortable relationship. There was, however, no intimacy beyond the physical, and in the end that was what broke them up.

"Hello, Joe."

"Valerie," he said, and then, "you look great." He hadn't expected to say that, but it was the truth. Her hair had grown longer and she'd lightened it. She was fit and lovely, as always, but since he hadn't seen her in some time it had a greater impact on him.

"Thank you. You're looking well. How is the—how are you?"

"I'm fine." He knew she'd started to ask about the diabetes, and then stopped herself. It was so awkward between them that it was painful.

"Shall we go in?" he asked.

"Yes, of course," she said. "That's what we're here for, after all."

They walked up the walkway to the door together. The house was mostly brick, two stories, one of the larger ones on the block. There was a winding driveway that ended at a two-car garage, and in front of the closed garage door was a BMW, probably last year's model. The license plate said BABE.

He let Valerie ring the bell and she said, "I called and let them know we were coming."

"Good."

They waited patiently, awkwardly, for the door to open. When it did, Keough was sure that the woman standing there belonged to the license plate on the BMW.

Seventeen

THE WOMAN WHO opened the door was trying very hard to live up to the name on the license plate. She was mid-thirties, but was wearing enough makeup to make you think she was trying to hide wrinkles earned by at least forty years of living. Certainly not bad looking, but trying way, way too hard.

"Yes?"

"Mrs. Logan?"

"That's right."

"I'm Valerie Speck. You called me about Brady—"

"Oh, yes," the woman said, "Miss Speck. And is this . . ."

"Detective Joe Keough. May we come in?"

"Well . . . of course," she said, backing away uncertainly. "My husband is not home from work yet—"

"Is Brady here?" Keough asked.

"Yes," she said, closing the door. "He's in the backyard. I'm terribly sorry to bother you with this, Detective Keyho—I mean, Keough. I know you must be busy with more important—"

"It's all right, Mrs. Logan," Keough said. "What Brady wants is important, too."

"Yes, well . . . my husband isn't here, but . . ." She was obviously nervous about something.

"Here's my badge," Keough said, producing it, "and my ID, if it makes a difference."

She peered at them, but he had his doubts about how much she was able to retain.

"I suppose it's all right . . . come this way."

She led them from the entry foyer into a large living room, and then across the room to a large set of sliding doors. Through the glass Keough could see Brady sitting on the ground playing with something.

"Shall I go with you?" Mrs. Logan asked.

Keough looked at her and said, "I think I can handle this, Ma'am."

"Joe—" Valerie said.

"I got it, Val."

He slid the door open and stepped out before either woman could object further. He crossed the patio and started across the grassy backyard toward where the boy was crouched. Off to one side was a set of swings, and a seesaw.

As he approached, the boy seemed to sense him and looked up. There was no fear in his eyes, but there wasn't much of anything else, either—except maybe sadness.

"Brady?"

The boy didn't answer, but he didn't look away. The dump truck in his hands was forgotten.

"Do you remember me?"

Brady nodded. For a moment Keough thought he wasn't going to speak, but then he said, "Detective Keyhole."

"You wanted to talk to me, right?"

Brady nodded.

"Well, I'm here," Keough said.

Brady bit his lip and looked unsure for the first time. He looked past Keough to where Valerie and Mrs. Logan were watching them through the glass.

"Don't worry," Keough said, "they can't hear us. Why don't we go and sit on the swings and talk there."

Brady thought it over a minute, then nodded. He stood up and surprised Keough by taking his hand. The boy seemed to have grown a foot since Keough saw him last, and it seemed to be mostly legs.

They each sat on a swing, Brady's feet dangling. He stared down at them while Keough waited to see if he would start talking. He was wearing a T-shirt, jeans and sneakers, and his hands were black from playing in the dirt with the truck.

"Brady?"

"Huh?"

"Now that I'm here, are you sorry you asked for me?"

The boy shrugged.

"I could leave," Keough said, making as if to get up off the swing.

"No!" Brady turned his head and stared at Keough, who could now see the fear in the boy's eyes, along with the sadness. He settled back down on the swing.

"What is it, son?" he asked. "What's wrong?"

Brady bit his lip again, then asked, "Can you stop someone from doing something . . . without putting them in jail?"

"Well . . . that sort of depends on what they're doing."

Brady took some time to think about that.

"What are they doing, Brady?" Keough asked.

"Hurtin' somebody."

"Somebody you know?"

Brady nodded.

"And you want me to stop them?"

"Yes."

"But you don't want me to put them in jail?"

Brady shook his head.

"Well . . . I don't know what I can do, Brady, until I know exactly what's going on. Do you understand?"

"Yes."

"So tell me," Keough said, "who's being hurt?"

Brady stared down at his shoes and said, "Mommy Logan."

"Your foster mother? Brady, is she being hurt?"

"He hits her."

"With his fists?"

Brady nodded.

"Well," Keough said, "if somebody is hitting your foster mother, Brady, I can certainly stop them."

"You can?" Brady looked at Keough hopefully.

"Of course. That's what I do."

"Without putting him in jail?"

"Well . . ."

"You can't put him in jail!" Brady said urgently. "That would ruin everything."

"Okay, settle down," Keough said. "Why don't we see what I can do before we talk about jail, all right?"

"All right."

"Just tell me who it is that's hitting her," Keough said, with a sinking feeling that he already knew, "and we can start from there."

Brady fell silent again.

"Brady? Do you know who's hitting her?"

"Yes."

"And will you tell me so I can help?"

"Yes."

"All right, then. Who is it?"

Brady looked at him with big, solemn brown eyes and said, "Daddy Logan."

Big surprise.

Eighteen

"THAT EXPLAINS THE heavy makeup," Valerie said. "To cover the bruises."

"I thought she was wearing a little too much, but then women do that when they get to a certain age."

She looked sideways at him. "And what age is that?"

He hesitated, then said, "Whatever age Mrs. Logan is."

"She's about my age."

"Well . . . she looks a lot older than you do."

"Good save."

The jokes were falling flat—maybe because of Brady's accusation, or perhaps because the awkwardness was still there between them—so they gave up.

"What else did he say?" Valerie asked.

"He's afraid that if I put Mr. Logan in jail he won't be able to live there anymore."

"Why would he want to, if Mr. Logan is violent?" she wondered. Then she caught her breath as a thought occurred to her. "Did you ask if Mr. Logan had ever struck him?"

"I did," Keough said. "The answer was no. But I think if Logan had hit him he wouldn't want to stay there."

"You're probably right," she said. "But . . . do you believe him?"

He glanced at her briefly before returning his gaze outside the window. They were sitting in a St. Louis Bread Company in the Sunset Hills Plaza shopping center, each with a regular coffee in front of them, rather than something fancy, like a latte. That was one of the things he had liked about being involved with her: her tastes had matched his . . . most of the time.

"I have to make a decision, Valerie," he told her. "Either I believe everything he tells me, or nothing. But I can't pick and choose."

"So then you do believe him?"

"Supported by your observation about her makeup," Keough said, "I choose to, yes."

"Just because I said—"

"She's a good looking woman," Keough said. "Why else would she need that much makeup?"

"So what are you going to do?"

"Brady wants me to get Mr. Logan to stop without putting him in jail."

"Because he wants to keep living there."

"Apparently."

"Well, I have to tell you," Valerie said, "if you find out that Mr. Logan is indeed beating his wife, I can't in all good conscience leave Brady in that house. I wouldn't be doing my job."

"That's up to you," Keough said.

"And what about you?" she asked. "If he is beating his wife can you let him off with a warning? Do you think that would stop him? Would you be doing *your* job?"

Keough continued to stare out the window, playing with his coffee cup. He found that looking at Valerie distracted him. She looked too good. He hadn't realized how much he'd missed her until he saw her getting out of her car. Now, with her this close, he also realized that he had missed the way she smelled.

He looked at her now, though, so she would be able to see that he was serious.

"I have to consider that little boy, just as you do, Valerie," he said. "I have to factor that into my decision about what to do."

"But wouldn't it be your job to arrest him if you found out he was beating her?"

"Not necessarily," he said. "I wouldn't be able to do anything if she didn't sign a complaint."

"And, like most battered wives, she probably wouldn't," Valerie observed. "I knew she was too nervous when we got there. She was probably afraid of what her husband would do if he found out she let us in while he wasn't home."

"That's what I was thinking."

Valerie frowned. "I looked into their background before I placed Brady there," she said, shaking her head. "There was no indication of anything wrong. If there was I would never have placed him there. . . . Never!"

He reached out and placed his hand on hers before he knew what he was doing.

"Nobody would blame you for this, Val," he said. "You did your job."

"If anything happens to that little boy *I'll* blame me," she said, easing her hand away from his.

He drew his hand back and said, "I'll check and see if Mrs. Logan has ever filed a charge against her husband. If there was a history of abuse, though, you probably would have found it when you did your background check."

"And when will you actually talk to Mr. Logan?"

"Within the next couple of days," Keough said, "after my background checks. If this is really going on I don't want to leave Brady in that environment any more than you do."

"But he wants to live there," she said. "He wants a home so badly. His heart will be broken if we take him out of there."

"Well," Keough said, "I say better his heart than something else."

Nineteen

WHEN THE CASKET was removed and all the mourners had left for the cemetery, Andrew Judson remained behind at Judson's Funeral Home. His work was done and now it was up to the preacher/priest/rabbi to complete the service and the cemetery to complete the burial.

Judson took a deep breath after locking the doors. He was alone in the place, now, and that was the way he liked it. As a child he had been left alone in this building many times by his parents, who never allowed the fact that they had a small child to interfere with their lives. During all that alone time he managed to explore every inch of the building, and eventually he chose the basement as his favorite place.

The basement was where the bodies were prepared for their showing. In those days his father had a small staff, and sometimes when his parents were away employees would be working downstairs on the cadavers, and let him watch. Other times there was nobody in the building but him and a cadaver or two, and he would become friends with them. He'd talk to them, touch them, comb their hair. As he got older and moved into the business with his father he became more fascinated by the females. The first pair of breasts he'd ever touched were stone cold. Later, in his teens, when he finally got to touch the warm breasts of a live girl he found he preferred the dead ones.

He was in his thirties now and had no friends save the ones in the basement. He would pour his heart out while preparing them to be viewed, but in the end they always left him, like today. Their families took them away from him and buried them in the ground. After that he'd always have to make a new friend.

He turned off the lights and made his way to the stairs that led to the basement. Halfway down he could feel the welcoming cold from below. His friends liked it cold.

Presently he had some new friends waiting for him down there and now that everyone was gone he was free to talk to them. One of them had to be prepared for a wake that started tomorrow. His other new friends, however, were a long way from being waked. It would be a very, very long time before they would leave him, oh yes. He'd finally figured out how to make friends and keep them close.

The only problem was that he didn't have enough new friends. He needed more, and soon he'd have to go out and get another one. That was the way he made new friends now, one at a time.

Once downstairs he went to the left, to the room where the new cadaver was waiting. His other friends were in a room to the right. He'd go see them later. Right now he had a friend who needed to be prepared for his grand departure.

Twenty

WHEN KEOUGH ARRIVED home he grabbed a Boulevard beer from the refrigerator. He wasn't supposed to be drinking beer because of his diabetes, but he kept a few around for occasions like this. He also realized that he had not taken his pills yet so he grabbed some crackers from the cupboard, ate a few, then washed them and the pills down with the beer. Screw it.

Seeing Valerie had been harder than he'd thought, and talking with Brady harder still. As if that kid's life had not been hard enough with his mother killing his father and being sent to prison for it, he was probably going to be bounced from yet another foster home. He was trusting Keough to fix the problem without that happening, but if the accusation was true, that didn't seem very likely. The next time the boy had a problem, Keough wondered if he'd think to call "Detective Keyhole" again.

Although Keough was now referred to as "The Mayor's Cop," he was still a member of the department. That meant he had access to department facilities. He tossed the empty beer bottle into the trash, went to the phone with the phone book and called the Sunset Hills police station. He got on the phone with a Detective Knoxx, identified himself and told him what he wanted. The man promised to check and see if any complaints had ever been sworn out for spousal abuse by a Mrs. Logan against a Mr. Logan at the address Keough gave him. He also promised to get back to Keough as soon as he could. He hung up on the other detective feeling stupid, because he didn't know the Logans' first names. Seeing Valerie had thrown him off his game and he hadn't thought to ask.

He went to the freezer to get something for dinner, chose a Marie Callender's chicken fried steak dinner. When he had popped it back into the microwave for the last of several steps of preparation he decided to bite the bullet and call Valerie. She answered after one and a half rings.

"Val, it's Joe."

"Oh, hi!" she said, with what sounded like forced brightness.

"I was just getting my dinner ready and had a thought—"

"Oh, Joe," she said, "I really don't think that would be a good idea. I mean . . . I know it was kind of rough seeing each other today and I think we both handled it really well, but I'm not ready for dinner."

Now he knew she'd been waiting for him to call, and he also knew that he'd had no intention of inviting her to dinner. He was just calling for some information, but he didn't want to embarrass her, so he said, "Well, you can't blame a guy for trying, can you? But since I have you on the phone . . ."

He went on to ask her for the first names of the Logans, and also the name and address of the company where Mr. Logan worked. She read the info to him—apparently she'd taken Brady's file home with her, or had a duplicate—and he wrote it all down.

"I've also checked in with their local police to see if they have any record of responding to domestic abuse calls at their address," he explained. "I'm waiting for a call back."

At that moment his microwave beeped that his dinner was ready, and since he was sitting in the kitchen she was able to hear it. She knew enough about him to know he liked to nuke his dinner when he was alone.

"What was that?" she asked.

"Um, nothing."

There was a moment's hesitation, and then she said, "Oh my God . . . I've embarrassed myself, haven't I?"

"Val—"

"That was your microwave," she said. "You're making dinner."

"Val—"

"I have to go, Joe," she said hurriedly, and hung up, completely mortified.

He hung up, feeling badly, but to call her back would only make it worse. He had to let her come to terms with her *faux pas* before they spoke again.

He was taking the dinner out of the microwave when the phone rang. Wondering if it was Val, he set the tray on the counter to cool and answered the call.

"Hello?"

"Detective Keough?"

"That's right."

"Detective Knoxx, from Sunset Hills."

"Well, that was quick."

"Sorry, but it's not. I've been called away from my desk, and wanted to let you know I wouldn't be able to get back to you tonight."

"That's no problem," Keough said. "Get to it when you can."

"I can dig it up tomorrow morning."

"Why don't I stop by and get it?" Keough asked.

"You know where we are? We've got a great new complex on Lindbergh."

"I know where it is. What time?"

"Come in about ten?" Knoxx said. "We serve a pretty good cup of coffee here."

"How about nine?" Keough asked. "I'm supposed to be at a press conference at ten in East St. Louis."

"East St. Louis? We don't have enough crime for you on this side of the river?"

"They just came up with something very . . . interesting."

"Well, why don't you come in at eight thirty, then?" Knoxx

suggested. "I'll probably be back here later tonight and I can find the info then. I'll have it ready by morning."

"I don't want to keep you away from your family—"

"What family? I'll see you at eight thirty, Detective."

Keough hung up, either on a man married to his work, bitterly divorced—or both.

Twenty-one

THE SUNSET HILLS Municipal Complex was located at the corner of Lindbergh Boulevard and West Watson Road. Founded in 1973, the facility it presently occupied was fairly new, and shared the complex with other city departments. They had twenty-four police officers and seven civilians working there. The vital statistics were given to Keough by Detective Knoxx minutes after he'd been directed to the investigative office, where the man was waiting for him. Knoxx seemed inordinately proud of the new facility, as if he'd had something to do with choosing the location and building it.

"Sorry," he said, after a moment. "I get carried away sometimes. See, my old man was one of the original ten officers when the department was first started in seventy-three."

"I can see why you'd be proud, then."

Knoxx sat forward in his chair and it groaned beneath his weight. He was carrying way too much extra baggage for a man who appeared to be in his thirties. He reached for a file folder and opened it on the desk in front of him.

"I ran your guy through the system and came up empty," he said. "If he's beating his wife she's never made a complaint."

"I guess the hospital's my next stop, then," Keough said.

"I did come up with something for you, though."

"What's that?"

Knoxx took a piece of paper from the file and floated it across the desk to Keough.

"There was one complaint made against your man, Michael Logan, for assault."

Keough picked up the copied report but asked, "Assault against who?"

"A minor," Knoxx said. "Her name was Amy Witherspoon. Fifteen years old."

"What kind of assault?"

"Physical," Knoxx said, "sexual."

"Rape?" Keough looked down at the report now.

"Sexual abuse," Knoxx said. "She was the family baby-sitter. Apparently, when he was taking her home one night he got grabby. Left bruises on her arms, fondled her breasts, tried to kiss her. Scared the kid to death."

Keough scanned the report for a disposition on the case and found it. "She dropped the charges?"

"Her parents made her," Knoxx said.

"It doesn't say that here."

"I remember the case," the other man said. "The parents were afraid of scandal, and I can't prove it, but I think your man bought them off."

So if the charges were dropped and Michael Logan was never prosecuted, it wouldn't have come up in Valerie's background check of the pair as possible foster parents.

"Is this for me?" Keough asked, holding up the copy.

"Take it." Knoxx waved it away. He sat back, causing his chair to protest again. "Anything else I can do?"

"The address of the complainant is blacked out of this report," Keough said.

"Doesn't matter," the Sunset Hills detective said. "The family moved away."

Keough looked again at the report, located the date. It was two years old.

"I don't suppose you know where they moved to?"

"Out of state. Beyond that, you got me."

"Well," Keough said, "I want to thank you, Detective Knoxx."

"Just call me Knoxx," the man said, hauling himself to his feet and sticking out his hand. Keough stood and accepted it. They had exchanged only matching nods of the head when he'd entered the office. "I know your reputation, Detective Keough."

"Is that a fact?"

"Is this something big you're working on?" the man asked. "We don't get very much of interest around here to work on. Maybe I can help."

"Actually," Keough said, releasing the man's hand, "this is kind of a favor for a friend, but if I think of anything you can do I'll let you know."

"I'll be here," Knoxx said.

Keough started for the door, then stopped and turned.

"Knoxx, do you remember Michael Logan at all?"

"Sure do," Knoxx said. "Arrogant sonofabitch. Never bothered denying he made a move on the girl. Didn't admit it, mind you. But he never denied it. He just seemed real sure of himself, sure that nothing would ever come of it."

"And he was right."

"I'd like him to slip again," the other man said, "so I can be there to catch him."

"If this pans out," Keough said, "and he slips, I'll give you a call so you can be there."

"I'd appreciate it," Knoxx said. "Like I said, Detective, anything I can do."

"Joe," Keough said. "Just call me Joe." He waved with the hand that was holding the report. "Thanks, again."

"My pleasure."

Keough checked his watch as he walked out of the building to his car. He still had time to get to East St. Louis and meet with everyone before the press conference started. In the car he paused to stash the report in his glove compartment before he started the engine and pulled out of the parking lot.

Twenty-two

KEOUGH HAD SCOPED out the building enough the day before to be able to enter the East St. Louis Municipal Building without passing through the lobby, where the press conference was to take place. When he got to the investigation office Marc Jeter was waiting impatiently.

"You're late!" he said, anxiously.

Keough checked the clock on the wall, saw that it was 9:40. He'd said he'd be in by nine.

"I had another stop to make," Keough said. "Where are the sergeant and the chief?"

"In the chief's office. I'm to take you there as soon as you arrive."

"Okay, then," Keough said. "Lead the way."

He followed Jeter down a hall until they came to a door marked CHIEF OF POLICE. He knocked and they entered. A woman who was obviously the chief's secretary said, "Go right in, gentlemen."

Jeter took the lead and they entered the chief's office, where Sergeant Benson gave Keough a hard look.

"You're late."

"I've been told that. I had another matter to see to this morning."

If the sergeant expected him to apologize, he hid his disappointment well.

"Detective Keough, this is Chief Adam Clark."

Clark stood and extended his hand. He was a barrel-chested black man with a grip like iron and a palm as dry as sandpaper. His age was hard to guess, but Keough put him around fifty. He was wearing full uniform, but he eschewed personal adornment. No awards, no medals: just his badge, buttons and bars.

"Detective Keough," he said. "I've heard a lot about you. I'm happy to have you helping us on this."

"It's my pleasure, sir." Keough eyed the clock. "Shall we go and address the press?"

"If you don't mind," Clark said, "I'd like to do most of the talking."

"It's your department, sir."

"If I feel there's a need for you to say something I'll toss it over to you."

"That works for me."

"Ben?" Clark looked at his investigative supervisor.

"I'll follow your lead, sir."

"Good," Clark said. "Then let's get to it."

"If you don't mind, sir," Keough said, "I think Jeter should come along and be seen."

"I have no objection."

Clark left, followed by Benson. Keough and Jeter brought up the rear.

"Do you have the photos?" Keough asked.

"Shit! They're on my desk."

"Quick, go get them."

As they passed the investigations office Keough waited while Jeter slipped inside and retrieved an envelope with photos of the two dead women. It took only a few hurried steps for them to catch up to the other two men.

* * *

The press conference went off well enough. Chief Clark introduced the participants, but did all of the talking in the beginning. He explained about the two murders and the importance of identifying the two victims. At one point Jeter held up both photos—clear, black-and-white 8 x 10 headshots taken at the morgue—for the cameras.

"Are the television cameras getting this?" the chief asked.

The members of the TV media assured him that yes, they were getting it. A couple of the members of the fourth estate looked away when the photos were held up. Although the photos were head shots, the faces were battered.

Finally, when it came to questions and answers, the conference started to take a turn. The speakers identified themselves by the name of their newspaper or TV or radio station.

"Chief?"

"Yes?"

"*Southern Illinois News.* Isn't Detective Keough a member of the St. Louis Police Department?"

"Yes, he is," the chief said. "He was kind enough to agree to give us the benefit of his expertise."

"KMOX, Chief. Are you saying that your own department is not equipped to handle this investigation?"

"I'm not saying that at all."

"KDST, Chief. If that's not the case, why is Detective Keough here?"

Just for a moment the chief faltered, as he did not want to come off too defensive. Keough hurriedly stepped in, hoping the man would not mind.

"I happened to be available," he said, stepping up to the podium of microphones.

"KPLR, Detective Keough. Aren't you assigned to the mayor's office, these days?"

"That's right."

"Then why would you be loaned out to East St. Louis to head

up their investigation?" The young blonde from KPLR was persistent.

"First of all, I am not 'heading up' this investigation," Keough said. "Detective Jeter here is in charge of this investigation. Secondly, I have been loaned out to East St. Louis, in an advisory capacity, as a matter of courtesy between cities. I am, after all, very experienced."

No one could argue that point.

"I think that's enough—" the chief started to say, but he was interrupted.

"*Post-Dispatch*, Chief. Can we ask Detective Jeter some questions?"

Clark turned to look at Keough and Jeter. The young detective swallowed hard but Keough put his hand on his back and gently nudged him toward the microphones.

"F–first question?" Jeter said.

"Jesus," Jeter said, later.

The chief and the sergeant had gone back to their offices after dutifully shaking hands all around for the cameras. Keough could not tell from looking at Clark whether or not the man was angry that he had stepped in when he did. He did get a dirty look from the sergeant, but both superiors went back to their offices without a word.

"How you doing, Kid?" Keough asked, as the crowd dispersed.

"Hmm?" Jeter said. "What?"

"You did okay," Keough said. "No need to worry."

"Oh, I wasn't worried," Jeter said.

"Then why—"

"Jesus," Jeter said, again. "That Mandy Moon from KPLR. Have you ever seen a prettier mouth on a woman?"

Twenty-three

THE PHOTOS WOULD not hit the print news until the next day, but Keough knew reports of the photos would make the radio that afternoon, and the press conference and photos would make the evening TV broadcasts. The news of the second pregnant woman would finally be out.

"We can't just sit here," Jeter said, seated behind his desk.

"You're right," Keough said. "We need our own room, away from the everyday operations of this department. When the phone rings I want to know it's for us."

"And how do you propose to get that?"

"Simple," Keough said. "Ask."

For the second time that day, Keough presented himself to the chief's secretary. She used the phone to check with the chief before letting Keough enter the man's office.

"What can I do for you, Detective?" Clark asked from behind his desk. He had removed his jacket and draped it over the back of his chair, and rolled up his shirtsleeves to reveal a dock-worker's forearms.

"I wanted to apologize if I stepped on your toes, chief—"

"Nonsense," the man said. "I hesitated and you stepped in and took over very ably. I should have thanked you for it." But he hadn't, and Keough still wasn't sure that he just did.

"Was that all?"

"No, sir." He made his request for a room and phone lines of their own until the investigation was over.

"We have a room that's used for writing reports," the chief said. "I'll set you up in there. The officers can write their reports elsewhere for the time being. Is that good enough?"

"If it's what you've got, I'll take it," Keough said. "We'll need it set up in time to take calls on the hotline number we gave out at the press conference."

"You'll have it this afternoon."

"Thank you, sir."

"Anything else?"

"No, sir, that's it."

"Carry on, then."

"Yes, sir."

Keough left the chief's office, realizing that he was batting .500 as far as the locals were concerned. It was an embarrassment to the chief and the sergeant that he was here, but not to the mayor and certainly not to Jeter—the detective assigned to the case.

Returning to the investigation office, Keough explained two things to Jeter. One, that they'd be getting what they wanted by evening; and two, that he had something else to do.

"I'll come with you—" the young detective started, but Keough cut him off.

"This is personal, Marc," he said. "I'll be back in a few hours. I just have to go and talk to someone."

"Well, what do I say if the chief or the sergeant comes looking for you?"

"Tell them I'm out," Keough said, "and that I'll be back in a few hours."

"But—"

"That's all you have to say," Keough said. "Our hotline won't be connected until tomorrow, anyway. When I come back later on we'll set up our office the way we want it."

"And how's that?"

"I tell you what," Keough said, wanting to give the young man some busy work. "You know where the report-writing room is. You see to it. Have it set up any way you want, as long as there are tables, chairs and a telephone. It's got to be comfortable, yet efficient, because we'll be running our investigation from there. Got it?"

"Okay," Jeter said. "I've got it, but—"

"I'll be back in a few hours."

He got out the door before Jeter could stop him with one more "but."

He got in his car in the parking lot and pointed its nose towards St. Louis. Michael Logan, Brady's foster father, worked downtown, which would make it easy to stop in and see him and get back to East St. Louis in a matter of hours.

He wasn't at all sure yet what approach he was going to take with Logan. From what he'd learned about the man so far a direct approach might be the best way to go. If Logan got off on beating his wife and sexually harassing young girls, he was certainly not the type of man who had a hidden agenda.

Twenty-four

ONE OF THE perks of being on the mayor's staff was that Keough had a pass to park in any of the downtown municipal parking lots for free. He took advantage of that and parked in a lot on Walnut, just down the block from the building where Michael Logan had his office.

In the lobby he found the listing for Logan's architectural firm on the twelfth floor. When he got there Logan's name was on the glass door along with several others. Apparently, he was a partner.

He entered and presented himself to a receptionist. She was young, pretty, brown-haired and the owner of a ready smile. The nameplate on her desk said she was Stephanie Gion.

"Good morning," she said. "Can I help you?"

"I'd like to see Michael Logan, please."

"Do you have an appointment?"

"No," he said, "no appointment." He took out his badge and showed it to her. "Tell him it's Detective . . . Keyhole."

"Keyhole?" She repeated it with a half smile, like she thought she was being put on.

"That's right."

"Really?"

"Really."

She picked up the phone and dialed three digits. "There's a policeman here to see Mr. Logan. He says his name is . . . Detective Keyhole. Yes, really. I'll hold." She covered the receiver. "His secretary is asking him."

"Thank you." After a moment she dropped her hand from the receiver. "All right. Yes. I will." She hung up. "Mr. Logan has agreed to see you."

"Thank you."

She furnished him with directions through the halls and he followed them to the letter. He came to a doorway with a woman standing in it.

"Detective Keough. My name is Karen Johns, Mr. Logan's secretary."

"Miss Johns."

She extended her hand and he shook it. She was a large woman, professional looking, the kind of woman a man like Logan could probably have working for him without being tempted.

"Mr. Logan is waiting in his office. This way, please."

She led him through what was probably her office into one beyond. A man was seated behind a huge desk—one that Keough thought was way too big for one man . . . with a normal-sized ego.

"Detective . . . Keough, I believe?" the man said, standing. "I'm Michael Logan."

"Mr. Logan."

Keough stood silently, waiting for Karen Johns to leave. She didn't.

"Um, is this about Brady?" Logan asked. "And your visit to my house yesterday?"

"In a way."

Logan frowned. He was dark and intensely good looking, almost like Pierce Brosnan on steroids.

"I don't understand."

"Well, if Ms. Johns would leave us alone I could explain."

"Ms. Johns is my private secretary," Logan said. "I have nothing to hide from her."

Keough smiled. "I have." He turned to her. "Ms. Johns, would you leave us alone, please?"

She seemed conflicted about what to do and looked to her boss for assistance.

"It's all right, Karen," Logan finally said. "You can go."

"Yes, sir." She left the room, closing the door behind her.

"I didn't appreciate having to do that, Keough," Logan said, abruptly. "I don't hide things from her. Just what was it you thought she couldn't hear?"

"Well, for one thing, that you beat your wife."

Logan had probably had a lot of practice denying the accusation. He didn't flinch. Wifebeaters often convince themselves of their own innocence. They usually lay the guilt off on the wife.

"W–what?"

"Or how about that you sexually harass and abuse young girls?"

That one got to him. "I was never charged! How did you know about that?"

"I have connections."

Logan puffed himself up to the point that Keough thought his suit would burst. "Are you investigating me?"

"Mr. Logan," Keough said, "I'm here to warn you never to lay your hands on your wife—or any other woman—in anger, or . . . in . . . lust." The last word sounded melodramatic even to him, but he'd gotten himself worked up and couldn't think of another one.

"I—what's going on? Has my wife been talking to you?"

"No," Keough said, "your wife has said nothing."

"Then who . . . what . . . I don't understand."

"It's a simple warning," Keough said. "If you don't curb your violent side, your . . . *deviant* side . . . you'll have to deal with me—and I can't be bought off."

Logan stared at him for a few moments, then suddenly adapted the arrogant attitude that had so irked Detective Knoxx of the Sunset Hills Police.

"Is that a fact?" the man asked.

"It is."

Logan came around his desk and walked towards Keough. He stopped an arm's length away. "Am I to understand that you are here in an unofficial capacity?" he asked.

"If I were here officially, Logan," Keough said, "you'd be in handcuffs."

Logan smirked and Keough was suddenly filled with the urge to lay him out. The man was taller and more musclebound than he, and probably knew his way around a gym. It was doubtful, however, that he'd ever had a fight in the street. It might have been interesting.

"So, if I was to physically throw you out of my office," Logan said, "I'd just be throwing *Mister* Keough out, right? Not *Detective* Keough?"

"I see where you're going with this, Logan," Keough said, "and don't even think about it. Any time you lay your hands on a police officer, whether he's on duty or not, it's a crime."

"Lucky," Logan said, after a moment, "for you."

"This has been a courtesy call on my part, Logan," Keough said. Then he got melodramatic again. "The women of St. Louis—and that includes your wife, and fifteen-year-old girls— are under my protection. You touch one, or make an improper advance, and I'll be all over you."

He turned and walked to the door. "And next time," he added, "I won't ask your secretary to leave the room."

Twenty-five

BY THE TIME the evening newscasts came on Keough and Jeter were in their "Task Force" office. Efficient but small, it was a six-by-ten room with one table and two chairs, and a telephone with several lines coming into it.

"This is where you write your reports?" Keough had asked when he first saw the room.

"The patrol guys use it," Jeter had explained, then added, "one at a time."

Now they sat in the chairs and watched the news on the eighteen-inch color TV Jeter had managed to forage from somewhere in the building. "No cable," he'd said when he walked in, carrying it, "but we'll be able to see Mandy Moon." Keough preferred Katherine Jamboretz when it came to local anchors and reporters, but since Moon had been at the press conference she'd be the one to watch tonight.

Jeter had also managed to find a standing bulletin board/chalk board, to which he'd pinned photos of the victims, and some key pages from the reports. His crowning achievement, though, had been bringing in a state-of-the-art IBM computer with the latest Pentium processor. "I, uh, borrowed it," he explained, "using the chief's name."

Jeter had spent his afternoon wisely and well, and Keough told him so. "We'll do fine from here, Marc," he said, patting the young man on the back. "Just fine."

Jeter looked proud at having successfully set up his first task force office.

The press conference was carried on all the stations, starting with the earliest news reports, and they watched at least a portion of each one, although Jeter insisted on watching the entire KPLR segment.

They all had the facts straight, except one reporter suggested that maybe "Detective Keough's involvement would be a little more than advisory, given the apparent youth and inexperience of the detective actually assigned to the case."

"What inexperience?" Jeter complained.

"You kept leaning in and bumping your mouth on the microphones," Keough reminded him. It was a common problem with people who were inexperienced with microphones. They tended to get too close.

"Oh, that. . . . Well . . ." Jeter touched his bottom lip, which he'd split the first time he'd bumped a mike.

"Never mind," Keough said, using the remote to turn off the TV. He grabbed his jacket, preparing to leave for the day. "At least the photos are out there, and the phone number. Damn!"

"What?"

"We're going to need a civilian to man these phones when we're out of the office. I forgot to tell the chief."

"Leave that to me," Jeter said, hurriedly. "I know just the gir—uh, the person for the job."

"She'll probably have to volunteer," Keough pointed out.

"Believe me, that won't be a problem."

"Is she competent?"

"Very, I guarantee it."

"Okay, then," Keough said, standing up, "have the, uh, person in here tomorrow morning. If we get some early calls we'll probably want to check them out right away."

"All of them?"

"All of them."

"What about the crank calls?"

Keough stood in front of the bulletin board and looked at the photos of the two dead women which had been taken in the morgue. "We don't have anything, Marc," he said. "We'll have to check out every one before we call them cranks."

"Jeez—"

"Unless, of course," Keough said, turning away from the board and heading for the door, "they're obviously crazy."

"Yeah," Jeter shouted after him, "but whose call is that gonna be?"

"Mine!" Keough said, and waved a hand behind him without looking.

When Keough got home to the Central West End he stopped a moment to look at the house he'd been living in. A friend had arranged for him to house-sit for as long as the owners were away, so he always knew it was a temporary residence. However, it had now been almost two years and the owners showed no desire to return. He found himself thinking more and more of this house as home, even though he hadn't opened all the boxes from his initial move from New York. Lately, as his thoughts turned to possibly moving away from St. Louis, he knew that he would probably miss this house—and the Central West End, with its eclectic shops and restaurants—more than he'd miss the city, itself.

He started up the walk to the front steps and was almost there when he noticed two shadows on his porch. They came forward into what was left of the light as he reached the steps, so he could identify them—Detectives Angela Mason and Jack Gail, from Internal Affairs. Mason was in her forties and since the last time he'd seen her the bags beneath her eyes had become even larger. Gail was in his thirties and still looked like a fast tracker, although maybe he was stuck in IA for a while, now.

"To what do I owe this . . . pleasure?" Keough asked, looking up at them.

"Need you to take a ride with us, Keough," Mason said.

"Am I under arrest, Detective?"

"No," she said, "we just need your help with something. Being a big shot in the mayor's office doesn't preclude you from helping the rest of us lowly cops, does it?"

"That depends."

"On what?" Gail asked.

"On whether or not what you want entails sticking my own butt in a sling."

"You got something to be guilty about, Detective?" Mason asked.

"Not today."

"That's funny," Mason said. "Today is what we're concerned with."

"Meaning what?"

"There's a dead body downtown," she said. "Seems he was murdered in a parking garage, right near his car."

"And IA is working a murder?"

"We get involved whenever a cop is involved, Detective," she said. "You know that."

"And I'm involved in this one?"

"You tell us."

"I can't tell you a thing until you tell me who's been murdered."

"Fella named Michael Logan," Jack Gail said.

"That name ring a bell?" Mason asked, with a smirk.

Twenty-six

KEOUGH SAT IN the backseat of the IA detectives' car, if only for the perverse pleasure of having them drive him home again. He was also able to focus better on his situation. The obvious questions the detectives would ask would concern what he was doing at Logan's office that day, and what they had talked about. If he told them that he was there because the man made a habit of beating his wife, that would make Mrs. Logan the prime suspect. If he didn't tell it would make him an immediate target of investigation—but he was already a suspect in the eyes of Detectives Mason and Gail. They had been after him ever since they had tried to get him on a sexual harassment charge last year. Even Harriet Connors had told him that when they'd had their drink at the Morgan Street Brewery.

As they reached downtown and pulled into one of the municipal lots, Keough noticed that it was the same one he'd parked in. That meant the parking lot attendant would remember him and his mayor's staff ID. When they went up a separate ramp, he realized Logan's office had been in one of the downtown buildings that had a deal with a public parking lot for a private floor.

When they parked and got out Mason said, "You were pretty quiet back there. Working on your story?"

He smiled. "I fell asleep."

They walked toward the other end of the parking lot and he could see the yellow crime scene tape cordoning off a section that encompassed about half a dozen parking spots. One car, a new BMW, was parked and some people stood around it.

"When was the body found?" he asked.

"A couple of hours ago," Mason said. "The attendant heard a shot and came running."

"A couple of hours?" he asked. "And you got to me already?"

"You were identified right away by the receptionist and the private secretary," Gail said.

"And the parking lot attendant said there was a man here with an ID from the mayor's office," Mason added.

"You guys were pretty quiet in the car, too," Keough said. "No questions?"

"Later," Mason said. "We offered to pick you up and bring you here for the detective assigned to the murder to question you, first."

"And that would be . . ."

They reached the car and ducked beneath the tape. A man Keough did not recognize turned to face them. Two other men, apparently from Forensics, continued to work in and around the car. From Keough's vantage point he could see a broken driver's side window and blood on the front seat. Someone had apparently approached the car and shot Logan right through the window.

"Record time, Detectives," he said. He was a large, beefy man in a rumpled suit, who could have easily played a sleazy P.I. on TV

"We told you we'd bring him back," Mason said.

"Any trouble?" the man asked.

"He came willingly enough."

"Why wouldn't I?" Keough asked. "I guess I was one of the last people to see the victim alive—although he still had most of a workday ahead of him when I left."

"We'll get to that," the rumpled cop said. "I'm Detective Eddie Burns; I'll be working this homicide. You're Detective Joe Keough?"

"That's right."

Burns did not offer to shake hands. That wasn't a good sign.

The big man turned to the two IA detectives and asked, "Would you like to stay while I question him? Might save you some time duplicating my efforts."

"Sure, why not?" Mason asked. "Thanks."

Keough frowned. There was entirely too much cooperation going on between Burns and the Internal Affairs detectives. It was looking worse and worse for Keough by the minute.

"I assume I was brought here to help in this investigation?" Keough asked.

"To help?" Burns replied. "Oh, that's right. You're the one with the big reputation as a homicide man. You're some kind of special mayor's cop now, aren't you?"

"Some kind."

"Well, Detective," Burns said, with heavy emphasis on the word *Detective*, "you've been brought here because you were identified as having been to see Mr. Logan today. So you're here to be questioned as a private individual, not here to work the case as a cop. Is that clear?"

"Crystal," Keough said. "I've got enough of my own work, as it is."

"Fine," Burns said. "Now that we've got that straight, why were you here to see Mr. Logan?"

"It's a private matter."

"There are no private matters in a homicide investigation, *Mister* Keough," Burns said. "You know that."

"Look, Burns," Keough said, "I don't know what your problem is, but whether I'm here in an official or an unofficial capacity my name is *Detective* Keough, to you."

Burns glared at Keough for a few moments. His eyes had a yellow cast to them and Keough could smell cigar smoke all over him.

"You're not going to get anywhere being antagonistic, Detective Keough," Burns finally said.

"Funny," Keough said, "I was just going to say the same thing to you."

Twenty-seven

KEOUGH AND BURNS glared at each other for a few moments with Mason and Gail looking on before Keough decided to break the stalemate.

"Look," he said to Burns, "let's start over. Do you want to talk to me about my relationship to this victim?"

"Yes."

"Then get rid of them," he said, pointing to Mason and Gail.

"They're going to want to talk to you, too."

"Let them do their own job."

"Now, wait a minute—"

"Hold on a second," Burns said, holding his hand up to Gail like he was a traffic cop again. "He's got a point."

"What point?" Mason demanded. "Look: we brought him here for you."

"And you still haven't told me how you knew his whereabouts and how you got here so fast," Burns said to her.

"That's . . . I can't tell you that."

"Well then why don't you and your partner take a walk down to the other end of the parking lot for a while?"

"Hey, look—" Gail started.

"I'll let you have him when I'm finished."

"You can't—" Mason tried, but Burns didn't let her get much further, either.

"*My* crime scene, Detectives," he reminded them. "Until a supervisor gets here I'm in command."

They glared at him, gave Keough an even dirtier look, then moved away towards the other end of the parking lot, where they put their heads together and began talking earnestly.

"A supervisor hasn't been here?" Keough asked.

"Been and gone, called away on something else," Burns said. "He'll be back. Now, as to you: are you going to answer my original question?"

"Look, Detective," Keough said, "I was here earlier today very briefly, had a conversation with the victim, and left."

"His secretary said you made her leave the office."

"It was a private conversation."

"About what?"

Keough hesitated.

"Damn it, Keough! You're impeding a homicide investigation. Cop or no cop, I'll throw you in a cell!"

Keough considered his options, then reached into his pocket and brought out his cell phone. He'd rescued it from his glove compartment before getting into the IA detectives' car.

"Let me make a call," Keough said. "Maybe I can save us some time, and further argument."

Burns gave a disgusted snort and said, "You'd better be calling a lawyer." He turned and walked back to the car.

"Not quite," Keough said, brought up a number on the phone's LED screen, and pressed speed dial.

As if he sensed Keough there, Burns turned away from the technician he was speaking to and faced him.

"Here," Keough said, holding his phone out. "Somebody wants to talk to you."

Burns eyed the phone suspiciously, then took it impatiently and barked, "Hello!" He listened for a moment, then said, "Yes, sir, I know who this is . . . Yes, sir . . . I understand . . . but, sir, this is a homicide investigation . . . Yes, sir, I know he is, but as of this moment he's a suspect . . . No, sir, I can't arrest him now . . . Yes, sir, I understand . . . Yes, sir . . . No, sir, I don't need to hear it from the chief. He's my boss and you're his boss. Your word is good enough . . . Yes, sir . . . Uh, you're welcome, sir . . ."

Burns ended the call and tossed the phone to Keough, who caught it with one hand.

"Called in the big guns, huh, Keough?"

"Look, Burns," Keough said, "I just need some time. Like the mayor told you, I'll come in and talk to you tomorrow, but I've got to check on some things, first."

"You going to call in your friend the mayor to take care of them, too?" the other man asked, pointing to Gail and Mason.

"They're idiots," Keough said, putting his phone back in his pocket. "I can handle them myself."

"I'm supposed to be flattered that you called in the mayor to handle me?"

"I don't want to 'handle' you, Burns," Keough said. "Believe it or not, I want to help you."

Burns pointed a finger at Keough. "In my book you're a suspect, Keough. Don't forget that. If you did this, I'll take you down."

"Fine," Keough said. "I can live with that."

Burns dropped his hand and scowled. "The mayor said I was to let you view the crime scene and ask whatever questions you wanted, so go ahead."

"Thank you."

Keough approached the car and looked it over, then had a few words with the technicians. He found out that the body had been removed after the supervisor had arrived.

"One shot to the head," one of the men told him, pointing a rubber-gloved finger to his left temple, "here. Through the window."

Keough bent over to look into the car again. "The window on the other side isn't shattered."

"No," the man said, "the bullet apparently did not exit."

Couldn't have been a large-caliber gun then, Keough surmised. Anything a cop carried would have gone right through, and Burns knew that—unless he suspected that Keough had used a backup weapon.

Keough turned and saw Burns being besieged by Mason and Gail. He wondered if Burns was explaining to them about the mayor. He turned and walked over to join them.

"I have a few questions, Detective Burns."

"Go ahead."

"Jesus Christ!" Mason exploded. "You're gonna answer *his* questions?" Burns ignored her, as did Keough.

"You said the parking lot attendant heard the shot?"

"That's what he said."

Keough turned, looked around. "We're on level two?"

"That's right," Burns said. "Private parking for the building Logan's firm is in."

"The bullet didn't exit Logan's head."

"I know that."

"Well then, it must have been small caliber."

Burns sighed. "Tell me something I don't know."

"He wouldn't have heard one shot from a small-caliber gun," Keough argued.

"So?"

"So if he heard a shot, it must have been from another gun, not the murder weapon."

"You're saying Logan got off a shot after he was shot in the head?" Burns asked. "Then where's his gun?"

"I'm saying," Keough replied, "that somebody wanted the body found quickly. They used one gun to kill Logan, then fired another, larger-caliber gun to get the attendant's attention."

Burns stared at him. "So you're saying . . ."

"Unless the shooter took it with him," Keough said, "there's a spent bullet around here somewhere."

"Unless you're the shooter," Mason offered.

Keough stared at her for a few moments, and then said,

"That's right, Angela. Unless I'm the shooter." He looked at Burns. "You working out of Major Case?"

"That's right."

"Captain McGwire can vouch for me."

"McGwire's gone," Burns said. "Took early retirement months ago. Had something to do with a divorce." Keough had not heard that about his former commander.

"You need somebody else to vouch for you besides the mayor?" Jack Gail asked incredulously.

"Burns," Keough said, pointedly ignoring Gail, "I'll be in your office tomorrow at three."

"Fine."

Keough turned his attention to the two IA detectives. "You ready to take me home?"

"Fuck you," Mason replied.

"But don't you have some questions for me?"

"We'll find you," Gail said, and the two detectives turned and walked away.

Keough looked at Burns, who said, "I'll have someone take you home."

"Thanks."

"Keough . . ."

"What?"

Burns seemed to run a few possible responses through his mind before he finally shook his head and said, "Nothing. Just don't fuck me on this, or mayor or no mayor, I'll have your ass."

Keough took a moment, then said, "That's fair."

Twenty-eight

KEOUGH FOUND THE West End comforting. There were days when he took the time to walk through it from end to end on Euclid Avenue, pausing at the hub of it all, Maryland Plaza, where diners sat outside during all but the winter months—and even during some of those—enjoying the simple fare of Culpepper's, the more formal offerings of Bar Italia or the coffee creations of the Coffee Cartel. Nine times out of ten, though, when he finally decided to sit and eat he would end up at the southernmost end, between MacFarland and Delmar, at the Welsh bar, Dressel's.

He had the policeman who drove him home drop him off at Dressel's instead of home. He ordered their cold roast beef sandwich—the best in town—the homemade chips, and a bottle of Newcastle. It was times like this he particularly missed his partner, Al Steinbach. He could sit and eat and talk to Al about anything, which was amazing to him, since they really hadn't been partnered all that long. In fact, he'd been with Al only a few months longer than he'd been with Valerie, and he had never gotten to that point with her—or with any woman, for that matter. It was a byproduct of being a cop. Your closest relationship always ended up being with your partner.

Well, the only partner he had now was young Detective Jeter, who was so fond of quoting Mark Twain. He wondered what Twain would have to say about the mess he'd gotten himself into now? Not only was he a suspect in the murder of Michael Logan, but the IA types were on his butt again.

Tomorrow he'd have to talk to Valerie again, and also to Mrs. Logan, before he went to Detective Burns and told him everything. Hopefully, once he explained it all, he'd be taken off the suspect list. He also hoped, for Brady's sake, that Logan's wife hadn't killed him; although what good that would do the boy he didn't really know. It seemed a foregone conclusion now that Brady would have to go back on the waiting list for a foster family, the poor kid.

He finished his dinner and left a generous tip for the waitress. He hadn't kidded around as much tonight as he usually did. Maybe that in itself would have been tip enough.

When he got back to the house he decided it wasn't too late to call Valerie, even though it felt as if it had already been a forty-eight-hour day.

"Oh my God!" she said when he told her that Michael Logan was dead. "Has his wife been told?"

"I don't know," he said. "It's not my case."

"God," she said, "somebody should be there with her—"

"It's not your case either, Val," he reminded her.

"Maybe not, but . . . my goodness, the poor woman! She's lost her husband, and I'm probably going to have to take Brady away from her."

"Probably?" he asked. "Val, I've got to tell you, she's going to be one of the suspects in his murder."

"One of them? Who are the others?"

"Well . . . me, for one."

"Make some coffee," she said. "I'm coming over."

"Bring bagels," he said.

* * *

She made good time. The coffee was ready and they spread the bagels out on the kitchen table and ate them with butter—him—and cream cheese—her, while he told her the events of the day.

"I'm so sorry," she said, when he finished.

"About what?"

"Well," she said, "you've got enough on your hands with these terrible murders of pregnant women—I saw the press conference, by the way. Very impressive."

"Thank you, ma'am."

"But then I have to go and call you, get you involved in . . . in this."

"Val, there was no way we could know that Michael Logan was going to be murdered."

"Do you really think his wife could have done it?"

"I can't form an opinion on the few words we had with her when we went to see Brady," Keough said. "I'm going to go and see her again tomorrow."

"And then what?"

"And then I'll go tell Detective Burns everything I know and get myself out of this," he answered. "You're right about one thing. I do have enough to do with my own case."

"Have you gotten very far?"

"Not at all," he said. "Hopefully, after the press conference, someone will call us tomorrow who knows one or both of those women. Once they're identified, we can start a meaningful investigation and maybe stop this guy before he hits again."

"You think he's going to hit again?"

"Count on it," he said. "I never knew a serial killer yet who stopped at two."

Andrew Judson watched the report of the press conference on KPLR's nine o'clock news with interest. None of the men who spoke impressed him, except for Detective Keough. This man stepped up and took charge confidently. He would be a daunting opponent—and an opponent was what he would be. After tomorrow, Keough would be doing everything in his power to keep Judson from making new friends.

That wasn't something that Andrew Judson was going to allow to happen, though. Not now that he'd just gotten started.

Twenty-nine

KEOUGH HAD A leftover bagel for breakfast the next day, toasting it. While he waited for it to brown he sniffed the air in the kitchen. Valerie's scent hung there, the Ocean Breeze that she wore. It hadn't been there in a long time. He found that he liked it.

He drank his coffee and ate his buttered bagel over the sink, thinking back to last night. They were both concerned for Brady's welfare, as well as his safety, and that had seemed to take away some of the awkwardness from between them. He had walked her to her car and they had touched hands briefly before she left. Nothing more, and yet that seemed like a big step to him.

Maybe, he thought, dumping the last of the coffee down the drain, when this was all over . . .

He had to go to East St. Louis before seeing Mrs. Logan—whose first name, he had found out from Valerie, was Kathy. The murders of the two women had to take precedence over the murder of Michael Logan, even if he was a halfhearted suspect in that one. And that was all he felt he was. Even those IA bozos couldn't really think he'd waited in the parking lot to shoot and kill Logan right after having met with him.

He was going to have to stop and see Kathy Logan on his way to meet Detective Burns. That meant he'd either have to keep his cell phone on him, or take Marc Jeter along.

As he entered his and Jeter's new task force office a pretty blonde girl looked up at him from one of the desks and smiled.

"Hi," she said.

"Good morning."

"Are you Joe Keough?"

"That's right."

She stood up—revealing herself to be opulently outfitted with curves—and stuck out her hand. Luckily she was wearing office clothes rather than a T-shirt, which would have been filled to bursting.

"I'm your civilian volunteer, Jenny Sykes."

"Ah," he said, taking her hand, "Marc's friend."

"He's a sweetie," she said. "He went out to get some donuts or bagels."

"Good," he said. "So you're manning the phones?" "Manning" was a ludicrous term to use for this Pamela Anderson–like young lady.

"Yup—and it's been ringing off the hook since I got here at eight A.M." At that moment it rang and she gave him a look that plainly said, "See?" and answered it.

He walked to the other desk and put his own container of coffee down on it. He had the feeling that this was the unseen girl he'd heard Jeter give the extra bagel to the other day. Couldn't really blame the guy, after all. He just hoped that she was as competent as Jeter had said she would be.

Seated once again, she hung up the phone as he was taking the lid off his coffee, turned in her chair and held out a handful of message clips to him. Some were pink, some were yellow.

"These are the calls that have come in so far today."

He accepted them, ignored them for the moment and asked, "What's with the colors?"

"Pink are the ones that sounded more legitimate to me," she said. "Yellow are the ones that sound like cranks."

He looked at her instead of at the slips. "Are you qualified to make that distinction, Jenny?"

"I've worked here for four years," she said, without rancor. "I started out as a dispatcher, and I was a good one. I was eventually moved into the office. I'm good at what I do, which a lot of the time is crime statistics. I know my stuff, Joe, but I guess you'll have to decide for yourself, won't you?"

"I didn't mean—" he started, wondering why he was instantly on the defensive.

"That's okay," she said. "I didn't take offense. You don't know me. It's understandable you'd wonder about my competence, but I think you know by now that Marc is very serious about his job. He wouldn't have recommended me for this position if he didn't think I was competent enough."

"Yes, I see that," he said. He also saw that upon closer inspection, and ignoring her obvious physical attributes, she was not as young as he had first thought. She was a woman, not a girl, and she was probably a woman who was constantly challenged to prove herself because of her extraordinary appearance. It must have been hell for her in the beginning, working around a bunch of cops who didn't know her beyond what they could see. It might have only been marginally better, now.

"I appreciate the initiative, Jenny," he said. "It might make things go a bit smoother."

"Thank you," she replied. "That said, I've made an appointment for a man to come in and see the two of you this morning. He should be here at . . . well, in about ten minutes."

"What's it about?"

"He claims he can identify one of the girls he saw on TV last night," she said.

"And what relation does he say he is?"

"Well," she said, slowly, "he said that she might be his wife."

"Oh, boy . . ."

Thirty

KEOUGH WAS ACTUALLY hoping to get a quick hit on the press conference's TV coverage, but this was even more than he'd bargained for—if it turned out to be true.

Jeter got back five minutes before the man arrived. His name was Allan Barnes and he shuffled into the office as if he was afraid someone was going to jump on him. Maybe he was afraid that the victim would turn out to be his wife, and was putting off finding out as long as possible.

Keough studied the man as he entered. In his thirties, shoulders hunched, head down, he appeared even mousier than he probably normally looked. Because of the way he hunched, his height was difficult to estimate, but he must have topped six feet. He wore a white shirt buttoned to the neck and a pair of gray Dockers.

"Mr. Barnes?" Keough asked.

"Um, yeah," Barnes said, keeping his voice down.

"This is my partner, Detective Jeter," Keough said. Jeter nodded. "And you spoke to Miss Sykes on the phone."

Jenny smiled at him, which in itself would have lifted the spirits of most men.

"Have a seat," Keough said. He almost offered the man coffee, but about the only thing Jeter hadn't procured for the office was a coffee maker. Keough had noticed, while waiting for Jeter to return with the bagels, staplers on each desk, a paper cutter in one corner on top of a two-drawer file cabinet that hadn't been there last night, and a box of hanging file folders under a desk.

"Mr. Barnes," Keough began, gently, "you told Miss Sykes on the phone that you thought one of the victims was your wife?"

Barnes nodded and said, "Betty. Um, Elizabeth, but everyone called her Betty."

"Sir . . . which woman are we talking about?"

Barnes looked directly at Keough for the first time and it was obvious that the man was on the verge of tears. His eyes swam with moisture behind small wire-rimmed glasses. He was in his mid-thirties, and constantly ran his hands—first one, then the other—through thinning brown hair. Keough wondered if the man had been plucking it out little by little all these years with the habitual movements.

"Can you look at the photos again, up here on the bulletin board?" Keough asked.

"Um . . ." Barnes said. His eyes darted to the board, then away, then back to it, then away. Keough could see he was going to have to be careful the man didn't fall apart on them.

"Perhaps you can come up to the board and look at them again. I know it's difficult, but . . ."

Barnes didn't move. He looked around the room, at Jeter, at Jenny, back at Keough, anywhere but at the bulletin board.

"It looked like her," he said, finally, "last night, on the TV I mean . . . you know how they say the camera adds ten pounds? I wonder if that's true of pictures that are shown on TV? Huh?"

Helplessly, Keough said, "I really don't know, sir. Maybe if you looked at the photos now . . ."

"Yes," Barnes said, "yes, of course," but he still made no move to stand up.

Jeter stepped forward and touched the man's shoulder. "If you'll step over here, sir?"

Barnes looked up at Jeter, who placed a gently insistent hand beneath one of the man's elbows. Keough and Jenny watched as Jeter got the man to his feet and steered him over to the photos on the bulletin board. If the man collapsed now, Keough wondered how they'd ever get him to the morgue for a final ID.

"It's difficult, I know," Jeter said, as he and the man reached the board. "Take your time, sir."

Barnes stood in front of the bulletin board without lifting his head. Keough couldn't tell if he was staring at his shoes or trying to lift his eyes to the photos without moving his head. He looked at Jenny and the look on her face was so sad it hurt. She was on the edge of her seat, but was she hoping that it was his wife, or it wasn't? For his part he was conflicted, as well. If it was his wife the poor guy was going to go to pieces. If it was his wife, then they would have something to work with.

Barnes was wearing a windbreaker, and he had his hands thrust deeply into his pockets. His angular body seemed to be as tight as a kite string subjected to a strong updraft. Oddly, Keough remembered that the last time he'd put a kite in the air was a few days after Steinbach's death.

"Mr. Barnes?" Jeter said.

Barnes took a deep breath, and then raised his eyes to the two photos. After a few moments he simply started to shake, and then his legs went. Jeter grabbed him, but if Keough had rushed to his other side the man would have struck the floor. He looked like a bag of bones. They dragged him back to the chair and sat him in it. He sat there with his eyes shut tightly and then started muttering, "No, no, no, no, no," until it was all running together.

"Jenny, get some water," Keough said. He looked at Jeter. "I guess we've got an ID."

Both he and Jeter looked up at the two photos on the board. One of those women was Elizabeth Barnes. They needed her husband to recover enough to tell them which one it was.

Thirty-one

EVENTUALLY, ALLAN BARNES recovered sufficiently to identify the second woman as his wife, Elizabeth Barnes.

"Mr. Barnes," Keough said, "you understand that in order to get a positive identification we'll have to take you to the morgue to, uh, view the, uh, your wife."

"Yes," Barnes said, "yes, of course."

Keough walked Barnes out into the hall and put him on a bench outside the door. "We'll be right with you, sir."

Barnes just nodded and stared down at his shoes.

"Marc," Keough said, going back into the office, "let's take him over to the—"

"I can do that, Joe," Jeter said. "There's no point in both of us going, is there?"

"No," Keough said, "I guess not."

Jenny touched Keough's arm and said, "There are a few more people coming in today."

"What?"

"I didn't think you'd be wanting to drive all over Illinois and Missouri to talk to them," she said. "I arranged for as many as I could to come in here, instead."

He turned and looked at her and said, "That was probably a

good idea. Thanks, Jenny." Then he looked at Jeter. "I'd like to get the first victim identified today, if we can, so you take Mr. Barnes to the morgue and I'll stay here and interview people."

"Okay."

Keough decided to walk Jeter and Allan Barnes out to Jeter's car. By the time he returned there were three men and two women lined up outside the office, claiming to have recognized the two victims either from the photos they'd seen on a TV news report or in the morning paper. Keough realized he hadn't even had time to check the newspapers, yet.

He told the people he'd be right with them and went inside the office. Jenny had the *Post-Dispatch* and the *Southern Illinois News*. Both papers had put grainy black and white photos of the two women on the front page. He didn't see how anyone could recognize anything from them, and he was right.

By the time Jeter returned from the morgue with Allan Barnes Keough had interviewed eleven people who thought one of the pictures in the paper was of their wife, sister, neighbor, friend or grocery store checkout girl. In every case they were wrong, and glad of it.

"I left him out in the hall," Jeter said, as he entered. "He's pretty shook up."

"It's definite?" Keough asked.

"Yup," Jeter said. "That's her."

"Okay," Keough said, "then we've got some more questions for him."

"Shall I bring him in?"

"Find us another room, where we can question him without being disturbed," Keough told him.

"You think I can find an empty room, just like that?"

Keough spread his hands and said, "I just have to look around me to know that you're the great appropriator, Marc."

"Flattery will do it every time," Jeter said. "Come on. I know a room that's almost always empty."

"Don't mind the bars, Mr. Barnes," Keough said as they entered the cell block. "This is simply the only place we could find to talk with you undisturbed."

He tossed Jeter a look and the young detective just shrugged. This was the best he could do.

"I'm not under a–arrest?" Barnes asked.

"No, sir," Keough said, "you're not under arrest. Why would you be?"

"I th–thought the husband was always the f–first suspect," he said. "I mean, in all the movies . . ."

"Well, that's sometimes the case, sir," Keough said, "but not in this instance."

"Why not?"

"Well, because of the other girl."

Jeter had brought in some wooden chairs so they wouldn't have to sit on stainless steel bunks.

"I—I didn't know her," Barnes said.

"Exactly," Keough said, "so you'd have no reason to kill her. We need to find someone with reason to kill both women, Mr. Barnes."

"I don't know who'd want to kill my Betty," Barnes said. "And the baby? W–what happened to the baby?"

"That's what we're trying to find out."

"Y–you mean—you didn't find the baby?"

The one fact that had not been released to the public was that the two women had been pregnant.

"I'm afraid not, sir."

"Then—then sh–she might be alive, somewhere?" His face brightened, as if he thought he might be able to salvage something from this horror.

"I don't want to give you any false hopes, Mr. Barnes."

"Please," Barnes said, passing a hand over his face, "call me Allan. It—it'll just make things easier."

Keough took a moment to compose his thoughts, and studied

Barnes at the same time. His brown hair was thin and lifeless, his nose broad, the flesh beneath his lower lip thick. His blue eyes appeared bloodshot and wet. His hands were his best feature, with long, graceful fingers and well manicured nails.

"All right, Allan," Keough said, "suppose we start with a simple question."

"Okay."

"When was the last time you saw your wife?"

"About a week ago."

"And when was the last time you spoke to her?"

"A–about a week ago."

Keough and Jeter exchanged a glance. "She's been gone a week?" Jeter asked.

"That's right."

"Mr. Barnes . . . Allan," Keough said. "Can you tell us why your wife was gone a week and you never reported her missing?"

Barnes looked at them both, his eyes wide and totally without guile. The question did not seem to surprise him in the slightest.

"Because she was never missing," he said, as if it made perfect sense.

Thirty-two

IT WAS A simple enough statement. Apparently, Betty Barnes had gone to visit her mother with the intention of staying for a couple of weeks.

"She wasn't due for a month or so," he explained, "so we didn't think it would be a problem."

"I see." Keough had never been married, never had a pregnant wife—or girlfriend, for that matter—so he had no idea if this was normal thinking for a couple or not.

"Jesus," Barnes said, putting his hands to his head, "I'll have to tell her mother. What am I gonna say?"

"It's always hard," Keough said.

They got Barnes's address along with his phone number, and then the same information for his mother-in-law. He said she lived in Lebanon, which did not explain why his wife was found in a Fairview Heights garbage dump.

They let Allan Barnes leave after he shook hands with both of them and said, "Thank you."

"That's all right, Mr. Barnes," Keough said.

"You are going to catch this . . . this monster, aren't you?"

"We're going to do our best," Jeter replied.

"I hope it's good enough," the man said, and left.

When Keough and Jeter got back to the task force room there was another line of people outside the door which extended down the hall. Jenny was on the phone, looking harried. She waved her hands wildly at them until Keough walked over to stand by her while Jeter spoke with the people outside.

"What is it?" he asked.

She covered the phone with her hand. "I have a man on the phone who says he's sure one of the dead women is his wife."

"So? Have him come in."

"Joe," she said, "he says his name is Allan Barnes, and that his wife is Elizabeth Barnes."

"What?"

She shrugged.

"Must be a crank," he said.

"Unless . . ." she held the phone out to him.

"Allan Barnes" left the East St. Louis Municipal Building, walked to his car and got behind the wheel. He flipped down the driver's side visor so he could look into the mirror. Carefully, he removed the putty from inside his nose, which had widened and flattened it, and then from inside his bottom lip. It was the same putty he used when he did cosmetic surgery on the cadavers that were left in his care at the funeral home. After that he removed the wig of sparse brown hair to reveal his own dark, thick locks. After that he removed contact lenses from his eyes, revealing their own brown color.

Andrew Judson knew he was talking a chance removing his disguise right there in the parking lot. Either one of the detectives could have come out at any moment, but that just added to the excitement.

He'd wanted to size up Detective Keough face-to-face, and since he still had Elizabeth Barnes's wallet he had access to most of her personal information. It was not hard to impersonate her bereft husband for the two detectives. The contact lenses had been very uncomfortable, but had done their part, making his eyes appear red and watery from crying.

With "Allan Barnes" now lying in tatters in the seat beside him he turned the ignition key and calmly drove his own car out of the parking lot. He gazed into the rearview mirror as he pulled away and was almost disappointed that neither Keough nor the younger man, Jeter, had come out.

Thirty-three

"WAIT A MINUTE," Sergeant Ben Benson said, holding his hands up. He looked at Keough, Jeter and Jenny in turn before continuing. "You mean you had him here? You had the killer here—in a cell, no less—and you just let him walk out?"

"We don't know that for sure, Sarge," Keough said, as the task force spokesman. "We won't know anything for sure until the other Allan Barnes comes in. Maybe we just had a crank impersonating the husband."

"Do you really believe that?" Benson asked.

Keough hesitated, then said, "No, I don't."

"Tell me what you think?"

"My instinct says it was him," Keough said, tightly, "and I follow my instincts quite a bit. I think the sonofabitch walked in here bold as can be, probably to size me up after seeing me on television. I think he came in here and made a fool out of me."

"Why would you think that?"

"I tend to temper my instincts with something . . . intangible," Keough explained. "It's that intangible something that tells me it was him."

"Why would you think he was trying to make a fool of you?" Benson asked. "You weren't pointed out as the head of this task force. In fact, it was made clear that Jeter, here, was assigned the case."

"Well . . ." Keough said, realizing the man was right.

"Don't start taking this personal, Keough," Benson warned. "Don't start thinking it's you against him." Benson's anger melted a bit from the heat of Keough's obvious discomfort. "That'd be an arrogant . . . attitude to take."

Keough could almost hear the other word that Benson had edited from his remarks at the last second. An arrogant "New York" attitude. It irked him that the man might be right.

"I didn't have to take him at face value, and I did," Keough said. "I should have asked him for ID, and I didn't."

"*We* didn't," Jeter said. "I drove him to the morgue and back, remember?"

Both Benson and Keough turned to face Jeter. "What was he talking about, Marc? All that time?" Keough asked.

"That's what I was about to ask," Benson said.

"His wife—I mean, the dead woman. He was . . . remembering things, you know? Happy times, happier memories? Man, his act was good!"

"It sure was," Jenny said. "He had me feeling sorry for him. He should get an Academy Award for his performance."

"Okay," Benson said, "okay, he probably would have taken me in, too, then, if he was that good." That was magnanimous of him, Keough thought. The sergeant looked at Keough. "He was trying to make fools of all of us."

"You know, I stared right at him the whole time."

"At least you got a look at him," Benson said.

"That's what I mean," Keough said. "I stared right at him and I wouldn't know him. He was sweating the whole time, probably from wearing makeup."

"You think he was made up?" Benson asked.

"He's bold, Sarge," Keough said, "but he's not stupid. I don't think he'd walk in here and let us see what he really looks like."

"No, I guess not," Benson said. "Jesus, what am I gonna tell the chief?"

"I'll talk to him, if you like," Keough said.

"No," Benson said. "I'll do it. It's my job."

"Of course . . ." Keough said.

"What?" Benson asked.

"We don't really have to tell him," Keough said. "It's his department, his building, it'll probably just make him feel like he was made a fool of, as well."

Benson frowned, then said, "I can't believe I'm considering this. You mean not tell the chief that a serial killer was here in the building?"

"Why does he have to know?" Jeter asked, backing Keough's play.

"It'll put us on the defensive, Sarge," Keough said. "We'll be defending ourselves rather than doing our jobs."

"Jesus," Benson said.

"We're going to get this guy, Sarge," Keough said. "I guarantee it."

"How?" Benson asked. "How can you be so sure?"

"Because they slip up," Keough said. "They always do."

"So when is he going to slip up?"

"Maybe he already did," Keough said, "by coming in here, by trying to make fools of us. He's got me even more determined to put him away than I was before."

"Me, too," Jeter said.

Jenny remained silent and watched the three men. Her opinion would have no effect here.

They all watched Ben Benson grapple with the idea of keeping something from his boss. Keough wondered if this would actually be the first time the man had ever done something like this.

"If we don't tell him," the sergeant finally said, "then it never leaves this room."

"Absolutely," Keough said.

"Never," Jeter said.

They all looked at Jenny.

"Hey," she said, holding her hands up in surrender, "my lips are sealed."

"Ah, jeez," Benson said, "I don't know . . ."

"He gave us something else by coming in here, Sarge," Keough offered, hoping to finally sway the man.

"Like what?"

"Like an idea about him," Keough said, "about who he might be."

"How do you figure?"

"If his makeup job was so good," Keough said, "that means he's a pro."

"An actor?" Jeter asked.

"Or a makeup artist," Keough said. "At least it gives us someplace to start."

"An actor," Benson said.

"Oscar caliber," Jenny said.

Benson rubbed his jaw, then said, "Okay. I'll go along with this, for now. But if it gets out I'm going to have someone's head."

"Fair enough, Sarge," Keough said.

Benson looked at all of them, then shook his head at himself and his decision. He started to leave, then turned back.

"Let me ask you something, Keough."

"What's that?"

"If you wanted to keep it from the chief, why did you bother telling me?"

"Well," Keough said, "to tell you the truth, I didn't think of keeping it quiet until after I told you."

Benson scratched his head and said, "I kinda wish you had."

As Jenny went off to run an errand Keough and Jeter walked back to the task force office.

"Can I ask you something?" the younger detective asked. "This . . . intangible thing you talked about. I mean, I understand having an instinct but . . ."

"Sometimes," Keough said, "there are times when I just *know* something is right."

"Isn't that instinct?"

"To tell you the truth," Keough said, "I'm not sure. I think that when I follow my instinct I'm hoping I'm right. But this other thing . . . when I think back to it, Marc, I just *know* it was him, and he was laughing at us."

"So you don't just think it was him, or have a feeling, you know?"

"That's right."

They walked silently for a few moments and then Jeter asked, "What if you're wrong?"

"If I'm wrong," Keough said, "I guess I'll just have to stop believing in it."

"Instinct," Jeter said. "Mark Twain said it was 'petrified thought.'"

"Is that good?"

"Well," Jeter explained, "he followed that up by saying that it's 'thought which was once alive and awake but it had become unconscious . . . '"

"Well, I suppose that's true, then," Keough said. "Instinct is unconscious."

"And this . . . intangible?"

"Even more so, I guess."

"And do you believe that this is what makes you a good detective?"

"That, and a good understanding of the art of investigation," Keough said. "I believe in procedure, too, Marc, but you can't put all your faith in one thing."

As they approached the office Jeter asked, "So this intangible . . . this, like, seventh sense . . . does it ever tell you when things are wrong?"

Keough sighed and said, "All the time, Marc. All the time."

Only it hadn't been working—been switched "on"—while the killer had been standing right in front of him, had it?

Thirty-four

THIS TIME WHEN Allan Barnes came into the office the first thing Keough did was check his ID. When it was confirmed that he was the true Allan Barnes they went through the same routine and, amazingly, the real Barnes reacted almost identically to the phony one. This led Keough to wonder if the killer had known Allan and Betty Barnes.

Once again it was Marc Jeter who drove Allan Barnes to the morgue to identify the body. Keough called ahead to let them know they were bringing in another "relative," and asked that they not mention the first man. A knowing wink could almost be heard over the telephone line.

While Jeter was gone Keough asked Jenny if she could do a job for him, using the computer.

"Sure," she said. "My computer skills are at least as good as Marc's. What do you need?"

"Names and addresses of theater groups, theaters, theatrical stores—anyplace that would sell costumes and makeup."

"Illinois and Missouri, I presume?"

"Yes," Keough said. "At least our killer had something right when he came in."

"Which was?"

"That Allan and Betty Barnes lived in Missouri," Keough said. "That takes the investigation squarely into my backyard, so to speak."

"And he had all that stuff right about her going to see her mother," Jenny added. "Do you think he knew them, or did he just get all of that from talking to Betty before he killed her?"

"I was thinking he might have known them before," Keough replied, "but you've got a good thought there. What if this guy is so smooth and charming that he actually got these women to talk about themselves?"

"Aren't most serial killers charming?" she asked.

"Not the one we caught last year," Keough said, "but many are."

"You mean the Mall Rat? Isn't that what the papers called him?"

"That's right," Keough said. "He was a young man with no social skills, at all."

"Maybe not," she said, "but he sure saved me money by keeping me away from malls."

"What did you do with all the money you saved?"

"Put it in a jar and spent it all after you caught him, of course," she said. "It was my way of celebrating."

Keough could have thought of better ways for a girl like Jenny to have celebrated, but he pulled his thoughts off that track pretty quickly.

"I'll get to work on that theater information," she said.

"Any more visitors due in today?" he asked.

"No," she said, "but here are the names and addresses of some people who are expecting visits from you and Marc."

He accepted a sheet of 8½ x 11 paper with names, addresses and phone numbers typed on it. She'd apparently put the list into the computer and printed it out.

"Jenny?"

"Yes?"

"Did you also put the names and addresses of the people who came in today into the computer?"

"I did," she said, "just in case you wanted a full list. Do you want me to print that out?"

"No," Keough said, "just tell me what address the phony Mr. Barnes gave."

She brought the list up on the screen and he leaned over her to take a look. She was wearing a blouse that buttoned up to her neck, so there was no danger of her thinking he was trying to sneak a peek. He did notice, however, that her hair smelled very fresh and clean.

"The real address," she said, gazing up at him. "Probably got it from her wallet?"

"I'm sure," Keough said.

"I wonder what he would have said if you had asked him for ID?" she said.

"Probably that he was so upset he left his wallet home. Get on those theatrical addresses, will you, Jenny?"

"Sure thing. As soon as I have something I'll print it out."

"Thanks."

Keough took a seat at the other desk in the room and looked at the list of names and addresses she had given him. Eleven of them, five on this side of the river, six on the other. She even had them grouped that way, top and bottom. Jeter had been right in "drafting" her for this job. He tore the sheet in half, set the bottom half down on the desk with a stapler on top of it so it wouldn't blow away, and folded the top half and tucked it into his wallet. Then he stood up and grabbed his windbreaker from the back of his chair. The weather was turning chilly as a cold front threatened to bring in some rain.

"Jenny, when Marc gets back tell him I left him his half of the list, okay?"

"But . . . he's coming back with Mr. Barnes, isn't he?"

"He knows what to ask Barnes," Keough said, "and if I think of any more questions, the guy lives in Missouri. I'm going to go and interview the rest of the names on the Missouri side."

"Okay," she said, "I'll tell him."

"Thanks."

"If you don't get back before I go I'll leave the theater list on the desk for you."

"Great," Keough said. "You're the best."

"So they tell me," she said, and went back to her computer.

Thirty-five

IN THE PRIVACY of his car Keough fumed. He didn't like being made a fool of by the killer, and he didn't like having Sergeant Benson take him down a peg. But the man had been right. He was taking this personally, and maybe that was his New York rearing its ugly head again.

The phony Allan Barnes had pulled his stunt so early that Keough had most of the day ahead of him to think about it. They had questioned other people in the building, but no one else had even seen—or noticed—the man while he was there. What a pair of brass balls he must have had to pull a stunt like this.

Keough had to put the amazing incident behind him for now and get on with his day. He was in something of a quandary. On one hand he hoped the other victim would also end up being from Missouri, because that would put both of them on his home turf, so to speak. However, that would make dumping them in Illinois . . . well, even odder. On the other hand, if the first victim was from East St. Louis or, at least, Illinois, that would make it more than just a dumping ground.

But when it came right down to it, the first body could have been dropped into the Mississippi from anywhere north, having simply gotten "snagged" around East St. Louis. Finding out where they each lived and where they were supposed to be would give him—them—a place to start.

In his car, driving over the bridge to Missouri, he fished the cell phone out of the glove compartment and using his thumb, dialed Valerie's number. By the time she answered he was getting on Highway 44 and heading east.

"Joe, I spoke with Kathy Logan today," Valerie said, excitedly. "She's ready to see you."

Keough closed his eyes and shook his head. If it was anyone else—anyone he worked with—he'd be chewing them out, right now. "Val, why did you talk to her?"

"Well . . . I had to call and say something—"

"Val," Keough said, "if she killed him she's going to be on her guard with me, now."

"You think she killed him?" Valerie asked, shocked.

"She's a suspect, Val," Keough said. "Everybody who knew him is a suspect, but especially his wife."

"I—I didn't think—I'm sorry—I wanted to talk to her about Brady, and we started talking, and I just mentioned that you would be coming to see her—"

"All right, all right," Keough said, "we can't do anything about it now."

"Shall I call her back—"

"No!" he snapped. "Don't talk to her again. I'll just . . . drop in on her. I have another call to make in that vicinity, anyway." One of the addresses on his list was in Affton, not far from Sunset Hills.

"Joe, I'm so sorry—" she stammered. "I guess I just didn't think."

"Okay," Keough said. "I'll talk to you, soon." If she wanted him to forgive her, or tell her it would be all right, she was out of luck. He broke the connection, then dialed the number of someone in the St. Louis Police Department that he had checking missing persons reports in Missouri. Jeter said he could do that from his computer, but since Keough had access to the St. Louis P.D. facilities, he was determined to use them.

"I got a hit, Joe," his contact said. "The description fits. This guy reported his wife missing last month."

"Give me a date." He wrote it down. "Now the name and address." Wrote that down, too. A car behind him beeped him because he'd slowed down while talking on the phone. He was turning into one of those people he hated, talking on cell phones in their car.

"Okay, thanks," he said. "I owe you." He hung up, then turned off the next exit and pulled into the first parking lot he saw, a Burger King. Once he had the engine off he dialed the task force number.

"Jenny?"

"Joe? What's wrong?"

"Nothing," he said. "Is Marc back yet?"

"Not yet."

"He was checking missing persons, had some kind of program running on the computer."

"Wait . . . the missing persons thing, right?"

"Yes. Can you access it and see if he got any results?"

"Sure, hold on."

He heard the keyboard clacking, then silence before she came back on.

"He had it set up to spit out any reports that matched the description . . . and we got one."

"Where?"

"Your side of the river."

"Give it to me."

"It's on your list already, Joe."

That was the next thing he was going to check. Now he pulled it out and saw it, fourth on the list. "I've got it. Thanks, Jenny."

"Sure. I'm still working on those theater groups."

"Good. I'll be in later. See you then, or tomorrow."

He hung up and just sat there for a moment. Using a pen he checked which addresses he'd go to first, listing them one through five. The hit happened to be the Affton address. He decided to go there first. If it was a match he wouldn't have to go to the others, and he could swing by the Logan house and talk to Kathy Logan.

He started the engine and drove through the drive-thru window. He got a chicken sandwich and a diet Coke. He pulled into a parking spot again and wolfed it down there, then took his pills because he knew he'd forget later. He got out to dump his trash, then started the engine, pulled out of the lot and got back on Highway 44.

Thirty-six

"HOW DID YOU sleep last night?" Dr. Jerry asked.

"Fine."

"No dreams?"

"No," he lied.

"Well . . . that's good."

"I suppose."

They sat in silence for a few moments, and it was Dr. Jerry who began to fidget. "How is business?"

"Fine."

"Doing . . . well?"

He smiled. "People are dying."

The statement made Dr. Jerry fidget even more—that and his patient's eyes.

"You know, you come here to talk and you hardly ever say a thing," the doctor said.

"I come, don't I?"

"I suspect the only reason you come is because your father made it clear in his will that the only stipulation is you see me or you lose the business."

They sat in silence for a few moments, and then he said, "That might not be so bad."

"Mightn't it?"

He thought about all his friends who had come and gone, and the friends who were still to come. He didn't want to give up the business but he didn't want the snooty Dr. Jerry to know that, either.

The doctor's name was Gerald Todd, but when Judson started going to him ten years ago as a teenager the man had tried to make friends with him and said, "Just call me Doctor Jerry." Since then Judson was sure the doctor was afraid of him. He continued not only to call him but to think of him as "Doctor Jerry."

One time, a few years ago, Dr. Jerry had said, "Don't you think it's time you started calling me Doctor Todd, Andrew? Like an adult?"

Judson had simply smiled and said, "You'll always be Doctor Jerry to me."

After Andrew Judson left the office the doctor watched from the window to make sure the young man drove away. When he was sure Judson was gone he poured himself a stiff scotch. He never scheduled a patient immediately following Judson, because he needed time to recover from his sessions with the boy.

But Judson wasn't a boy any longer, he was a man and as such was even more frightening than before. Even when Judson was a teenager the doctor was unnerved by his young patient. It did not take long, after beginning treatment, that Dr. Gerald Todd realized there was nothing he could do. Andrew Judson was an unredeemable sociopath who would probably kill one day.

Dr. Jerry poured himself a second scotch. Every once in a while he worried that it would be him Judson killed, but the fear wasn't enough for him to give up the checks that came in from the father's estate. Benjamin Judson had been very smart. If Andrew stopped coming in to see Dr. Jerry he would lose the family business, and Dr. Jerry would lose a large part of his income.

So, for as long as Andrew agreed to come, he would see him,

and he would have two scotches after every session to calm his nerves. It was just a lucky thing that the young man's work brought him into close contact with more dead people than living ones.

Judson had gone straight from the police station to Dr. Jerry's office. He thought that was appropriately ironic—or maybe it was poetic. He wasn't sure.

When he left Dr. Jerry's office and drove home to the mortuary he still had the remnants of "Allan Barnes" on the seat next to him. He stopped at the first public trash can he saw and deposited the putty and wig into it, then continued on home.

Talking with the women had certainly come in handy. It had given him all the information he'd needed to impersonate Allan Barnes. Also, it had soothed them and made them think he wasn't really going to kill them. Silly women, how else was he going to get their babies if he didn't kill them? After all, that's how he was born, that's how they had to be born. He'd heard it time and time again from his father, whenever the old man would get mad at him.

"They gutted your mother and killed her for this?" the old man would ask. "She gave up her life so I could have a son like you?"

More times than he could remember his father had wished him dead instead of his mother, but it simply had not happened that way. She'd died giving birth. Andrew Judson had no idea that there were actually women who had their babies through C-section and lived. If he had known that, maybe it would have made a difference.

Then again, maybe not.

Thirty-seven

KEOUGH KNOCKED ON the door of the house in Affton, on Heege Street. A man answered, opening the inner door and staring at him through the storm door.

"Mr. McKay?"

"Yes?"

"I'm Detective Keough." He pressed his badge and ID to the window. "You called us about your wife?"

"Is she dead?"

"Can I come in so we can talk about it, sir?" Keough asked.

The man didn't move. Keough couldn't make him out very well due to the glare on the window.

"All right," the man said, finally unlocking the storm door. "Come in."

"Thank you, sir."

The man's name was Bruce McKay. He had reported his wife missing a week ago, after she had been gone a week. He didn't offer Keough anything to drink. They sat in a cheaply furnished living room and talked about his wife, Mary Ellen, for half an hour.

* * *

Keough stopped his car outside of the Logan house in Sunset Hills and turned off the ignition. He got the cell phone out of the glove compartment again and called Jenny. She told him Jeter was there and put him on the phone.

"McKay was our guy," he told the younger detective. "I just came from his house."

"Why'd he wait so long to report her missing?"

"He said they had a fight, she went off to cool down."

"A week? That sound funny to you?"

"He said they did that, sometimes. They'd argue, and one or the other would leave for a while."

"And that sounded okay to you?"

"You ever been married?"

"No."

"Ever lived with a woman?"

"No."

"Me, neither," Keough said. "I don't know if it's right or not. I guess we'll find out."

"Is he going to ID the body?"

"He's coming in tomorrow morning."

"I have to go to the morgue again?"

"Don't worry," Keough said. "I'll take him. Have you checked any of the others on your list?"

"Three," Jeter said. "The other three weren't home. I got a couple of guys whose wives left them, I think, and another who can't find his sister. I guess I don't have to check the other three. They'll just be some other poor slobs who are having trouble with their women."

Here it comes, Keough thought.

"Twain said '. . . a woman will never do again what she has done before.' When are men going to realize that?"

"Do it on the phone, as a courtesy," Keough said, ignoring the quote. "I mean, they called in, they must be worried about something. At least we can put their minds at ease."

"What about your other ones?"

"I'll do the same," he said. "I'll call them when I come in."

"When will that be? I mean, in case the sergeant or the chief asks," Jeter said.

"In a while. I've got something else to do, first."

"Okay," Jeter said, then added, "maybe at some point you'll tell me what this something else is that you're working on."

"It's personal," Keough said, then relented and added, "but I'll fill you in when I see you."

"Okay," Jeter said.

Keough broke the connection, and instead of putting the phone back into the glove compartment he left it on the seat. He figured if he was lucky someone would steal it.

There were unsightly cracks in the thick makeup on Kathy Logan's face when she answered the door. He wondered why a woman who obviously spent so much time in front of a mirror could not have seen them.

"Oh," she said, putting one hand up to her neck, "it's Detective . . . I'm sorry, all I can remember is Keyhole."

"It's Keough, Mrs. Logan," he said. "May I come in?"

"If this is about Brady I'm afraid he's . . . gone."

"Is he?"

"They came and took him this morning."

"Was it Miss Speck who came?"

"No, Val wasn't with them," Kathy Logan said.

"I see. Well, it's not about Brady, although I'm sorry to hear . . . um, it's about your husband, Mrs. Logan."

"Oh," she said again, but this time instead of putting her hand to her neck she put a fist to her mouth.

"I'm sorry," he said, "I know this is difficult. May I come in?"

"I—I already talked to a Detective. . . ." She groped for a name, again.

"Burns?"

"Yes," she said, "yes, like the actor . . . no, no, that's not right, is it . . . he said . . . he said it wasn't like the actor. . . ."

"Right," Keough said. "It's with a 'D.' I realize you've already spoken to him, but I wonder if I might come in a moment, anyway? I have some questions of my own."

"Of your own?" she asked. "I'm sorry, I don't understand. Val said you were coming by, but I thought it concerned Brady."

They had already established that he was not there about Brady, so he let that pass.

"I saw your husband yesterday afternoon, Mrs. Logan," Keough said. "I spoke to him at his office."

"You went to Michael's office?" she asked. "Whatever for?"

"Well, I wanted to talk to him about . . ." Keough wasn't sure what to say. He certainly wouldn't be getting Brady in any trouble if he told the truth, since the boy was out of the house, now. "Mrs. Logan, I went to talk to him about . . . beating you."

She gasped. "What?" Her eyes darted from side to side, as if checking for neighbors who might be within earshot.

"Do you really want to talk about this on the doorstep, ma'am?" he asked.

"No," she said, "no, certainly not! Please come inside."

Thirty-eight

KATHY LOGAN DID not offer Keough any refreshments, as had been the case with Bruce McKay. However, while McKay's demeanor had remained one of resignation, Kathy's surprised Keough.

"What the hell do you mean by insinuating that my husband beat me?" she demanded.

"Well . . ." Keough said, still not wanting to come right out and say that Brady told him, "I just assumed . . . there were signs . . ."

"What signs?"

"Well, the heavy makeup—to cover the bruises."

She put her hand to her face, then pulled it away hastily.

"I'm sorry if you don't like the way I use makeup, Detective Keough," she said, "but that in no way means my husband—"

"He didn't deny it."

That stopped her. "What?"

"When I went to his office to warn him away," he continued, "he never denied it."

"You're telling me my husband admitted that he beat me?"

"No," Keough replied, "what I said was, he did not deny it."

She was wearing a pair of tight fitting capri pants and an

equally tight top, both the same shade of pink. If she'd been expecting him to come because of Valerie's call, then she had dressed for him. There was no doubt she had a trim, health spa body, and as women went she was on the tall side. Her bare arms looked well-toned, even muscled. She was obviously a strong woman, one you wouldn't think would allow herself to be subjected to abuse.

"Wait a minute," he said.

"I don't know what you're thinking," she said, "but I don't think I like it. I want you to leave."

"Just another minute—"

"No," she said, "I'd like you to leave, and I believe that as a policeman you have to comply—unless you've come here to arrest me."

"I just wanted to—"

"You just wanted to give me a motive for killing my husband," she said, cutting him off. "If he used to beat me up then I must have wanted him dead, right? Well, I'm sorry to disappoint you, Detective, but my husband did not beat me up."

"Mrs. Logan—"

"*I want you out of my house!*" she screamed. She rushed to the door and yanked it open.

"All right, all right," he said. He didn't need her calling Burns, or anyone else, to complain about him. "I'm going."

He was barely out the door when she slammed it behind him, hitting him nice and solidly on the ass.

Driving back to East St. Louis to resume his workday Keough realized that Brady might have been wrong—actually, he and Brady might have been wrong. He hadn't really asked the boy if he ever saw Michael Logan beat his wife. The boy may have simply heard the sounds of fighting and assumed that was what was happening. What might actually have been occurring could have been quite different.

He grabbed the cell phone from the seat next to him and

dialed Burns's office number, which he knew by heart because it used to be his own. When someone answered he identified himself and asked for Burns.

"Burns."

"It's Keough. I'd like to stop in and see you, if that's okay."

"*Okay?*" the other man demanded. "I expected you hours ago."

"I've been busy," Keough said. "I'm working a double homicide—"

"Well, I'm working a homicide, too, Detective," Burns said, "or have you forgotten?"

"I haven't forgotten," Keough said. "Look, I'm on my way back to East St. Louis—"

"Did they ship your ass to the other side of the river, now?" Burns asked.

"Temporarily," Keough said. "I can explain when I get there. Look, why don't you meet me outside and we'll go someplace. I'll buy you a drink—"

"I don't drink during the day."

"Some coffee, then," Keough said. "Do you drink coffee?"

"Incessantly—but the real stuff, nothing fancy."

"Fine," Keough said, "I'll buy you some coffee and we can exchange facts."

"Facts?" Burns asked. "You got facts you think I'd be interested in?"

"I've got some thoughts I think you'd be very interested in. In fact, I think you'll be downright fascinated."

Burns hesitated and then asked, "Does this have to do with my case, or yours?"

"You might be interested in mine, I don't know," Keough said. "But what I've got to say has to do with yours."

"All right," Burns said, "okay, I'll meet you out in front of the building. You know where it is, right? Oh, that's right, you used to work here before you went off to work for the mayor—and now he's sent you over to East St. Louis."

"Wait for me out front," Keough said, "and we'll talk."

Thirty-nine

KEOUGH STARTED TO pull up to the first coffee place he saw, which happened to be a Starbucks. Burns objected.

"There's a St. Louis Bread Company a few blocks up," he said. "That's as fancy as I get."

Keough relented and drove the extra blocks. When they were seated they each had a regular coffee, and Burns had soup in a bread bowl.

"Might as well have some lunch while you're boring me," he said.

"I'm ready to tell you why I went to see Michael Logan yesterday," Keough said.

"So talk."

Keough told Burns about Brady, going back to when he had first met the boy. Then he filled him in on current events, ending with his visit to Logan.

"Did he admit to knocking his wife around?"

"No," Keough said, "but he didn't deny it—but I went to see his wife today and something else occurred to me."

Burns was bringing his spoon up to his mouth and stopped, giving Keough a sharp look. "Are you messing with my case, Keough? I talked to Mrs. Logan already. Now granted, with this new info I'll have to talk to her again. I mean, what with her husband knocking her around—"

"That's just it."

Burns put his spoon down and looked annoyed. "*What's* just it?"

"Brady didn't ever *see* Michael Logan beat his wife, he heard the fights." He recalled this from his interview with Brady that the boy had never said he "saw" the violence.

"So?"

"So," Keough said, "when I mentioned to Mrs. Logan today about her husband beating her she got mad and threw me out of her house."

"Sounds like a smart lady."

"Burns," Keough said, "what if Mr. Logan wasn't beating Mrs. Logan up? What if it was the other way around?"

"What?" Burns sat back in his chair now, looking disgusted. "A woman beating up a man?"

"Don't be such a chauvinist, Burns. It's been known to happen, you know."

"You saw Logan," Burns said. "Did he look like a man who would let a woman beat up on him?"

"I guess that would depend on the woman. I found out something else about him, too." He told Burns about the charge of sexual abuse that had been dropped.

"And what happened to the family?"

"Moved away."

"To where?"

"I don't know."

"Then what good is that information?"

"I think if Logan was the kind of man who picked on young girls, then a full-grown woman like Mrs. Logan could probably handle him."

Burns thought it over. "She is a healthy looking woman, I'll give you that."

"A little too much makeup for my taste."

"Hadn't noticed that, myself," Burns said. Different strokes,

Keough thought. "Okay, so first you tell me Logan is kicking his wife around, which gives her a motive to kill him, and then you tell me she was knocking him around. Are you thinking this takes away her motive?"

"Well if she's the one beating him up, where's her motive for killing him?"

Burns leaned over his soup bowl again, then sighed and pushed it away. He looked at Keough and shook his head. "Why would you even think of this?"

That was what Valerie had asked him when he called and asked her a question, then explained why he was asking . . .

"I don't think I know another man who would have thought of that," she said.

"Why not?"

"Joe," she said, "a normal, red-blooded American male would never consider this—and if a man *was* being beaten up by a woman, he'd never admit it."

"I guess I'm not a normal American male, then."

"Tell me something I don't know," she'd said . . .

"Okay, so you gave her a motive and then took it away," he said to Keough. "I've still got *you* being pretty intense when you went to see him, according to his assistant."

"Intense enough to come back and ambush him?" Keough asked. "Kill him with—what? A twenty-two? Then fire a thirty-eight or a Glock to attract the attendant's attention?"

"I don't know."

"Well, I do," Keough said. "I had no reason whatsoever to kill him, and if I did I sure wouldn't call attention to it."

"And if his wife didn't, either, who did?"

"Maybe," Keough said, "he's accosted some other girls along the way, as well. Could be one of them did it, or one of their men—a father, or a husband."

"So basically," Burns said, "you fed me all this just to muddy the waters?"

"You know, I thought maybe I was helping you out by telling you something you didn't know," Keough said. "Apparently you think I'm trying to cover for myself."

"Maybe you want to get the mayor on the phone again?" Burns asked. "He might have some kind of explanation I can buy." He stood up. "I think you better take me back to my office."

On the way back to Burns's office the man asked, "What's this case you're working on in East St. Louis?"

Keough explained it to him, and also explained how recent developments had brought the focus to the Missouri side of the river.

"Sounds like a bad one," Burns said. "Good luck."

Keough pulled in front of the office and killed the engine, then turned to face Burns.

"Look, talk with Detective Knoxx at the Sunset Hills department. He's got some opinions about Michael Logan."

"Okay," Burns said, opening the door, "I'll do that."

He closed the door and started to walk away, then came back. Keough started the engine and rolled down the passenger side window.

"Look," he said, "officially, you're a suspect, because it's proper procedure."

"I understand that."

"Unofficially, I don't really think you did it."

"And I appreciate that."

"But," Burns added, "officially, if I find out you did do it, I'm going to be real disappointed in you—and I'm going to come down on you as hard as I can."

Forty

AFTER ANDREW JUDSON left Doctor Jerry's office he went to get lunch at his favorite restaurant, a place in Fairview Heights where the waitresses knew him and served him, but didn't talk to him. He disliked being talked to by strangers, especially while he ate. He was unaware of the fact that they didn't talk to him because he scared them, but if he had known he probably would have gone there even more often.

When he returned to the funeral home he was surprised to see someone waiting by the front door. A woman, one who looked familiar, but he couldn't place her until he got up real close.

"Hello," she said.

"Hello."

"I, uh, do you remember me?" she asked. "The mistress from the funeral?" Her tone said she was making fun of herself.

"I remember."

"You kept me from making a fool of myself."

"It's all right," he said. "We all get distraught, sometime."

"I don't think I thanked you properly."

"It's fine," he said. "You don't need to."

"Oh, well, I thought . . . maybe, if you weren't busy, we could have . . . a cup of tea?"

"Actually, I just had lunch," he said.

"Oh, I see."

But there was something in her voice, in her face that made him say, "But a cup of tea would be nice," before he knew what he was doing. Then he realized why. She was pregnant.

"Oh, wonderful."

"In fact," he said to her, "if you'll come inside, I'll make it."

"That would be . . . nice," she said. As he put the key in the lock of the front door she kept talking. "I just . . . it's been hard, with no one to talk to . . . and you were so kind last time . . . I thought . . ."

He swung the door open, stepped aside and said, "Come right in."

Forty-one

KEOUGH AND JETER spent the rest of the early evening calling the other people on their lists, listening to their stories and assuring them that the dead women were not their loved ones. Jenny was still there when Keough arrived. Before leaving she reminded him that she had put some printouts on the desk for him.

As Keough hung up the office phone on his last call Jeter did the same with his cell phone.

"Okay," he said, "we did our good deeds for the day. Now what's our next step?"

"Mr. McKay is coming in to view the body tomorrow," Keough said. "I'll take him over and try to get some background on his wife during the ride there and back. Why don't you go call Mr. Barnes and do the same. Let's find out who these women's friends were, who they confided in."

"Okay," Jeter said, "that's tomorrow. What about the rest of tonight?"

"Well," Keough said, picking up a sheaf of paper from the desk, "there are these printouts to go through."

"I've got a better idea," Jeter said.

"What?"

"Why don't you tell me about this other thing you're working on—not that this isn't enough to keep you busy."

"It's a personal thing," Keough said, "or it was. . . ." He went on to tell Jeter about Brady, right from where he first met the boy up to the murder of Michael Logan. He left out the relationship with Valerie. He wasn't quite ready to share that much with his young partner.

"Wow, so you're a suspect?" Jeter asked. "That's . . . wild."

"Yeah, it is."

"So what are you going to do about it now?"

"Nothing," Keough said. "I may have already muddied the waters. I'm going to let Detective Burns do his job, and you and I are going to do ours."

"So we're taking this investigation across the bridge to St. Louis?" Jeter asked, anxiously.

"No," Keough said, "I think it would be more correct to say that the investigation is taking us to St. Louis. In fact, why don't you wait here tomorrow while I go to the morgue with Mr. McKay, and then we'll both go and see Mr. Barnes and ask him the same questions. Once we know who both women confided in we'll check them out and see if they have any idea where these two women went—especially the first one, McKay."

"She went upriver, for some reason," Jeter said, "unless someone killed her downriver and drove her there to get rid of her."

"I think anybody dumping her body in the river wouldn't expect her to be found. I doubt they'd drive upriver with a corpse. At least, I hope they didn't. What we don't need is for this to get more confusing."

"I hear you."

"Hey, I've got a question," Keough said. "No criticism, just curiosity, if that's okay."

"Sure, man, go ahead."

"How come it took your computer search so long to come up with that match on the McKay girl?"

"Oh, that's easy." Jeter moved some papers around on the desk and came up with one he wanted, then another. "Look at this one . . . and then this one."

Keough squinted, then raised his eyebrows. "There's a dollar sign on this one."

"Right. It's a dollar sign instead of a letter S," Jeter said. "Somebody typed it in wrong, and it fucked up the whole search. I was sitting here looking at the stuff and it suddenly jumped out at me. So I put it in again with a correction, and up it—"

"Okay, never mind, I get it. Somebody screwed up. That's all I needed to know. Anything else is just going to go over my head." He handed the two sheets back to the younger man.

"Well, should we get to that list tonight?" Jeter asked, indicating the printouts in front of Keough.

"No," Keough said, looking down at the list of addresses in front of him, "most of these are businesses and I'm sure they'll be closed now. We can check them out tomorrow, too, while we're in St. Louis."

"And the ones that are on this side of the river?"

"We'll have Jenny call them."

"And ask them what?" Jeter said. "If a mad killer has bought any makeup lately?"

Keough rubbed his face. "You've got a point there. What do we ask any of them?" They both fell silent and then Keough broke the reverie. "Go on home. We can worry about it tomorrow."

Jeter got up, retrieved his jacket from the back of his chair. "What about you?"

"I'll hang out here a while," Keough said. "Maybe look over this list. I just might be able to eliminate a few places."

"You want to get something to eat?"

"No, thanks. I'll head home in a little while."

"Well, okay," Jeter said, moving towards the door. "I have a feeling this investigation is going to really get moving tomorrow."

"I hope you're right," Keough said. " 'Night, kid."

" 'Night, Joe."

"Oh, by the way, thanks for dressing down a bit." Jeter had actually left his tie home and had worn a polo shirt underneath his jacket. "Makes me feel a little less like a Target shopper."

"Where *do* you shop, anyway?"

"Never mind."

Forty-two

SHE ASKED FOR it.

This one was different that way. She flaunted her swollen body, paraded around in next to nothing for all to see. She was on his table, all swollen belly and milk tits. He hadn't wanted her, but her actions insisted, and now she was secured to the table and gagged and ready to be "prepared." Her eyes were wide with fear, an incredible amount of white showing until he thought her eyes would almost pop out.

"We didn't have time to talk," he said to her, "I like to talk to the women before . . . but then you would never talk to someone like me, would you?"

She nodded, but he didn't believe her.

"Oh, no," he said, "just prance about almost naked, your windows wide open. It's disgusting, a woman in your condition doing that—but then you did it before you were pregnant, didn't you? So why not after, isn't that right?"

Now she shook her head, but he didn't believe anything she had to say—even if it was said with nods and shakes of the head.

"Women like you are degenerates. You don't deserve to be pregnant, to give birth. I know, because I was birthed by one degenerate, and then raised by another. And I knew they were warped, even if they didn't. My father told me all about my mother. And of course, he was always proving himself, day in and day out. I saw him down here with the cadavers, when he was supposed to be preparing them—especially the women . . . women like you."

He ran his hand up over her belly and then to her tits. He squeezed her nipple, causing a large drop of milky fluid to leak from it, and a tear to drip from her eye. He stared at her with wild eyes.

"You don't deserve to carry this life-giving fluid—but I'll take care of that. I'll take care of everything, don't you worry."

The last part was not meant for the woman. He ran his hand down over her belly again, touching her ever so gently, talking not to her, now, but to the life inside of her.

"Don't you worry," he said, leaning over her, "I'll take care of you better than anyone would."

He turned away and walked to the table with his tools—the tools of his trade. But first, even before any of that, he turned back to her holding a pump not originally designed to extract breast milk, but sufficient for the purpose. She began to squirm, to try to scream. The cords stood out on her neck, but her cries were muffled by the gag.

He approached the table again and placed his right hand on her belly. She flinched, but he rubbed her gently, with reverence reserved not for her, but for the life inside of her.

For his new friend.

Forty-three

WHEN KEOUGH GOT home that evening his message light was flashing three messages. The first was from the mayor—his mayor—wanting a progress report. The second was Detective Knoxx from Sunset Hills, wanting to know if there was anything else he could do to help. The third message was from Valerie. He decided to return both the mayor and Detective Knoxx's calls in the morning, before he left for work. As for Valerie . . . he was still pretty upset with her for talking out of turn to Kathy Logan. On the other hand he wanted to know what had happened to Brady, so in the end he decided to call her before he did anything else. Besides, she sounded pretty contrite on the machine.

"Oh, Joe," she said, when she answered. "I—I wasn't sure you'd call me back. You seemed so angry."

He decided not to address that. "I was wondering where Brady was, Val, and how he's doing? I talked to Kathy Logan and she said they had come and taken him this morning."

"To tell you the truth I was pretty angry about that myself," she said. "I wanted to go and get him so he'd at least see one friendly face."

"What did they do with him?"

"He's in a shelter."

"Shit!" he swore.

"I know, the poor baby," Val said. "I'm making it my personal mission in life to find this boy a home, Joe. I don't understand the trouble I'm having. He's a perfectly adorable little kid."

"Yes, he is," he found himself agreeing.

"I wish I could take him myself, but . . ."

They usually liked to place the children in homes that had both a mother and a father. He knew that. He had even thought once or twice about taking the boy himself, but gave that idea up pretty quick. Notwithstanding his ability to get along with Brady, he just wasn't cut out to raise a child. He knew that. Marriage seemed out of the question for him, as well. What did that leave? Just work.

"Joe?"

"I'm sorry," he said. "I drifted off. I've got a lot on my mind. I just wanted to find out if Brady was all right."

"Well, he's fine, physically," she said. "That's about all I can say."

"That's something, I suppose," he replied, lamely.

"How did it go with Kathy—Mrs. Logan?" she asked.

"She threw me out."

"Why?"

"It might have been because I told her she was a murder suspect," Keough said. "Also, because I asked her about what Brady told me."

"About her husband beating her? Wasn't it true?"

He hadn't intended to talk to her about it, yet he found himself imparting his theory about who was beating whom.

"Wow," she said. "Are you sure Brady never saw the violence?"

"No, I'm not sure," he said. "I keep rehashing the last conversation I had with him."

"Maybe you could talk to him again."

"No, I don't think so," he answered. "It's not my case, and I've got enough on my hands with this other thing. Besides, I could be wrong."

"Anything happening on the other case?"

"No." It didn't concern her, and back when they were together, discussing those kinds of cases was an unspoken taboo between them. She got enough misery at work dealing with neglected kids. The inability—or unwillingness—between them to discuss their work was just another nail in the coffin of their relationship.

"I have to go, Val," he said.

"Can we . . . talk again, Joe?"

"Sure," he said. "I'll call you."

He was about to hang up when she blurted, "I'll call you if I place Brady somewhere!"

"That'd be good. Thanks."

He hung up and decided not to think about Valerie or Brady any more this evening, or even Michael and Kathy Logan. Let Burns do his job and solve that murder. He had his own problems.

After he had changed into jeans and a T-shirt he went in the kitchen. As he was checking out the contents of his freezer, the doorbell rang. He glanced at the clock. It was after six. Every once in a while the UPS man or a mail truck would stop by this late. Maybe his friend Mike O'Donnell had written another true crime book and sent it to him. Or perhaps it was another royalty check from the Kopykat book. O'Donnell kept sending them no matter how Keough protested, and he usually had to sign for them.

He left the kitchen and walked to the front door. When he opened it he saw his neighbor from across the street, Jack Roswell. The older man and he occasionally played chess. It was while helping Jack out with a medical problem that Keough had discovered that he had diabetes—an ailment Jack Roswell shared. The old man tried to help Keough deal with the idea of having the disease.

He opened the door. "Hey, Jack. What's up?"

"Wanna get a drink, and somethin' ta eat?" the old man asked. "Saw you pull up a while ago, thought maybe you hadn't eaten yet."

"A drink, Jack?" Keough asked.

"Dressel's," Roswell said.

"What about—"

"I'm gonna cheat tonight," Roswell said, cutting him off. "Wanna cheat with me?"

"Sure," Keough said, right away. "What's the point of cheating if there's no one there to see it, right?"

"You got it."

"Just let me grab a jacket."

Forty-four

DINNER WITH ROSWELL might have kept his mind off of everything, but as usual the old man had a way of getting Keough to spill his guts. Keough realized during the conversation that losing both Steinbach and Valerie last year had not left him completely without a friend.

They shared a basket of chips while they worked on their Newcastles, and Roswell listened intently while Keough told him about both cases.

"Seems to me," Roswell said when Keough was done, "the one you should be working on is the dead husband."

"Why's that?"

"'Cause that's the one might put your ass in a sling."

"Which is exactly why I shouldn't be working on it," Keough said. "A detective loses his objectivity when he's personally involved in a case."

"I know what you mean. What about you and the woman?"

"Which woman?" For a moment Keough thought maybe Roswell had seen Marie Tobin leaving his house the other morning.

"You and that lady, Valerie?"

"Oh," Keough said, "that ended last year, Jack."

"And it ain't gonna start up again because of all this with the kid and the husband?"

"No," Keough said, "I don't think so."

"Too bad. Seemed like a nice lady."

"She is, Jack," Keough said. "Too nice to be tied up with me."

Roswell finished his Newcastle and started looking for the waiter to order another.

"Hey, that's it," Keough said. "You said one."

"Now you sound like my daughter."

"Well, she'd never forgive me if I let you do too much damage to yourself."

"Speaking of damage," Roswell said, "takin' your pills?"

"I am," Keough said, then added, "when I remember."

"Any numbness in your fingers?"

"No."

"How are your eyes?"

"Fine."

"And what about—"

"Jack," Keough said, "now you're sounding like my mother."

"See?" Roswell asked. "Ya don't like it either, do you?"

After a second beer for each of them they walked back to their block.

"Speaking of your daughter," Keough said, "how's that going?"

"She's still driving me crazy, her and those hellspawn kids." Keough knew Roswell loved his daughter, and his grandkids. According to him, though, they started to wear out their welcome after about half an hour. The son-in-law, he said, he could take. Snuck him a beer every once in a while.

"When am I going to meet her?" Keough asked.

"Oh, believe me, you don't wanna meet her," Roswell said. "She'd take one look at you, dump her husband, and then she'd end up living with you and the kids right across the street from me. That'd be more than you and me could take."

"I thought you said she was good-looking."

"She is. She's a looker, even if she does have her mother's child-bearing hips, but I still wouldn't wish her and those kids on you—or on my worst enemy, for that matter. . . . And kid, you ain't that."

The old man patted him on the back affectionately and Keough realized that Jack Roswell was really the only person in his life right now that he genuinely liked.

"What about this new partner of yours?" Roswell asked as they stopped in front of Keough's house.

"He's okay," Keough said. "Eager to learn, smart . . . he's just too free with the Mark Twain quotes."

"Huh? Mark Twain?"

"He loves him."

"Didn't you say he was black?"

"That's right."

"And he likes Mark Twain?"

"Why not?"

"I didn't know black folk liked Mark Twain," Roswell said. "I mean, all that 'Jim the slave' stuff an' all. I didn't think they'd like that, you know?"

"Black folks?" Keough asked. "Jack, have you been watching *All In the Family* on Nick at Night again?"

"That was a damn shame, Archie Bunker passin' away like that," Roswell said. "That man was a TV icon, what with *All In the Family* and *In the Heat of the Night*."

"Well," Keough said, "he and both shows will live on forever. Seems like they're on every channel as it is."

"Take my advice, Joe," Roswell said, as he started across the street, "work on your case, but don't forget about coverin' your ass on that other one. Ain't nobody gonna pull your bacon out of the fire but you. Remember that."

"Good night, Jack."

Keough went inside, marveling at how the old man had suddenly shifted gears, enabling him to get away with a last minute word of advice. But his bacon wasn't in the fire . . . or was it?

Forty-five

KEOUGH STARTED THE day by taking Mary Ellen McKay's husband over to the morgue to view her body. After the proper ID was made, he had to wait until the man composed himself to bring him back to the municipal building. Once there the man broke down again and it was a good half hour before he was ready to get into his car.

"How is he?" Jeter asked when Keough came back inside.

"He's okay to drive home," Keough said. "Don't know what he'll do when he gets there."

"What did you tell him about releasing the body?"

"I told him I'd call and let him know when we were done with them—with her."

"We're not done?"

"I asked the ME to go over both bodies again," Keough said. "Just in case he missed something. Then we'll release them to the family." He also had something else in mind, but didn't want to share it with his partner, at the moment.

"What are you hoping he'll find?"

Keough shrugged. "Something—anything."

"What about a list of her girlfriends?"

"Two," Keough said, holding up a slip of paper. "He said the three of them were very close, but he didn't know what they could tell us that he didn't."

"Guess he hasn't heard of girl talk," Jenny said.

"A woman will tell her girlfriends things she won't tell her husband?" Jeter asked.

"Please!" Jenny said. "Oh . . . you weren't kidding?"

Jeter looked at Keough, and then back to Jenny. "No."

"You're such a sweet man, Marc," Jenny said, with an affectionate smile. "The answer is yes, yes, a thousand times yes. Women will always tell their best girlfriends everything."

"Everything?" Jeter asked.

"With no exceptions."

"And not their husbands?"

"Come on, Marc," Keough said, "husbands and wives lie to each other all the time."

"Well, yeah . . . I mean, I know when it comes to crimes and things, but . . . what about normal stuff?"

Keough looked at Jenny and said, "One of us is going to have to talk to our boy, here, about the facts of life."

"Well," Jenny said, rolling her eyes, "I hope he already knows about those."

She got up and left the office, both men watching appreciatively until she was out of sight.

"When are you going to make your move?" Keough asked.

"My move?"

"Why else did you recommend her for this job if it wasn't to get her into the same office?"

"Because I thought she'd be good at it," Jeter said. "I thought she'd be an asset to the investigation. I thought—"

"When are you going to make your move?"

"I can't, now," Jeter complained.

"Why not?"

"She thinks I'm naive!"

"Well," Keough said, "let's hope you know more about computers. I want you to run a program, or a search, or whatever you call it."

"What kind?"

"I want to know if and when there are any more reports of missing pregnant mothers."

"That's not a problem," Jeter said. "It's already running as part of my original program. As soon as something new comes in, we'll know it."

"How will we know?"

"Well, I'd have to bring the program up to check for hits, but . . . oh, I see. Wait a minute."

Jeter sat himself down at Jenny's desk and started typing on the computer keyboard.

Keough sat down at the other desk and took out his lists. The first, which Jenny had made for him, consisted of theaters and places selling theatrical materials. The second was Bruce McKay's list of his wife's two friends. While Jeter worked at the computer Keough made a call to Allan Barnes and got a list of girlfriends from him, as well. This one was longer than McKay's list. Apparently Elizabeth Barnes had more friends than Mary Ellen McKay did—five, to be exact. Barnes said he didn't know how well the women knew each other. Keough thanked him and hung up.

"No hits since yesterday," Jeter said, turning away from the machine. "I'll let it run."

"All right," Keough said absently, looking at the lists.

"What's our next move?"

"I've just been thinking about that," Keough said. "There are too many places on this theatrical list for us to check, even if we split up. It'll take days."

"Don't some serial investigations take weeks, or even months?"

"Or years," Keough added, "but I don't think your boss wants this to be one of those. We don't have the luxury of extra men to run down every lead. We'll have to cut some corners."

"I don't think we'd get more men if we asked," Jeter said. "The chief doesn't want to tie up the entire department on this."

"One more dead woman and he will," Keough said.

"Are you suggesting we wait—"

"No, of course not," Keough said. "I'd like us to catch this maniac before he kills again, but I doubt we will. At least when he does hit again we'll have some fresh ground to cover. For now we'll have to go over old territory."

At that point Jenny walked back in and Jeter got up to give her back her chair.

"Jenny, we need your help," Keough said.

"That's what I'm here for, Joe," she said, seating herself. "What do you want me to do?"

He held out her list. "Call all these places and ask them one question."

"Just one?"

"That's it," he said. "Ask them if they know anyone who is exceptionally talented with makeup—almost a magician with it."

"Oh, I get it," she said, accepting the paper. "We're going to isolate that angle?"

"Exactly," Keough said. "The makeup job on the killer when he came in here was too good. He's got to be a pro."

"I'll get right on it. What are you and Marc going to do?"

"Marc is going to talk to Mary Ellen McKay's girlfriends," Keough said, giving Jeter the slip with the two names and addresses on them.

"These are in St. Louis," Jeter complained.

"I'll tell you how to get to them and how to get back," Keough said. "I just got a similar list from Allan Barnes on the phone while you were on the computer. His wife had five close friends, and I'll check them out."

"All today?" Jenny asked.

"I hope so," he said, then added, "if I find them at home."

He took time to write down directions for Jeter and handed them to him. "Can you understand these?"

Jeter read them over and said, "Right, I've got it. What do I do when I've talked to them both?"

"Come back here and make some notes," Keough said. "And check your missing persons program again. I'll meet you back here when I'm done."

"Are you going to have your cell phone on you in case I need to call?" Jenny asked Keough.

"He usually keeps it in the glove compartment of his car," Jeter said, giving Keough up.

"I'll compromise," Keough told Jenny as she gave him a look. "I'll keep it on the seat next to me. I'll be in and out of the car enough that you should be able to get me."

"All right." She turned to Jeter. "And you?"

The young black detective took his cell phone out of his pocket and said, "I always have it on me."

"Good."

"Let's get moving," Keough said. "Jenny's got lots of calls to make and we've got lots of people to see."

"Good luck!" Jenny called out to them as they went out the door.

In the parking lot Keough again went over the directions he'd given Jeter. They weren't the quickest routes around St. Louis, but they were the most direct, without any fancy shortcuts. When Jeter again assured him that he understood Keough watched the younger man drive away, then got into his own car. He had just started the motor when his cell phone rang. Jenny, he thought, checking on him.

"Hello?"

"Uh, Detective Keough?"

"That's right."

"Detective, this is Kathy Logan."

"Hello, Mrs. Logan."

"Look, I know you probably don't want to talk to me after the way I treated you yesterday, but I would really like to meet with you."

"Mrs. Logan," he replied, "if you have something to say about your husband's murder you should be talking to Detective Burns. He's in charge of the investigation. I'm really not part of it."

"No, I—I'd really like to talk to you," she said. "Val gave me your cell phone number—she wouldn't give out your home phone. I—I told her it was important—and it is."

Keough frowned. He had just decided that morning to ignore Jack Roswell's advice about working the Logan murder and put all his time and effort into the killings of the pregnant women. Now Kathy Logan was wheedling him to get back into the investigation of her husband's murder.

"Please . . ." she said.

"All right, Mrs. Logan. Where would you like to meet?"

"I—somewhere out of the way. Not a restaurant, but . . . I know. Do you know where the Laumeier Sculpture Park is in Sunset Hills?"

"As a matter of fact, I do." He didn't know it by name, and he had never been there, but he knew where it was.

"When can we meet? I'm free all day, but the sooner the better . . ." She let her voice trail off, leaving the time to him.

"I have some other stops to make today, Mrs. Logan," he said. "How about two o'clock?"

"All right, that's fine."

"Yes," he said. "All right. I'll meet you at the sculpture park at two, then."

"Meet me by the *Aurelia Roma* fountain in front of the museum gallery."

"Fine." He didn't know what that was, but he'd figure it out.

"I appreciate this, Detective," she said. "You won't be sorry."

"I hope not," he said, and broke the connection.

Before heading out he dialed a number from memory. Keough didn't deliberately try to memorize numbers, it was just a fact that he did. This one was to the St. Louis Medical Examiner, Dr. "Smiley" Donaldson, so dubbed because he always had a smile at the ready.

"Keough? Haven't heard much from you since you joined the mayor's staff. What can I do for you?"

"I've been loaned out to East St. Louis to look into a couple of murders, Doc. I'd like you to take a look at the reports."

"What's the matter with their ME?"

"Do you know him?"

"We talking about Eddie Meeks?"

"That's the guy. He looks a little . . . slipshod to me, Doc."

"Eddie? I'd never call him that. What happened?"

"He missed something."

"Something obvious?"

"Let's just say something you wouldn't have."

"And you found it?"

"Yes."

"Excuse me for saying so, Keough," Donaldson said, "but you're kind of rare in that respect. I think you'd find stuff I missed."

"I appreciate the compliment, but—"

"I'm going to have to pass."

"What? Why?"

"Because, as I said, I know Eddie Meeks. He's a good man. Give him a chance. Trust his reports."

"Doc—"

"Look," Donaldson said, "if things really go south on you give me a call, but right now I don't think I want to butt into another man's case. Can you understand that?"

Keough hesitated, then said, "Sure, okay, Doc. Thanks, anyway."

"I wish you luck."

Keough broke the connection, sat there for a few moments with the phone in his lap. He started to put it in the glove compartment, then remembered his promise to Jenny and dropped it on the seat next to him before starting the car and pulling out of the parking lot.

Forty-six

KEOUGH MANAGED TO interview two of Elizabeth Barnes's girl-friends before his two o'clock meeting with Kathy Logan. Both friends said they didn't have any idea where Betty might have gone if she hadn't gone to her mother's. One of them said she didn't think Betty was particularly happy in her marriage, or with the fact that she was pregnant. He'd go over the interviews with Jeter later. He put them behind him for the time being and headed for his meeting with Kathy Logan.

Keough knew the sculpture park was not far from Sunset Hills Plaza shopping center. He drove along Lindbergh until he saw the sign for it, then turned off the main drag onto Rott Road. He was surprised to find it was still a bit of a drive, and even more surprised when he arrived and found it to be a fairly large park and museum.

He parked and got out, noticing how the parking area was virtually surrounded by metal sculptures. He chose a path and began walking, following the wooden street sign to the museum gallery. Along the way were receptacles holding maps of the park, and he picked one up.

As he approached the building he put aside the case of the mutilated pregnant women for the moment and concentrated on Kathy Logan, who was standing with her back to him in front of a fountain. Mounted in the center of the fountain was a white stone sculpture of a nude woman. Beyond Kathy Logan he could see a string of huge balls that looked like a giant dirty pearl necklace. He checked his map and laughed when he read that it was called *Ball? Ball Wall? Wall!* by an artist named Ernest Trova. The sculpture Kathy Logan was standing in front was—as she had said—titled *Aurelia Roma* by Walter Dussenberry.

Logan was in the act of turning, looking around her, when she eventually spotted him and stopped. She was wearing jeans and a T-shirt that molded themselves to her tennis-toned body. To her credit, since their last conversation, she had apparently lightened up on the makeup.

"Sorry I'm late," he said, as he reached her. "I've been doing interviews all morning."

"That's all right," she said, shrugging. "I like it here. It's quiet. I often come here to be alone."

With less makeup she looked softer, prettier and younger.

She looked at his hands. "You didn't bring your lunch."

"Didn't have time to stop."

"I'm sorry."

"That's all right," he said. "I'll get something when we're finished. What was it you wanted to talk about, Mrs. Logan?"

"Can we sit?"

They had the option of a wooden bench or a porch with umbrella-covered tables and chairs. It was a mild day, so they sat on the wooden bench next to the fountain. From that vantage point he found himself looking at a hugely fat Roman soldier across the lawn from them.

"Detective Keough," she began, "I didn't kill my husband."

"That's not something you should be telling me, Mrs. Logan, but Detective Burns."

"Perhaps," she said, "but for some reason it's important to me that you believe me."

"Okay, then," he said, "convince me."

She looked away from him, gazing out at the sculptures. "You were right about my husband and me," she said. "We had a . . . a volatile relationship."

"Define volatile."

"At times I'd become . . . angry with him, and I would . . . lash out," she admitted.

"Hit him? With what? Your hands? Fists? Lamps?"

"Anything that was close by."

"And did he hit you?"

"No," she said, "never."

So Brady had been wrong, which meant he hadn't seen the violence, only heard it, and misinterpreted it.

"So you see, I had no motive to kill my husband," she said. "He never laid a hand on me."

"But you did lay hands on him, Mrs. Logan," he said. "That still gives you a motive."

"But . . . why? I thought I would only be considered to have a motive if I was a . . . a battered wife."

"As the batterer instead of the battered," Keough said, "you're prone to violence."

"Yes, but . . . not with a gun."

"The kind of violence you describe could easily have escalated into that in the eyes of the law, Mrs. Logan," he said.

She raised her arms, then dropped them to her sides. "Then my confession here means nothing?"

"Not exactly," he said. "You see, I do believe you."

"You do? Why?"

"Let's just say my instinct tells me you didn't do it," he said. "But tell me, what set you off?"

"He . . . cheated on me, constantly. When I found out I would become angry, and lash out at him."

"And then what would happen?"

She looked away, as if the next part shamed her.

"We would . . . have sex. You see, the violence aroused him . . . it aroused both of us."

"And so you'd have sex, and then you and he would fall back into the same pattern until he cheated again?"

"Or got caught."

"And how often did he get caught?"

"Every single time."

"So do you think he wanted to get caught?"

"I suppose so. It all sounds so . . . sordid, now."

"Mrs. Logan—"

"Can you call me Kathy?" she asked, turning a pleading eye on him. "Would that be . . . against some rule?"

"No," he said, "and it wouldn't be against any rule for you to call me Joe."

"Thank you, Joe."

"Kathy, when your husband cheated was it always with the same woman?"

"No," she said. "Different women."

"How do you know?" he asked. "Did he give you names?"

"No," she said, "but I could smell them on him, and they smelled different."

"You mean you never smelled the same fragrance on him?"

"Well . . . yes, on occasion I would smell something familiar."

"And did you know anyone who wore that particular scent?" he asked.

"No," she said, "I don't think—why is this important?"

"Because if he had a regular woman, and she got tired of having him go back to you time and again . . ."

". . . then she may have killed him!" she finished.

"Exactly."

She turned to face him and grabbed his arm excitedly. Her eyes were bright for the first time since he'd met her.

"What can I do?"

"Think back," he said. "Try to identify a fragrance for me, and try to connect it to someone I can talk to."

"You? Or Detective Burns?"

He grimaced and against his better judgment said, "No, don't call Detective Burns with this. He might not agree with my method of identifying a potential suspect. Call my cell phone number if you think of anything, and then we'll talk." He didn't really think anything would come of this, but it gave her something to cling to—if she didn't kill him herself.

Her grip on his arm tightened. "I can't tell you how much this means to me."

Impulsively she leaned in and kissed him on the mouth. For just a moment their lips pressed together warmly, firmly, and then suddenly he thought of Marie Tobin, and how as nice as sex with her had been, he'd regretted it later. He pulled away from Kathy Logan's kiss as gently as he could, trying not to insult her.

"I'm sorry," she said, a little breathlessly, "that was silly of me."

"It was just a kiss of gratitude."

"Yes," she said, "it was . . . I guess."

He stood up and helped her to her feet.

"Give it some thought and get back to me. Can I walk you to your car?"

"No," she said, "I'll stay here, walk around a bit. It will help to clear my head."

He didn't know if she meant because of the kiss, or simply in general. "Well, all right," he said, checking his watch.

"You go ahead," she said, "you've got work to do. I—I can't tell you how much I appreciate this, Joe. I feel so much better having talked to you."

"There is one more thing you should do, Kathy."

"I know," she said, "I should call Detective Burns and tell him about the relationship my husband and I had."

"Yes," Keough said. "He may go at this another way and find an angry mistress."

"Yes, all right," she said. "I'll call him when I get home."

"And I'll wait to hear from you." He gave her his home number.

"Joe?"

He'd started away, and now turned back.

"About Brady? I'm sorry it didn't work out. He's such a sweet little boy."

"Yes, he is."

"You like him, don't you? I could tell by the way you talked to him when you were there."

"Yes, I do like him. We have a sort of history."

"You're not married, are you?"

"No."

"And you and Val are—"

"Friends."

"I see," she said. "So I guess it wouldn't be possible for you to take him."

"No," he said, "that's not an option, Kathy. I wouldn't . . . I'm just not father material."

"I wouldn't be so sure of that if I was you."

He smiled at her, then turned and left the park.

Forty-seven

THE REST OF the afternoon was a bust. Keough did not find any of the remaining three girlfriends at home, and they lived in neighborhoods miles apart, which was why he'd left them for the afternoon.

After leaving the last home, which was all the way out in South County, he paused by his car to decide what to do next. It was almost five and he was feeling shaky. He never did get to lunch, he hadn't taken his pills today, and his sugar was probably low rather than high. That was something he didn't understand about diabetes. It's a disease that manifests itself by forcing the blood sugar to increase to sometimes dangerous levels. However, there were times during the day when the sugar could be too low. Usually when that happened, like now, he felt weak and shaky. For the life of him, though, he could not "feel" when his sugar was too high. Either that or he simply refused to admit it.

In any case he had to get something to eat, if only so he could take his pills, which needed to be consumed with a meal. He decided he could afford to make a few calls before choosing a place to eat. The first was to Jenny at the office.

"We're still getting calls from people who say they can identify the dead women, Joe."

"All right, we'll have to issue a statement confirming we've succeeded in identifying them. Have you heard from Marc?"

"He found one of the women this morning and interviewed her. He's been tracking the second one ever since. She was supposed to be in her office, but she works for a real estate outfit, so she was out showing a house. He went out there—well, he's been a step behind her for hours, it seems."

"That's okay," he said. "He only had two to talk to, he can afford the time."

"Where are you now?"

"I'm out in South County, in Mehlville. How are you doing with that list?"

"I've got six names, addresses and phone numbers of people for you to talk to. They all say they have this person who is just amazing with makeup."

"Think any of them are the same person?"

"I don't know," she said. "I guess that'll be for you to find out. After all, you're the detective." Her tone was teasing.

"So I've been told. Okay," he said to her, "I'll get something to eat here and then I'll be in."

"Right."

He broke the connection, considered calling Jeter, thought the young detective might think he was checking up on him, then decided he'd make the call just to "compare notes."

"I haven't found her yet," Jeter said, "but I'm getting closer."

"Okay," Keough said, "give it another hour then meet me at the office. We'll compare notes in detail then."

"Right."

They each broke their connection and Keough kept the phone in his hand. Call Valerie? No reason to do that unless he wanted to talk to Brady again. He did owe the kid at least another conversation. He'd asked Keough to stop the fighting and—whether he'd done it or not—the fighting had now stopped—only Brady wasn't in the house, anymore.

He dialed the mayor, but got a secretary, who said His Honor was out of the office and unreachable. After a moment he asked her to simply give the mayor the message that things were "progressing."

He broke the connection, then called Knoxx at the Sunset Hills Police Department and found him in.

"Glad you called back," Knoxx said. "I was wondering if you thought about my offer to help."

Keough started to answer that he had thought about it and didn't need help, but he stopped himself. Depending on how long Jenny's list of theatrical places was it might be useful to have an extra set of flat feet, so to speak.

"I might have something for you to do, Detective—"

"Just call me Knoxx," the man said. "Everyone does."

"Okay, Knoxx," Keough agreed. "Like I said, I might have something but it would be legwork, and I wouldn't want to interfere with your own workload."

"I got nothing right now," Knoxx said, "and as for legwork I'm pretty good at it, appearances to the contrary."

"I've got to go back to my office and coordinate some things," Keough said. "Can I call you tomorrow? When will you be in?"

"Doesn't matter," Knoxx said. "Here's my home number. Call me anytime. I live alone, and can't sleep worth a shit."

"Okay," Keough said, jotting the number down in his notebook. "I'll definitely call you tomorrow."

This was good, he thought as he dropped the cell phone on the seat next to him. He might be able to expand his task force without making an official request to do so.

He went in search of the nearest Steak 'n' Shake.

When Keough walked into the office Jenny looked up at him and the expression on her face said something was wrong.

"What?" he asked.

"They found another one, Joe," she said. "The report just came in from a radio car about half an hour ago. I tried your cell but it was busy, so I called Marc. He's on his way—or he might even be there."

"Where? And what do we have?"

"A dead woman found along the Greenway Trail, in Belleville."

"Belleville?"

She nodded. "There are eight counties that make up Southern Illinois, and we usually know what's going on with each other. They know about this case over there, and when they got the call on the body and saw what it was they notified us."

"Wow," he said. "That's what I call cooperation."

"Is that unusual where you come from?"

"Very. Now, tell me what the Greenway Trail is?"

Forty-eight

BY THE TIME Keough reached the site, Marc Jeter was there, as well as several Belleville uniformed police, holding people back. He showed his badge to one of the uniformed cops and was allowed beyond the crime scene tape. Jeter looked up in time to see him coming. There was another man standing with him, older, wearing plainclothes and sporting the ruddy complexion of a drinker, and still another man apparently crouched over the body.

"Joe," he said, nodding at the man next to him, "this is Detective Metfield."

Metfield reached out and shook Keough's hand. "I don't envy you this," he said. "It's gruesome as hell."

Keough moved closer so he could take a look. He ended up looking over the third man's shoulder. The man turned a tanned and well-lined face to take a look at Keough.

"Joe, that's Doctor Grace, the ME."

"Part-time," Grace said. "Are you the man in charge?"

"To tell you the truth, Doctor, I'm not sure of the protocol," Keough said. He turned and looked at Detective Metfield.

"I've got orders to turn this over to you," the man said, "and I do so gladly."

Keough looked at Dr. Grace. "I'm in charge, then."

"I've talked to the ME in East St. Louis," Grace said, standing up. "Quite by accident, actually. We go to the same club." Grace was portly, didn't look like an athlete. Keough didn't ask what kind of club. It didn't matter.

"He talked about this to you?" Keough asked.

Grace suddenly looked like he was caught talking out of school. "Well . . . actually, only about one of the, uh, women . . . we do compare notes, you know."

"Sure," Keough said. This was not good, but this was not the ME he was angry with. "Same MO, then?"

"Looks like," Grace said. "This baby seems to have been ripped from her."

"Damn," Keough said.

"This is what we wanted, isn't it?" Jeter asked. "A fresh case, a fresh crime scene?"

Keough turned and looked at him. "Maybe what we needed, Marc, but sure as hell not what we wanted." He turned back to the doctor. "Doc, how fresh is she?"

"I'd say she was killed within the last thirty-six hours."

"Damn," Jeter said. "That's way fresher than the others."

Keough gave him a warning glance and the younger detective decided to clam up, just in case those around them thought they looked at this as good news.

"Can I take her?" Grace asked.

Keough looked at Detective Metfield.

"I've got everything I need," Metfield said. "I talked to my sergeant and he said to go along with whatever you want."

Keough kept forgetting that in these small municipal departments sergeants ran the detectives. In New York it would be a chief of detectives.

Keough examined the grass around the body. It had been pretty well trampled, probably by whoever found her as well as the uniforms who had responded, and now by the medical examiner, himself—and that reminded him.

"Have you had a tech go over the area?" he asked Metfield.

"We have a man who does that," Metfield said. "He took photos, looked for evidence."

"Bag anything?"

"I—I'm not sure."

"Well, if he did have him ship it over to me with the photos, and the negatives."

"Okay."

"Who found the body?"

"A couple of joggers."

Keough looked around. The path was a little bit away from where they were standing at the bottom of an incline. The killer might very well have rolled the body down.

"Not easy to see from up there."

Metfield opened a notebook.

"One of them admitted he came down here to take a leak," he said.

"Were both runners men?"

"Yes."

Keough looked at Jeter. "Have you talked to them?"

"Not yet."

"Where are they?"

"Outside the tape," Metfield said. "I've got a uniform with them."

"Talk to them, will you?" Keough said to Jeter. "I still want to look over this scene."

"Right." The young black detective started up the incline.

Keough looked at Grace. "Can your men remove the body with a minimum of additional damage to the scene?"

"Detective Metfield indicated that his man had already photographed the scene—" Grace started, defensively.

"Easy, Doctor," Keough said, "I'm not blaming anyone for anything. I'd just to like examine the scene myself with as little additional contamination as possible."

Grace said, "I'll tell them to watch their big feet."

"I'd appreciate it."

Keough stepped back to allow the ME's men in. He watched

as they bagged the body and then lifted it and started up the incline. He knew he wasn't going to get much from this scene, but he'd give it a try, anyway.

"I'll send my reports to you," the ME said.

"Would you send them to Doctor Meeks, as well?" Keough asked. "I'd like him to look them over."

"Of course," Grace said. He fidgeted a bit, looking reluctant to leave. "Look, Detective. Er, what I said about Doctor Meeks—"

"He shouldn't have said a word, Doctor," Keough said. "You both know that."

"I don't want to get him in trouble—"

"I'm not his boss," Keough said. "I can't do a thing to him."

"Yes, well . . ."

"Good day, Doctor," Keough said. "Thanks for your help."

Grace scowled, then turned and trudged up the incline.

"Somebody's ass is gonna get reamed," Detective Metfield said.

"Maybe," Keough said. "Isn't it a little late in the day for jogging?"

"Most people jog when they can," Metfield said. "For many, it's morning. Some do it after work."

"Mmm," Keough said. "I suppose."

"You need me for anything else?" Metfield asked.

"I need one man, if you can spare him," Keough said. "And keep the tape in place until I'm done looking around."

"Okay," Metfield said. "I'll leave a man and tell him to hold folks back until you say so."

"Fine."

"If I can help . . ." Metfield said.

"I'll call." Keough shook the man's hand. "Thanks for the cooperation."

"No problem."

As Metfield walked up in the wake of the others Keough turned and found himself alone with the crime scene. He didn't expect to find much, but he started his examination, anyway.

* * *

When he had finished he and Jeter walked back to their respective cars.

"This one's different," Jeter said.

"Tell me why?"

"He didn't hide this one. He wanted it found."

"And that means?"

"He's challenging us," Jeter said. "Challenging you. He's getting bolder."

"Good." Keough was approving of the younger man's deductions, not the fact that the killer was challenging him.

They reached Keough's car and he opened the door. "How much bolder can he be than walking into the police station?"

Jeter scowled and said, "Good point."

Forty-nine

HE STEPPED BACK and regarded his handiwork. With the use of putty he had built the cadaver's face back up to its normal size, and with more putty managed to hide the scars from where he'd peeled the face back in order to get beneath it. He grew up playing with tools of cosmetic surgery the way other children grew up playing with Silly Putty and Play-Doh.

"Another masterpiece," he said, touching the dead man's face. He leaned over so he could speak into the cadaver's ear. "Another masterpiece for someone to bury."

What other artist, he wondered, had so much of his work buried in the ground?

He looked at the clock on the wall. It was almost time for him to meet Julia for dinner. He didn't know why he had agreed to meet her, but he had and he always kept his word.

He went to the stainless steel sink in the corner and washed his hands and arms. He knew he should have showered and gotten the smell of cadavers off of him completely, but if she wanted to have some sort of relationship with him she was going to have to get used to the smells of his profession.

He dried his hands, took one last look at his handiwork, then said to the dead man, "I'll be back to finish you later, my friend."

He walked to the table, looked down and smiled. "I've made you better looking in death than you ever were in life."

He left the room, turning off the light and closing the door behind him. He paused at the stairs to look over at the other closed door, the one that led to the special room, and then went upstairs. He had someone waiting for him, and she was alive.

That was very rare.

When he entered the restaurant she was already there. What did she see in him, he wondered? Was there an attraction here, or was it just a matter of need? With her lover dead, and now carrying his child, was Julia Cameron just in need of some kindness?

As he walked across the room towards her table he could see the glow from within. How many months along was she? Five, had she said? And not showing much, yet. Four months to term, three more months before the child would be ready for him.

That last one, the slut he'd left by the path to be found, she would be his last for a while. He had a live one, here, to nurture and bring along. This was something new, and he didn't want to blow it.

This one would be his crowning achievement.

Fifty

IT WAS 9:00 P.M. before Keough was ready to leave, and allow Jeter to go home. However, he'd sent Jenny on her way after returning from Belleville.

They had returned to the office once Keough completed his fruitless examination of the crime scene. As he had surmised almost immediately it had been hopelessly trampled and compromised before his arrival, as had the grounds around it. The killer had done one of two things. He'd either rolled the body down the incline, in which case there would have been nothing to find around her anyway, or he'd walked down and placed her there. If that was the case, any footprints had been obliterated.

When they returned to the office they exchanged notes about their day's efforts.

"I ran around like a chicken without a head for most of the day, trying to track down this woman Louise Proctor."

"The real estate woman?"

"Right," Jeter said. "Never did catch up to her. In fact, since I don't know St. Louis that well I kept getting lost. I thought I'd show up at her office bright and early tomorrow and catch her before she went out again. Apparently, I guess she's a real go-getter."

"What about the woman you did talk to? Another professional type?" Keough asked.

"No, a housewife. I found her home with a toddler. Said she thought the McKays were the perfect couple."

"Don't they always."

"What did yours say?"

Keough briefly went over his interviews with Elizabeth Barnes's friends, Angela West and Laura Scandal. They didn't give them much to go on. Both described her as quiet, but not particularly happy in her marriage. Neither had ever met her husband, but from what they'd been told they didn't like him.

"Did he beat her? Abuse her?"

"*Mistreat* was the word they each used," Keough said, "but it sounded like typical husband stuff. Never helped her, overworked her, even though she was pregnant. You know, didn't help keep the place clean, still made her do the shopping. Nothing really helpful. One of the other three might give us more, when we find them."

"What are we going to do about this new one, now?" Jeter asked.

"We'll get the reports tomorrow. You or Jenny will run her through the computer, and we'll run her prints through NCIC. Maybe we'll get lucky. But until we identify her, we'll have to keep working on the other two."

"I'll find that real estate woman tomorrow," Jeter said, again.

"And I've still got those three friends of Elizabeth's to find, but we also have to go to Lebanon to talk to her mother. Where is Lebanon, anyway?"

"About eight miles east of Fairview Heights."

"So he either grabbed her in Lebanon and dumped her in Fairview Heights, or—what would take her to Fairview Heights?"

"I don't know. Shopping?"

"Well, there's no point in speculating," Keough said. "We'll ask her mother tomorrow. We'll see her first."

"Together? What about the real estate woman? If I don't catch up with her early I might never find her."

"We'll do that together, too," Keough said. "I fact, we'll stick together all day tomorrow."

"Well, good," Jeter said, with feeling.

"Glad you won't be getting lost again?"

"Glad I might actually get to learn something by watching you."

"Is that flattery?"

"No."

Keough studied the younger man for a few moments and then said, "No, I guess it's not. Why don't you go home and get some rest. Be back here tomorrow at eight."

"What about the theatrical list Jenny made? Eight locations?"

"Six in Missouri and two in Southern Illinois," Keough said. "I've got somebody to take care of that for us."

"You got the chief to give us another man?"

"Not exactly." Keough explained that he had a volunteer from another department who was going to help them. "I just have to call him tonight or tomorrow and give him the list. He'll do the preliminary interviews. If anything sounds promising, then we'll go in and check it out."

"Sounds good," Jeter said. "We can use the extra legs."

"You got that right," Keough said.

"What about your problem? Did you leave it alone, like you planned?"

"I tried to," Keough said, "but somebody changed my plan."

"A woman?"

"A woman and a kid."

"Can I help with that?"

"No," Keough said. "I just want you to concentrate on one thing."

"Well, if you change your mind . . ."

"Thanks, Marc."

Jeter said good night and headed for home. As soon as he was gone Keough dialed the home number Detective Knoxx had given him.

"Yeah?" Knoxx's voice called out too loudly.

"Knoxx? It's Joe Keough."

"Hey, Joe! Gladta hear from ya."

"Am I interrupting something?"

"A party." Keough listened but could not detect any background noise. "Just me and my friend."

Keough caught on. "Which friend? Jack Daniel's?"

"No, nothing that hard," Knoxx said. "John Courage."

"Good beer."

"You know good beer?"

"I do."

"We'll have to hoist a few."

"Maybe when I'm finished with my cases," Keough said. "You still want to help?"

"Definitely."

"Sober enough to write down some addresses?"

"Wait," Knoxx said. "Let me put my friend down and pick up a pen."

"Knoxx," Keough said, "don't fuck with me."

When Knoxx spoke again his tone was a few decibels lower.

"Don't worry, Joe," he said. "I'm only about a sheet to the wind. Takes more than that to induce early morning amnesia. I'll do the job for you."

"Okay, then," Keough said. "Take down these names and addresses, and then I'll tell you what I'm looking for."

It took a few minutes for Knoxx to get it all written down, and then a few more for Keough to explain.

"Have you got all that?"

"Every word," Knoxx said.

"Then why don't you get some sleep and an early start tomorrow?" Keough said. "Take down my office number here—and do you still have my cell number?"

"I do."

"Then I appreciate the help, Knoxx."

"I'll be in touch tomorrow night to let you know how many of these I was able to hit in one day."

"I expect it to take a few days."

Knoxx laughed and said, "We'll see."

Keough said good night and hung up. He sat at the desk for a few more minutes, thinking about the new girl. Her stats would be on his desk in the morning, with any luck. If they could identify her quickly, they might actually have a fresh trail to follow.

Tomorrow could bring some answers, or a lot more questions.

Fifty-one

WHEN HE WAS eight he walked in on his father fucking the body of a dead nineteen-year-old cheerleader. The old man took the belt to him, then said, "You'll learn. When they're dead they don't yell at you, or tell you your dick is too small!"

The only thing he learned was that his father was a sick man who sometimes abused his friends in the basement of the funeral home. In all the times he'd gone down there and looked at the nude bodies laid out, ready to be prepared, he'd never touched them. He talked to them, made friends with them, but had never touched them, not even the prettiest girls, like that cheerleader.

He did learn something about his father, though. In spite of being a disrespectful pig in the basement, he was the most charming of men when he was upstairs, dealing with live clients. The parents of that cheerleader had thanked him profusely for the wonderful job he had done on their daughter, totally unaware that he'd screwed their "little girl" prior to embalming her.

But once his father was dead and he took charge of the business, that sort of abuse never happened again. The basement became a safe haven for his friends, until they were stolen away and buried.

Of course, he revealed none of this to Julia Cameron during

their talks. None of his father's past, or of his own present. And although they had seen each other now three times, he still had not touched her. He was pleased to learn that this did not bother her. She told him she was impressed that he was so "respectful." This from a woman who was carrying a dead man's bastard.

Some of them had all the nerve!

Fifty-two

KEOUGH MET JETER at the East St. Louis Municipal Building the next morning, and even before Jenny put in her appearance they were gone, taking his car to Lebanon to see Elizabeth Barnes's mother. Keough was annoyed that the reports on the new victim were not yet available.

"That rat bastard!"

They were sitting in the living room of a small A-frame house in Lebanon, listening to Elizabeth's mother cursing out her son-in-law. After they had showed their credentials she had invited them in to sit and talk. She offered no refreshments. She was giving them what they wanted, though—talk.

"Why do you call him that, ma'am?" Jeter asked.

"Because he is, that's why."

Elizabeth's mother was named Cora Daniels. Keough didn't think in all his years of interviewing people he'd ever met a Cora before. It wasn't a name you ran into a lot in New York. This Cora was fifty-five or so, thickly built and probably always so, with big solid breasts, butt and thighs. Her hair was dark, shot with gray, her fingers blunt, nails chewed to the quick.

She noticed Keough looking at her nails and held up her hands. "There was a time my nails were long and well tended. Not anymore, though."

She brought her hands down on her thighs with a loud slap. She was sharp, having spotted his appraisal, so perhaps her observations would be helpful.

"Mrs. Daniels—"

"Just call me Cora, Detective," she said, interrupting Keough. "I haven't really been a Mrs. since Elizabeth's father ran off and left me to raise her on my own, twenty years ago."

"Never married again?" Jeter asked.

"And give another man the chance to do that to me?" she asked. "No way. When I give a man the time of day now it's for sex only, and then I choose to move on." She gave Jeter an amused look. "You think it's odd for a woman my age to still have sex?"

"Uh, no, I didn't—I mean—"

"I've embarrassed him," she said to Keough.

"He's young."

"You're not embarrassed?"

"Not by talk of sex, Cora."

"You can see me having sex?"

Keough stared at her and said, "Vividly."

Now there was just the hint of embarrassment on her part, and she used hospitality to cover it up. "Would either of you like something to drink?"

"No," Keough said, "we really just want to talk about your daughter and her husband."

"That rat bastard!" she said, again.

"So you said," Keough pointed out, "but you didn't say why."

"Because," she answered, "he didn't have the common decency my old man had to leave."

"I thought you were, uh, bitter about your husband leaving," Jeter said.

"Best thing he ever did for me," she said to Jeter. "Do you know why?"

"No, ma'am."

"Because I have friends whose husbands stayed with them," she said, "and all they did was kill them slowly. I've seen my friends waste away while catering to their men, and I was watching the same thing happen to my daughter."

"She didn't want to leave him?" Keough asked. He wondered if Angela West and Laura Scandal had been wrong about Elizabeth wanting to leave her husband.

"She didn't," Cora said, "until she became pregnant. Then she got smart."

"So when she came here to stay with you," Keough asked, "it was to leave him?"

"No, not then," she said. "She came here to talk about it."

"Ask advice from her mother, maybe?" Keough said.

"Yes," Cora said, "not that I should be giving anybody advice about how to run their life. I told her to have the baby, let him pay all the bills, and leave his ass. I told her she could come here and stay if she wanted, with the baby."

"That was very generous," Jeter commented.

"She's—she *was* my daughter," Cora said. "I didn't have a choice. Nothing generous about that."

"So when she left here she was going back to him?" Keough asked.

"That's what I thought." Cora looked directly at Keough. "She was here for four days, and then she left. Is he saying she never got back home?"

"That's what he's saying."

"And he didn't report her missing?"

"He thought she was here."

"You didn't report her missing," Jeter pointed out.

Eyes flashing, she said, "I thought she was with him."

"Did you call to check?" he asked.

"No," she said, "I don't call there. We don't talk, him and me."

"So," Keough said, "he thought she was here, you thought she was there . . . and where was she?"

She lit a cigarette with shaky hands that reminded him of

Angela West again. Thinking of Angela West reminded him suddenly of Angela Mason, the IA detective. He wondered when he'd be hearing from her, again.

"Did he kill her?" Cora demanded, bringing Keough back to the present after his momentary lapse. "Do you think he killed her?"

"We don't really," Keough said.

"Why not?"

"Because we have two more women killed the same way," Keough said, "we think by the same man. Would Allan have any reason to kill other pregnant women?"

"I don't know what he'd have reason to do," she said, taking a long drag on her cigarette. "Oh God, two other mothers have lost their daughter and grandchild?"

"Yes, ma'am," Jeter said.

"Stop calling me 'ma'am' for Chrissake."

"Yes, ma'—um, I mean, yes."

She looked at Keough again, ignoring Jeter. "What do you want from me?"

"We just wondered if Elizabeth might have said anything to you about other men."

"Other men?" she snapped. "What are you talking about? Elizabeth didn't run around. I wish she did. Maybe she would have found somebody better than that asshole. Although as long as it was a man . . ." She let the rest of her comment go unsaid. She had an obvious low opinion of men as a gender. "Are either of you married?"

"No," Keough said, and Jeter just shook his head.

"Good," she said, "do women a great big favor and don't marry one. You'll just make them miserable."

Jeter started to comment but Keough stood up and said, "We won't take up any more of your time, Cora."

"If you don't mind," she said, "I won't see you to the door. My legs feel kind of weak, at the moment."

"That's fine," Keough said. "We'll let ourselves out."

She nodded, sucking on the last of her cigarette, then stubbing it out and reaching for another one. "Elizabeth was my only child," she said, around a fresh cloud of smoke. "I raised her myself and she was a good girl. You know, some women like me—the kind who like sex?—they don't ever want to be called a grandmother, you know? I was looking forward to it. When you catch the sonofabitch who killed her you'll let me know, right?"

"I'll let you know personally, Cora," Keough said. "You have my word."

She glared up at him and he knew just what she was thinking—the word of a man. Unfortunately, he didn't have any other kind to give.

Fifty-three

THE NEXT STOP was the real estate woman who was friends with Mary Ellen McKay. Her office was in Webster Groves, not far from the Affton home Mary Ellen shared with her husband Bruce. Not far when measured in miles, but a long distance if measured by income bracket. Webster Groves was a fairly affluent area with large homes and expensive shops and restaurants. The realtor Louise Proctor worked for had an office on Lockwood, right in the center of a bank of shops that included an antique dealer and a furniture store. Actually, to Keough the antique place was more of a trendy junk store.

During the drive Keough and Jeter had discussed their visit to Cora Daniels.

"Man, has she got a hard-on for men, huh?" Jeter asked.

"Lots of women do," Keough said, "after they've been abandoned by one."

"Yeah, but, man . . . I mean, get over it, right?"

"Easier said than done in some cases, I guess."

"At least she thinks we have some use, though," Jeter said. "Can you imagine someone that old having sex regularly?"

"How old are you, anyway?" Keough asked.

"Come on," Jeter said, "you've got to admit—"

"What does Mark Twain have to say about the charms of older women?"

Jeter thought a moment, then said, "I don't know." He seemed annoyed that he couldn't come up with a quotation. Keough figured that would keep him quiet for a while on the subject.

"Well, we've got the word of two people now—her mother and her friend, Angela—that she was thinking of leaving her husband."

"But we don't suspect the husband," Jeter said.

"You always suspect the spouse," Keough said, "but in the case of a serial victim, not seriously."

"So who do we suspect?"

"Everyone else."

They parked down the street from the Realtor and walked back.

"I wish the reports on yesterday's victim were ready," Keough said. "I wanted to read them early."

"We're dealing with an ME from Belleville," Jeter reminded him.

"Good point."

"You think the freshness of this victim is important?"

"I think everything about this victim is important," Keough said, "the similarities and the differences."

"Well, the freshness is a difference," Jeter said, "and the fact that she was pregnant and the baby was taken from her—"

"Torn from her."

"—*torn* from her," Jeter amended, "is a similarity. What would be more helpful, if the ME comes up with more of one, or the other?"

"At this point," Keough said, as they reached the front door, "anything would be helpful."

They entered and stopped just inside. There were six desks and only one was occupied, by a woman.

"Not going to be here," Jeter said in a whisper. "We can't get that lucky."

The woman appeared to be about the same age as Mary Ellen McKay, so Keough said, "You can't get that lucky. I can."

"I chased this woman all over St. Louis yesterday," Jeter said. "We're not going to get this lucky."

"Excuse me?" Keough said.

"I'm sorry to keep you waiting," the woman said, searching for something on her desk. "I'll be right with you."

"Are you Louise Proctor?"

She looked up then and said, "Yes, I am."

"I don't believe it," Jeter said.

She was still leaning over, which made her long dark hair fall like a curtain across her face.

"Do I know you?"

"I'm Detective Keough. This is my partner, Detective Jeter."

She stood up and pointed at Jeter. "You were looking for me yesterday."

"Yes, ma'am."

"I'm sorry, I had a really busy day. It was an outside day."

"Outside?" Jeter asked.

"I spent most of it outside," she said. "We take turns. Today I'm supposed to be inside."

She bent over and started searching again. She brushed the curtain of hair back, but it fell forward again. It was a gesture that always appealed to Keough on attractive women, and Louise Proctor qualified.

"Luck," Keough said, to Jeter.

"Did you say something?" Proctor asked.

"What are you looking for?"

She stood up and put her hands on her hips, an exasperated gesture. "It doesn't matter. What can I do for the police?"

"It's about Mary Ellen McKay," Keough said.

"Oh, God," she said, "Mary Ellen . . . that poor girl."

"Could we have a few moments of your time?"

She looked around, said, "I just opened the office—late, if you must know. I haven't made coffee. Can we walk down the street? I really need some if I'm going to talk about this. In fact, if we could take a ride there's a coffee shop just a little—um, actually it's on Big Bend, but not far—"

Keough could see how nervous she was so he said, "We can take our car, and we'll bring you back when we're through. Is that okay?"

"That'll be fine," she said, with relief. "I'll just lock up."

Fifty-four

SHE TOOK THEM to a small combination bookstore and coffee shop that was not part of a chain. Keough was able to get plain black coffee while Jeter got a latte and Proctor a hot mocha concoction. It occurred to Keough—as it had before—that many of his conversations with people took place over food or drink, or both—or was this just the case with everyone?

Louise Proctor told them that she first met Mary Ellen McKay when she and her husband came into the office looking for a home.

"I wasn't able to help them," she said. "I had nothing in their limited price range, but I was able to refer them to a realtor in Affton."

"And that's where they bought their home," Keough said.

"Yes," Proctor said. "After they made the deal Mary Ellen called me. She wanted to take me to lunch as a thank you. I accepted, and we became friends."

"Were you friends with her, or with both of them?"

Proctor shifted in her chair uncomfortably. Keough's eye went to the realty emblem on her blue blazer. It was gold, and he could not for the life of him make out what it was supposed to be.

He averted his eyes, then, before she could assume he was looking at her breasts.

"Mr. McKay and I never . . . connected," she finally said.

"Why was that?"

"Honestly?"

"Please."

"He's a pig," she said. "A moment ago you were looking at the emblem on my blazer, weren't you?"

"Yes, I was."

"You see? I knew that. I also knew that when he was looking at me he was always undressing me. He'd stare very blatantly at me, even in front of her."

"Did he cheat on her?"

"He did."

"And she knew?"

"Yes."

"Before or after her pregnancy."

"Before and during."

"Was she unhappy?"

Proctor sat forward, leaned her elbows on the table.

"That's the odd thing. She wasn't. She seemed to think that this was the way men were—or the way they were supposed to be."

"Did you tell her different?"

"I tried. My own husband is very loving and supportive of my career," she said.

"And what did she think?"

"She thought that my husband was the odd one. I couldn't convince her otherwise."

"They did fight, though."

"Constantly. She also thought it was part of being married."

"But this time she ran away?"

"No," Proctor said, "they employed what she called a 'cooling off period' when they fought. Sometimes he left, sometimes she did."

"And where would she go?"

Proctor shrugged. "Someplace different every time. Once she came and stayed with me. Another time she went to a hotel."

"And where did he go?"

"Who knows? To a girlfriend's?"

"Miss Proctor—"

"Louise, please."

"Louise, did their fights ever become physical?"

"No," she said, "not that I know of."

"You never saw her with a bruise?" Jeter asked.

"No, never. She insisted that he didn't beat her—but I always thought there were different types of abuse."

"I agree," Keough said.

She checked her watch and said, "I really have to get back. I opened late, as it is. My boss will flip."

They drove back and pulled up in front of her office. She slid to the passenger side of the backseat and put her hand on the door handle.

"I hope I was of some help to you."

"Everything is helpful, Louise," Keough said, from behind the wheel.

"I hope so," she said. "I miss Mary Ellen. And I have to admit, I thought her husband did it."

"These murders are particularly brutal, Miss Proctor," Jeter said. "If you say he was never violent . . ."

"I see your point," she said. "I just keep thinking. She was very happy about being pregnant, was looking forward to being a mother. And now . . ."

"We're going to find out who did it, Louise," Keough said. "You can count on it."

"Well, if I can help any further, just let me know."

"We will."

She opened the back door and started to step out, but stopped with one foot on the ground.

"Have you talked to her other friends?"

"We got your name and one other from her husband when we asked who her friends were." He told her the name of the other woman, whom she did not know. "Do you know any others?"

"No, I'm sorry," she said, and got out of the car. She stopped short, though, turned and leaned down to look in the window past Jeter to Keough.

"What about her group?" she asked.

"Was she in group therapy?" Keough asked.

"Well, not that I know of," she said, "unless she saw it as therapy. I was referring to her theater group."

Fifty-five

WHEN JETER ASKED Louise Proctor why she remembered the name of Mary Ellen McKay's theater group she said, "It has an odd name. Besides, I take an interest in my friends."

Now, as they drove away from her office, Jeter wrote in his notebook and said aloud, "The Black Box Group. I've never heard of it."

"Neither have I, but it shouldn't be too hard to find."

"Now?"

Keough thought a moment, then said, "Let's stick to our schedule, Marc. Also, I've got Knoxx on the theater groups. Maybe this one is already on his list."

"So we're going to go looking for the other friends of Elizabeth Barnes?"

"That's what we're going to do right now."

"Okay," Jeter said, closing his notebook and retrieving the list, "geographically or alphabetically?"

Before Keough could reply, his cell phone rang.

"Get that for me, will you?"

Jeter got the phone out of the glove compartment and said, "Hello?" Then he held it out to Keough. "It's Jenny."

"What's up, Jenny?"

"The chief and the sergeant," she said. "Both of their temperatures are up about this new murder."

"I left reports for them before I went home last night."

"Skimpy reports, they say," Jenny replied.

"Well, tell them we don't have an ME's report, yet."

"We do now," she said. "It just came in. Do you want me to show it to them?"

"No," Keough said, "just stick it in a drawer and hold it for me. I want to see it first."

"Okay."

"Is it from Belleville? Or our guy?"

"Belleville," she said. "Why would we have one from—"

"I asked the Belleville doctor to send it to ours to get an opinion," Keough said. "Okay, if you get something from Doctor Meeks do the same."

"What am I supposed to do if the chief or the sarge ask if the ME's report has come in?"

"Tell them the truth."

"That they have?" she asked. "Or that they have and you asked to see them first?"

"Both," he said. "Don't get caught in a lie, Jenny."

"Yes, sir."

"See you later."

He handed the phone to Jeter, who stashed it in the glove compartment again.

"She'd lie if you asked her to, you know," he said.

"I'm not asking her or anyone else to lie for me," Keough said. "Remember that."

"Okay."

"Back to the friends," Keough said. "Let's take them geographically. Read me the addresses."

Fifty-six

"I'VE MET A woman."

The doctor looked across his desk at Andrew Judson. "Have you, now?" He was wondering what had brought his patient back so soon.

"Yes."

"Who is she?"

"Just someone who came to a funeral," Judson said. "She came back afterward, looking for me."

"Ah!"

"What's that mean?" Judson asked. "Ah?"

"Just that I'm listening."

"You say it a lot."

"I listen a lot," Dr. Todd said. "When you talk, which isn't often, Andrew."

"Well, I'm talking now, aren't I?"

"Yes," Todd said, "about this woman. What's her name?"

"What does that matter?"

"Well, if you're dating her—"

"I didn't say anything about dating," Judson asked, agitated, "did I?"

"Well, no, I just assumed—"

"We've just had coffee together," he said, "and lunch, that's all."

"But if she came looking for you it means she likes you," Todd said, "doesn't it?"

"You're the expert on what things mean, not me," Judson said. "How do I know what she's thinking? She's a woman, isn't she?"

"And what does that mean?"

"It means that men don't know what women are thinking," Judson said. "Isn't that true?"

"Well," Todd said, "that is the case sometimes, unless the woman is being completely honest—"

"What?" Judson asked. "When have you ever known anyone to be completely honest?"

"Well, I—"

"And when have you ever known a woman to be completely honest?"

Doctor Todd felt that Judson was very close to losing control. Ranting and raving were okay, but losing control . . .

"Now, Andrew," he said, soothingly, "just relax. There's no need to get upset."

Andrew Judson stared across the desk at the doctor and was suddenly calmed by the knowledge that the man was afraid of him. He'd known it all along, of course, but at this moment it was particularly apparent.

"But I'm not upset, Doctor," Judson said. "As a matter of fact, I'm very calm at this moment."

Todd stared back at Judson and wondered when he should be more afraid of him: when he was upset, or when he was calm?

"Andrew . . . your feelings towards women? Have they . . . changed at all?"

"Why would they change, Doctor?" Judson answered.

Doctor Todd knew that Judson's feelings about women came directly from his father. What made Judson interesting—when you set aside the fear factor—was that he was not the textbook child of an abuser. Typically, the child of an abuser abuses, and while Judson's somewhat . . . skewed opinion of women was his father's, his attitude toward children was not.

"But do you still want children of your own?"

"Of course I do," Judson said. "Children are precious."

"And women?"

"Women are a necessary evil," the younger man said. "They are needed to bear children."

"Evil?" Todd repeated. "All women?"

"Oh, yes," Judson said, "and do you know who the most evil woman of all was?"

Todd sat back in his chair. Perhaps this would be some sort of revelation. "Who?"

"Lucy."

"Lucy . . . who?"

"Ricardo."

Todd was confused. "Andrew . . . who is Lucy Ricardo?"

"You know," Judson said, "*I Love Lucy*? The TV show?"

"Ah . . . you mean Lucille Ball?"

"I mean Lucy Ricardo," Judson said.

Todd wanted to get this straight. "You believe the character of Lucy Ricardo, from the classic television series *I Love Lucy*, was evil?"

"Incarnate."

"I'm afraid you'll have to explain that to me."

"Look at everything she ever did to ruin Ricky's career," Judson pointed out. "She was a no-talent, evil, selfish bitch—she even tried to sabotage his screen test to try to get herself in the movies. What kind of a woman does that to her husband?"

Todd thought, *A sitcom character*, but did not say it out loud.

"Well, let's put that aside for the moment," he said, instead. "Andrew, tell me about this woman you're seeing."

"She's pregnant."

That surprised Todd. He did not think that Judson had ever had sexual relations with a woman, despite the fact that he was almost thirty years of age.

"By you?"

"No, of course not by me," he said. "None of them have been pregnant by me."

"None of . . . them?"

Suddenly, Judson stood up. "This session is over, Doctor."

"But you still have time—"

"Good day," Andrew Judson said, and stormed out, his shoulders stiff, his back straight. The young man gave every impression of controlled fury.

Doctor Todd sat there a few moments, giving Andrew Judson time to get to the parking lot, then looked out the window and watched his patient drive away. He went immediately to the sideboard and poured himself a stiff scotch. He could not believe that the young man's disregard for women had extended to a television character—and a much beloved one, at that. He carried his drink back to his desk, sat down and unfolded his copy of the *Southern Illinois News*. His eyes immediately went to the headline: THIRD PREGNANT WOMAN DISCOVERED DEAD IN SOUTHERN ILLINOIS.

With shaking hands he reached for the phone and dialed the number of the lawyer for the Judson Trust.

Fifty-seven

WHEN KEOUGH AND Jeter returned to their task force office their asses were dragging.

"Wow," Jenny said, "you two look like you've been *running* all over St. Louis, not driving."

"I *feel* like I've been running," Jeter said, dropping heavily into a chair.

"What happened?" she asked.

Keough rested a hip on her desk and said, "These last three girlfriends of Elizabeth Barnes's are not cooperating."

"They won't talk?" she asked.

"They won't be found," he said. "We finally tracked one of them down and she had nothing to offer. She was a knockout, though, which might be why she stuck in Allan Barnes's mind, but she said she wasn't very close to Elizabeth, at all."

"And the other two?"

"Lead very active lives," Keough said. "We'll try to track them down tomorrow."

"What about calling them?"

"It may come to that," he said, "but usually calling someone first gives them time to rehearse what they want to say to the police."

"We did find out something interesting from the real estate lady, though," Jeter said.

"The one you chased all over St. Louis yesterday?" Jenny asked. "You mean Joe went with you today and she was there?"

"As luck would have it," Jeter said, defensively. "Anyway, she told us that Mary Ellen McKay was a member of some amateur theater group called the Black Box Group."

"Was that on the list you gave me, Jenny?" Keough asked.

"I think it was," she said. "I'll check it. I kept a copy."

He removed his hip from her desk and walked over to the other one, where Jeter was sitting.

"Where's the ME's report?" Keough asked, in the meantime.

"You're going to be real happy," she said. "Check your In box."

He did and found the ME's report, another report from Doctor Meeks with his opinion, and last but not least a fingerprint report on the dead woman.

"They got an ID?" he asked, excitedly.

"On our new dead woman?" Jeter asked, sitting up.

Keough looked the report over and said, "Gloria Lauren, a.k.a. Gloria Loving."

"A.k.a.?" Jeter repeated. "She had a record?"

"Prostitution," Keough said, handing the report to Jeter. "Also, she worked under the Loving name as a stripper."

"Add in Fairview Heights," Jeter said. "She's the first victim living over here, east of the Arch."

"Differences," Keough said.

"And similarities," Jeter added.

"Are you two talking code?" Jenny asked.

"Not really," Jeter said. "Just something Joe was telling me about being a detective, that sometimes differences can be as important to a case as similarities."

"It's on the list," Jenny said.

"What?" Keough was distracted.

"The Black Box Group," she said. "It's on the list. They're in Webster Groves."

"Have you heard from a Detective Knoxx?" he asked.

"Check your In box," she said, again.

He went back to the In box and found some pink message slips. Two of them were from Knoxx. He'd last called about an hour before. One of the slips was from Kathy Logan, who had called around lunchtime. There was another from a reporter with the *Southern Illinois News*.

"Okay," Keough said to Jeter, "change of plans for tomorrow."

"Which is?"

"We take up the chase on the new case," he said. "We'll go to Gloria's address and see if we can find a husband or a boyfriend."

"And what about the other two girlfriends of the Barnes woman? Don't they still have to be interviewed?"

"As a matter of procedure, yes," Keough said, "though I don't hold out much hope that they're going to know anything helpful."

"I could go and talk to them," Jenny offered.

"Out of the question," Keough said, rejecting the idea immediately. "You're a civilian, and this is a homicide investigation. I can't put you at risk."

"It was just an idea," she said.

"Besides," Jeter said, trying to soften the blow, "you're too valuable here."

"Speaking of being valuable," she said to Keough, "I kept the sergeant from sending out a search party for you."

"And how did you manage that? You didn't lie, did you?"

"Of course not," she said. "I told him you'd stop in and see him as soon as you got back. Was that a lie?"

"No," Keough said, "it wasn't. I'll go and see him now. You can go home if you want to, Jenny."

"I think I will," she said. "I've had a full day taking messages and filing." She was still miffed at being dismissed so abruptly.

"I'll walk you to your car," Jeter said.

"Whatever," she said, slinging her purse over her shoulder.

"See you back here," Jeter said, going out of the office behind her.

Her feelings may have been hurt, but Keough didn't think

there was anything he could do about that. She wasn't a cop and could not go out and interview people. That was just the way it was. Maybe Jeter could explain it to her better than he could.

He left the office and walked through the halls to the sergeant's office.

Fifty-eight

"JESUS," SERGEANT BENSON snapped when Keough knocked on his door and entered, "where have you been?"

"Working."

"Doing what?"

"Running down leads. It's what detectives do." Keough regretted the comment as soon as he said it, but he couldn't take it back.

"I don't need your New York attitude, Detective," Benson said. "I need to know what's going on."

"I've been keeping you and the chief in the loop, Sergeant," Keough pointed out. "Reports at the end of each day."

"Reports?" Benson asked. "You call hastily scribbled notes reports?"

"If it's the best I can do at the time, yes."

"And I didn't even get a hastily scribbled note this morning on yesterday's victim. Jesus Christ, another one?"

"This one is different."

"Different? How?"

"We've got her identified already."

Benson's eyebrows went up. "That is different. Who is she?"

"Her name's Gloria Lauren. She worked as a stripper named Gloria Loving."

"Around here?"

"I don't know where she worked. Maybe we'll find out when we get to her address tomorrow."

"Where does she live?"

"Fairview Heights."

From beneath knitted eyebrows Benson asked, "You will check in with the local police when you're over there, won't you?"

"Of course." Not just to go to her house, he added to himself.

"Well, give me the particulars on her."

"I would have written you a report tonight."

"I'll take a verbal."

"What about the chief?"

"Write one for him before you go home. He was on my ass all day. I'll send him a note."

"Fair enough." Keough ran it down for him, from the moment he got the call.

"Was the press there?"

"They must have been, if it made the papers today, but they didn't talk to me. I do have a message from someone at the *Southern Illinois News*."

"Don't return the call."

"I don't intend to," Keough said. "I don't check in with the press on my investigations."

"Unless the reporter's a friend, right?"

"You're referring to Mike O'Donnell, in New York. That was a special case."

"Why's that?"

"Because Mike was—and still is—a friend. We exchanged information."

"And he made you famous."

Keough hesitated, his first instinct to snap curtly. When he spoke he kept his tone well modulated.

"Sergeant, I didn't think we were going to have a problem when we spoke in the mayor's office that first day."

"I didn't, either, but you're not keeping me informed, Detective," Benson said. "You're running this investigation as if you're in charge."

Yes, Keough admitted to himself, he did have a big city attitude when he first arrived and found a hybrid small town/big city setup in St. Louis, with its "City" and "County" departments. But he seriously thought he had gotten over it—then, without warning, he could feel it rearing its ugly head and—just for this moment—he'd decide not to fight it.

"Fine," he said, standing up. "You want to run the investigation? Run it! It's yours. I'm out of here."

"What?"

Heading for the door Keough said, "You heard me. Take it, run with it, be a detective. I'm finished."

"Come back here!"

Keough kept going, out into the hall. Behind him he could hear Benson squawking, and the sound followed him out into the hall.

"Keough, get back here! You can't do this!"

Keough turned and faced Benson in the hall. It was after hours and there was a skeleton crew in the building, but he was sure they were being heard by someone.

"Why can't I? You want to be the detective, don't you? You want to run a murder investigation? Only if you knew how to do that I wouldn't have been called in, would I?"

Benson recoiled as if he'd been slapped.

"So go to the chief and tell him you're in charge now."

"I—I can't—"

"Then get off my back, Sergeant, and let me do my job," Keough said. "Yes, this is my investigation, and yes, I'm running it. I'm keeping you in the loop out of courtesy, because this is your department, but I'm not checking in with you. That would be counterproductive. You have nothing to offer this investigation and talking to you is wasting time I could be putting to better use."

Keough was out of breath. He'd vented, and having done so he now wished he was somewhere else. They couldn't fire him, because he didn't work for them, but they could call the mayor—his mayor—and report his behavior. What would happen after that was anyone's guess, but what would not happen was the serial killer getting caught. As it stood now, he was the only man who had a chance of doing that within in a reasonable period of time.

"Look, Sergeant," Keough said, "I'm sorry for my outburst, but I've got a fresh homicide and a good chance to catch this guy. I thought this was all about catching this guy."

"Well," Benson said, after a moment, "you've made it very clear that it's about *you* catching him, haven't you? Very well, *Detective*, you may consider that you have put me in my place."

With that Benson turned on his heels and walked stiffly back to his office. Beyond him Keough could see a man with a broom and a young woman with an armful of papers. The man looked bored, the woman stunned. Both had witnessed the entire exchange.

"Well," he said to himself, "that's the end of a budding friendship."

When he turned the hallway was empty and he walked back to his office.

Fifty-nine

"I HEARD YELLING echoing through the building," Jeter said when Keough entered the office. "Were you giving or getting?"

"Giving, I'm afraid."

"Are we still in business?"

"For the time being, I guess."

"Want to tell me what happened?"

Keough did, then said, "I guess I lost my patience."

"Sounds like it."

"Is that a criticism?"

"I'm agreeing with you," Jeter said. "You lost your patience. You think he'll pull the plug?"

"Does he *have* the pull for that?"

Jeter shrugged. "I've never tested him this way."

"Well then, it'll be interesting to see what takes precedence," Keough said, "catching a killer or soothing Sergeant Benson's hurt feelings."

"At the very least," Jeter said, "you haven't made a friend."

"I can live with that." Keough picked up the phone, and one of the pink phone messages from Detective Knoxx.

"What are you doing?" Jeter asked.

"Checking in with Knoxx before I leave. You can go home, if you want."

"Maybe I'll just wait," Jeter said. "You might want to get a drink after."

Keough studied the younger man, then said, "Yeah, you might be right."

Keough dialed the number and waited for the man to pick up. When he did he said, "Knoxx? Keough."

Knoxx reported that he had personally gone to six of the theater groups on the list and interviewed someone at each place. Unfortunately, it was not always the right person. He did, however, manage to get some piece of information at every stop.

"Figured I better make each visit worth my while," he explained.

"That's more than I did. What did you get?"

"Two of the places said they knew of a man who was like a magician with makeup."

"Did you get his name?"

"Names," Knoxx said. "Two different guys."

"Give me the names." More people to interview. Oh for the days of a fully appointed task force, he thought. He wrote both names down and then asked, "Are both these fellas actors, or what?"

"The second one is an actor. The first name I gave you is just a makeup man."

"Were any of these places you went to called the Black Box Group, in Webster?"

"No," Knoxx said, "but that one's on my list."

"How many more to go?"

"Two."

"Okay, look, I've got something else I want you to do. I'll take the last ones."

"You're the boss. What have you got for me, then?"

"A couple of nice young ladies," Keough said. "I'm having a hell of a time finding them. They're friends of one of the victims."

He explained to Knoxx what he wanted from each woman, and gave the man their names and addresses.

"Maybe you can get an earlier start than I can and catch them at home. Apparently, they live alone and have very active lives, because we never found anyone home to even ask where they were."

"Okay," Knoxx said. "Maybe I'll try some neighbors."

"Fine, do that," Keough said, "and thanks for what you did today."

"I'll check in with you tomorrow, then."

"Just leave a message if I'm not in, like today. I'll get back to you." He didn't bother telling Knoxx that by the same time tomorrow, the plug might have been pulled on the investigation—at least, on Keough's part of it.

He hung up on the man and turned to face Jeter.

"Got two names, an Andrew Judson and a Walter Kinney. Apparently they're both makeup experts. Kinney's an actor, though, and Judson a makeup man."

"Maybe one of them is also connected with the Black Box Group."

"That would be a nice connection," Keough said. "We'll find out tomorrow. I traded jobs with Knoxx."

"I heard," Jeter said. "Maybe he'll have more luck with the ladies, huh?"

"Maybe," Keough said. "Better turn off the computer."

Jeter turned, tapped a few keys, got permission to safely turn off the power and did so.

"Want to get that drink?" he asked.

"Marc," Keough said, "you might want to think twice before hitching your wagon to me after what I did today."

"You're the man behind this investigation, Joe," Jeter said. "I'm with you, good or bad."

"Yeah, but you actually work here."

"So? If they kick you back across the bridge I'll still work here—maybe."

"I don't want to be the reason you lose your job."

"What the hell?" the young man said. "Maybe you can get me a cushy spot on your mayor's staff."

Keough laughed and said, "I might be able to, at that. Okay, then, let's get that drink—but on my side of the river."

Sixty

THEY HAD ONE drink on the Landing, talked a bit about what they were going to do the next day, and then went their separate ways. It wasn't much, but Keough felt they had made more personal contact that evening than any of the other days they had worked together. Maybe it was because he had yelled at Benson and that was something Jeter would never do—no matter how much he wanted to. Or maybe it was just Marc Jeter's way of telling Keough he would back him, no matter what tomorrow brought. Whatever it was, Keough appreciated the gesture—even if it turned out be just that . . . a gesture.

When Keough got to his house the porch was in darkness, but he knew someone was there. In fact he even knew who it was, because he was expecting them sooner or later.

"Detective Mason," he said, even before walking up the steps. "To what do I owe this pleasure—again?"

Once he reached the porch he could see her, sitting there in a corner. She stood up and approached him.

"We need to talk."

He looked past her, but didn't see her partner. "Where's Gail? You out on your own tonight?"

"We're not joined at the hip."

"Or is he in a car down the block," Keough asked, "on the other end of a wire?"

By the look on her face—a fleeting shadow of something—he knew he was right.

"Are you coming inside, or do you want to take me somewhere again?" he asked. "Because I gotta tell ya, I'm real tired and not in the mood for a drive."

"We can go inside."

"Fine."

He unlocked the door, allowed her to go first and then followed. After all, she might have been IA, but she was still a lady—or a female, at the very least.

Once inside he turned on a light and tossed his keys on the table next to the phone. He could see the message light flashing "3."

"Are any of these messages from you?" he asked.

"No," she said, "I didn't call first—but go ahead and listen to them, if you like."

"No, that's okay," he said. "It might be one of my cronies trying to set up something crooked."

"Ha ha."

"I'd offer you something to drink but that would imply that this was a social call and that I might want you to be comfortable."

"Don't worry," she said, "it's not a social call." She was wearing a windbreaker over a T-shirt, and jeans. He knew there had to be a microphone on her somewhere.

"Testing, one, two, three," he said.

"What?"

"Let's get on with it."

She reached inside her jacket and came out with a regular white number 10 envelope. From it she extracted what looked like a snapshot and handed it to him. He accepted it, and examined it. It was a picture of him and Kathy Logan sitting together in the sculpture park.

"That's you kissing the wife of Michael Logan," she said, "the murder victim."

"So what?" he asked. "It's not my case. To me she's just a woman, not a suspect."

"How about an accomplice?"

He contrived to look as if he was thinking that over, then shook his head and said, "Naw, I don't like that one. Here's your picture back." She took it. "Is that it?"

"You don't want to try to explain this?" she asked.

"I don't think it needs to be explained—not to you, anyway."

"You're kissing a murder victim's wife."

"Actually, to be accurate, she's kissing me."

"And you don't think that needs to be explained?"

"Like I said," he repeated, "not to you, and not to your partner." He took a quick step towards her and grabbed the bottom of her jacket, spreading it. She backed away quickly and he released her.

"Don't put your hands on me."

"I can't believe you came into my house with that picture and a microphone and expected me to break down and confess."

"Do you have something to confess?"

Keough folded his arms and stepped back. "You don't have anything on me so you're willing to have me confess to . . . anything?"

"You were seen in Michael Logan's office the afternoon he was killed," Mason said. "His assistant said you did not have a friendly attitude."

"I always have a friendly attitude, Angela," he said, using her first name in a familiar manner. "You of all people should know that."

"What?"

"Come on, sweetie," he said, "turn off that mike and come to Daddy. All is forgiven."

She narrowed her eyes and said, "You're crazy."

"You mean that one night we had meant nothing to you?"

"We never had a night!"

"You promised to keep me out of jail if I slept with you," he said. "Now you're telling me you don't remember?"

Her hand went down to her waist, on the left side, betraying where the microphone was. "That'll never work, Keough," she said. "Nobody would ever believe that you and I slept together."

"No? Don't tell me you're—"

"That's enough!" she said. "I'm leaving."

"I'll walk you to the door," he said, but she already had it open and was out on the porch. He walked to the doorway. "Sorry you didn't get what you wanted," he called after her.

"Fuck you!" she yelled.

He took some focaccia bread from the back of the refrigerator, removed it from the plastic wrap and studied it. Rosemary, onions and no sign of mold. He put it in the microwave and removed some cheese and olives from the refrigerator, as well. Add his last Boulevard and it was the best he could do for dinner.

Sitting at the table munching, he wondered what Mason had been fishing for. Was it just the Michael Logan murder? Or something else? Obviously, she and her partner had been watching him, and they must have been good at it because he hadn't spotted them. They snapped his picture meeting with Kathy Logan—just when she was giving him an appreciative kiss, apparently—but had they shown it to Detective Burns? Probably not. If they had he would have been on the doorstep with Angela Mason. So the question was, were they going to show it to Burns?

Sixty-one

KEOUGH MET BURNS at the door with a cup of coffee when the man rang the bell at quarter to eight.

"You were expecting me?" Burns looked at the cup in his hand, puzzled.

"I knew Mason would call you," Keough said. He walked into the kitchen and Burns had no choice but to follow. "I don't have much in the house for breakfast. Haven't had time to shop." At that moment the two halves of an English muffin popped up from the toaster. "I'll split this with you."

"Forget it," Burns said. "The coffee's enough."

Standing at the counter, Keough buttered the muffin and took a bite, then turned to face Burns.

"What the hell is this about a photo of you and my victim's wife?" Burns demanded.

"Mrs. Logan called and asked to talk to me," Keough said. This reminded him that he hadn't yet returned his last call from her, but he didn't mention that to the other detective. "We met at the park over in—"

"I know where it is," Burns said, interrupting him. He put his cup of coffee down on the kitchen table, untouched. "What did she want?"

"She wanted to tell me that she didn't kill her husband," Keough said. "I told her that was the kind of thing she should be telling you."

"She has, several times," Burns said. "So what? That's all she had to say?"

"I advised her to call you after she spoke to me. Did she?"

"Yes."

"And she told you about the domestic violence?"

"What domestic violence?" Burns asked. "He never laid a hand on her."

"But she hit him."

"That's what you call domestic violence?"

"Don't tell me you think it's only domestic violence when the husband beats the wife?"

"Don't go getting progressive on me, Keough," Burns said. "So she hit her husband with a frying pan or something once or twice. So what?"

"That's what I told her," Keough said. "So what? She insisted on telling me that since her husband never struck her, she couldn't be a viable suspect in his death."

"And what did you tell her?"

"I told her to tell it to you."

"And then the two of you started making out in the park?"

"We weren't making out," Keough said. "I listened to her and she was grateful, so she leaned over and kissed me. It was over in a second—but that was long enough for Mason and Gail and their surveillance equipment to catch it on film. She came here last night, showed me the photo and waited for me to confess to something."

"Why does she have a hard-on for you?"

"You'd have to ask her that," Keough said. "I had to field a sexual harassment beef on the last case I worked before going into the mayor's office. It was bogus, and got dismissed, but she doesn't seem to want to give it up."

"Probably because she's a woman," Burns said. He looked at the coffee he'd laid on the table, picked it up, took a testing sip to see how hot it was, then drank half of it down. "Okay, I buy it. She's got it in for you—but do me a favor, huh? Stay away from my suspects?"

"Believe it or not," Keough said, "I have been. I've been working my own case."

"Well, keep working it." Burns put the cup back on the table.

Keough walked him to the door and asked, "By the way, am I still a suspect?"

Burns turned and looked at him. "I'll tell you what I know you've told people a million times when they ask that question—everybody's a suspect until an arrest is made."

"Fair enough," Keough said.

"By the way," Burns said, on his way to the door, "we searched that parking lot with a lint brush. There was no bullet from any other gun."

"Another theory shot to hell," Keough said, with a shrug. "It happens."

Sixty-two

"YOU'RE PANICKING FOR no reason at all, Gerald," David White told Dr. Gerald Todd. White was the attorney for the Judson estate, the man who oversaw the payments that were made to Todd as long as he was seeing Andrew as a patient.

They were in White's law office in Fairview Heights. The attorney was seated behind his desk, regarding the doctor calmly. Todd had phoned him the day before, after his session with Andrew Judson, but the lawyer had refused to see him until this morning at nine A.M. The psychiatrist had arrived in an agitated state.

"Look," Todd said, "you haven't talked to Andrew Judson every week for ten years. I have."

"Careful, Doctor," White said. "Don't reveal anything that's privileged."

"I'm not!" Todd said. "I'm just telling you what I read in the papers."

"Pregnant women have been killed," White said. "I've read it. Why does that lead you to believe that Andrew Judson might have something to do with it?" White leaned forward. "Can you answer that without violating your professional ethics?"

Todd opened his mouth to answer, and then stopped. Could he? He wasn't sure.

"Take your time, Doctor," White said, looking at the clock on his desk. "I don't have any appointments until ten."

"David," Todd said, "all I'm saying is that this is something that we should consider. The boy has problems with women."

"Pregnant women?"

Todd chose his words carefully. "There's an incident in his past, yes." He could not reveal that the incident was Judson's own birth, which had resulted in the death of his mother.

"But do you have any reason to believe that Andrew would kill any woman, let alone a pregnant one?"

Todd wanted to scream, *The boy is crazy!* Instead, he said, "Not really."

"Doctor," White said, "what would you have me do?"

Todd stared across at David White. He'd met the attorney a little over ten years ago, when the arrangements had been made for him to see the Judson boy. The father had employed the attorney to employ the doctor. White had been a partner in another firm, then, a lawyer in his thirties looking for that one client that would enable him to open his own office. Andrew Judson's father, Benjamin, turned out to be that client. Ben Judson had quietly built himself a small fortune in the stock market while running his family owned funeral parlor. When he became David White's client, allowing White to handle his business affairs, the attorney had been able to leave the firm he was with and open his own office. Similarly, when Andrew Judson became "Dr. Jerry's" patient, he had been able to stop sharing an office with two other doctors and go out on his own.

"Just between you and me, Doctor," David White had told him at the time, "Ben Judson is something of a cash cow. He's willing to pay you twice the going rate to take on his son as a patient."

"Why so much?" Todd asked.

"Frankly," White had said, "because no one else will take him."

Todd had not asked why. After his first session with the boy, however, he knew why—but he also knew he wanted the money, so he accepted the new patient.

Ben Judson died the following year and David White became the executor of his estate.

"As long as you keep seeing Andrew," he told Todd at that time, "you will continue to be paid two and a half times the going rate."

Todd had wondered at the time how much White was getting from the estate. As he looked around him at the small but impeccably furnished office, he figured the attorney was making out all right.

Suddenly, it was as if White knew what Todd was thinking.

"Gerald," he said, "this has been pretty easy money for the two of us all these years, hasn't it?"

Not so easy, Todd wanted to say, when he had to look into the eyes of Andrew Judson every week, but what he said was, "I suppose."

"Why would you want to rock the boat now?"

"But David . . . what if he is killing these women?"

The lawyer sat back in his chair again and gave the doctor an exasperated look. "Gerald," he said, "bring me some evidence that Andrew Judson is a killer and maybe then I'll call the police."

"You won't take my professional opinion?" Todd asked. "Just call them and ask them to investigate?"

"No," White said, "I won't do that."

"Why not?"

"Because it's my job to look after my client's interests."

"Ben Judson was your client, and he's dead."

"I still have a responsibility to his son," White said, "and to his estate."

And to the exorbitant fee you're undoubtedly drawing from the estate, Todd thought.

"And so do you, by the way," White said. "If I find you went to the police, or anyone else, about this I'll see to it you lose your license. Understand?"

"I understand," Todd said, meekly.

"Now, if that's all you had on your mind?"

Todd hesitated, then stood up and walked slowly to the door.

"Doctor?"

"Yes?"

"Take my word for it," David White said, "there's still plenty of milk left in this cash cow."

Todd nodded dumbly, and left.

Sixty-three

JETER DROVE HIS car with Keough in the passenger seat, since it was the younger detective who knew his way around Southern Illinois. They had the Fairview Heights address of the third victim, Gloria Loving, and Jeter drove right to the neighborhood.

Both Jeter and Jenny had been in the office already when Keough arrived that morning. Keough stopped just inside the door and looked around.

"Are we still in business?"

They both looked back at him.

"Doesn't look like we're shut down yet," Jeter said.

Keough looked at Jenny. "No messages from Benson? Or the chief?"

"Nothing," Jenny said.

"So what do we do?" Jeter asked. "Go to the chief's office?"

"No," Keough said, "what we do is not ask for trouble. Let's just get going to Gloria Lauren's address and talk to her husband."

So they left Jenny to "man" the office while they pursued the facts behind the third murder.

* * *

Keough took the time to read the ME's new reports in the car. The man agreed that the third victim fit with the first two. In fact, he had checked the bodies further and had found other similarities—marks indicating that, in some way other than "ropes, more likely manacles" all three women had been similarly bound.

"Listen to this," Keough said, and read it aloud to Jeter.

"What's it mean?"

"Well, all three women were immobilized, somehow."

"I know that, but how? Using what?"

"He doesn't say."

"What else does he say?"

Keough read further and then said, "Jesus."

"What?"

"He thinks that 'some kind of pump' was fastened to Gloria Loving's breasts to apparently 'remove her breast milk.'"

"Ugh! Does it really say that?"

"Yeah, it does," Keough said. "I don't have the kind of mind to make up something like that."

"What about the other two women?"

Keough read further. "He's not sure about the first one, but says similar marks were found on the second woman's nipples. The first body had too much damage to the breasts to tell."

"Got to be, though," Jeter said. "He's taking their babies, and their milk? And then killing them? This is getting sicker and sicker."

Keough closed the folder and tossed the reports onto the back seat. "You got that right."

They suspended any further discussion about the ME's reports and parked near a fire hydrant in front of Gloria Lauren's house. It was an older home, in need of repair but not exactly run-down. The homes around it had been maintained at a much better level. As they walked toward the door Keough noticed someone watching from a window next door but couldn't see if it was an adult or a child.

When they reached the door Jeter rang the bell and the two detectives waited. Jeter rang again and then looked at Keough.

"Left for work already?"

"Maybe," Keough said. "Let's try next door."

"Here?" Jeter pointed to the house on the left.

Keough pointed to the right, where he'd seen someone at the window. "There."

They walked down the path, over to the next house and up the path again. The grass in front of the Lauren house was dried and patchy, but they didn't want to trample over the other house's well kept lawn.

At the door Jeter rang the bell and they waited.

"Nobody here, either?"

"Somebody's home," Keough said. "They were peeking out the window when we got here."

Jeter rang again, then knocked on the storm door. Finally, they heard a lock disengage and the door opened. They were separated by the storm door from a blowsy looking faded redhead in a house dress. The screen airbrushed her face so that Keough could see she'd had better days before her looks faded, hidden beneath pouches and behind lines.

"I hear y'all," she said, "y'all don't have ta knock the door down."

"Ma'am," Jeter said, "we're from the police. I'm Detective Jeter and this is Detective Keough."

"Y'all got IDs?"

They both produced identification and held them to the screen so she could see them.

"I'll talk to y'all," she said, "but I can't let y'all in. The place is a mess." She held the house dress tightly around herself. Keough guessed she was about ten years younger than Elizabeth Barnes's mother in Lebanon, but she had lost her sex appeal, while the older woman had somehow maintained hers.

"That's all right," Keough said, "we can talk from here."

"What about?"

"Your neighbor."

"Hank?"

"His wife, I think," Keough said. "Gloria Lauren?"

"Gloria who?"

"Gloria . . . Loving?"

"That slut?" the woman asked. "She ain't married to nobody, let alone Hank."

"But does she live next door?"

"Oh, she lives there, all right," the woman said. "Walks around naked all day, in front of the windows. Gives the men in this neighborhood a real show, she does."

"But," Jeter asked, "isn't she pregnant?"

The woman looked at him and smirked. "That don't stop her. Belly out to here, she still got them milk titties out to here, too, if y'all know what I mean? Men love 'em."

"Ma'am," Keough said, "we're looking for the man who lives next door."

"That'd be Hank—Henry Bowen."

"Is he the owner of the house?"

"That's right."

"And Miss Loving, she's not his wife?"

"No," she said, as if that were the most ludicrous thing in the world to suggest.

"Then why does she live with him?" Jeter asked.

"Because she's one of his girls."

"His girls?" Keough asked. "You mean he has more than one girlfriend?"

"Not girlfriend," she said. "Girls. Ain't you listenin'?"

"I'm trying to, ma'am," Keough said. "What do you mean she's one of his girls?"

"His girls," she said. "His strippers."

Keough got it. "Are you saying Mr. Bowen owns a strip club, and she's one of his employees?"

"That's what I been sayin'," she complained. "What kind of detectives are you, anyway?"

"The confused kind, I guess, Mrs. . . ."

"Bonaconte," she said. "I'm Lydia Bonaconte."

"Mrs. Bonaconte," Keough said, "Could you tell us the name of the strip club Mr. Bowen owns, and where it is?"

"How the hell would I know that?" she asked. "I look like somebody who goes to strip clubs? Or works in one?"

"No," Jeter said, "of course not."

"Why of course not?" she demanded. "You don't think I coulda worked as a stripper if I wanted to?"

Jeter gave Keough a nervous look and said, "Uh, I don't know, ma'am."

"Well, I coulda," she said. "I used ta have a good body, you know—and not that long ago." She folded her arms beneath her generous, if somewhat floppy, breasts.

"I'm sure you did, ma'am," Keough said. "Would your, uh, husband know about the club?"

"I'm sure he would," she said. "He knows where all the strip clubs are—him and his buddies."

"Would he be home?"

She made a face and said, "He's always home. I'll get him."

She left the door open as she went to get her husband. Jeter took the opportunity to lean over to Keough and ask, "If he's married to her, why is he always home?"

Keough just shrugged.

Sixty-four

LEO BONACONTE DID, indeed, know where Henry Bowen's strip club was, as well as all the other strip clubs in Southern Illinois.

"We just need to know the location of the one," Keough said, "and the name."

"It's called the Diamonique Club," Bonaconte said. He was in his early fifties, his slovenly, faded appearance a perfect compliment to his wife's. "It's in Sauget." Another Southern Illinois community. He told them how to get there, his directions perfectly clear.

Before they left, Keough said, "Mr. Bonaconte, is there anything you can tell me about your neighbors?"

The man looked behind him, then stepped outside and pulled the front door closed.

"Gloria was Henry's top act until she got pregnant," he said to them, keeping his voice down. "She's got a killer body, even pregnant. Huge tits, if you know what I mean."

"We know." He wasn't exactly being subtle.

"When she got pregnant he took her in to look after her," Bonaconte said. "That's all I know."

"What about her walking past the windows naked?" Jeter asked. "Is your wife right about that?"

"On, yeah," Bonaconte said, with a light in his eyes.

"Which windows, sir?" Jeter asked.

"All of 'em," Bonaconte said. "She wasn't shy, that girl, and she hated clothes."

"A nudist?" Jeter asked.

"Huh?" Bonaconte gave him a blank look.

"Never mind," Keough said. "We have what we wanted, Mr. Bonaconte, Thanks."

They walked back to their car.

During the drive to Sauget Jeter asked, "What did that tell us?"

"A lot, actually."

"Like what?"

"Like it's possible the killer lives here."

Jeter looked surprised. "Is that a leap of logic, Joe?"

"I'm known for my leaps of logic, Marc," Keough admitted, "but I don't think this is one of them."

"What do you mean?"

"She walks around in front of the windows," he said. "That's how she caught his attention. I think he noticed her and couldn't resist. That's why he took another victim so soon, and why we have a fresh case to pursue. She was an impulse kill."

"Wow," Jeter said. "Okay, yeah, I can see that."

"He either lives here," Keough said, "or he passes by here often enough to have seen her. And he couldn't resist, that's why he took her so soon after the second one."

"So what do we do, stake out the house? The neighborhood?"

"No point in staking out the house," Keough said. "She's already dead. As for the neighborhood, let's see what Mr. Bowen has to say about all this, first. Maybe he noticed something."

"What if he hasn't even noticed that she's gone, yet?" Jeter said. "We still don't have a missing persons report in the computer."

"From the way Leo Bonaconte's eyes lit up when he talked about her, I'd think Bowen would notice."

"He owns a strip club," Jeter said. "He deals with lots of girls every day."

"If she was his headline act and he took her in to take care of her while she was pregnant," Keough said, "then he knows she's missing."

"Then why not report it?"

"Maybe he thinks she left on her own," Keough said. "We'll find that out when we talk to him."

"Have you ever been to any of these clubs?" Jeter asked.

"A couple in Brooklyn," Keough said, "that's all. You?"

"A few in Collinsville," Jeter admitted, seemingly embarrassed. "One or two in Sauget."

"Something you want to tell me?"

"I was in a friend's wedding party once," Jeter said, "and we club-hopped one night. I won't know if this was one of the clubs until I see it . . . and then maybe not. We were all pretty drunk. If we went to this one towards the end of the night . . ."

"I get the picture, Marc," Keough said.

Jeter fell silent.

"Why so embarrassed?" Keough asked. "So you went club-hopping one night."

"I kinda enjoyed it," the younger man said. "The music, the smells, the girls."

"You're a young guy, Marc," Keough said. "You're allowed to enjoy looking at naked women."

Jeter didn't respond.

"Unless Mark Twain had something to say about that?"

"No," Jeter said, seriously, unaware that Keough was teasing him. "Nothing. After that night I checked."

Sixty-five

THE DIAMONIQUE CLUB was not one of the biggest strip joints in Southern Illinois, or even in Sauget. In fact, it wasn't even the largest one on the block. There were three clubs clustered on a triangle-shaped patch of land, one larger than the Diamonique and one smaller.

Jeter parked the car in front of the club, near several other cars. It was too early for the place to be open, but maybe not too early for the boss to be at work. At least, that's what they were hoping. They didn't want to have to chase him all over Southern Illinois as they had chased some of the other victims' girlfriends all over St. Louis.

They approached the front door, tried it and found it open. Before they could enter, though, another car pulled into the gravel parking lot and stopped alongside Jeter's. The detectives waited to see who would get out. It turned out to be a blonde in sweats, her long hair pulled back in a ponytail. As she came closer they could see that she was not wearing any makeup. An off duty stripper, Keough assumed.

"You boys are anxious," she said, smiling at them. She looked like a fresh-faced twenty-two-year-old for the moment, but

Keough knew that would change. Tons of makeup and acres of naked flesh would do it. "We don't open for hours."

Keough produced his badge and showed it to her.

"Wow," she said. "Are we being closed down before we even open today?"

"We're looking for your boss, Miss," Keough said. "Henry Bowen?"

"Hank is probably inside," she said. "He was going to be checking out some new girls this morning. Come on in."

When they opened the door to enter they were assailed by the loud, driving beat of a song Keough did not recognize. The place was brightly lit, instead of being dark, as many strip clubs were. However, that might simply have been because it wasn't open for business.

"Sounds like he's already auditioning," she said.

"Is that what you're here for?" Keough asked.

"Oh no," she said, "I already work here. Hey, wait."

"What?"

She turned to face them. "Am I gonna get fired for letting you guys in here?" she asked, yelling to be heard. "Is Hank in trouble?"

"No trouble," Keough said. "We just have some news for him."

"What kind of news?"

"I think we'll wait to talk to him about it."

She shrugged and said, "Come on, then. I'll take you to him."

Keough tapped her on the shoulder and put his mouth by her ear so he could be heard over the music without shouting. She smelled like soap.

"Just point him out!" he said loudly. "That'll do."

"Fine!" she shouted back.

As they got deeper into the club they saw a girl up on one of the three stages, dancing, and several other girls standing around waiting their turns. A man was sitting in a straight-backed chair in front of the stage, presumably grading the performance. From the back he looked wide, and he had a bald spot at the crown of his head. There was also a cloud of smoke around his head that looked like it was coming from a cigar.

"That's Henry!" the girl shouted to Keough, pointing.

"Thanks."

She waggled her fingers at him and went off to wherever off duty strippers went off to.

Jeter started forward but Keough put his hand on his arm to stop him. The young detective looked at him and Keough just shook his head. They stayed where they were until the girl finished her audition.

"You got any experience givin' lap dances?" Bowen asked the girl.

"Um . . . no," she said, standing totally relaxed with her hands behind her back and not a stitch on.

Bowen looked around until he spotted one of his own girls.

"Patsy, c'mere," he called.

Patsy was a tall, lanky brunette with great legs, a killer butt, and small breasts. She was wearing something filmy and white so that her large brown nipples were very much in evidence.

"Yeah, boss?"

"Take this girl in the back and show her how to give a lap dance."

"Okay, Hank."

Bowen looked at the new girls again. "After Patsy shows you how to do it you're gonna come back and give me one. If I like it, you're hired."

"Thank you, Mr. Bowen."

"Thank me after I hire you," Bowen said.

The naked girl gathered up her clothes and then followed the brunette into the back.

"Who's next?" Bowen called out.

Before any of the other stripper hopefuls could call out Keough said loudly, "I think that would be us, Mr. Bowen!"

Sixty-six

BOWEN TURNED IN his chair to look at Keough and Jeter, then stood up and approached them. He had a belly that matched his width, a dark stubble peppered with gray, and he smelled of cheap cologne. Pudgy fingers on each hand sported flashy rings, three on the right and two on the left. The collar of his short sleeved white shirt was open and Keough was somehow relieved not to see any chains around the man's neck.

"You got some ID?"

They both displayed their badges. The man had pegged them on sight as cops. That was good. He'd been around the block a few times and they wouldn't have to establish that first.

"What did you think of her?" Bowen asked. He was looking directly at Keough.

"I'd hire her," Keough said.

"She's got great tits. It's all gonna come down to the lap dance. What's this about, boys?"

"Gloria Lauren."

"Gloria?" Bowen frowned. "Where is she?"

"Can we go someplace and talk, Mr. Bowen?" Keough asked.

"That bad?" Bowen asked.

"I'm afraid so."

"That means she's in the morgue."

"Yes, sir."

"The girl in the papers?"

Keough said, "I'm afraid so."

Bowen seemed to think it over for a few moments, then said, "Okay, let's go to my office."

He led the way to a door in the back that opened into a small office with a desk, a file cabinet and one extra chair.

"Sorry," he said, seating himself behind the desk. "I can get another chair—"

"That's okay," Jeter said. "I'll stand."

Keough sat opposite the man.

"Tell me," Bowen said, and Keough did. He didn't hold anything back because he wanted to see how Bowen reacted. When he told him about the baby the man didn't flinch. Not his, Keough thought.

"Shit," Bowen said. "Now I'll have to replace her permanently."

Just to confirm his suspicion Keough said, "I assume the child wasn't yours?"

"You assume right."

"How long has she been missing?"

"I didn't think she was missing," Bowen said. "I thought she just went out two nights ago and didn't come home yet."

"Did she do that a lot?"

"Hell, yeah," Bowen said. "That's how the dumb cunt got pregnant in the first place."

"You don't seem too upset that she's dead," Jeter said.

"Look," Bowen said, "I'm sorry she's dead, all right? But business is business. I gotta compete around here, and she was my top draw before she got herself knocked up."

"You took her in when she got pregnant," Jeter said.

"Just protecting my interest, Detective," Bowen said. "Don't read anything into that. I don't sleep or get involved with strippers."

"We talked to your neighbor, Mrs. Bonaconte."

"Nosy cunt," Bowen said. "What'd she have to say?"

"She claims Gloria used to prance around in front of the windows nude, even while she was pregnant."

"She's got that right," Bowen said. "Gloria'd put on a show at the drop of a hat if she thought somebody was looking."

"And did a lot of men look?"

"Word got around," Bowen said. "Men came, they looked. Some were just passing by and they looked. When they saw her they stood rooted to the spot. Gloria was that good."

"Anybody come around more than once?" Keough asked.

"Fucked if I know," Bowen said. "Probably some of the neighbors, like Leo Bonaconte. He was always lookin' out his window hopin' to see somethin'."

"And did he?"

"Gloria used to tease him," Bowen said, "by not dancing when he was looking."

"Did he get pissed off about it?"

"You think Leo killed her? Not a chance. If he was gonna kill somebody he'd kill that ol' lady of his."

Keough didn't pursue it. He had already eliminated Leo Bonaconte as a suspect. Bowen was right about his neighbor. "I'd like to get into your house, Mr. Bowen."

"What for?"

"I want to look out all your windows."

"You think the killer's a neighbor?" Bowen asked. Then his eyes widened. "Hey, wait. You thinkin' this killer is the same that killed those other girls?"

"It's possible."

"And he lives around me?"

"Or passes your house."

"That dumb, dumb cunt," he said. "She attracted the guy?"

"It's a possibility," Jeter said.

"When can we get inside?" Keough asked.

"I can't leave the club now," Bowen said. "I got auditions, as you can see."

"Maybe you could give us the key?" Jeter asked.

"Not a chance. I mean, no offense, but not all cops are honest, if ya know what I mean."

"Just a minute—" Jeter started, but Keough cut him off.

"We'd like to do it tonight, Mr. Bowen," Keough said. "Why don't you give us a time?"

"I usually take a break from this place between five and seven. I wanna be here later, when it gets busy."

"How about six?" Keough asked. "We'd only need to be inside for a few minutes."

"Okay," Bowen said. "Make it six. I would like to see you catch this bastard. Hey, you think my other girls are in danger?"

"Any of them been dancing in front of your windows?" Keough asked.

"Naw, only Gloria."

"Then I don't think you have any worries." Keough stood up. "We'll meet you at your house at six."

"Fine."

Jeter opened the door and went through. Keough stopped short and looked at Hank Bowen again.

"If you weren't the father, Mr. Bowen, do you have any idea who was?"

"She wouldn't say," Bowen said. "I'm guessing just some guy she had a one nighter with."

"Did she have a lot of one nighters?"

"That's all she had," Bowen said. "She didn't believe in relationships. She thought men were good for only one thing."

Keough decided that could only be one or two things, so he didn't ask the man to clarify the statement.

"All right, Mr. Bowen," Keough said. "You can go back to your auditions now."

"Not too many left, really," Bowen said, getting up from behind his desk. "If that chick out there can lap dance I'll hire her, but there ain't nothin' out there that's gonna replace Gloria Loving. That'll be a whole different kind of audition."

He followed Keough out and saw him and Jeter to the door.

"Look, fellas," he said, before they left, "I know I come off like an asshole, but if I can help ya, I will. I don't like seein' girls get tore up like that."

"We appreciate it, Mr. Bowen," Keough said. "We'll see you at six."

Sixty-seven

WHEN THEY LEFT Sauget Keough told Jeter to get on 255 and drive into Missouri. He wanted to see if they could check out the theater groups before returning to Fairview Heights and Hank Bowen's house.

"He sure didn't seem all broken up about this poor girl," Jeter said, his tone heavily laced with disapproval.

"He's a businessman, Marc," Keough said, "and those girls are his inventory, nothing more."

"You approve of that?"

"I didn't say I approve," Keough said. "I just understand, that's all."

"I wonder how he would have felt if we'd shown him pictures?" Jeter said. "I mean, he had that girl living in his home."

"Forget about it," Keough said. "We only need him to let us into that house tonight. Somebody spotted that girl through a window, I feel sure of it."

"Leap of logic," Jeter said, again.

"You've got to learn to go with your gut, Marc," Keough said. "I follow procedure in an investigation, but sometimes it comes down to instinct. Petrified thought, right?" He was giving Jeter his "Twain" back.

"What else is your gut telling you?"

"That this is the case to concentrate on."

"You mean forget about the other girls?"

"I mean if we find the killer of this girl we find the killer of all three," Keough said. "Why divide our attention at this point? The thing to do is work the fresh case."

"So why are we driving to these theater groups?"

"Because we started this line of investigation and I want to see it through," Keough said.

"And what about Knoxx and the other girlfriends?"

"Same thing," Keough said, "but after today we're going to concentrate on who killed Gloria Lauren."

"And are we going to tell the chief and the sergeant what we're up to?"

"I'll send them a report telling them just enough to keep them satisfied," Keough replied.

"Why do I have a bad feeling about this?"

"You don't have to go along with me on any of this, Marc," Keough said. "Make up your own mind."

"Oh, I have," Jeter said. "I've come this far with you, I'm going to go all the way—even though I have a bad feeling about this."

"Don't worry about it," Keough said. "When we find the killer everybody is going to be happy, and you're going to be a hero."

"Me? Why me?"

"Because it's your case," Keough said. "Officially, you're the detective assigned. When it gets solved, you're going to get the credit."

"But we can share the credit."

"That's okay," Keough said. "I prefer it this way."

"Well," Jeter said, "the people who matter will know what you did."

"And they are?"

Jeter grinned and said, "You and me."

* * *

They were halfway across the bridge when Keough asked to borrow Jeter's cell phone.

"Where's yours?"

"In my car."

Jeter unclipped the phone from his belt and handed it over. "Who are you calling?"

Keough reached behind him to grab a file folder off the backseat and open it.

"I want to call ahead, make sure there's somebody at these places to talk to us," Keough said. "I don't think we have the time to waste trying to track people down, anymore."

"Why? What's changed?"

"As I said before," Keough answered, "I think this latest victim was an impulse kill."

"And?"

"Our man is apparently losing control," Keough said. "His killing may escalate now."

Sixty-eight

HE WAS FEELING very calm. This was the first time he'd had a guest upstairs from the funeral home—in his home. The last time she'd been there he'd made tea downstairs.

Julia Cameron looked around. "This must have been an odd place to grow up." She'd been too shy to mention this last time, but felt emboldened by the fact that he had invited her back.

"Why?"

She looked at him. "I mean, all the dead bodies . . . in your home."

"The bodies were down here, and we lived upstairs." He did not mention the basement to her. Not yet. That would come later. He wanted to surprise her.

She turned to look at the two viewing rooms.

"Is there a body here now?"

"No," he said, "but there is to be a showing later today. I'll have to bring the body up . . . soon."

"Who is—was it?"

"A young boy," he said. "Six, I think."

"How did he die?"

"Naturally," Judson said. "A heart attack."

"God! How sad for the mother."

"For the entire family."

They remained silent for a moment, as if in memory of the boy.

"Would you like to see the upstairs?"

"Oh yes," she said, "I would love to see where you grew up."

She was so beautiful . . . but not as much as she would be in a few months, when she was about eight along.

"This way," he said.

It was very odd, he thought, as he followed her up the stairs, but since the last one—that naked cow—he hadn't had the Urge again. Usually, he had to fight the Urge every day, but lately he had not been feeling it. He wondered if being around Julia Cameron had anything to do with that. He was certainly having feelings around her he'd never experienced before. After all, here he was taking her upstairs to see where he lived, where he grew up, where he interacted with his father—if you could call it that.

And he had taken the time to prepare her surprise.

Sixty-nine

FOR WHAT SEEMED like the first time in days, they were having some good luck. Keough's calls were fruitful, and they were able to contact someone from each theater group.

The first was the Black Box Group. Keough got a phone message that gave out two other numbers and through one of them he got hold of the same woman Knoxx had spoken to, named Roseanne Hogan. She told Keough that the group really had no office, and that he should come to her home in Clayton.

When they arrived she ushered them in and explained further.

"You see, there are several of us who run the group, and we use our own home phone numbers for the business of taking reservations and selling tickets."

"And where is the theater located?" Keough asked.

"Oh, there is no theater."

Roseanne Hogan was very theatrical in her appearance. In her forties, she had obviously gotten herself ready for their visit, with expertly applied makeup, freshly dabbed perfume and a very chic pantsuit that was apparently designed to hide a generous posterior. Keough wondered why she'd wear pants, at all, if she was worried about that. Her deep red lipstick contrasted starkly with her makeup-induced pale pallor. Jenny would later confide to Keough that red lipstick was "back in."

"I'm sorry?" Keough said. "I thought you were a theater group."

"Yes, we're a group, but we don't have our own theater," she said. "You see, we can't afford the rent to have our own permanent theater, so we move our performances around."

"To where?"

"Wherever we can get a space," she said. "Wait." She got up and left them alone in her living room for a moment.

"I'm confused," Jeter said.

"So am I," Keough said, "but I don't think this part is important. Let's see if we can get her to move on."

The woman returned with a flyer, done on maroon paper for some reason, and handed it to Keough.

"That's the ad for our next performance. We're having it in the basement theater of a church, which we will turn into our black box."

Keough couldn't help himself. "And what is a black box theater?"

"Basically, we present the performance in a black room. It prevents any distraction from the players, you see."

Keough wasn't sure he did, but he handed the flyer to Jeter and went on.

"Mrs. Hogan—"

"Roseanne," she said, "please."

"Roseanne, Detective Knoxx spoke to you about a makeup man who works with your group?"

"Yes," she said, "Andrew Judson. He's quite brilliant."

"Tell me, is he part of the group? Or does he work for you?"

"He donates his time to work with us on makeup," she said, "but he's not part of the group, per se."

"I see. And has he had training with makeup?"

"Oh, yes, of course," she said. "He can alter the appearance of anyone, making them seem older, or younger, or just . . . different."

"I see. Would you have an address for him?"

"Has he done something wrong?" she asked, looking concerned.

"No," Keough said, "he hasn't done anything wrong that we know of, but we think he might be able to help us with some inquiries."

"Well," she said, "I don't actually have an address for him. He gave us a post office box so we could send him flyers, and he actually calls me when he has the time to work on a project."

"I see. So that would mean you don't have a phone number, either."

"I'm afraid not."

"Didn't you ever find it strange that you can't contact him?" Keough asked.

"Detective, I don't care how strange he is, or wants to be," she replied, frankly. "When someone that talented wants to donate time to our theater group, I'll take him on his terms."

"Yes," Keough said, "of course you will."

Keough obtained a description of Andrew Judson from Roseanne Hogan before rising to leave, but then she laughed. "Of course, I don't know that I've ever really seen the real him, if you know what I mean."

"Yes," Keough said, "I do know what you mean."

She walked them to the door. "I'm sorry I couldn't be more helpful."

"We appreciate your cooperation, ma'am," Jeter said.

"Of course," she said, as they started down the outside steps, "there is one other thing I could tell you about him."

"And what would that be?" Keough asked, turning to look up at her.

"Well . . . his business. Would it help you to know that he is in the mortuary business?"

"Mortuary?"

"Yes," she said, "quite against type he did mention one day that he ran his own funeral home, and did everything himself."

"Everything?" Jeter asked. "Like . . . embalming?" the black detective asked.

. "Well, yes . . . I suppose so."

Keough looked at Jeter and said, "And, I suppose, all cosmetic work, as well."

"Yes, I believe so," she said, and then excitedly asked, "Say, do you think that might be where he learned how to use makeup?"

"Yes, ma'am," Keough said, "I think that just might be."

Seventy

WHEN JULIA ENTERED Judson's room she saw that the wall was plastered with movie posters.

"Horror films," she said. Just an observation, no judgment. Judson was used to hearing people's judgments of him in their tone of voice.

"Yes," he said. "It's the makeup I'm interested in."

She saw more Lon Chaney movie posters than any others, but more contemporary films were represented as well, like the *Elm Street* films and even some *Star Trek* films.

"No monsters." Another observation. "I mean, like *Alien*, or *Predator*?"

"It's not monster makeup I'm interested in," he said, moving to stand in front of a Lon Chaney poster. "That's just putting a rubber mask on someone. I'm more interested in the changes you can make to someone's actual face, to make them look different. For instance, the makeup work they did on Marlon Brando in *The Godfather*."

She looked around. There was no *Godfather* poster, but she knew what he meant.

As she stood there studying the walls, he studied her. In profile there was just the hint of a belly. She was not a large woman, and he had been surprised when she'd confided that she was more than six months along. She was obviously one of those who did not carry low—like that cow across the backyard. She pranced around naked with her big belly and her swollen tits, just begging to be noticed. Judson knew that taking her had been a bad idea, but there hadn't been much he could do about it. When the Urge came over him . . .

But he'd gotten rid of her in Belleville. Dumping the first one in the river had been a mistake. The Mississippi had not claimed her, as he'd hoped, nor had it taken her to the ocean. Hoping to cause confusion he had left the second one in an East St. Louis garbage dump, and now the third in that Belleville park. He probably should have been getting rid of them across the river, in St. Louis. After all, the first two had lived in St. Louis. Wouldn't taking one from here only serve to confuse the police further?

It seemed very clear to Judson now, even though there were times when his brain got kind of muddled. For instance, by the time his mind had cleared enough for him to realize what was going on, that pregnant cow from across the way was already on his preparation table. He had no recollection of grabbing her from the house, or of dragging her across the yard to the rear of the funeral home. Anybody could have seen him, but no one had. Apparently, the incredible good fortune that had been with him in transporting the other women was still there.

Once he accepted the fact that he'd grabbed her, he'd had no choice but to finish her up and then get rid of her. His response to seeing her naked in her window for the umpteenth time had been ill-timed and ill-advised, but at least he'd come out of it with a new friend.

And now here was Julia, in his room, looking at his posters, simply radiant with that inner glow that pregnant women get. As he stared at her he was particularly aware of the fact that he did not feel the Urge. Was that because she was not far enough along to incite it in him? Or was it because she was different? He was aware of some unusual feelings inside him when he thought of her, or when he was with her. He was not sure how to interpret them or react to them. He wondered if Doctor Jerry would be able to help him with that.

Could it be possible that after all these years the man could actually be of some help?

Seventy-one

"GODDAMNIT!"

Jeter turned his head and looked at Keough, who was sitting in the passenger seat.

"What did we forget?" he asked.

" 'We' didn't forget anything," Keough answered. "I did. I forgot to answer some phone messages I had."

"Want my cell?"

"No," Keough said, "I'll return them later. Let's just keep going." He felt bad that he had not returned Kathy Logan's call from a couple of days ago. They hadn't spoken since their meeting in the sculpture garden, but he had been very busy with these murders. Maybe later in the day.

They were on their way back to Southern Illinois to keep their appointment with Hank Bowen. They had made their second theater stop of the day and hadn't come up with anything of great interest. What they learned about the second name given Keough by Detective Knoxx, Walter Kinney, was that Kinney was an actor who enjoyed doing his own makeup, assisted others with theirs—and was seventy-two years old.

"So I guess we can concentrate on this Judson guy," Jeter said.

"Unless we believe we have a seventy-two-year-old serial killer."

"It's possible, isn't it?"

"Oh, anything's possible, but let's call it highly improbable for now."

"So what do we do, stake out his post office box?"

"We don't have much choice," Keough said.

"If he's the killer won't he stay away from it? Change his routine?"

"Why? Changing it would make him look suspicious. He'll keep to his routines in order to look normal—that is, if he ever knows we're on to him."

"So which one of us gets to sit on his P.O. box until he shows up?" Jeter asked.

Keough smiled and said, "Guess."

Jeter winced and said, "Low man, again."

But before they could even think about sitting on someone's post office box they had to finish what they started that day. Jeter drove back to Fairview Heights to the home of Henry Bowen and parked in front. They got out, walked to the front door and rang the bell. It only took moments for Bowen to answer his door.

"Right on time," he said. "Come on in."

"We appreciate your cooperation, Mr. Bowen," Keough said.

The house had obviously been furnished by a man. Nothing matched. The sofa and chairs all looked comfortable, but they were from different sets and different periods.

"Mr. Bowen, the information we have—"

"From my nosy neighbors, right?"

"—is that Gloria paraded around in front of the windows nude," Keough finished. "Can you tell us where she did that?"

Bowen spread his arms and said, "Pick a window."

Keough looked at Jeter. "I'll take the downstairs windows," the young detective said.

Keough turned to Bowen. "Can you show me the upstairs?"

"This way."

Keough followed Bowen up the stairs to the second floor.

"How many bedrooms do you have up here?"

"Three," Bowen said. "One's mine, the other two are guest rooms."

"Did Gloria go into your room?"

"Never," Bowen said. "That'd be the one place she didn't prance around naked."

"Can you show me which room was hers?"

"Right down the hall, on the left. The one on the right isn't being used. Actually, the only rooms she used up here were her bedroom, and the bathroom."

"How many bathrooms?"

"Two," Bowen said. "I have one in my bedroom, and then there's one at the end of the hall, which she used. Look, I got some business to do in my office downstairs. You can look anyplace you like. Just let me know when you're done."

"We'll do that, sir," Keough said. "Thank you."

Bowen nodded and went back down the stairs. With him gone the opportunity was too good to pass up, so before looking at the rooms Bowen said Gloria did use, Keough decided to look at the rooms the man said she didn't use.

He started with the master bedroom.

Bowen's bedroom reflected his taste by emulating the theme of the downstairs—nothing matched. The bed was huge, king-sized—a four poster. The dresser and chest of drawers were of entirely different styles, and neither matched the wood of the head- or footboards.

He checked the closets and the drawers very quickly; there was nothing to indicate a woman had ever used the room. Bowen was probably telling the truth. He had not had a sexual relationship with the victim—or he'd cleaned all her stuff out of his room. He took a quick look out the window—which afforded him a view of the street in front of the house—and then got out of there before Bowen could catch him.

Next Keough took a look at the unoccupied guest room. It was dusty, and had obviously gone unused for quite some time. He left that room and walked to the bathroom. There were signs a woman had been there. Hair products sat on the counter, and other feminine items were on the lip of the tub, including a razor, a bottle of bath beads and a douche bag.

There was a skylight in the room, but it was small and over the bathtub. No one could have seen her through it unless she got up there and hung herself out of it.

Finally, he went to the other guest room and stood just inside. On the dresser was a mirror and a collection of perfume and nail polish bottles, brushes, combs, lipsticks—all the items you'd expect to find in the bedroom of a woman. The quilt on the bed was plain, not something a woman would buy, but then she had only been living there for a short time, as a boarder.

He went through the drawers as a matter of course and found nothing. Eventually he worked his way to the window. It overlooked the backyard, and beyond that was the parking lot of what appeared to be a small business. The only vehicle parked in the lot at the moment seemed to be a hearse. She could easily have been seen from any of the windows across the way, or by someone standing in that parking lot.

Finished with his examination of the second floor, Keough went back to the stairs and down to the first floor. He found Jeter waiting for him at the bottom.

"Anything?" he asked.

"Several of the windows in front afford a view of the street, and vice versa. The side windows offer views of the houses on either side. I would have been able to see through the windows but they were all curtained—unlike these."

"No curtains," Keough said, "because it's a man's house."

"So if she wanted to walk around naked it'd be easy to see her," Jeter said. "What about upstairs?"

"Not as many opportunities," Keough said, "except for the window in the bedroom she was using. It looks out over the backyard, and one building beyond that has a parking lot behind it."

"Parking lot? Is it a business?"

"Could be," Keough said. "It's a house, and a big one. There's a hearse in the backyard. Could be a . . ." He stopped and stared at Jeter.

"A funeral home?" Jeter asked.

"We couldn't get that lucky," Keough said.

"Why not?" Jeter asked. "We've been chasing our tails, trying to find people to question for days. So why not?"

"Well," Keough said, "let's find our host and ask him."

Seventy-two

THE SIGN OVER the front door said JUDSON FUNERAL HOME.

They had not let on to Hank Bowen how interested they were in his neighbor. Keough had been very offhanded when he asked the man what the building was.

"It's a funeral home," Bowen said. "Family owned and run, I think. I don't know that much about it. Some of the other neighbors might, though—like that nosy bitch next door."

Instead of asking the woman next door, Keough decided that he and Jeter should take a walk over there and check it out themselves.

"I can't believe it," Jeter said, excitedly.

"Take it easy, Marc," Keough said. "This may not be the guy."

"It's too much of a coincidence, though, don't you think?" Jeter asked. "We get his name from the theater group, and then we end up in the house right behind his building."

"All we know is that he likes to do makeup for actors in his free time," Keough said. "We don't even have enough for a search warrant."

"But if he just lets us in . . ."

"That's what we're about to find out," Keough said.

* * *

When they approached the front door they found it locked. Keough had been hoping it wouldn't be, since it was a business.

"Not going to get much walk-in business this way," Jeter commented.

"There's a doorbell," Keough said, and rang it.

They waited as patiently as they could, but after several minutes passed he rang it again.

"The hearse is in the back," Jeter said. "If it's a small family operated business, how many hearses could they have?"

"I don't know," Keough said. "I'm not up on my funeral home etiquette."

After several more minutes Keough rang again.

"Maybe I should go around the back," Jeter suggested.

"No," Keough said, grabbing his arm, "let's stay together." Losing his partner last year was still with him. It hadn't been his fault by any means, but he didn't want to take any chances. "We'll give it a few more minutes and then we'll both check the back."

Jeter shrugged. It was fine with him either way. Keough was glad the younger man had not taken his reaction as an insult. It was to his credit that his ego had not been tweaked.

They were just about to turn to walk around back when the lock in the door clicked and it opened.

When the doorbell started ringing Andrew Judson was downstairs. Sweating slightly, he took the time to stop in the bathroom, wash his face and refresh himself. The first ring of the bell had set things in motion, the second ring had added a touch of frenzy to the situation. Now he needed to calm things down.

When he opened the door and saw the two men on his doorstep, he recognized them immediately from the police station.

* * *

The first thing Keough looked at when the man opened the door was his eyes. That's when he knew. Although his total appearance was different from the day he'd come to the station in his makeup, the eyes were the same.

You couldn't hide those intense eyes even with lenses.

This was the guy—Keough knew it.

Seventy-three

THE ONLY AUDIENCE for this meeting between Detective Joe Keough and Andrew Judson was Detective Marc Jeter. The young man could almost see and hear the tension crackling in the air between the two men as their eyes met.

"Yes?" Judson asked. "Can I help you?" After a beat he added, "Are you bereaved?" Jeter thought that Judson was probably close to his age, perhaps a couple of years younger. He seemed, however, very self-possessed and assured.

"Well," Keough said, "in a way we are."

"I don't understand," Judson said.

At that point Keough took out his badge. "I'm Detective Keough and this is Detective Jeter. Are you Andrew Judson?"

"I am."

"You own this funeral home?"

"I do, yes."

"Mr. Judson, may we come inside and ask you a few questions?"

"About what?"

"One of your neighbors is missing, Mr. Judson," Keough said. "We thought you might want to help find her."

"Well, my goodness yes," Judson said. "Why didn't you say so in the first place? Please come in."

Judson backed out of the doorway to allow the two detectives to enter. When they did he closed the door and turned to face them.

"Which of my neighbors is missing?" he asked.

"Gloria Lauren," Keough said.

"I'm afraid I don't—"

"Also known as Gloria Loving," Keough added.

"Loving?" Judson asked, looking amused. "Really?"

"You don't know her?"

"I'm afraid I don't."

"It's the house directly behind yours."

Judson frowned. "I thought that was Mr. Bowen's house—oh, I see."

"Do you?" Keough asked.

"Yes, indeed. You're talking about one of Mr. Bowen's . . . ladies, I suppose you'd call them. The, uh, one he has living with him at the moment?"

"The pregnant one," Keough said, watching Judson's face very carefully for a reaction.

"Yes," the man said, without a tick.

"Mr. Judson," Keough said, looking around the entry foyer of the funeral home, "we understand Miss Lauren was given to walking around in front of the windows, ah, buck naked."

"Yes."

"Yes, you understand?" Keough asked. "Or yes, you've seen her?"

"I've heard some talk," Judson said, "but I've never actually seen her, myself."

"Is that a fact?"

"Yes, it is."

"But . . . the window to her room is right across the parking lot from here." Keough said, pointing in that direction. He even took a few steps that way. "Where would your own bedroom be, Mr. Judson? I assume you live upstairs?"

278

"I do, yes," Judson said, "but I'm afraid my bedroom window overlooks the front, not the rear."

"Ah, I see."

Judson looked at Jeter then, as if wondering if the other man would ever speak. Jeter didn't give the man the satisfaction of a nod, or even a change of expression. The look in Judson's eyes gave Jeter a chill.

This is the guy, he thought.

"So you see," Judson added, looking back at Keough, "I couldn't have seen anything."

"You never look out your back windows?" Keough asked.

"Rarely," Judson said. "I have guest rooms there, but at the moment I have no guests."

"Mr. Judson, I see a hearse in the parking lot," Keough said. "Where do you park your own car?"

"I have a garage on the side of the house. But at the moment I don't own another vehicle."

"Ah."

Keough had noticed the garage, with its closed door, when they drove up.

"And on this floor you have your, uh, chapels?"

"Yes."

"Are you, uh, showing anyone at the moment?"

"Not as we speak," Judson said, "but soon. I'm preparing someone for showing tomorrow."

"Ah," Keough said, "and that would be downstairs?"

"Yes, it would."

"Would you mind if we took a look down there?"

"Yes, I would."

"And why is that, Mr. Judson?"

"It would be disrespectful to the dead," Judson said, "and an invasion of my privacy—that is, unless you have a warrant."

Keough looked at Jeter and for the first time spoke to him. "Everybody always wants a warrant."

Jeter shrugged and said, "Television."

"Gentlemen," Judson said, "I'm afraid that's all the time I have right now. In the event that you do return with a warrant I would be happy to give you a tour of our facilities."

"Would you?" Keough asked. "Happily?"

"Why, yes," Judson said. "You don't think I have this Gloria person down there, do you? I'm afraid my tastes do not run to strippers."

Keough was tempted to say, "What do they run to, then . . . pregnant women?"

Instead, he said, "Oh no, sir, we know where she is right now. She's in the morgue."

"How sad," Judson said.

He and Keough went back to staring at each other and Jeter shifted nervously. He had realized that, up to the moment he spoke, he'd been holding his breath—and now he was doing it again. With a concerted effort, he began to breathe. He'd never been in the presence of a serial killer before. He found the experience stifling. It was as if he thought that breathing the same air might somehow contaminate him.

"Yes," Keough said, "it is. Well, we've taken up enough of your time. Thank you for talking to us."

"You're welcome." Judson opened the front door for them. "If there's anything else I can do—"

"I'll certainly let you know, Mr. Judson," Keough said. "In fact, I think I can guarantee you we'll be talking again."

"I'll look forward to it."

"So will I."

Jeter studied the two men for a moment, then he and Keough were outside and the door was closed—and he was holding his damn breath again!

Seventy-four

"HE LOOKS SO normal," Jeter said, "except for his eyes."

"They all looked normal," Keough said. "Women said Bundy was so handsome. Berkowitz looked like a normal shlep."

"Except for the eyes."

"Manson eyes," Keough said.

"That's it!" Jeter cried. He slammed his drink down, spilling it and attracting the attention of some of the other customers. "Exactly."

They were in a bar. Neither of them knew where it was. After leaving the Judson Funeral Home they started back to the office but then Keough told Jeter to find a bar. "I need a drink."

"I'm so glad you said that," Jeter replied, and found a bar.

It was the end of the day. People getting off work were stopping into this, their local bar, and they were giving Keough and Jeter curious looks as they sat together at a corner table.

"What about his height, Joe?" Jeter asked. "He must be six-four, at least. When he came to the office—"

"He was slouching," Keough reminded him, "almost bent forward, Marc. Actors—good actors—can even alter their physical appearance—and he is a good actor."

"What if he takes off now?" Jeter asked.

"He won't."

"What if he does?"

"Then he'll take his business somewhere else, too," Keough said, "and we won't have to deal with his shit."

"And would that suit you?" Jeter asked.

"No," Keough said, "it would not. I want to see this through to the end, and that means putting that smug sonofabitch away."

"He *was* smug, wasn't he?"

"No," Keough said, "that's just the way we remember it. Oh, he's smug, all right, but he wasn't while we were there. He was acting again, only this time without the makeup."

Jeter looked across the table at Keough, aware that his hands were shaking a little. At least he was breathing.

"It is him, isn't it, Joe?"

"It's him," Keough said. "I'd swear to it. It's in his eyes. It's him."

"But as far as he knows we were just checking with the neighbors and he was one of them, right?"

"No," Keough said, "we took a turn today, Marc. No more stumbling around looking for girlfriends or theater groups. This is him."

"So how do we get him?"

"We'll start with his background, check his business contacts, see if he's got any family," Keough said. "When we get back, Marc, I want you to use your trusty little computer and run him through the system. Get me every damn thing you can on Andrew Judson."

"You got it," Jeter said. "And what are you going to do?"

"I've got some phone calls to return," Keough said, pushing his half-finished beer away. "Come on. Let's get to work."

His first instinct after the police left was to run, but he quelled that. If they'd had anything on him—anything at all—they would have arrested him. They had nothing, so running was not an option. He decided to examine the situation. They had come because of his error in taking that pregnant cow from the house behind him. Her fault, her fault, her fault. She had not only raised the Urge in him, she had incited it. He'd had no choice, and now he would have to deal with the consequences.

Detective Keough knew, though. He was convinced of that. It was in the way the man looked at him. He knew, but he couldn't prove a thing. The detective had only wanted to repay what Judson himself had done to Keough, beard him in his own den. The situation was still completely manageable.

But there were more pressing matters to attend to at the moment than even the police coming to his door. He made sure the front door was locked and went down to the basement. He ignored the locked door to his left, went past the preparation room and continued on to the room all the way to the right. He needed a key to unlock the door. He entered, closed the door behind him and used the key to lock it again. Then he turned to look at Julia Cameron.

She was standing with her back to the wall, glaring at him, nostrils flaring with either anger or fear. Whichever emotion it was, it made her even more beautiful—but thankfully, did not yet inspire the Urge.

"Are you crazy?" she demanded. "Wha–what's going on? The doorbell rings and all of a sudden you grab me and drag me down here—"

"It was time, Julia," he said.

"Time? Time for what?"

"I couldn't let someone being at the door interfere with what had to be done," he went on, ignoring her question. She was sweating, perhaps from struggling with him as he dragged her down the stairs and thrust her into the room, or from screaming and banging on the door, which would have gained her nothing as the room was soundproof.

"For me to take care of you."

"Andrew," she asked, "I don't know what you're talking about, or what you're doing."

"You came to me, remember?" he asked. "After the funeral?"

"You were nice to me," she said. "I thought you were a nice man."

"We had tea, we ate together, and you came here."

"I just needed someone to talk to."

"No," he said, "you need someone to take care of you—you and the baby."

At the mention of her baby she wrapped her arms around herself, as if to protect the child. "My baby?" Her voice was hardly a whisper. "Don't touch my baby."

"I'm not going to touch your baby," he said. "I'm going to take care of both of you. This will be your home from now until you deliver."

She looked around the room, then. While she had been banging on the door, demanding to be let out, the room's contents had not registered with her. There was a queen-sized bed and a chest of drawers, as well as an overstuffed armchair.

"I furnished it for your comfort," he said. "I'll be bringing your meals down to you."

"You can't do this, Andrew," she said. "It's—it's kidnapping!"

"Believe me, Julia," Judson said, "kidnapping is the least of my worries."

"But—but—you're breaking the law!"

"I'll give you some time to think about it," he said. "You'll see I'm doing the right thing. Your lover is dead, the man who was taking care of you. You need me."

"I don't need you or any other man!" she snapped, but her words sounded empty even to her. She had been a kept woman for at least two years, and she had sought out Andrew Judson after the funeral of her lover, believing him to be a man she could talk to. She had to at least take partial responsibility for her present predicament.

"I'll be back later," Judson promised. "I won't ever leave you down here very long without coming to see you, even when I'm working."

"Andrew!" She screamed and rushed him. He caught her by the arms and held her tightly.

"Don't ever do that!" he shouted into her face. His vehemence shocked her, robbed her of all her anger in that moment. He released her and she backed away from him. "You could have gotten yourself hurt. Don't ever do that again!"

Seventy-five

WHEN THEY GOT back to the office, Jeter jumped on the computer to find out everything he could about Andrew Judson.

"What's going on?" Jenny asked when Jeter indicated she should move away from the computer.

"We got him," was all Jeter said, so Jenny looked to Keough for more.

"Jenny, get me an appointment with the sergeant, the chief and the mayor as soon as possible."

"Today?"

"That would be ideal."

"But . . . if you got him—"

"We think we know who he is," Keough said. He decided to explain it to her rather than brush her off like a file clerk. "We can't prove it. I just want to update them on the situation in person."

"Okay," she said. "I'll get on it."

They had two phones—one on each desk—and two phone lines. He told her to use the second desk, and he went out to his car to get his cell phone. Once out there, he decided to stay outside and make his calls.

* * *

The first call was to his boss, the mayor of St. Louis. He had to wait a while, but he finally got him on the line.

"This is how you keep me informed?" the man asked.

"You're hard to reach, sir," Keough said.

"You reached me from that parking lot the other night," he said. "What happened with that murder?"

"I'm not working that murder, remember?" Keough asked. "I'm a suspect."

The mayor snorted. "What about East St. Louis? You were supposed to keep in touch."

"I left you messages."

"*A* message, Joe," the mayor said. "I got one message. Okay, forget it, Fill me in."

He did, right up to the Judson Funeral Home.

"You've got him, then," the mayor said. "Good. Wrap it up and come home. I've got some things—"

"This is not something I can wrap up in one day, Your Honor," Keough said, interrupting. "We need proof."

"Bring him in," the mayor said, "get him off the streets and let East St. Louis's district attorney do his job."

"I don't have enough evidence for him to do his job," Keough said. "When I do I'll make an arrest, and then I'll come back and go to a party with you, or a parade, or whatever."

"My life is not all parties and parades, Joe."

"Look," Keough said, "you got me into this, now let me do the job right. . . . Sir."

The mayor heaved a great sigh on the other end of the line. "Okay, Joe. You're right, I did get you into this. So go ahead and finish the job."

"Yes, sir."

"And Joe?"

"Sir?"

"What are the chances of you getting arrested for that other thing? I mean, really."

"That depends, sir."

"On what?"

"On who gets the last word on it," Keough said. "Internal Affairs still has a hard-on for me from last year. If they get their way I'll go down for this murder. However, if the investigating officer, Detective Burns, gets his way, maybe not."

"Maybe?"

"Well, he's not a hundred percent sure about me."

"I'd like to be a hundred percent sure about you, Joe," the mayor said. "Did you do it?"

"What do you think?"

The mayor sighed again. "I think maybe I'd better look at having you over there in East St. Louis as something of a vacation."

"For you or me, sir?"

"What do you think?" the mayor asked, and hung up.

The second call was to Kathy Logan.

"I've been calling you for days," she said.

"I'm sorry—"

"Don't you pick up your messages?"

She sounded like a wife. He took a deep breath. "Mrs. Logan, I've been working on a particularly difficult serial murder case—"

"All right!" she said. Then in a calmer tone, "All right, Detective Keough. Yes, I know. I just thought you had a sort of . . . vested interest in the murder of my husband."

"I do, Kathy," he said, making his own tone gentler. "After all, I'm one of the suspects."

There was silence at the other end, and then: "That's what I wanted to talk to you about."

"I'm listening."

"I was visited by a detective, a woman named Mason," Kathy Logan explained. "She showed me a picture of us kissing in the park. She said that if I confessed to her that you killed my husband she'd see to it that I got a reduced sentence."

"What did you say to that?"

"I told her she was ridiculous."

"Well, you got that right."

"Who is she? She doesn't work with Detective Burns. I called and asked him."

"She's an Internal Affairs detective who is out to get me, Kathy."

"Then why was she following me? Taking pictures of me?"

"She wasn't following you, she was following me. Look, don't worry about her. She was just trying to scare you. She didn't, did she?"

"She did," Kathy said, "out of my wits. . . . But it made me mad, too."

"I'll take care of it," he said. "She won't be back."

"Joe?"

"Yes."

"You don't think I killed Michael, do you?"

"No, I don't."

"And I don't think you did."

"Thank you."

"So can you tell me something, then?"

"What?"

"Who did?"

"I don't know, Kathy," he said, "but Detective Burns will find out."

"You could find out," she said. "I know you could. I went to the library. I—I read up on you. You're an expert."

"So they say."

"I mean, I know you're busy with this other case, but it would really mean a lot to me if you could find out who did it."

"Kathy . . ." he started, but stopped. He sighed and realized he sounded just like the mayor when he did that. "I'll see what I can do."

"Really?"

"Yes, really," he said. "If I just sit down and think about it I might come up with an answer."

"How could you do that?"

"I'm the expert," he said, "remember?"

"Yes. . . . Oh, and I'm sorry if my . . . kissing you got you into trouble," she apologized.

He smiled and said, "Well, that kind of trouble I think I can handle."

"I'm no good at flirting," she said. "I never have been. Are you?"

"Fair."

"I shouldn't be doing it, anyway," she said. "Not with my husband dead, and not with you."

"Probably not."

"I'm—I feel better now that you called."

"I'm sorry it took so long."

"This other case," she said, "are you close to catching the person who did it?"

"Closer than I've ever been," he said, "but not quite there yet."

"It must get very . . . frustrating, sometimes."

"Not sometimes," he said. "Often."

"Well . . . I'll let you go, then."

"Kathy, if I find out anything about Michael, I'll let you know."

"All right, thank you."

"And I'll see that Detective Mason doesn't bother you anymore."

"All right. Good-bye, Joe."

" 'Bye, Kathy."

He broke the connection and heard a high-pitched whistle, the kind it usually takes two or four fingers in a mouth to make. He turned, expecting to see Jeter, but it was Jenny standing in the doorway of the municipal building. She waved to him to come closer and he waved back, walking toward her.

"They're waiting for you," she said, when he reached her.

Seventy-six

KEOUGH STOPPED BY the office long enough to offer Jeter the opportunity to go into the mayor's office with him and face Mayor Emery, Chief Adam Clark and Sergeant Benson. Jeter decided to stay right where he was, working on the computer.

When Keough was ushered into Emery's office, all three men's eyes were riveted to him. Emery's were hopeful that this man had managed to solve the biggest problem his administration had ever faced. The sergeant's eyes were hateful, hoping Keough was there to admit his abject failure. And the chief's eyes were curious and interested, with no ulterior motive behind them.

"Gentleman," he said, without preamble, "I believe we've identified the killer."

All three men started to speak at once and Keough used hand motions to quiet them down.

"If you'll give me a chance," he said, "I'll explain it all to you."

And they did. They all sat back, watching him expectantly, and listened. As he told them about the investigation and where it had led Mayor Emery began to get excited, Benson appeared unhappy and the chief continued to look curious and interested. He was the one, Keough knew, who was going to ask the intelligent questions.

Finally, when Keough was done explaining about Andrew Judson it was Mayor Emery who demanded, "Do you have him in custody?"

"No, sir, I don't."

"But why not? You said you've identified him. What are you waiting for, man? Arrest him and I'll call a press conference—"

"Chief?" Keough said, interrupting the highest-ranking official in the room. "Would you explain it to him, please?"

"Mr. Mayor," the chief said, "I believe the detective's point is that at the moment there's no evidence to hold this man Judson on. If we were to arrest him now the D.A. would not be able to get a conviction."

Emery looked at the chief, then back to Keough.

"He'd get kicked free, Your Honor," Keough said. "Back on the street to kill more women."

"So you've identified him but you can't touch him?"

"That's basically it."

"Then what do we do?"

"We investigate him," Keough said. "I've already got Detective Jeter doing a background check on him as we speak. We'll put all our effort into getting him, Mr. Mayor, into gathering the evidence we need to nail him."

"I have a question, if I may, sir?" Benson said, finally speaking up.

"Yes, all right, Sergeant," Emery said. He sat back in his chair and put his hand to his head, as if fighting off a migraine.

Benson stared directly at Keough and asked, "What if it's not him?"

"What?" Emery asked, coming alert.

"It's him," Keough said.

"But what if it isn't?"

"What are you talking about, Sergeant?" Mayor Emery demanded.

Benson looked at Emery. "If he's wrong and he keys on this man, then the killer goes free to kill again."

The mayor looked confused. He wasn't quite sure who to look at now and finally settled on his chief of police.

"Chief?"

Adam Clark looked at his sergeant, then at his boss, and finally at Joe Keough.

"Your Honor," he said, "I'm inclined to go along with Detective Keough on this. After all, we did get him over here for his expertise. We're wasting his time—and ours—if we don't give him his head on this."

Emery looked at Benson, who averted his eyes. With his boss going against him, he had nothing more to say.

Mayor Emery heaved a great sigh—sounding very much like another mayor Keough knew—and said, "Very well, Detective Keough. Go on with the investigation the way you see fit. And since Sergeant Benson doesn't seem to be in agreement with you, I suggest you simply report directly to the chief from this point on."

"Yes, sir." Keough stood up. "I'll get back to it, then, if I may."

"Of course," Emery said. "Chief? Could you stay for a moment?"

"Yes, sir."

Keough turned to the chief. "Sir, I'll also need some surveillance on him."

"In what form?"

"Plainclothes, two men, twenty-four hours."

The chief winced. In a department where personnel was limited fulfilling this request would not be easy.

"For how long?"

"Hopefully no more than a couple of days. After we've finished our background checks, Jeter and I can take it over."

"And how long will you watch him?" the mayor asked.

"Until he makes a mistake," Keough said, "and we can nail him."

"All right," Clark said, "I'll see what I can do. I may have to put some uniformed men into plainclothes, though."

"That's fine," Keough said. "I just want them to watch him."

"And if he makes a move to run?"

"Then they call me, and they call for backup, and we'll grab him and worry about the consequences later."

"How does that differ from arresting him now?" Emery asked, still smarting from having his suggestion overridden.

"We'll only grab him if he makes a mistake," Keough said, "or if he forces our hand by trying to run."

"Or if some new evidence arises," the chief added.

"Right," Keough said.

"Oh, very well . . . I'll bow to your combined experience, gentlemen."

Keough made for the door and then realized that Benson was right behind him. Once out in the hall the two men faced off.

"Congratulations," Benson said, bitterly.

"Look, Sergeant—"

"You've managed to completely undermine me in my own department."

"I didn't mean to—"

"Don't bother," Benson said, and walked away, stiffly. Keough gave him time to get far enough ahead and then followed in his wake, since they had to go in the same direction.

"What's going on with Benson?" Mayor Emery asked Chief Clark.

"He was against this from the beginning, Mayor," Clark said. "I guess maybe he doesn't like being left out of the loop."

"He didn't leave me much choice, did he?"

"I suppose not."

"Well, he's lucky."

"How so?"

"If this thing blows up in somebody's face," Emery said, "it's going to be in Detective Keough's, and his boss's, the esteemed mayor of St. Louis, and not ours."

Clark frowned. "You'd hang him out to dry?"

"If he's wrong?" Emery asked. "And one more woman dies? Or more than one? In a heartbeat."

Clark didn't comment.

"Don't get soft on me now, Adam."

The chief waited a moment before answering, then said, "Oh, don't worry, Your Honor. I won't get soft."

"Good," Emery said. "Stay on Keough, then. Ride him. I want results and I want them now. So do the mayors of Belleville, Collinsville, Fairview Heights and the rest of our Southern Illinois community. Everyone is on edge about this."

"Yes, sir."

"And keep him and Benson apart," Emery said.

"What about Jeter?"

"What about him?"

"He's our man, sir."

"Don't worry about Jeter," Emery said. "He'll come out of this fine, no matter what happens. I'll take care of him. That's what I do, Adam: I take care of all of us. Remember that."

"Yes, sir."

"You and I must stay on top of this, Adam," Emery said. "When the time comes we're going to have to move fast."

"Yes, sir."

Clark turned and left without looking back. No, he wouldn't go soft, but right at that moment he wasn't sure which way he'd go if—and when—push came to shove.

Seventy-seven

WHEN KEOUGH RETURNED to the office both Jenny and Jeter stopped what they were doing and looked at him expectantly.

"Jenny, you can go home," he said.

"Are we still in business?" she asked. "Do I come back tomorrow?"

"Oh yeah, we're still in business," he said. "See you in the morning."

"I was on hold—"

"We'll start over in the morning, Jen," Keough said. "It's okay."

She shrugged, then hung up the phone and stood up. She bade them goodnight and left.

"What happened?"

Keough took the seat Jenny had vacated. "I have to tell you something," he said, "before we go any further."

Jeter turned his chair away from the computer screen and gave Keough his full attention. "What's on your mind?" he asked.

"I've got the okay to continue this investigation as I see fit," Keough said.

"That's good, isn't it?"

"It is, but I'm also reading between the lines."

"Meaning?"

"Meaning I've learned to read faces, read the looks that men are passing around the room, thinking they're going over my head."

"And?"

"If this goes wrong, Marc, I'm going to be hung out to dry. If you work with me on this and it goes sour you might get hung out there with me."

"How do you mean?"

"I've been given my head to do as I see fit. If it goes bad I'm going to take the blame. Some of that blame will rub off on my boss, but he can handle it. Some of it might rub off on you. Can you handle that?"

Jeter thought a moment. "I can do whatever—"

"Think it over tonight, Marc," Keough said, cutting him off. "Let me know in the morning."

Jeter's first instinct was to argue, but he fought that down. "All right."

"Why don't you go home?"

"I'm doing a search on Judson."

"Can we leave the computer on all night?"

"Sure," Jeter said.

"And the search will be completed by morning?"

"The answer should be waiting for us."

"That's fine, then."

"I've got more to do, Joe."

"I know, Marc," Keough said, "we've got a lot to do. We'll have to check on Judson's parents—"

"I ran the business through the system," Jeter said. "Both parents are dead and the business was left to him."

"No siblings?"

"None."

"What are you searching for now?"

"Paper trail," Jeter said. "Driver's license, social security number, arrest records—anything that's got his name down on paper should come up."

"Okay," Keough said. "I've got some suggestions, but let's save them for morning. You'd better go, I'm expecting company."

"Who?"

"Your chief," Keough said, "if I've read the man right."

"He's a decent guy, Joe, from what I've seen."

"All the more reason for you to go," Keough said. "If he does come he'll want to talk alone."

Jeter made a face and said with distaste, "Politics."

"I know," Keough said. "I hate them, too."

Jeter got up, gathered his things—jacket, gun and a briefcase—and headed for the door.

"One more thing, Marc."

"Yes?"

"You're part of this department," Keough said. "There's a possibility that no matter what happens you'll be protected."

"And you?"

"Oh, no," Keough said. "I'm out there on the limb with no net. If Judson's the wrong man I'll go down. If he's the right man and he gets off, I'll go down."

"But that wouldn't be your fault."

"Kid," Keough said, "it's *all* going to be my fault."

"That sucks."

"That's the job."

"So why do it?"

"Because beyond all the politics, I want this scumbag. I want to take him down and make it stick."

Jeter put his stuff down on the desk and looked at Keough. "Let me ask you something, now."

"Shoot."

"Suppose he does walk, for whatever reason?" Jeter asked. "And we can't touch him. What do you do to get justice?"

"You can't always get justice, Marc."

"Twain said 'The rain falls upon the just and the unjust alike; a thing which would not happen if I were superintending the rain's affairs. No, I would rain softly and sweetly on the just, but if I caught a sample of the unjust outdoors I would drown him.'"

"If I read that right, you're asking me if I'd blow him away?"

"I guess so."

Keough hesitated, then said, "I'll go on to the next case."

"And let him walk? And kill again?"

"The next case, Kid," Keough said. "There's always the next case."

Now it was Jeter's turn to hesitate. He collected his things again, said, "I don't know if I could do that," and left.

After a moment Keough said to no one, "Neither do I."

Seventy-eight

KEOUGH SAT AND watched the computer screen until—as Jeter had predicted—the screen went blank and into sleep mode. Moments after the screen went dark the chief appeared in the doorway.

Keough almost said, "I've been expecting you," but decided that would sound arrogant. He didn't want to be accused—again—of having a "New York attitude."

"Good evening, Chief."

"The others gone home?"

"Yes, sir," Keough said. "I wanted them well rested for tomorrow."

"And you?"

"I was just about to leave."

"Can I have a moment?"

"Of course."

Clark entered the room and took the chair in front of the computer. He looked around the room. "We didn't give you much space to use."

"It's got what we need," Keough said. "Something on your mind, Chief?"

Clark turned his chair so he was facing Keough head on. "I wanted to warn you to watch your back, Keough."

"I'm always watching my back, Chief," Keough said. "It's a lesson I learned a long time ago."

"It's a good lesson," Clark said.

"Any particular reason why I should practice it right now?"

Chief Clark studied him for a few moments, then leaned back, his expression changing.

"You were expecting me, weren't you?" he asked. "That's why you're still here."

"Well . . ."

"Then you know why I'm warning you."

"Chief," Keough said, "I know what you're warning me about, but I couldn't really know why, could I?"

"Look," Clark said, "I was against this from the beginning— oh, not the way Benson was against it. I just wished we could solve this thing ourselves, but I admit it got out of hand and we needed help. That's where you came in."

Keough remained silent, gave the man time.

"But I'm not on the same page with my boss on this." Clark was struggling with his words and Keough decided to try to make it easy on the man.

"Chief," Keough said, "Emery wants to take the credit if I nail this guy, and wants me to swing alone if I don't. I know that."

"And you'll still do the job?" Jeter had asked him the same question a little while ago.

"I started this with my eyes open," Keough said. "I'll finish it the same way."

"I can't—if this goes sour—are you damned sure about this?" Clark asked. "That this Judson is the guy?"

"I'm sure."

"How? If you don't have the evidence to nail him, how can you be so sure?"

Keough hesitated, then decided to tell the man the truth.

"It's his eyes, Chief," Keough said. "I've looked into them

twice now. The first time was when he walked in here in disguise, and the second time was earlier today. I recognize those eyes."

"You're that sure?"

"I'm dead sure."

Clark shook his head. "It must be nice to be that confident about something."

Now the older man was starting to reveal some things about himself Keough really didn't want to know.

"Chief," Keough said, "I'm going to do the job I signed on to do. I just need everyone else to do the same."

"Well," Adam Clark said, "that doesn't sound like too much to ask." He stood up, the chair groaning as he lifted his weight off of it.

"I just need one thing from you, sir."

"And what would that be?" the chief asked.

"Jeter," Keough said. "I've given him an out, but if he chooses to stay with me on this, I want him protected."

"No problem."

"I need your word," Keough said. "He's got the makings of a good detective."

"You've got my word, Keough, that I'll do what I can . . . for Jeter."

"Thank you, Chief." His meaning was plain.

"Go home and get some rest yourself, Detective," Clark said. "Sounds to me like you've got a big day planned tomorrow."

"Yes, sir," Keough said. "I'm on my way."

Clark nodded, turned and was gone.

Keough waited a few minutes, then shut off the lights in the office and left.

Seventy-nine

ANDREW JUDSON UNLOCKED the door and entered. The tray of food was right where he'd left it, untouched. Julia was sitting on the floor in a corner of the room. She refused to eat his food, sit in his chair or lie in the bed he had provided for her.

"You're not helping yourself with this attitude," he said.

She didn't look at him, and didn't answer. It was okay with him for now. This was only the first day. Tomorrow she'd be hungry and want to eat, and she'd be sleepy and want to lie down. He could afford to let her have her way, make her little statement for now.

He reached for the tray and, at the last minute, removed the carafe of water and the glass, setting them aside.

"I'll leave the water for you," he said. "You'll get thirsty during the night."

He picked up the tray, backed out of the room, set it on the floor, closed and locked the door, then picked up the tray again and carried it up two flights of stairs to the kitchen.

In the face of the arrival of the police he'd come up with what he thought was a bold plan. Julia would not be ready for him for months. He intended to be inactive for that time. Because he had Julia to take care of, he thought he could fight off the Urge if it came over him. Knowing the police were waiting for him to make a mistake would help him with that. In the past he had not been able to resist the Urge—not since that first time. But he planned—and hoped—that it would be different.

He didn't have to worry about anyone looking for Julia. With the other women, he'd known that he had a certain amount of time before husbands would report them missing. With this one, though, there was no husband, no boyfriend, no mother—no one to file any kind of report. There was also no connection to him, whatsoever, which had not been the case with the other two. His connection to them had been tenuous, at best, and perhaps it had been what led the police—Detective Keough—to his door, but it was clear the man had no evidence. All Judson had to do was be careful the rest of the way—more careful than he'd been up to this point.

For that to happen he had to control the Urge when it came, and not allow it to be the other way around. He did not want the Urge to go away, he simply wanted to learn to master it. Once he did that he'd be . . . well, invincible.

Julia Cameron wanted to make her statements, but she had been unable to turn off the light. She didn't even want to use Andrew Judson's electricity, but she could not bring herself to sit in the dark. There were no windows, and no light coming from beneath the door. She couldn't stand the thought of complete darkness.

And since the light was on she was able to stare across the room at the water carafe. There had been ice cubes in it when he first brought it down, but the ice had since melted. Still, there was condensation on the outside, leading her to believe that it was still cold—or at least cool. She had a raging thirst and the water was calling to her. You're using the light, it said, why not drink the water? She'd been able to resist the food, because any thought of eating made her nauseous. She craved the water, though. She imagined how it would feel coursing down her throat, perhaps even cleansing the taste of fear from her mouth. And, after all, she was using the lights.

She got to her feet slowly, her knees cramped from sitting in the corner so long. Her shoulders and back hurt from being hunched so tightly. She walked across the room, hating herself the whole way, but she finally reached the water, poured herself a glass and started drinking. The sheer pleasure of it was almost orgasmic.

She'd make another statement tomorrow to make up for her weakness today.

Keough pulled something from the freezer for dinner when he got home, not noticing what it was. Almost anything would be ready after six or eight minutes in a microwave, so it really didn't matter. He unwrapped it, put it in and then took a beer out. It was a brand he didn't usually drink, but it was all the way in the back and was cold. He had to do some shopping. Household errands had gotten away from him during this past week of working this East St. Louis case—in addition to getting involved with the Logan murder.

He took a few sips of the cold beer, grimaced and poured the rest of it down the drain. Just as well. As a diabetic he shouldn't be drinking beer. He got himself a glass of ice water and sat at the kitchen table waiting for the final two minutes to count down on his dinner. He wanted to give the Logan murder some thought, but he couldn't. His mind was completely taken up by the East St. Louis murders, and Andrew Judson, not to mention the political shenanigans that were going on. If he couldn't nail Judson his boss was going to come out looking awfully bad.

The more he thought about Judson, though, the more convinced he became that he was right. In the morning he'd find out Judson's background, whether or not he had a record. Since he'd inherited the family business, they'd be able to check with the probate court and find out who the lawyer was. Talking to the father's lawyer might give them some insight about the son, and his background. If Harriet Connors was on this case she would have been working on a profile of the man.

Thinking of Agent Connors reminded him that he still had a decision to make regarding her offer. Did he want to leave St. Louis and join a special unit that—despite what she said—was probably going to be run by the FBI? Did he want to move to a new city for the second time in a couple of years, and start all over again?

Of course, if things turned out badly on this case the decision might be made for him. By the time the press and the two mayors were done with him he might be lucky to have Harriet Connors's new unit take him in.

He got his dinner from the microwave and frowned at it. He ate just enough bites so he could take his pills with it. That done, he got rid of the rest down the garbage disposal and tossed the tray into the trash.

He filled his glass with water again, added ice and carried it into the living room. He hadn't checked his messages when he got home, so he looked at the machine now. These days it was a relief when the red message light wasn't flashing.

He sat in a chair and sipped his water, thinking about the Judson case. He was looking forward to the next morning, when he could get started actively investigating the man. He hoped Jeter would decide to keep working with him. Between the two of them and Jenny he thought it might only take a couple days to get a picture of Andrew Judson. Not a profile, as the FBI liked to call it, but a good picture.

You could always tell more about a person from a full picture than you could from a profile.

Eighty

WHEN KEOUGH ARRIVED at the office the next morning Detective Marc Jeter was there, waiting and ready. Jenny hadn't come in yet.

"Let's get this show on the road," Jeter said.

"Wait a minute." Keough stopped him by laying his hand on the other man's arm. "You were supposed to think things over—"

"I've made my decision," Jeter said.

"Are you sure?"

"You're not the only one who has something inside that tells you when you're doing the right thing, Joe."

Keough studied Jeter's face for a few moments, then nodded. "Okay, then. Did we get anything?" He looked at the computer.

"I can fill you in on the way."

"On the way where?"

"I checked with the probate court and got the name of the attorney who executed the will," Jeter said. "I figured you'd want to talk to him first thing."

Keough had been right when he'd told the chief the night before that Jeter had the makings of an excellent detective.

"Let's go, then," Keough said. "I'll drive so you can navigate and fill me in."

"Deal."

They headed for the parking lot, and Keough's car.

They drove to the Fairview Heights law offices of David White, and were shown into his office after identifying themselves.

"That will be all, Helen," White said, from behind his desk. "Gentlemen, you have fifteen minutes; I'm due in court in thirty."

"We'll try and make it brief, Counselor," Keough said. "We're interested in a client of yours named Andrew Judson."

"I don't have a client named Andrew Judson."

"You're the attorney of record on the probate of his father's will," Jeter pointed out.

"Exactly right," the lawyer said. "I was Benjamin Judson's lawyer and the executor of his will. I do not nor have I ever represented Andrew Judson. In fact, I don't believe I've seen the boy twice in ten years."

"Not a boy, Counselor," Keough said. "He's a man now."

"I'm afraid I'd have to take your word for that, Detective."

"So you really can't tell us anything about him?"

"Not at all."

"But you can tell us who to talk to, right?"

White drummed his fingers on his desk for a few seconds, pushing his lips in and out. Keough looked around the office. It was small, but elegantly furnished. He wondered how a lawyer so young—and for a lawyer, forty-five or so was still pretty young—could afford a one-man operation like this.

"Are you gentlemen at liberty tell me what this investigation is about?" White asked.

"Of course," Keough said, "if it will speed us along. It's about murder, Counselor—the murder of three women . . . so far."

"Ah," White said, nodding his head thoughtfully, "those pregnant women."

"That's right."

White frowned. Keough wished at that moment he could read minds.

"And what does Andrew Judson have to do with that?"

"He's part of an ongoing investigation, Counselor," Keough responded.

"That's just a clever way of saying he's a suspect, isn't it, Detective?"

"Do you practice criminal law, Mr. White?" Keough asked.

"Most of my practice is civil, but I have been known to dabble."

"Mr. White, who do you suppose we could talk to about Andrew Judson who would have the answers you obviously don't?"

"Well, there's no more family, so I guess you'd have to talk to Dr. Todd."

"His physician?"

"His psychiatrist."

"He's seeing a psychiatrist?" Keough asked, surprised. "Willingly?"

"Alas, no," White said. "It was a stipulation of his father's will. As long as he continues to see Dr. Todd he maintains control of the family business."

"And as long as he continues, Dr. Todd gets paid?" Keough asked.

White smiled. "Very astute."

"And by the same token, Counselor," Keough asked, "you also continue to be paid?"

"As long as I am executor of the will, yes," White said. "That would not stop if Andrew were to stop seeing Dr. Todd and lose the business. I'm afraid my position is, er, rather secure."

"Tell me, Counselor, is Mr. Judson's estate large?"

Again White smiled, this time a cat-that-ate-the-canary smile. "Large enough, sir."

"Well." Keough looked at Jeter. "I guess we'd better go and see Dr. Todd." He looked back at White. "Would you have his address?"

"Of course." The lawyer began going through his desk drawers. "I believe I have one of his cards somewhere . . . ah, here it is." He came out with an embossed business card done on gray stock.

"Thank you." Keough gave the card to Jeter.

"If I can help you any further," David White said, "please don't hesitate to call."

"We won't," Keough promised. He and Jeter started for the doorway, and as Jeter went through it Keough turned back to the lawyer.

"Tell me, Counselor," he asked, "if something happened to Andrew . . . if he were to die . . . what would happen to the estate?"

"I'm afraid it would be disbursed to many different charities."

"And the bulk of it?"

"There would be no bulk," White said. "It would be disbursed equally."

"Ah," Keough said, "then in that case you would be out of a job, wouldn't you?"

"As I said," White replied, "you are astute."

White sat down behind his desk after the police had gone. He considered calling Dr. Todd and warning him, but decided not to. No matter what happened his position would be secure. What he had neglected to tell Keough was that while the estate would be disbursed to many charities, over the past ten years he had managed to get himself hired by most of those charities to oversee their affairs. So whatever happened to the Judson money, he would continue to be in control of the bulk of it.

He decided simply to adopt a wait and see attitude.

Eighty-one

"FAIRVIEW HEIGHTS," JETER said when they got into the car.

"What?"

"The lawyer, his office is also in Fairview Heights."

"It's all starting to center around here."

"But only one of the women was from here."

"That was his impulse kill," Keough said. "The one he truly couldn't help, couldn't resist at the time."

"His one big mistake."

"Let's hope so. But there's still something odd."

"What's that?"

"Well, after an impulse kill you'd expect the killer's activities to escalate."

"Are you profiling?"

"It's just a fact," Keough said. "It's like starting a rock rolling downhill. It's just going to pick up speed. But Judson was real calm when we talked to him. Way too calm. This one may not only go beyond the profiling, but beyond common sense, as well."

"I guess we'd better go and see what his shrink has to say."

Jeter started the car and pulled away from the curb.

* * *

During the drive to the doctor's office Jeter went over Andrew Judson's file with Keough.

"No sheet on him," he said. "If he's displayed any violent tendencies over the years, he's managed to stay out of jail."

"Maybe his father's money bought him off," Keough said. "Any arrests with no convictions?"

"Nothing," Jeter said. "He's clean. No parking tickets."

"Any vehicles registered to him?"

"No, just a hearse registered to the business."

"Then he's been transporting the bodies in the hearse," Keough said. "It's a great cover, but on the other hand somebody would remember seeing a hearse at a garbage dump or the Greenway Trail, don't you think?"

"Maybe he's got another vehicle that's not registered to him."

"Could be. All we saw at the funeral home was the hearse, though." They'd even peered in the window of the garage next to the house and found it empty.

"What about education?"

"He went to Wash U," Jeter said, "but didn't finish. Went into the family business with his father."

"What was his record like?"

"His academic record was poor," Jeter said.

"What about his social record? Belong to any clubs? Have any friends? Girlfriend?"

"It appears he was a loner," Jeter said. He glanced at Keough. "That fits most profiles."

"Yes," Keough said, "that does, but what else? Did he abuse animals when he was younger? Set any fires? Any psychological cries for help?"

"Not that I found."

"So, no friends, and no girlfriends. Any trouble with girls?"

"The file's in the back seat," Jeter said. "I think I printed out something on his record that had to do with a girl."

Keough reached back and grabbed the file. He flipped the

pages, came to what he wanted and then looked at Jeter, who could feel Keough's gaze.

"What?"

"Something about a girl, all right," Keough said. "A dead one."

"Right, right," Jeter said. "They found him with a dead girl. . . . Doing what?"

"Found him with a dead girl, period," Keough said. "Apparently she died of natural causes, was fairly popular in school and consequently was waked there. Security guards found him during the night . . . well, it says here just sitting by the coffin holding the girl's hand."

"No arrest."

"Right." Keough looked at Jeter again. "I bet Daddy's money bought some silence on that one."

"What do you think he was doing with her—or *to* her?"

"I don't know," Keough said, "but I think we'd better find out. After we talk to the doctor let's take a ride to the university. It was only about eleven years ago. Maybe somebody there still remembers him, and the incident."

"We could get the girl's name and check with her family, too," Jeter said.

"Good idea."

"This might be a break, Joe," Jeter said. "If we find out he was, uh, doing something to the girl, it'll give him a prior history."

"Yeah, and there's something else I'd like to find out, too."

"What's that?"

"I'd like to know if this girl was pregnant at the time of her death, wouldn't you?"

Eighty-two

WHEN GERALD TODD'S receptionist showed Keough and Jeter into the man's office the doctor looked nervous. He stood up but remained behind his desk. He appeared to be very close in age to the lawyer, David White, but his tastes in furnishing were not as expensive. Keough found himself wondering if Dr. Todd had been handpicked by White for the job.

"Dr. Todd? I'm Detective Keough, and this is my partner, Detective Jeter."

"Gentlemen," Todd said. "Uh, what can I do for you?"

"May we sit?" Keough asked.

"Oh, yes," Todd said, "Sorry. Please, have a seat."

The detectives sat down in front of the doctor's desk and Todd settled down behind it. He put his hands together on top of the desk, fidgeted a bit, then finally put them in his lap. Still not comfortable, he put his hands on the desk again, but kept them apart.

"What can I do for you?"

"Did you get a call from David White today?" Keough asked.

"White? David? Uh, you mean, the lawyer?"

"Yes," Keough said, "the attorney for the estate that pays you to see Andrew Judson as a patient."

The doctor blinked rapidly, as if a breeze had just blown into his eyes. "This is about Andrew Judson?"

"Yes," Keough said. "We just came from Mr. White's office, but he couldn't offer us any insight into Andrew Judson's character."

"Insight?"

"Into the kind of man he is."

Todd sat there staring at the two detectives, who stared expectantly at him. His mind was awhirl. Why were they investigating Andrew? Because of the women who had been killed? What had White told them? That Todd suspected that his patient might have killed those women? And what was he supposed to tell them? He couldn't break his doctor/patient confidentiality without losing his livelihood—but what if Andrew actually was the killer?

"Doctor?" Keough said.

"Yes?"

"Can you tell us *anything* about Andrew Judson?"

"Detective," Todd said, slowly, "he is my patient."

"That much we know, Doctor," Keough said. "You haven't asked us why we're investigating him. Do you know what that indicates to me?"

Todd swallowed. "What?"

"That you already know."

"Know? Know w—what?"

"That your patient, Andrew Judson, has killed three women."

"That's . . . absurd."

"He hasn't confessed to you that he's killed three women?"

"Confessed?" Todd asked. "I'm a doctor, Detective, not a priest."

"All right, then," Keough said, "let me use another word."

And then he blanked for a moment, because he was watching the doctor so intently, and because his heart was racing. The doctor's reaction was only reinforcing what he already felt, that they had the right man.

"Confided," Jeter said.

"Yes," Keough said, thankful to the younger man for coming to his rescue. "Has he confided to you that he's killed three women?"

"Even if he had," Todd said, "I would not be able to tell you, Detective."

"All right, Doctor," Keough said, "then what can you tell us?"

"Nothing specific," Todd said. "He, uh, has issues . . . which I, uh, cannot discuss."

"Issues? With women?"

"I'm sorry, but I—"

"Let me ask you a question you *can* answer, Doctor."

Todd closed his eyes. "All right."

"Do you think Andrew Judson needs the service you've been providing for . . . how long?"

"Ten years . . . or so."

"Okay, you've been seeing him for ten years. Has he needed therapy that long?"

"I believe so."

"And does he still need to see you?"

"Yes." Todd seemed to appreciate that there were questions he could actually answer.

"And this has nothing to do with the money being paid to you by his father's estate?"

"Of course not."

"And would you discontinue his treatment if you were convinced he was cured?"

"We're not talking about a cure here, Detective," Todd said. "Perhaps you're not aware of what it is I do."

"Perhaps not, Doctor." Keough folded his hands in his lap and shrugged his shoulders. "Why don't you enlighten us, then?"

"It is not I who decides when a patient is 'cured,' as you put it. I leave it to the patient to decide when they no longer are in need of my services."

"But this is a different case, isn't it?"

"How do you mean?"

"You know what I mean, Doctor," Keough said. "The estate

pays you as long as Judson continues to come here, isn't that right?"

"Well, uh, yes," Todd said, "that is correct . . . essentially."

Keough stood up and leaned over the desk. The doctor pushed his chair back but it stopped when it struck the wall behind him.

"Doctor, let's stop tap dancing around," Keough said. "You can save us all a lot of trouble by telling us whether or not Andrew Judson killed those women!"

"I don't know!" Todd snapped, and suddenly he looked very guilty, as if by uttering those three words he had broken his Hippocratic oath.

"You don't know?" Keough asked. "You mean you think so, but you're not sure?"

Todd remained silent, staring up at Keough.

"Come on, Doctor," Keough said, "just a nod, it's not going to hurt and we won't tell anyone."

Todd stared up at him a bit longer, then lowered his eyes and shook his head. "I can't help you, Detective, I cannot do anything I do not think is in the best interest of my patient."

"You don't think stopping him before he kills another woman is in his best interests?"

"I'm telling you," Todd said, and when he looked at Keough this time his eyes were pleading, "I don't know that he killed three women. He has not confided to me that he's killed anyone."

Keough looked at Jeter over his shoulder, then back to the doctor when his partner simply nodded at him.

"Doctor," he said, menacingly, "if this maniac kills again and you could have stopped it, I will come back here for you."

"Y–you can't threaten me!" Todd said, accusingly. "You're a policeman!"

"I'll leave my badge at home." Keough took his business card out of his pocket and placed it on the desk in front of the man. "If you think of anything you want to tell me, call that number."

Keough straightened and turned to face Jeter. "Let's go."

The younger detective got up and headed for the door.

"W–what are you going to do now?" Doctor Todd asked.

"Why do you ask, Doctor?"

"Are you going to—to arrest Andrew?"

"We don't have any evidence to arrest him on, Doctor," Keough said. "What we *will* do is go and have a talk with him. Maybe I'll even tell him that you sent us."

Suddenly, Todd's eyes bugged out and he seemed to burrow back even deeper into his chair.

"You can't do that!"

"Have a nice day, Doctor."

Outside Jeter asked, "What do you think?"

"He's scared shitless of his patient," Keough said, "that much is obvious. I also think he's afraid that Judson did kill those women, but he honestly doesn't know for sure."

"You think he'll call you after he thinks it over?"

"I hope so," Keough said. "We could sure use his testimony stating that Judson is at least capable of murder. He'll probably call the lawyer and the two of them will hash it out."

"You think the lawyer knows?"

"I don't think anyone *knows*, Marc," Keough replied. "But I think they both suspect he's a maniac. Maybe they've both been waiting for this day to come, knowing that the gravy train would be cut off sooner or later."

"My God," Jeter said. "Do you think they'd protect him to try and keep the money coming?"

"I think there are a lot of things people would do for money, Marc," Keough said. "A lot of things."

Eighty-three

"SHE WAS PREGNANT," Keough said. He was speaking to Jenny. They were in the task force office, having just returned from the Washington University campus. After leaving Dr. Todd's office, Jeter had called on his cell phone to tell her where they were headed, and why.

"God!" she said. "How'd you find out?"

Jeter sat down and said, "There was a woman working in the office there who remembered. She's worked for the university for over twenty years and is retiring soon, so she decided to talk to us."

"What else did she say?"

"That there was a cover-up, sure as we're sitting here," he said. "She's not clear what happened, but she says there was some fancy footwork."

"Her words?"

"Oh yeah," Jeter said. "This is one cool old lady. She said she thought Andrew Judson might have been 'fiddling' with this girl's body."

"Fiddling?" Jenny looked at Keough. "Joe? Do you have enough to arrest him?"

"We have plenty to arrest him," Keough said, "but not enough to convict him."

"What more do you need?" she asked.

"Some evidence would be nice."

She hugged herself tightly. "It's scary just thinking about him out there."

"Just don't get pregnant and you should be fine," Jeter said.

"No danger of that," she said.

"No boyfriend, these days?"

"Flying solo," she said, "and I'm going to keep it that way until this is all over."

Keough could see Jeter wasn't exactly happy to hear that, but then the younger man hadn't exactly been aggressive in his pursuit of her. But he had more to worry about than his partner's love life right now.

"I'm going to get today's interviews down on paper for the chief," he said. "You two can leave, if you want."

"Fine," Jenny said. She stood up and straightened her clothes out by tugging on them. Keough wished she'd leave. "I have to meet some girlfriends. See you both tomorrow."

"Good night, Jenny."

" 'Night, Jen," Jeter said.

Keough took the chair she'd just vacated and turned it away from the computer toward the typewriter.

"What did we find out today?" Jeter asked. "The lawyer and the doctor didn't say much."

"We just have to read between the lines," Keough said. "I think they both know what Andrew Judson is. We just have to prove it."

"And as soon as we do they're both off the gravy train."

"Right. Couldn't happen to two nicer guys."

There were a few moments of silence that were broken when Keough inserted a piece of paper into the typewriter and moved it into position. He tapped the keys a few times and then stopped.

"Are you still sure about all this, Joe?" Jeter asked.

"I've got to be sure, Marc, or going after him isn't the right thing to do."

"But . . . I mean—"

"I know what you mean," Keough said, turning to face him. "Yes, I'm sure. Everything in me tells me that Judson is the guy. I'm also certain that the doctor is afraid of him, and that the lawyer isn't exactly on the up and up."

"Is any lawyer?"

"Maybe not," Keough said, "but that doesn't enter into my thinking here. I think this specific lawyer will try to protect his income stream. If I'm right, he built his practice on this one client. I'd like to know where Ben Judson got all of his money. Can't be from that small funeral home."

"I can find both of those things out tomorrow," Jeter said. "There's got to be a record somewhere of the source of his money."

"Well," Keough said, "work your computer magic tomorrow morning and see what you can find out about all three of them— Ben Judson, David White and Gerald Todd."

"Right."

"Then in the afternoon we'll take over the surveillance on Judson." He turned back to the typewriter and tapped a few more keys.

"What do we do if he doesn't run, and doesn't go after another woman—ever?"

"Sometimes it happens," Keough said. "Sometimes a serial killer will just stop. If that happens and there's no evidence yet, then he walks. With any luck, he never kills again. He got it out of his system."

"How often does that happen?"

"Not often, profilers say."

"But you have your own theory?"

Keough stopped typing and looked at Jeter.

"Okay, yeah, I do," he said. "There are supposed to be five hundred active serial killers across the country at any one time."

"Five *hundred*?"

"Active and unidentified. And that's according to the FBI. I believe the bulk of them will never be caught because, eventually, they stop. Also, any of them could be active, then stop, and never have been noticed."

"You mean like that case of yours in New York? The Kopykat? If you hadn't noticed the slight difference in MO then one man would have been blamed for all those murders."

"And the other would have gone free—and there's no guarantee he would have stopped."

Jeter frowned. "I feel a little like Jenny, now. This is chilling stuff. There could be a serial killer living next door to any of us that no one knows about."

"Go home, Marc," Keough said. "We're going to be starting heavy surveillance tomorrow. I'll want us to do at least twelve hours, then we'll get someone else to take over during the night. Eventually, you and I may split it up and do the twenty-four hours ourselves."

Jeter stood up and stretched. Keough could hear the bones pop in his lower back.

"How long is your boss going to let you work on this?" he asked.

"That may not be the question."

"What do you mean?"

"The question might be, how long is *your* boss going to let me work on this. Sooner or later, if we don't get this guy, the FBI is going to have to be called in. One more victim, and it'll be out of our hands."

"Only if we tell them about it."

"Don't kid yourself," Keough said. "With all the computer checks you've been doing? NCIC, serial killer data banks, DMV, plus the publicity . . . they know about it already. They're just waiting."

"Well, that may not be a bad thing," Jeter said. "We are working pretty shorthanded."

"I don't think your mayor would agree with you."

"Well," Jeter said, "I'll get in early tomorrow and start searching the computer for info."

"I'll see you then."

"Take it easy on that typewriter," Jeter warned. "The person I stole it from is going to be real pissed if I return it broken."

Eighty-four

THERE WAS ONE message on his phone when Keough got home, and it was from a frantic Kathy Logan.

"He called me, Joe! He called me today. Please, please call me back when you get this message."

He didn't know who she meant, and he had put off returning her last message for so long that he felt he should call her immediately, even before getting comfortable. He managed to toss his jacket on a chair before dialing.

"Oh God, Joe," she said, when she heard his voice. "I'm so glad you called." Relief was plain in her tone. "Can you come over right away?"

He looked at his watch. It was after seven. All he'd wanted to do was have some dinner alone and think about the day's events.

"Kathy, unless this is really important—"

"He called me, Joe," she said, anxiously.

"Who called you?"

"The man who killed Michael." She was breathless, not like someone panting after a run, but like someone who simply could not catch their breath.

"What?" If she *had* killed her husband, this could be a ruse to throw the investigation off. Maybe she thought he'd call Burns with this news. "Who was it, Kathy? What did he say?"

"He called me here, Joe. At home. Can you come over? I'm so scared to be here alone."

"When did he call?"

"This afternoon," she said. "I've been out most of the day. I thought that would be better than staying home, but it wasn't. I kept thinking that somebody was following me so I came back and called you and locked all the doors and windows and—"

"Kathy, slow down!" he said, stopping her. "All right, look . . . I'll be right over, okay?"

He heard her take a deep breath. "That would mean a lot to me, Joe, and I know you probably just got home and you haven't eaten. I'll make it up to you by cooking for you. How's that?"

He was hungry enough to say, "That sounds fine, Kathy. I'll be there in a little while."

He hung up, not knowing if she was just being paranoid or if she was trying to use him to throw guilt off herself. He didn't seriously think she had murdered her husband, so he couldn't see the harm in going over there. And if she was going to cook, that was just a plus. He could give his microwave the night off.

She answered the door on the first ring of the bell, and when she grabbed his arm he could feel the tension in her. She practically pulled him inside, slammed the door and then hugged him. He could feel her body vibrating like a tuning fork. She was wearing jeans, a sleeveless top and no makeup. She looked younger than he'd seen her, and prettier, but there was nothing sexual in their embrace.

"I'm sorry," she said, releasing him and backing away from him. "I know they could be out there taking pictures but . . . I just needed to hold onto someone, you know?"

"It's okay," Keough said. "I don't think those idiots are out there taking pictures." He put his arm around her and walked her into the living room, where they sat together on the sofa. Their clasped hands rested in her lap, but there was still nothing carnal in the air. She was frightened, and very happy that he was with her now.

"Okay," he said, "it's time you told me who called."

"I did tell you," she said. "The man who killed Michael."

"Yes," he said, patiently, "you did tell me that, but who is he?"

"Well, I don't know." She looked puzzled, then realized what he was saying. "Oh, I see . . . no, it's not someone I know . . . although the voice was familiar, now that I think of it. . . ."

"So he never identified himself?"

"No."

"What did he say?"

"He said . . . well, I still have it on the machine. Do you want to hear it?"

"You didn't talk to him?"

"No," she said, "he left a message on the machine."

"Whoa, wait a minute," he said. "The killer left a message on your answering machine?"

"That's right."

Now he had some doubts. What kind of killer would leave a message on a phone machine? Only one of two kinds—the kind who wants to get caught, and the kind who doesn't exist. Up to this point he didn't feel she had enough of a motive, but even more than that it was his instinct again. He just didn't *feel* that she was guilty.

But what if she had an accomplice? A lover? And he had left this message on her machine so the police would think he was the killer? What better way to throw them off? What if she'd called him over to hear the message so that he could testify about it to Detective Burns?

He stared at her for a moment. She seemed genuinely frightened. He'd never had the feeling she was playing him, but there was always a chance his instincts were wrong.

Wasn't there?

"All right, Kathy," he said, "let me hear it."

Eighty-five

"I JUST WANTED you to know I did you a favor, Mrs. Logan," a man's voice said. "I did us all a favor."

That was all.

"Play it again," Keough said.

He listened for any telltale background sounds, but there were none that he could discern. He had her play it a third time and listened to the words and the voice again.

"He's not disguising his voice," Keough said. "He sounds like he's speaking in normal tones. Do you recognize the voice?"

"Like I said before, it sounds familiar, but . . ."

Keough frowned. If he was being played, she was a pro. At that moment his stomach made a sound that could only be described—in mixed company—as rude.

"You're hungry," she said. "Let's have something to eat."

He didn't argue. They were in the kitchen, where the answering machine was, and the aroma coming from the pots on the stove was distracting to a man who was as hungry as he was.

"Sit down," she said, indicating the kitchen table. "We can talk while we eat. I hope you like sandwiches."

"I'm very simple in my likes and dislikes, especially when it comes to food," he said.

He sat down and she brought two sandwiches to the table. "I hope you like roast beef on a kaiser roll," she said. "I made this after you called. I put lettuce and not much else. I have mayo—"

"This looks great," he said, cutting her off.

"I don't have much to drink," she said, apologetically. "I haven't had time to shop—"

"Neither have I," he said. "Ice water would be fine."

She brought him the water as he was chewing the first bite. She knew how to make a sandwich. It was good.

"Thanks," he said, as she set down the water and then sat across from him.

"You're not eating?"

"I had my dinner," she said, "but you go ahead. I like to watch a man eat. Michael—" She stopped abruptly.

"It's okay to talk about your husband, Kathy."

"Oh, I was just going to say that Michael used to come home late from work and I'd cook for him and watch him eat . . . but that was a long time ago."

"How long were you married?"

"Fifteen years."

"You don't look old enough—"

"I'm forty-one," she said, "but it was nice of you to—"

"No," he said, interrupting her interrupting him, "I mean it, you don't look forty-one—"

"Without all the makeup?"

He felt his face flush. "I'm sorry about that."

"No," she said, "you were right. I *was* wearing too much. Nobody ever had the nerve to tell me before—not that I didn't know. Believe me, women know what they're doing, even when they look like they don't. I just had myself convinced it looked better."

"You look fine now," he said, "without makeup."

She put both of her hands to her face. "Well, at least you know I wasn't planning to seduce you. If I was I'd at least have some lipstick on."

He stared across the table at her. Her arms and part of her

shoulders were bare, and he noticed how smooth her skin was. There were some lines at the corners of her eyes, but other than that the skin on her face was just as smooth.

Suddenly she seemed to become aware that he was studying her and she blushed.

"I'm sorry," he said. He put the last of the sandwich into his mouth. "If you wanted to seduce me you could do it with your cooking."

"Would you like some more?"

"No," he said, "that's enough. It was very good."

"There's more—" she said, reaching for his plate.

"No," he said, grabbing her hands, "I've had enough."

They sat that way for a few moments and suddenly what had been an entirely non-sexual situation changed.

"We shouldn't—" she said.

"I can't—" he started, at the same time.

And then they were on their feet, in each other's arms. Their mouths fused together in a passionate kiss, her body pressed up against his. He moved his hands up her hips, then between them and underneath her shirt. Her breasts were heavy in his hands, the nipples evident through her bra.

"Come upstairs," she said, breathlessly.

"Kathy—"

"Come . . ." she said, taking his hands. "I swear I'm not a murderess trying to seduce you away from your suspicions. I'm just a horny old broad."

He laughed. "Not so old."

"But horny," she said, "really. It would be rude of you to turn me down."

"Well," he said, as she tugged on his hands, pulling him from the room, "I wouldn't want to be rude. . . ."

It was hours later. They were lying side by side and he noticed that he was breathing harder than she was. The sex had been . . . vigorous, just this side of rough. He had been forewarned, though, having been told the kind of relationship she'd had with her husband. They had made love with one small lamp on at her insistence. "I like to watch," she'd said. Well, he didn't mind, either.

He looked at her body now, which was glowing with a sweaty sheen. She was a fleshy woman, with large breasts and hips, and almost-chunky buttocks that he had spent a lot of time admiring. There was nothing as sexy, he thought at that moment, as a full-bodied, naked, glistening woman.

"What are you thinking?" she asked.

"Things that a man would think is sexy, but a woman wouldn't."

She turned her head on the pillow to look at him. "Meaning you don't want to tell me?"

"Meaning I don't dare."

"Good thoughts, though?"

"Very good."

"No regrets?"

"None now," he said. "Hopefully, none later."

"Why would you—oh, you mean Valerie?"

"No," he said, "I don't mean Valerie. She and I are just . . . well, I don't even know what we are, but we're not a couple."

"Oh," she said, "what happened?"

"It just didn't work out."

"How long were you together?"

"Not long," he said. "Less than a year."

She turned her head and stared at the ceiling. "At least you realized early that it was a mistake."

"Yes."

"It's a terrible thing to realize you wasted fifteen years."

"I can imagine."

"I should have gotten out years ago," she said. "It wouldn't have been hard, since we didn't have any children."

"Can I ask . . ."

"About Brady?" she said.

"That's what I was wondering, yes."

"That was actually Michael's idea," she said. "He thought having a child in the house might make things different."

"What was wrong, exactly?"

"Nothing a child could fix," she said. "Michael wasn't satisfied with me. He needed . . . more."

"I can't imagine that."

She smiled and looked at him. "You're sweet, but it became obvious to me soon after we married that he wasn't satisfied. I tried very hard. I tried everything that he wanted, almost. The rough stuff . . . that just sort of happened later in the marriage."

"Kathy, you don't have to . . ." He reached for her hands and she squeezed his tightly.

"It's okay," she said. "I might be giving myself a motive, I don't know, but it turned me on as much as it did him. The only time we had any satisfying sex lately was after, or even during, a fight."

"Well, I can testify to the fact that you don't need to be brutalized to enjoy sex."

She laughed and said, "You're so right about that. Michael didn't know how to be gentle, he really didn't know how to make a woman feel good. He was always so concerned with his own feelings. I thought all men were like that, but you're not."

Keough wondered how totally honest she was actually being. If she was dissatisfied for fifteen years, wouldn't she have had an affair somewhere along the way?

"I thought about having an affair once or twice, but I found it wasn't something I could do."

"How did you decide that?"

"I met a man, and we talked about having an affair . . . and I just couldn't do it." She squeezed his hand again, then rolled over, pressing her breasts against his arm. "You're the only man I've slept with other than my husband since I got married. I don't know if you believe that or not, but it's true."

She rolled over on top of him and kissed him. He put his arms around her and slid his hands down to cup her smooth, muscular buttocks.

"Your eyes are so beautiful," she said. "Brown and hazel. And you smell so . . . What is that you're wearing?"

"It's called P.S."

She nuzzled his neck and inhaled, her lips just barely touching him. "It's wonderful. I feel so safe here. I've never had that with a man before."

She slid off of him, content to lie beside him. He put an arm around her so she could settle against him with her head on his shoulder, her breasts flattened against his side. They were both still slightly damp from their exertions, but it didn't matter. She felt warm and good against him, and her body had ceased the tuning fork action he'd noticed when he first arrived. In fact, he thought that they were both probably completely relaxed for the first time in days, maybe longer.

So much so that they fell asleep that way.

Eighty-six

WHEN HE WOKE up, the digital readout on the night table clock told him it was one A.M. Kathy was still sleeping on his shoulder and he was surprised that he still had feeling in his arm. He was also surprised by how good she felt there. The whole time he was with Valerie, whenever they slept together, he'd found that he couldn't wait for her to fall asleep so he could reclaim his arm. Maybe that should have been the tip-off he needed that their relationship wasn't going to work.

He lay there with Kathy on his shoulder, wondering what woke him up. Then it came to him. A voice. The voice belonged to Detective Burns, and it was telling him that there had been no extra bullet fired in that parking garage when Michael Logan was killed. If there had been, the forensics unit would have found it, or some evidence of it. A hole in the wall, a flattened slug. But they'd found nothing. That meant the only shot fired that night had been from the twenty-two that killed him.

And that told Keough a lot.

He slid his arm out from beneath Kathy and slipped out of bed without waking her. He grabbed his clothes and his gun, left the bedroom and went back downstairs to get dressed.

She'd left the coffee pot on so he poured himself a cup before switching it off. The coffee hadn't burned, but it would have by morning. Armed with the cup, he fished out Burns's business card and dialed his home number. He got an answering machine and left a message.

"I'm going to the parking lot where Michael Logan was killed, Burns," Keough said. "I have an idea and I think you should meet me there whenever you can. Hopefully, you'll get this message soon. It's about . . . one fifteen A.M."

He hung up, hunted down a pad of paper and a pen and wrote Kathy Logan a note. In it he promised to call her, and told her he had to leave because he had some work to do.

That done, he left the house quietly, got into his car and started driving downtown. He didn't know if the parking lot would be open. Some of them closed overnight, others put their gates on automatic. Some of them let cars out but not in. He didn't know what kind this would be, but maybe he'd be able to get inside. He needed to be at the scene; he thought he was putting it all together.

He might have made more progress earlier, but for eight or nine days now he'd been working on the serial case. Some serial investigations went on for months, but this one only *felt* like he'd been at it for months.

As he got on the highway to head downtown he noticed the headlights behind him because the beams were high—not bright, but elevated. It made them memorable, and it seemed to him they'd been behind him since Kathy's house. It could have been the IA detectives in one of their private vehicles. Maybe they had been outside Kathy's house taking pictures. He'd been in the house long enough for them to make a certain assumption that would make them very happy. They'd try to bury him with it.

He thought briefly about Mason's offer to join the special unit. Why should he stay in St. Louis when these IA assholes obviously had it in for him? They'd be on his ass until they could charge him with something that would stick. And what if this serial thing blew up in his face? Yeah, maybe it was time for a change. Maybe there was a reason he still had so many unpacked boxes.

Okay, he told himself, forget about Internal Affairs, forget about the serial killer, and concentrate on this for a while. Maybe that was all he really ever needed to do was concentrate on this. The solution seemed fairly simple once he looked at it. One shot from a twenty-two, not one from the smaller caliber and then a second shot from a larger one. It made a difference—all the difference in the world. It was almost as if the killer wanted to get caught.

He got off the highway at Market and worked his way through the empty downtown streets toward the parking lot. He found the parking lot and pulled in. There was no metal door or anything closing it off, but as he pulled up to the arm it did not rise automatically. There was a ticket dispenser, but when he pressed the button nothing happened. He got out of the car and walked around behind his vehicle. He looked up. There was a metal door there, but someone had left it up. The parking lot was supposed to be closed. The yellow lightbulbs that illuminated it were probably supposed to be on, but the place should have been locked up. He walked around to the exit side and found that the arm would not rise automatically there, either. Definitely supposed to be closed.

He turned and started walking up the ramp to the second level, and then to the third, which was where Michael Logan had been killed. There were still a few cars there, perhaps belonging to night workers—cleaning crew, watchmen, whatever. There was an emergency door which he walked to and opened. He stepped into the stairwell and let the door close behind him. When he tried to get back in he found it locked. He walked down the stairs to the first level, where he was able to get out through another door. It left him back by his car and the attendant's booth.

He went to the booth and looked inside. There were a few paperback books, a clipboard, some old newspapers and cigarette butts on the floor. He sat on the attendant's stool and closed his eyes. He imagined that someone on the third level was being shot with a twenty-two. He couldn't hear it. Not one shot from a small caliber gun. When he opened his eyes the man was standing there. He had a twenty-two in his hand and it was pointed at him.

"It had to be you," Keough said. "No way you would have heard the shot. The only way you could have reported the body was if you killed him, then made the call to nine-one-one."

The man, tall, dark-haired, in his forties, could have been the attendant who'd been on duty when he himself had parked there one day. He wasn't sure.

"It took you long enough," the man said. "I've been leaving this lot unlocked for days. The owners find out and I'll get fired."

"You've been waiting for me to come?"

"One of you," he said. "You're a cop, aren't you? A detective?"

"Yes."

"I thought I recognized you from the other night, when you were all here."

"Was that you who was following me tonight?"

"Yes," he said. "I've been outside Mrs. Logan's house for a few nights."

"You made the call?"

"Yes."

"You frightened her."

"I didn't mean to," he said. "I just . . . wanted to let her know that she was free. That we all were."

"All of who?"

"All of us who have been damaged by her husband."

Keough looked at the man and found haunted eyes staring back at him.

"How were you damaged by Michael Logan? And for that matter, who are you?"

"My name is Frank Witherspoon," the man said, "and Michael Logan killed my Amy."

Eighty-seven

AMY WITHERSPOON WAS the babysitter Michael Logan had . . .

"Raped," Frank Witherspoon said, "he raped her."

"But the report—"

"We didn't want anyone to know," Witherspoon said. "Her mother and I convinced her to say he abused her, but then . . . in the end . . . we didn't even want to push that. We just dropped the charges and left town."

"So then how did he kill her?"

"We moved to Denver, Colorado," Witherspoon said, his eyes filling with tears. "I thought we could put this behind us, but we couldn't. She had nightmares, she stopped eating. We took her to a psychiatrist, but that didn't help. It just kept getting worse. My wife . . . her mother . . ." He sobbed and flexed his hand around the gun, which Keough was watching nervously. ". . . Finally, she couldn't take it anymore. She left us, and it was just Amy and me." He shook his head as tears rolled down his face. "I—I couldn't do anything for her. I didn't know what to do. . . . I'd already made so many wrong choices. Finally, she committed suicide . . . took a bottle of pills, and left me a note. It said, 'Daddy, it's not your fault.'" A huge sob wracked his body but he maintained his hold on the gun, and his focus on Keough. "Not my fault."

"So you came here . . ." Keough said, in an effort to keep him talking.

"Not right away," Witherspoon said. "I ruined what was left of my life, first. I drank, I was arrested several times for drunk driving, I lost my job . . . and then I decided there was only one thing I could do to redeem myself."

"Kill Michael Logan."

"I came here, got a job at this garage and waited for my chance."

"Why not just go to his house and kill him?"

"I went there first . . . but they had a child living with them. When I saw that I decided to do it this way. It wasn't hard to get this job; it's minimum wage. I started to see him every day when he drove into or left work."

"He didn't recognize you?"

"My hair was lighter and I had a mustache when I lived here," Witherspoon said. "Besides, he's the type who never looked at me twice when he drove in or out. He ruined my daughter and destroyed my family . . . and it finally killed my Amy."

"Wait a minute," Keough said. "I heard that your daughter was the baby-sitter for the Logans . . . but they don't have a child. They never did."

Witherspoon choked back another sob. "I didn't know that . . . then! She told me she was going over there to baby-sit. It went on for a year."

"Are you telling me that Michael Logan was having sex with your daughter for a year and you didn't know about it?"

Keough's vaunted instinct, in which he put so much stock, was telling him nothing about whether or not Frank Witherspoon was going to shoot him. He felt he had to keep the man talking until he could get a handle on what he was going to do, or until someone came along.

"I—it wasn't a year," Witherspoon said. "She was going over

there for about . . . about four months. She liked Kathy Logan and . . . and Michael paid attention to her."

"And you didn't?" Keough asked, on a hunch.

"I was busy . . . so busy . . . with my practice."

Keough thought he remembered from the report that Witherspoon was an attorney.

"So you paid little or no attention to your daughter. What about your wife?"

"Busy," Witherspoon muttered, "so busy . . ." and Keough didn't know if he was talking about himself now, or his wife. It was becoming clear to Keough what had happened, though. Virtually ignored by her own parents, Amy Witherspoon had found a childless couple who would pay attention to her, Michael and Kathy Logan. She probably went over to their house for dinner, and for talks. Maybe Kathy Logan even took her shopping. And maybe Michael Logan listened to her, and talked to her, the way her father never did. And then maybe the relationship changed. However it had happened, it sounded as if there were more people to blame than just Michael Logan. Maybe this was part of what was haunting Frank Witherspoon. He'd had more to do with the deterioration of his family than he wanted to admit.

But this was not the time to bring this up to him.

It was a cool night, but both Keough and Witherspoon were sweating to the point where drops of perspiration were dripping from their chins.

"So one night you saw your chance," Keough prompted.

"One night?" Witherspoon repeated. "I'm such a coward. There were plenty of nights when I had the chance—but that night I finally got up the nerve."

"You knew the nights he worked late."

"Yes," Witherspoon said, "and I made sure I worked those shifts."

"So that night you went up and waited by his car . . ." If he was a lawyer in court he'd be reprimanded for leading the witness, but here he was just trying to keep him talking.

"I didn't want to be away from the booth for too long," Witherspoon said. "It was my alibi, you see. I knew, though, what time he came down, so I went up with only minutes to spare, waited for him to get into his car and then I . . . I shot him. I wanted to talk to him, to make sure he knew who I was and why I was killing him, but I couldn't. I just . . . I just walked up to the car and pulled the trigger. He never saw it coming."

"And then you ran back down here, waited a while before calling nine-one-one."

"Yes," he said. "I told them I'd heard a shot, that I'd gone up to investigate and found him dead."

"That was a bad lie, Frank," Keough said. "You couldn't have heard the shot from down here, not if you used that little gun."

Witherspoon gestured with the gun. "I didn't know that. I—I don't know what else I could have done. This is the only gun I had."

"Well," Keough said, "maybe you wanted to get caught, Frank." Maybe, Keough thought, that's the final punishment the man wanted for himself.

"I guess that's why I've been waiting for you . . . or for someone . . . to come."

"That's why you left the lot open, so someone could get in one night."

Witherspoon gestured with the gun again. It wavered now, not held nearly as steadily on Keough as it had been a few minutes before.

"I even slept here, in the booth," Witherspoon said. "Nobody knew. I've been waiting a few nights . . . and now you're here."

"And now you want to give yourself up, don't you, Frank?"

"I—I don't know—"

"*Police! Hold it right there!*" Detective Eddie Burns shouted. Keough could see that Burns had his Glock trained on Witherspoon's back. He didn't know how long the man had been there, listening.

"No, don't shoot!" Keough shouted. Witherspoon looked panicked, his eyes darting around in their sockets. "Calm down,

Frank. That's Detective Burns behind you and if you twitch he'll shoot you. Burns, Mr. Witherspoon wants to give up."

"Mr. Witherspoon," Burns called out, "drop the gun, put your hands in the air and turn around."

"Do as he says, Frank," Keough pleaded. "He doesn't want to shoot you." Keough didn't want to shoot him, either. The fact was that he'd been holding his own gun in his hand for most of the past few minutes that Witherspoon had been talking. The man had never tried to disarm him, and had not noticed when he slipped his gun out of his holster. Most of Keough's nervousness had not stemmed from his fear that the man would shoot him, but rather that he'd have to shoot Witherspoon.

"Come on, Frank," Keough said. "It's all over."

"You were wrong about one thing, Detective," Witherspoon said.

"What's that?"

"I wasn't waiting for one of you to get here to arrest me."

"Frank—"

Witherspoon turned suddenly, leaving Burns no choice but to fire. The bullet caught him in the chest and propelled him back into the booth, into Keough, who caught him and disarmed him at the same time. Burns rushed in, keeping his gun pointed at the man, as Keough lowered him gently to the ground. A great gush of blood spurted from Witherspoon's mouth, and then Keough felt the life go out of him.

"I had no choice," Burns said.

"No," Keough said, looking up at the other detective, "and I suppose neither did he."

Eighty-eight

IT TOOK MOST of the night for the scene of the shooting to be investigated and cleaned up. The ME examined the body and had it removed. Burns and Keough went to Burns's office to give statements. Keough had to explain to Burns why he'd gone to the parking lot, and what had happened between Witherspoon and Michael Logan, and both Burns and Keough gave statements to a shooting team.

When they first reached Burns's office Keough called Kathy Logan, woke her, and told her not to worry anymore. When he told her that Frank Witherspoon had killed her husband she said, "That poor man. I thought the voice on the phone sounded familiar. Was this because of Amy?"

"Yes." Keough promised to tell her the whole story as soon as he could, and hung up. He didn't want to have that conversation now.

After Burns and Keough had given their stories to the shooting team Keough sat down to give Burns a statement about Michael Logan. He noticed that the man's hands were shaking.

"Don't worry," he said, "it's a clean shoot. With your testimony and mine . . . I told them you saved my life."

"Thanks, but that doesn't make me feel any better about

killing him," Burns said. Keough respected the man for that statement. "Besides, I get the feeling now that you could have plugged him any time you wanted to."

"Maybe. The fact is he had a gun, and he turned on you with it. You had no choice."

"Coffee?" Burns asked.

When he returned with a plastic foam cup for each of them, he seemed to have regained his composure.

"Okay, suppose you tell me why you called me and then went down to that parking lot?"

"I've been so wrapped up with my own case that I hadn't given this one much thought. Tonight I did."

"And?"

"I realized the only one with the opportunity to do this was the parking lot attendant. He had easy access, and he could not have heard the sound of that shot from his booth. Since he claimed that he had, he must have been lying."

Burns thought about it for a moment. "Simple . . . maybe too simple."

"Sometimes the simple things get overlooked," Keough said. "I went to the parking lot because I like to stand at the scene when I'm trying to work a case. I wanted to check the doors and stairwells, I wanted to stand in that booth. Witherspoon showing up there was pure luck."

"You said at the scene that he followed you?"

"Yeah, I saw headlights behind me, thought it might be Mason and Gail from IA. Turned out to be Witherspoon. Also, there's a phone message from him on Kathy Logan's machine you might be interested in. You'll be able to match his voice. He confesses on the tape. It supports his confession to me."

"I heard him talking to you," Burns said. "I guess my wife and I must've got home just after you left the message. I wasn't going to come, but then I decided why not? I was pissed because I thought you were working my case."

"Turns out I was," Keough said. "Sorry."

"Maybe if I'd gotten there a little later you would have blown him away instead of me." Burns realized immediately how that sounded. "Sorry."

"It's okay," Keough said. "It's never easy to pull the trigger."

"My first time," Burns admitted.

They finished up Keough's statement, filling in whatever blanks Burns might have missed listening from outside.

"I'm not asking how you knew about the message on Kathy Logan's phone," Burns said.

"She called me, played it for me. She was frightened."

"If you went there and IA was watching—"

"Fuck IA," Keough said. "Fuck Mason and Gail. I'm not sweating them, Burns."

Burns stood up, extended his hand. "Eddie. Just call me Eddie."

By the time Keough was through, he was already late in heading to East St. Louis. The red light on his answering machine was blinking madly with several messages. Kathy Logan? No, he'd promised to call her later. She was probably still asleep. Valerie? He hadn't spoken to her in a while. He would have ignored it and gotten a shower before heading out again, but it might have been Marc Jeter with something important. This was going to be a hell of a day, since he'd only had a short nap last night in Kathy Logan's bed.

Thd first call was from Detective Knoxx, and it had come in the day before. Knoxx had succeeded in interviewing the other three girlfriends of Elizabeth Barnes and was ready to give Keough a report. Keough was too tired to call the man back, especially since they were already keying their investigation on Andrew Judson. He put it off until later.

The next three calls were from Jenny—she was frantic. All of them had been left that morning, each more urgent than the one before.

"Where have you been?" she demanded when he called in.

"What's going on?"

"Marc had to go out with Sergeant Benson," Jenny said. "He had no choice. We got word from the chief and the mayor. We tried to get you. Marc had no *choice*—"

"Jenny," Keough said, cutting her short, "what are you talking about?"

She took a deep breath. "Marc, Sergeant Benson and some backup went to Fairview Heights to pick him up this morning."

"Pick who up?"

"Judson," she said, "Andrew Judson. They went and arrested him, Joe!"

"Fuck!" Keough shouted.

Eighty-nine

THE DOCTOR HAD warned her that the latter stages of her pregnancy would not be easy. In fact, she'd had some spotting over the past few days—the few days before Andrew Judson had imprisoned her. Stubbornly, however, she'd still insisted on leaving the house rather than confining herself to bed. Maybe, she'd thought, around the eighth or ninth month, she'd submit to bed rest.

But something was wrong now. She could feel it inside. She sat on the floor, her knees drawn up to her chest, waiting for Judson to come down again. He seemed very concerned about her baby, even though he was holding her prisoner. Maybe he would take her to the doctor.

The pain came slowly, started to get worse. She didn't know what time or even what day it was. She'd been drifting asleep and jerking awake so long that she wasn't even sure how long she'd been there.

But she needed to get out. Now that she knew something was wrong he would *have* to let her out.

Wouldn't he?

* * *

When they pounded on Andrew Judson's door that morning they woke him up. He came down the stairs in bathrobe, pajamas and slippers wondering who was at his door, and before he knew it he was on his stomach, hands being cuffed behind him by some uniformed cops. A white-haired man—presumably a superior— read him his rights. Standing off to one side and looking unhappy was the young detective who had taken him to the morgue when he was playing "Allan Barnes," but Detective Keough was nowhere to be found.

As they dragged him from the house and threw him in the back of a police car he thought briefly of the woman in his basement, and of his "friends." He wasn't worried, though. The cops had no evidence. They wouldn't be able to hold him, or search his premises—not legally. Someone had jumped the gun, made a big mistake. That was even more evident by the fact that Keough—the detective in charge—was not there. They'd obviously done this without him.

Boy, Judson thought, was he going to be pissed.

When they got him to the East St. Louis police station the press was waiting. Instead of taking him around back they walked him through the front door. The mayor's press secretary had notified them, and the mayor's orders to the chief were to "let him be seen." "We want this out in the open," he said further. "We want everyone to know that we've caught this bastard, and that we've cleaned our own dirty laundry."

Chief Clark agreed outwardly with his boss, but inwardly he knew this was a mistake. He should have put his foot down and fought it, but Mayor Emery had a way about him. He bulldozed his subordinates when he was on a roll, and he was on a roll today.

Clark was curious to see how Joe Keough reacted to this. Keough was not a man accustomed to being steamrolled.

It was going to be interesting.

Ninety

.

"I TRIED YOU at home, I tried your cell . . ." Jenny said as Keough walked in.

"Where do they have him?" he demanded. He was angrier still at having to fight his way through the press to get into the building. Not only had they arrested Andrew Judson without proper evidence, but they had leaked it to the press, as well.

"He's in the lockup."

"Where's Marc?"

"With the prisoner."

"Is he interviewing him?"

"I think Sergeant Benson is going to do that himself."

"Jesus." It was getting worse. "How the hell did this happen?"

"Marc and I got in about the same time this morning," she said. "The mayor's press secretary, Jack Powell, called and told Marc to come to the office right away. The next thing I know all hell is breaking loose. Somehow Marc got away to call on his cell phone and tell me to get ahold of you. I tried. I couldn't, Joe, I—"

"It's not your fault," Keough said. "I was involved in something else last night."

"You look like hell."

"Didn't get any sleep."

"So what are you going to do now?"

"My first instinct is to go into the mayor's office and call him an idiot."

"Ooh," she said, "that might not be smart."

"I know." He rubbed his burning eyes. It felt like someone else's eyeballs had been placed in his sockets. "Tell you what. See if you can get me the chief. Maybe he can get me in to see the mayor. Maybe there's a way to manage this."

"Manage it?"

"I know Judson's the killer," Keough said. "Judson knows I know. Maybe, if I conduct the interview, I can get him to confess."

"Do you really think you can?"

"I don't know," Keough said, "but it's the only chance we've got. There's not enough evidence to hold him. The D.A. will see that. So will Judson's lawyer. We'll never even get this to a grand jury. He's going to walk—unless he confesses."

Jenny shivered at the thought of Judson being back out on the street.

"Has anyone searched his place?" Keough asked. "The funeral home?"

"I don't know."

"All right," he said. "Just get me the chief. We'll start with him."

"Okay," Jenny said, picking up the phone. "What should I tell him?"

"Just get him on the phone," Keough said. "I'll tell him, myself."

Keough managed to get Chief Clark to meet him in Mayor Emery's office. Clark had made the call to Emery, as Keough felt he probably would not have been able to get through himself.

"All right," Emery said to Keough. "Get it off your chest—but remember who you're talking to." He sat back in his chair with his hands laced across his belly. The politeness of—what? ten days ago?—was gone, and he was now a very officious politician, granting a subordinate an audience.

Keough didn't have to ask whose idea the arrest was. Clark had already told him . . .

"There was nothing I could do to stop him, Keough," Clark had said on the phone. "He was bound and determined to make the arrest after he read your report about yesterday's interviews."

"I sent *you* a copy of that report."

"And I sent one to the mayor," Clark said. "He *is* the boss."

"I know."

"And don't hold this against Jeter," the chief went on. "He had no choice, either."

"I understand," Keough said. Clark was concerned about his job. He couldn't be blamed for that. "I'll see you in the mayor's office."

"I know who I'm talking to, sir," Keough said, calmly. "The politician who may have blown this case for good."

"Now listen here—," Mayor Emery started, but Keough cut him off.

"No, I think you'd better listen, Your Honor," Keough said. "I'm going to interview Judson and try to get him to confess to these murders. I think your D.A. will agree that's the only chance we have of nailing him and saving everybody's ass on this—including mine."

"Now look—"

"Your decision to send Benson and Jeter out to arrest Judson was wrong, Mayor," Keough said. "Dead wrong on so many levels I can't even begin . . ." He took a breath. "You got me over here to do a job and I was doing it. We would have gotten him eventually—but not soon enough to suit you, it seems. Now, without a confession we'll have to cut him loose, and how soon do you think he'll make a mistake then? I'll tell you . . . never!" Keough looked at Clark. "And you, Chief. You're a cop. How could you let him do this?"

"Chief Clark knows where his loyalties lie," Mayor Emery said to Keough. "Unlike some people."

"My loyalty right now is to the families of the victims, and to potential victims," Keough said. "And it's also to me. Don't think I don't know you were going to hang me out to dry if this went wrong. I'm going to try to make sure that doesn't happen." He looked at the chief again. "Keep Benson away from the prisoner. He'll make a mess of any interview he tries to conduct. Make sure the D.A. observes the interrogation. Have you got a two-way mirror in this pissant police station?"

"We've got one," Clark said, tightly.

"Good, use it. You watch, and the D.A. Oh, and Jeter. Nobody else."

Clark looked at the mayor. "What about—"

"Nobody else!"

"It's all right, Chief," the mayor said, magnanimously. "I have no desire to observe the interrogation. Give Detective Keough what he wants. Let's see if he can do what he says and save everybody's asses."

"Yes, sir."

"Half an hour," Keough said, standing up. "I'll be ready then." He started for the door, then stopped. He said to both men, "And no press until I say so." Not that he thought it would do any good. Emery was obviously not above doing whatever he pleased.

Keough left, slamming the door behind him.

"What if he's right?" the chief asked the mayor. "What if we can't get this guy without a confession—and we don't get one?"

Emery spread his hands and said, "Then we'll have to set him free, and he'll stop. Or he'll go somewhere else and kill women. Whichever way it goes, we will have taken care of business for our city, Chief. The killings will have stopped, and we'll all go about our business."

"And that will satisfy you?"

"Damn right that will satisfy me. And it better satisfy you, too . . . Chief."

Ninety-one

WHEN KEOUGH ENTERED the interrogation room Andrew Judson was seated at a table, hands clasped in front of him. He looked up and calmly met Keough's eyes. He was still wearing his bathrobe, pajamas and slippers, not having been given the courtesy of getting dressed. That was about the only thing Keough found to be in his favor. It was hard for a man to be truly comfortable when he wasn't dressed. Keough tossed a file folder onto the table, but remained standing so Judson would have to look up at him.

"Hello, Detective. I hope you're not too disappointed." His tone was soothing, probably his official "funeral director" tone.

"Disappointed?" Keough asked. "About what?"

"This arrest," Judson said. "I bet it wasn't your idea."

Keough thought for only a moment and decided to play it straight with Judson. "No," he said, "it wasn't my idea, and I *am* disappointed."

"I'm sorry. This must be your consolation prize, being allowed to question me."

"Well, once I heard about the arrest I sort of insisted."

"I'm flattered."

"Do you want coffee, tea, a cigarette . . . anything?"

"Oh, no," Judson said. "I don't expect to be here very long. My lawyer should be arriving soon."

Keough closed his eyes. "They gave you your phone call?"

"Oh yes," Judson said. "They did everything by the book."

Keough hadn't been told that. Suddenly, his internal clock accelerated. He had no idea how much time he had before the lawyer would arrive.

"Will you be alone? No bad cop to play off your good cop?" Judson asked.

"Just me, I'm afraid."

"You'll have to get me to confess before my attorney arrives, won't you?"

"It would be helpful, Andrew. Can I call you Andrew?"

"Oh, please do. I have the feeling that in another place, at another time, we might have been friends."

"You don't have a lot of friends, Andrew, do you?"

"More than you know." The look was smug.

Keough wished he could have gone right to Judson's place and searched both the funeral home, and the residence upstairs. But he didn't have the time. Their only hope was the confession. Searching the place would have to wait until later.

"Really? Men or women?"

"Both."

"I would have pegged you for a loner."

"Is that the profile? Should I be a loner? Dysfunctional?"

"You're not dysfunctional?"

"No."

"Why are you seeing a psychiatrist, then? A Dr. Todd?"

"You've talked to Doctor Todd?" There was only the hint of a hesitation, there.

"Oh yes. Dr. Todd, and David White, your father's lawyer."

"Then you know why I'm seeing a psychiatrist."

"Well, we know that you have to see him to keep your business," Keough said. "What we don't know is why your father insisted you stay in therapy, even after he was dead."

"Too bad you can't ask him."

"Maybe it had something to do with . . ." He trailed off, made a show of leaning over, looking through the folder for the name of the dead girl Judson had been caught "fiddling with" in college, even though he knew it. ". . . Bridget Murphy."

Judson stiffened slightly, but regained his composure. "That was a mistake."

"Was it?"

"I was holding her hand."

"Did anyone say different?"

"Lots of people."

"I didn't find anything like that in any files," Keough said. "In fact, I wouldn't have known anything if it wasn't for this nice lady who works in the administrative office."

"I was holding her hand."

"Even if you were doing more," Keough said, "your father had enough money to cover it up, didn't he?"

Judson laughed at that. "He had enough trouble covering up his own behavior."

"Really? Your father . . . misbehaved?"

"Constantly."

"What, with women?"

"He liked women."

"Live ones, or dead ones?"

Judson hesitated, then said, "Cold ones."

"Well," Keough said, as if confiding in the other man, "that never rules out live ones, does it?"

Judson didn't answer.

"How about you, Andrew? How do you like your women? Your girlfriends?"

No answer.

"Have you ever had a girlfriend?"

"I have one now."

"Oh? What's her name?"

"Julia."

"And Julia's alive?"

"Of course."

"Is she warm?"

"Very warm."

"And pretty?"

"Yes."

"Smart?"

"Very."

Keough leaned over so that his eyes were level with Judson's. "So tell me, what would a warm, pretty, smart girl like Julia be doing with a pervert like you?"

Judson stared back at him, his gaze unwavering, and then he smiled. Keough had interrogated a lot of criminals over the years, but the look in the other man's eyes at that moment chilled him.

He knew then, for certain, that Andrew Judson would never confess.

Keough left the interrogation room for a moment to talk to Jeter. Also in the room on the other side of the glass were Chief Clark and the district attorney, who was introduced as Pamela Kapper. He hadn't expected a female D.A. Clark introduced Keough as "the detective in charge of the investigation." Keough tried not to laugh.

"D.A.?" Keough asked. "Or assistant D.A.?"

Kapper, a polished, no-nonsense-looking woman in her late forties, said, "I'm the D.A."

"I'm going to need more time," Keough said. "We need to keep his lawyer busy when he gets here."

"We don't do that sort of thing in East St. Louis," Kapper said. "This man has rights."

"So did the women he killed, and their families."

"We don't know that he killed those women, do we?" Kapper asked.

"I know he did."

"But you can't prove it, can you, Detective?" the D.A. asked.

"No," Keough said.

"Do you have a chain of evidence for me?"

"No."

"One link?"

"No." They had some thin trails that might connect Judson to the victims if they'd had more time to investigate, but there was nothing indictable.

"Then get me my confession, or I'm cutting him loose."

Keough ignored the D.A. and looked at Jeter. "We need to search his premises before he gets out."

"Right."

"You'll need a search warrant." Keough looked at Kapper. "Can you facilitate that for us?"

"You'll never get one," she said. "You don't have enough—"

"Can you try?"

Kapper didn't like being cut off. "You need a confession, Detective," she said. "Even the suspect knows that. If you hadn't arrested him—"

"Hey," Keough said, cutting the woman off again, "I'm not the genius who wanted him arrested today, all right?"

"But you are the detective in charge, right?"

Keough took a deep breath. "That's right. Can you try for that search warrant?"

"Of course I can try . . ." Kapper said, but her tone added that it was a waste of time.

"And what about his lawyer?"

Kapper balked at that. "When he arrives he gets to see his client. Just on the off chance that we do go to trial, I'm not going to have it thrown out because I violated his civil—"

"Fine," Keough said. "Forget it." He gave Jeter what he hoped was a meaningful look, one the younger man would interpret correctly. He thought he saw a nod, but couldn't be sure.

"Okay," he said, "let me know when we have word on that search warrant."

He turned and went back in.

Epilogue

Two weeks later . . .

1

KEOUGH LOOKED AROUND the house at all the boxes. They were distinct from each other: the freshly packed and the still packed; the New York boxes and the St. Louis boxes.

He walked around, taking inventory. He had not accumulated very much "stuff" while living in St. Louis. "Stuff" was all that junk a person collected while living in one place for an extended period of time. "Stuff" was usually made up of things you don't need, things you could either pack or throw out while you're in the act of moving. Most people decide "what the hell," and pack it, and that's how stuff accumulates in attics and basements and garages of the homes they end up in at the end of the line—The House You Die In.

Keough had never felt like he was in that house—or "home"—and now he was starting to think he never would be. He certainly was not ever going to "settle down," have a wife and a family and a white picket fence. When he died, somebody—he didn't know who—would probably come into his apartment, or go into his storage unit, find his "stuff" and throw it out. Which is what he should have been doing now.

He walked through the house and ended up back in the living room. Living in St. Louis had changed him, the cases he'd worked on had changed him, as had the people he'd met. Steinbach, his partner for a short time until he died of a heart attack, had changed him. Jack Roswell, his neighbor and chess partner and sometime confidant had changed him. The two women he'd met and become close to—Valerie Speck and Kathy Logan—had changed him. And they had both lied to him, and disappointed him.

Valerie and Kathy were friends, and had been for many years. When Valerie told Keough that the little boy, Brady, wanted to talk to him, it hadn't been true. She had put that idea into Brady's head so that Keough would go and help her friend Kathy get out of what Val thought was an abusive marriage. Keough believed that everyone's first instinct was to lie. That was why Kathy had allowed Valerie to think she was a battered wife, when in reality she was the one perpetrating the violence in the marriage. Valerie had allowed Keough to believe Brady asked for him, when in reality Brady had not given him a thought until Valerie put it in his little head. She had lied about Brady, and about Kathy.

The signs had all been there. The women had referred to each other by their first names casually and often enough to tip him off. If he hadn't been so involved in the East St. Louis case, he would have noticed sooner.

Then, just when he thought he was getting close to Kathy Logan, he discovered that she had known all along about her husband having sex with the teenager, Amy Witherspoon. She had condoned statutory rape because it kept her husband busy and he didn't "bother" her for sex.

She hadn't killed her husband, he'd been right about that. What he'd been wrong about was thinking she wasn't playing him. She had been, in order to get his help. Valerie and Kathy both, in their own way, had been playing him. That realization made him feel stupid and embarrassed, which made it easier to decide to go ahead and make the move from St. Louis to Washington, where he would join the newly formed Serial Killer Unit he'd been invited into by Helen Connors. But even with that he felt he wasn't being told the whole truth. While she swore up and down it was not an FBI unit, he knew funding had to be coming from inside the Justice Department.

And talk about lying. The biggest liar he'd met the whole time he was in St. Louis was the mayor of East St. Louis, Will Emery. Even now, two weeks after they had been forced to let Andrew Judson go free, the man was taking bows for having stopped the killing in his city. He had never cared whether or not the killer was caught, only that the killings stop—or move elsewhere.

Keough was tired of the lying. He was packed up and ready to move to Washington. He didn't know what credentials he'd have—he'd given up his St. Louis P.D. status—but as long as he didn't lie to himself he was okay, and all he ever wanted to be was a cop—just not here, anymore.

The worst thing about being lied to, and believing people, was that now it made him doubt himself. What if the instincts he'd trusted for so many years were wrong? What if Andrew Judson was not the killer?

He checked his watch. He was supposed to go over to Dressel's with Jack Roswell so the old man could buy him a farewell drink or two. He had ten minutes before Roswell would be knocking on his door. A couple of beers, and then possibly a last game of chess. Keough was scheduled to fly out of Lambert tomorrow at two P.M.

His mind had been made up about leaving long before he had consciously admitted it to himself, but the moment Andrew Judson—still dressed in robe, pajamas and slippers—had walked out of the East St. Louis Municipal Building a free man with his lawyer, David White—that had clinched it. He'd called the airline that night and booked his flight two weeks in advance.

The next day he'd met with the mayor of St. Louis and

resigned. Nothing the man could say would change his mind. It was over. Realizing he'd been played by both women was just the topper on everything. The only two people he knew had never lied to him were Steinbach and Roswell—and, oh yeah, the kid, Jeter. The poor guy had been left even more disillusioned than Keough at having to let Judson go. Keough had worked eight hours to get a confession, eight hours during which Jeter had done all he could to distract the lawyer. But finally, the lawyer and the lady D.A. had gotten together and Judson was free.

After Keough and Jeter had watched Judson walk out they turned and came face to face with Pamela Kapper, who'd said to Keough, "If you worked in this department I'd have your badge."

"If I worked in this department," he'd answered, "I'd gladly give it to you."

He hadn't seen Jeter since that day. He'd tried calling him, but couldn't reach him. He'd called Jenny at work but she told him she hadn't seen him, either. He said good-bye to her, and thanked her for her help.

"I think this sucks, Joe," she'd said. "I'm afraid to walk the streets with that maniac out there."

"I don't blame you, Jenny." He had not been able to say anything encouraging to her.

When the knock came at his door he knew it was Roswell. As he opened the door to let the old man in, his phone started ringing.

"Gonna get that?" Roswell asked.

"Fuck it. Let's go."

He returned two hours later, after a few Newcastles and some homemade potato chips. Roswell had drunk more than he had and they'd decided against chess. "Don't want to ruin my record," the old man had said, "and finally lose a game to you because I'm drunk."

They shook hands in front of Keough's house.

"You're a good man, Joe," Roswell said. "Keep an eye on your diabetes, huh? And drop me a postcard?"

"I will, Jack. Thanks for everything."

And that was that. They both knew they'd probably never see or hear from the other again. There was almost an embrace—Keough thought the old man would have liked it—but it just wasn't Keough's style.

The light on his answering machine was blinking when he entered. He wasn't on the job anymore—at least, not until next week when he actually joined the new unit. There was really no reason for him to answer the phone. He'd even called Knoxx, not wanting to leave the man hanging, and told him the case was over. Knoxx told him he'd found one of the women, who told Knoxx that Elizabeth Barnes was also a member of the Black Box Theater Group. That established a tenuous connection between her and the suspected killer.

"It's over, Knoxx," Keough had said. "Even that's not enough to make a difference. Thanks, though, for all your help."

"Must suck, having him go free."

"Yeah," Keough said. "It sucks, all right."

So he'd even taken care of Knoxx, and Burns had no reason to call him since his case was solved. He'd spoken to Helen Connors already, and told her he was on his way. Who else could it be?

He had every right to think he could ignore the call, wipe it clean. Instead, he picked up the phone and listened to it.

"Joe? It's Marc . . . Jeter. I, uh, need your help. I think I may have fucked up big time. It's about seven now. No matter what time you get this don't call my cell, just get in your car and come over. I'll be here until you show up. I've got nowhere to go."

"Where the hell are you?" Keough asked the message.

"Oh, uh, I'm at the funeral home. . . . You know, Judson's Funeral Home. Get over here, partner. If you don't, I'm fucked."

Keough hung up. What the hell was the kid doing at Judson's?

* * *

He stopped his car in front of the funeral home. It was dark, outside and in. He walked around to the back first, saw that the hearse was parked there. What the hell was Jeter doing here? What had he been doing for the past few weeks?

He went back around to the front and approached the door. It was unlocked so he entered. Once inside he closed the door behind him. He'd turned in his Glock with his badge, but he'd brought his off-duty .38 with him, and took it out of his holster now.

It was quiet inside; some low-watt yellow lights were on outside of each of the chapels.

"Marc!" he called. Might as well let Jeter and/or Judson know he was there. He waited a few moments, then shouted again, but there was no reply. He could feel death in the building, and not from any previous funerals.

He checked each of the chapels and found them empty. He was about to go upstairs to check the living area, but instead something told him to go downstairs, to the basement. If Judson was hiding anything, it would be down there. He didn't have a warrant, but then he didn't need one. He was just a private citizen, trespassing where he didn't belong.

It took him a few minutes but he found the stairs to the basement. He'd been in a funeral home basement once, when his father died. It had fallen to him to make the arrangements, choose the casket. He'd seen his father there, lying naked on a stainless steel table, gray but for a red halo around his head, where he'd suffered an aneurysm. He'd hoped never to have to do that again. For him it felt worse than the morgue . . . and colder. The ten years that had passed did nothing to ease his nerves as he continued down the steps.

When he reached the bottom he found himself in a dimly lit area. There were doors on both sides, and ahead of him. A couple were ajar, with light coming from the other side.

"Marc?" he called. "It's Keough. You down here?"

There was a moment's hesitation, then he heard Jeter call out, "In here."

It sounded like it was coming from his right so he followed it.

"Marc?"

"Here, Joe," Jeter's voice responded weakly.

Keough approached one of the doors that was ajar and pushed it open with his gun hand. He entered, the .38 held out in front of him. The room was brightly lit, and Jeter was seated on the floor, his Glock in one hand, his cell phone in the other. His back was against the wall.

"You okay?" Keough asked.

Jeter looked at him and smiled. "You came. Yeah, I'm okay."

"Not hurt?" He'd found Jeter, but that was no reason to relax.

"No," he said, "I just can't seem to get up, you know? Thought I'd wait here."

"Where's Judson? In the building?"

"Right over there." Jeter jerked his head. Keough stepped into the room a little further so he could look around the door. He saw Andrew Judson lying on the floor with half his head blown off. Some of it, along with a lot of blood, was splattered across the wall in an odd Rorschach pattern.

"Marc," Keough said.

"Yep," Jeter said, "I blew his head off, Joe . . . and I did it in cold blood."

2

"I tailed him for two weeks," Jeter explained, "and he never even jaywalked. I knew it would be a long time before he made another mistake, so I decided justice had to be done."

"Jesus, Marc," Keough said. "You didn't have to kill him. He would have slipped up again. He wouldn't have been able to fight the urge to kill forever."

"I couldn't be sure of that, Joe. Listen, can you help me up? My legs are real weak. I—never killed anybody before."

The room they were in had obviously been set up for someone to live in, just barely. A bed, a chair, a dresser, a table and not much else. Keough holstered his gun and went to help Jeter up. He could feel the younger man trembling as he deposited him in the chair.

Keough noticed a bloody trail from a place against one wall all the way to the door, like someone had been dragged or had dragged themselves—it had obviously not been made by Judson.

"You want to give me those?" he asked. Jeter gave up his gun and cell phone. His hands were shaking. Keough tossed them on the bed.

"Marc. It'll be okay."

"I came here tonight to kill him, pure and simple," Jeter said, without apology. "I rang the bell. He answered it and I stuck my gun in his face. He laughed. You believe that? He thought I was here to arrest him again and he laughed because I probably had even less evidence than last time. I told him I was here to administer justice. I made him take me downstairs, because I figured that's where they would be."

"Where what would be?"

"His mementos," Jeter said. "All the profiling literature says that killers take keepsakes, you know? I wanted him to take me to them."

"And did he?"

"Yes."

"Then that was your proof."

"My proof, yes," Jeter said, "but not legal proof, you know? Just the proof that you were right, all along. Your instinct was right."

Keough felt an odd sense of relief for a moment.

"So what happened?" Keough asked. "Where are they? Why are you in this room?"

"He had a woman here," Jeter said. "That day we arrested him? She was down here, and she was alive. If we'd had a warrant and could have searched, we would have found her."

"What happened to her?"

"He said that when he got back he found her dead. Something had gone wrong with her pregnancy, and she had bled to death."

Keough looked now at the bloody trail on the floor.

"Yeah, he said she dragged herself to the door. He told me he never meant for her to die—not right then, anyway. He went on about how she was his perfect one and he was going to take care of her and deliver her baby for her."

"What about the mementos?" Keough asked. "Where are they?"

"In another room," Jeter said. "You're going to flip when you see . . . help me up. We'll go in there and you'll see why I finally blew the sonofabitch's head off."

Once again Keough helped Jeter to his feet. The younger man took a few hesitant steps, got his legs under him, and then was able to walk. He was still shaking, though. He led the way out of the room, across the basement to another chamber.

"That's the embalming room there," he said, indicating another door. "It's where he prepared all his clients for viewing. He told me his real goal in life was to do makeup for the movies. But because his father's will tied up the money with the business, he had to keep running it. There's a steel table in there where he probably tied the women down to . . . well . . ."

They came to another door that was ajar. It was different from the other doors in that it was metal, and had three locks on it.

"Looks like a vault."

"Brace yourself."

Jeter pushed the door open and they entered. Keough couldn't believe what he saw. The walls were lined with tables, and on the tables were large, transparent tubs, almost like oversized beakers. Inside each tub was a human fetus floating in some sort of yellow liquid.

"Oh my God!"

"The sick bastard thought that if he kept them like this, in some sort of a hybrid formaldehyde solution of his own making, that he would one day be able to bring them to life. To 'birth' them, he said."

"Jesus," Keough said, "Marc. There's . . ."

"Yeah," Jeter said, "there's nine of them. He's been at this a lot longer than we thought."

Christ, Keough thought. The room looked like something out of a sci-fi movie, with fetuses of varying sizes and shapes, floating in huge jars. If he had seen this himself, with Judson, he would have been tempted to kill the man, also. Tempted—but he didn't know if he could have done it.

"I had to do it, Joe," Jeter said. "It was justice. I couldn't let him walk away from . . . from this!"

"Oh, Marc . . ."

"And there's one more thing. Come here."

He led Keough across the room to what looked like a freezer door. He opened it and inside, on a table, was a woman's body.

"This is her, the woman he was holding in the other room," Jeter said. "Her name's Julia Cameron. He said she had no family, that no one was looking for her, so he kept her frozen. I don't know what he thought he was going to do with her."

He closed the door and turned to face Keough.

"I knew then I was going to kill him," he said. "I took him in the other room for . . . well, I'm not sure why. Maybe I didn't want to do it in front of them." He waved his arms at the bottled fetuses. "He called them his friends."

Keough stood speechless.

"So it's done," Jeter said, "and I was morally right to do it. Twain said 'The most permanent lessons in morals are those which come, not of book teaching, but of experience.' This is my experience, and I've learned from it."

"But . . . what have you learned?" Keough asked.

"Well, I can't be a cop anymore," Jeter said. Up to now, despite his physical reactions, Jeter's voice had been steady. Now it was beginning to betray his inner turmoil. "Not after what I've done. In spite of how right I feel I was, I have to give myself up and pay the price." He hesitated, then took a deep, shuddering breath. "Joe, I want you to take me in."

"Me?" Keough said. "Oh, no. I'm not even a cop anymore. I resigned."

"You what?"

"I'm leaving town," he said, "joining that new unit I told you about."

"You're still a cop."

"Not a St. Louis cop—not any kind of cop until next week."

"So make a citizen's arrest."

"No way," Keough said, "I'm not taking you in for this."

"Then you agree I was right?"

"Morally, maybe," Keough said. "Certainly not legally, but you know that."

"Then you have to take me in."

Suddenly, Keough was struck with an idea. "I don't know what I *have* to do," he said, "but I know what I'd *like* to do. It's just . . ."

"Not right? Morally?"

Keough hesitated. What he was about to suggest went way beyond the bounds of anything he'd ever done before—but considering what Jeter had already done . . .

"There's a way out of this, Marc, without turning you in—and also a way to make sure that Mayor Emery doesn't walk away from this clean."

"The mayor?"

"In a way," Keough said, "he's sicker than Judson was. He didn't want to catch the bastard, just dissuade him from killing or dumping his victims in East St. Louis. That's sick, political thinking. You know what's really been eating me up about this? That he was going to get away with it."

"So what are you saying?"

Keough looked around and shivered. "Let's get out of this room. In fact, let's get out of the basement."

They retrieved Jeter's gun and phone from the other room and went upstairs together. They found a small lounge. They sat close together, put their guns and the phone on the small table next to them, and spoke in conspiratorial tones.

"Okay," Keough said, "I think we can come up with a story that will get you out of this mess."

"Really?"

"Yes, but you'll still have to resign after a certain amount of time."

"Oh, of course," Jeter said. "I can't carry a badge, Joe. Not if I'm capable of . . . of this."

Keough frowned. He was going to help his young friend walk away from murder, but he chose not to think of it as either premeditated, or as cold-blooded. Maybe Jeter had come here to kill Judson, but Keough chose to believe he would not have done it if he hadn't been faced with the horror of what was in the basement. That was what pushed him over the edge. He also needed to get the young man to seek professional help, find someone he could talk to. He couldn't just take the law into his own hands and walk away. Nobody could.

"So what's the story?"

"We'll talk it out," Keough said, looking at his watch. "Then we'll call this in and wait for the locals to respond. When they get here you'll ID yourself, and they'll have to get someone from East St. Louis here, as well. But before anyone gets here we'll call it in anonymously to the newspapers."

"The papers? Why?"

"Because I want this to get out, Marc," Keough said. "I want your mayor to have to deal with the fact that he cut loose a murderer for political reasons, and it took one of his men to bring the killer to justice. Your department comes out looking good, but your mayor comes out looking very bad. God, how I hate politicians."

They spoke for fifteen minutes, Jeter doing more listening than talking. After they agreed in principle on a story they sat back and stared at each other for a few moments.

"Joe . . . I can't let you do this."

"Why not?"

"You'll be an accessory after the fact. I can't allow you to take that risk for me—"

"It's not just for you, Marc." Keough sat forward, elbows on his knees. "I want to do this, for me. It's legally wrong, I know. It might even be morally wrong, but looking at it logically . . . everybody wins."

Jeter sat quietly for a moment, then leaned forward as well. However, he put his head in his hands.

"Marc."

There was no answer, and then Keough became aware that Jeter was crying silently.

"Marc," he said, coming off his chair. He reached out to touch Jeter, stopped, then put one hand on the other man's shoulder.

"I didn't know . . ." Jeter gasped. "I didn't know it would feel like this. . . . '"

"It'll be okay, Kid."

Keough squeezed Jeter's shoulder, then put his hand on the back of the younger man's neck, pulling him towards him, until Keough was literally embracing him. They sat in the darkened funeral home that way for a few moments. The only sounds were Jeter's sobs. Then, still cradling his friend, Keough picked up the cell phone with his other hand and dialed nine-one-one.

ALONE WITH THE DEAD

ROBERT J. RANDISI

New York City is in the grip of a nightmare. A twisted serial killer called the Lover is stalking young women, leaving his calling card with their dead bodies—a single rose. And there's a copycat out there too, determined to do his idol one better. But the Lover isn't flattered. He's furious that some rank amateur is muddying his good name. As the nightmare grows ever more intense, one detective begins to suspect the truth. As his superiors close ranks on him, he realizes that his only ally may be the Lover himself.

___4435-8 $4.99 US/$5.99 CAN

Dorchester Publishing Co., Inc.
P.O. Box 6640
Wayne, PA 19087-8640

Please add $1.75 for shipping and handling for the first book and $.50 for each book thereafter. NY, NYC, and PA residents, please add appropriate sales tax. No cash, stamps, or C.O.D.s. All orders shipped within 6 weeks via postal service book rate. Canadian orders require $2.00 extra postage and must be paid in U.S. dollars through a U.S. banking facility.

Name_____
Address_____
City_____State_____Zip_____
I have enclosed $_____ in payment for the checked book(s).
Payment <u>must</u> accompany all orders. ☐ Please send a free catalog.
CHECK OUT OUR WEBSITE! www.dorchesterpub.com